Also by Ruth Frances Long

The Book of Gold

The Lore of Silver

Ruth Frances Long

HODDERSCAPE

First published in Great Britain in 2025 by Hodderscape
An imprint of Hodder & Stoughton Limited
An Hachette UK company

The authorised representative in the EEA is Hachette Ireland, 8 Castlecourt Centre, Dublin 15, D15 XTP3, Ireland (email: info@hbgi.ie)

1

A CIP catalogue record for this title is available from the British Library

Hardback ISBN 978 1 399 73161 4
Trade Paperback ISBN 978 1 399 73162 1
ebook ISBN 978 1 399 73163 8

Typeset in Baskerville MT Std by Manipal Technologies Limited

Printed and bound in Great Britain by Clays Ltd, Elcograf S.p.A.

Hodder & Stoughton policy is to use papers that are natural, renewable and recyclable products and made from wood grown in sustainable forests. The logging and manufacturing processes are expected to conform to the environmental regulations of the country of origin.

Hodder & Stoughton Limited
Carmelite House
50 Victoria Embankment
London EC4Y 0DZ

www.hodderscape.co.uk

To all my historian friends,
Sorry, not sorry.

Αἴσθου ποτὲ ὅτι κρεῖττόν τι καὶ δαιμονιώτερον ἔχεις ἐν σαυτῷ τῶν τὰ πάθη ποιούντων καὶ καθάπαξ τῶν νευροσπαστούντων σε.
Understand for yourself, then, that you have within you something stronger and more divine, for certain, than the passions that make you dance on their strings.
– Marcus Aurelius, *Meditations*

Worauf du nun (sage ich) dein Herz hängst und verlässest, das ist eigentlich dein Gott.
Whatever your heart clings to and confides in, (I say) that is really your god.
– Martin Luther, Der Grosse Katechismus, 'Das Erste Gebot'

The entire universe is like a lyre tuned by some excellent artificer, whose strings are separate species of the universal whole.
– John Dee, *Propaedeumata Aphoristica*

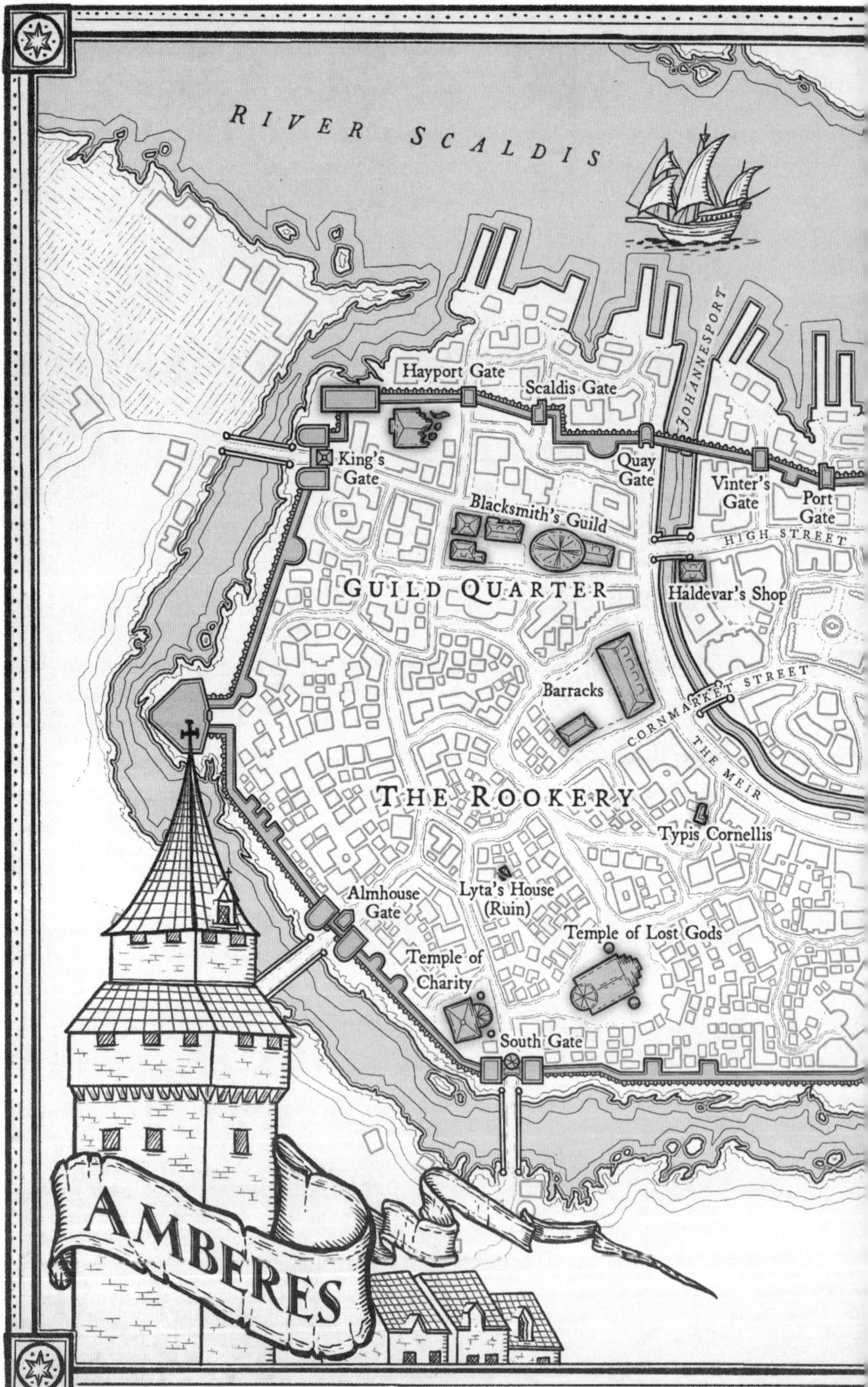
RIVER SCALDIS
JOHANNESPORT
Hayport Gate
Scaldis Gate
King's Gate
Quay Gate
Vinter's Gate
Port Gate
Blacksmith's Guild
HIGH STREET
GUILD QUARTER
Haldevar's Shop
Barracks
CORNMARKET STREET
THE MEIR
THE ROOKERY
Typis Cornellis
Almhouse Gate
Lyta's House (Ruin)
Temple of Lost Gods
Temple of Charity
South Gate
AMBERES

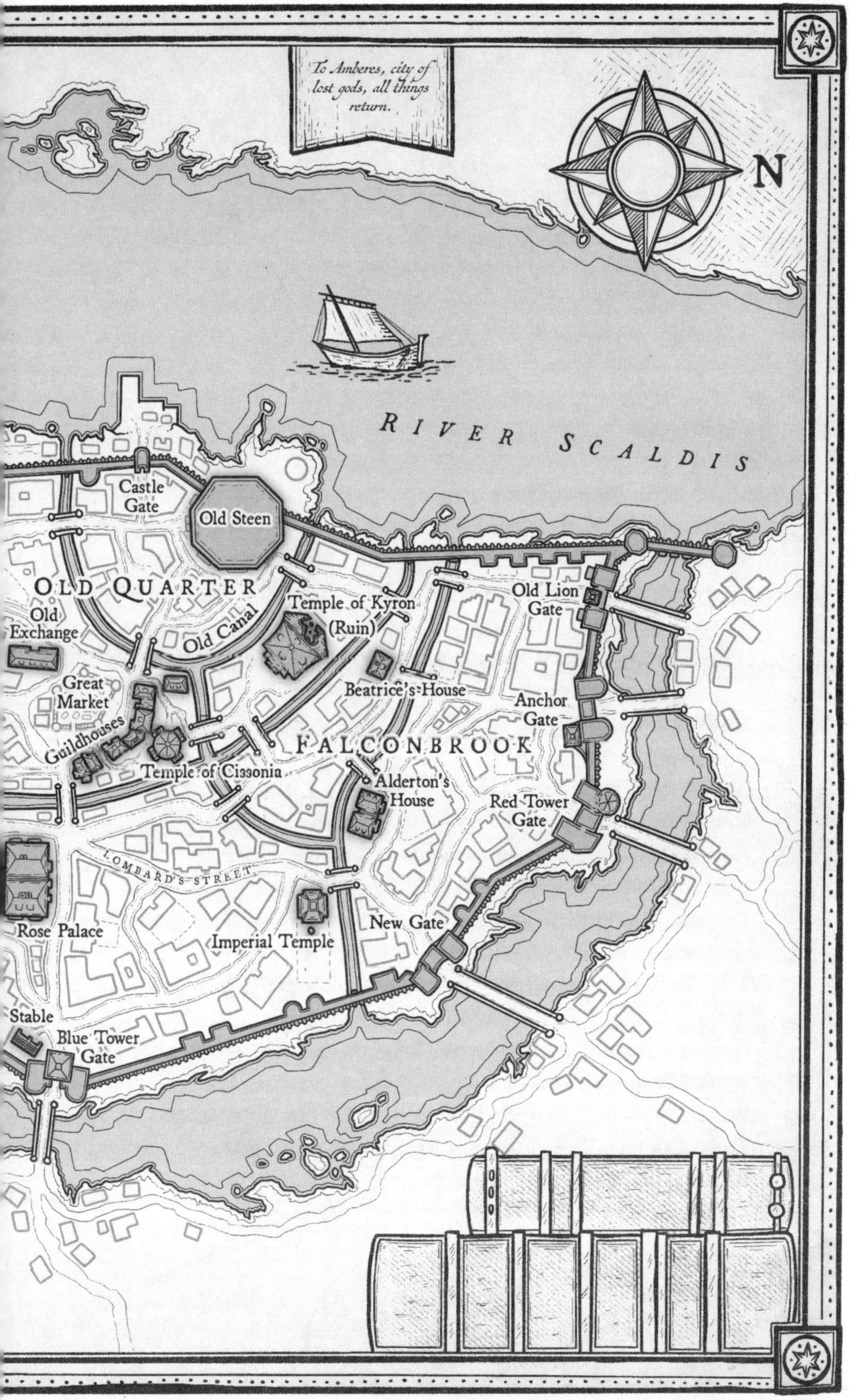
To Amberes, city of lost gods, all things return.
N
RIVER SCALDIS
Castle Gate
Old Steen
OLD QUARTER
Old Exchange
Old Canal
Temple of Kyron (Ruin)
Old Lion Gate
Great Market
Guildhouses
Beatrice's House
Anchor Gate
FALCONBROOK
Temple of Cissonia
Alderton's House
Red Tower Gate
LOMBARD'S STREET
Rose Palace
Imperial Temple
New Gate
Stable
Blue Tower Gate

Dramatis Personae

The Crew

Lyta Cornellis – a thief
Christopher (Kit) Cornellis – Lyta's brother, a printer
Sylvian Chant – a captain of the Royal Bodyguards, Lyta's former lover and partner in crime
Beatriz Alvarez – the Lady of House Alvarez
Benedictus (Ben) Alvarez – Seigneur of House Alvarez

Gods

Eninn the Trickster – God of Thieves
Cissonia – Goddess of Commerce, Patroness of Amberes
Kyron – the Warrior, God of Soldiers
Gloir – God of the Forge and the Hearth
Ystara – Goddess of Love
Nimyeh – Goddess of Wisdom
The August Imperator – the Imperator Eternal, the August One, God-Emperor of Caput Mundi
Druon Cissonius Antigonus – old god of Amberes, killed by Silvius Brabo, a lost god
Voseh – God of Decay and the End of All Things, a lost god
Tamfana – goddess of the lost Marsi tribe, a lost god
Rhiannon – Sovereignty Goddess of Albion

Nobility

Francisco – King of Castile, León, Aragón and the Greater Brabantine, the Soldier King, the Golden Lion of Castile
Annika – Queen of Castile, León, Aragón and the Greater Brabantine, youngest daughter of the Royal House of Vasa, Princess of Geatland
Carlos V – King of Castille, León, Aragón and the Greater Brabantine, Francisco's father, deceased
Iseult – Duchess of Montalbeau, deceased
Andras de Werve – Guildmaster of the Glorious Company of Blacksmiths, city alderman
Lancel Ursel – Count, Mayor of Amberes, city alderman
Charles – Lord Alderton, a lord of Albion
Viola Alderton – sister of Charles Alderton
Piers – Lord Stirling, a lord of Albion, alchemist
Juan Alvarez – Baron de Marasso, former general and companion of Francisco, cousin to Beatriz and Benedictus Alvarez

Church Imperial

The Magister of the Scholars' Tower in the Brabantine, deceased
Frater Caelinus – High Priest of the Imperial Temple in Amberes
Tiberius Octavius Aurelianus – First Prefect of the Praetorian Inquisitors
Silvius Brabo – ancient hero of the Church Imperial, killer of Druon Cissonius Antigonus, old god of Amberes

Royal Bodyguards

Elia Vasquez – General
Ivar Torren – Captain
Luca Juárez – Captain
Gabriel Montes – Captain

People of Amberes

Frida Elwynn – Lyta's former partner in crime
Ranulf Wray – master thief, Lyta's husband, deceased
Petrus Janlow – criminal gang leader in Amberes
Mattias Haldevar – spice trader, fence, former burglar, deceased
Jem Nyati – bookbinder, Kit's business partner
Molly Nyati – their accountant and Jem's wife
Rhea Cornellis – Lyta and Kit's mother, deceased
Prester Alaric – Vicar of the Seven Churches, High Priest at the Temple of Lost Gods
Florrie Stone – custodian of the Temple of Lost Gods, resident of the Rookery
Etienne du Lac – landlord of The Rack of Lamb Tavern in the Rookery, relic thief
Thomas Charnock – alchemist from Albion

CHAPTER ONE

Lyta

Amberes was never truly quiet, not the port city at the cross-roads of the world, but this early of a winter morning, with the chimes of Cissonia's first bells still echoing through the towers and rooftops, haunting the alleyways and near-empty wharfs like the wail of old ghosts, there was little activity. Snow smothered the usual sounds, muffling the world in white, or at least in that beige-grey sludge which approximated snow here. Lyta found it fundamentally unsettling. Her city, trade capital and port, beloved of Cissonia, Goddess of Commerce, was never still or silent at any hour. But who wanted to be out at the crack of dawn in the frozen heart of the Winter Solstice if they didn't have to be?

She certainly didn't.

The Vicar of the Seven Churches sat on the bottom-most step, sheltered by the arched roof of the narthex, his head bowed in desolation. His feet sank deep in snow, not that it seemed to bother him. He was younger than Lyta expected. The great title had been handed down only recently, and the last vicar had held it for twenty years. Said title was not quite as esteemed as once it had been.

Once, there had been more gods in Amberes than there had been stars in the sky—or so the old stories went. They each had temples and shrines and various other places for their followers to assemble. The Church Imperial had tried to wipe them out, but Amberes being Amberes clung to them stubbornly and, once the Church had been driven back, the remnants of those old religions crept back in. Some of them brought their gods with them. Some no longer had gods to pray to. And some found their gods wherever they could.

This high priest looked like little more than a scrawny boy dressed in plain, serviceable clothes which were still too big for him. Only the ornate bronze disc hanging from the cord around his neck gave him away. It dangled between his splayed knees, glinting dully in the midwinter light.

Breath misted the air in front of him so she knew he was still alive.

Lyta had slept late in her room above Kit's new printshop, face-down and dead to the world. At least there had been no nightmares. Not last night, anyway.

Kit had banged on the door of her room, a wretched expression on his freckled face which said he had not been so lucky. The curly riot of his red hair, more golden than hers, looked tangled and dishevelled, even as he tried to drag his fingers through it. She decided not to comment. He didn't appear to be in the mood for teasing.

'You're needed.' Even his voice sounded rough.

'Why me?'

'There isn't anyone else.'

So she was here, freezing, grumpy, and still only half awake, meeting the man who was apparently the last holy guide in the city for those whose gods were long gone. And she had no idea why.

As she stopped at the foot of the steps, the vicar looked up, his eyes hollow and dark-ringed, devoid of hope.

'You came,' he said.

'Well, . . . you asked nicely,' she replied, not sure what else she could say. Kit had done the asking, but she'd seen the note the vicar had sent. The words *desperate* and *no one else* had indeed been used and her brother had watched her read it in silence until she didn't have any bloody choice. She didn't want to be here. Temples were not her thing.

The Vicar of the Seven Churches tried to pull himself together, this man ten years younger than her and far from ready for the responsibility weighing him down. He dragged his cloak up around his thin shoulders and stood. Then he took a deep breath to steel himself and bowed to her.

'Mistress Cornellis, happy Solstice. May the last light of the lost gods shine on you and may—'

Lyta shushed him. 'That's really not necessary. Not for me.' She had met some of the lost gods and remained distinctly unimpressed. Their blessings were not worth their weight in shit. Eninn was the only one with half a brain left anyway. And even he . . .

The stirring in the back of her mind told her that her little god was daring her to finish that thought. She muttered a curse back at him.

The vicar carried on, stumbling over the end of the blessing anyway, though the words fell to an incomprehensible mumble, as if he couldn't believe she'd refused him and didn't quite know what to do about it.

'Want to show me what happened?' Lyta asked when he finally stopped.

The burden of it crashed down on him again, his face taking on that bleakness she'd seen when she arrived. Shoulders hunching, he nodded miserably.

Kit had asked her to come, Lyta reminded herself. That was why she was here. More or less the only reason. She didn't have time for temples and their dramas. But she was still trying to build on the new trust between herself and her brother and wouldn't do anything to jeopardise that. She was also meant to be stepping back and interfering less in his life, which did not come naturally to her. That seemed to lead to him interfering in hers instead, which didn't seem right. But as she had nowhere else to live since the house on Larch Lane burned down and he had taken her in . . .

Well, not quite true. Sylvian had offered. She could be living with him, in a palace, no less. Well, in the barracks, or whatever, as trusted servants, or as much as a queen could ever trust a thief, Lyta supposed. Ostensibly she was meant to be working for Annika, although there was precious little to do in that regard. Just keeping an eye on things in the city, on the nobles and the guildsmen and any other people Annika was interested in. She didn't need to report in. Mostly she talked to Sylvian or one of the other bodyguards. But if she moved into the palace, under the queen's thumb, at her beck and call probably, like he was, day and night . . . Lyta didn't want to think about that.

If there was one thing Lyta was sure of, it was her ability to fuck everything up when it came to Sylvian Chant.

Same with Kit if she wasn't careful.

So . . .

Here she was, with a smile. Almost. Ready to help, within reason. She knew the city, knew its underworld. She presumed at first someone had knocked over the poor box which, while being in bad taste, was common enough. She could probably find out who and have a quiet, stern word until it was returned. And while she was doing that, she was not thinking about Sylvian.

Though Lyta had lived most of her life in the shadow of this particular temple, she had never willingly stepped inside the place. Her mother, gods rest her, had been far too busy for temples, and besides, she had worshipped gods that didn't even have a place here. Not anymore. Or so she had said in Lyta's hazy memories. When she and Kit were orphaned, they'd been offered that same charity—food, old clothes, attempts made to find them shelter and a trade—that was basically what the temple did then and now. One of the largest in the city, the temple was lodged here in middle of the Rookery, the poorest quarter of Amberes, like a bone stuck in the city's throat. It had no riches, no significant patrons and struggled to get by, but still, men like the vicar tried to help those with even less.

It left her torn as to whether the temple was actually any use to the city. She and Kit hadn't needed it. She had a trade, however illegal, and they had made their own shelter, the two of them. For good and ill. Even from the beginning she could steal far better food and clothes than the temple offered.

There were always do-gooders haunting the shittier end of the city, looking for souls to save . . . or so they said. More often than not they were after the vulnerable to fleece, or victims to exploit.

What they gave away for free was often barely worth having. And what they asked in return? Well . . .

Eninn took a grim view of all of it and her little god had always steered her away from threats, albeit sometimes by a roundabout route, sometimes just as hazardous.

The Temple of Lost Gods was different. Kit said so and Kit wasn't actually as gullible as he appeared most of the time. He believed the best in people, not always wisely, but sometimes he was right.

Inside, the temple was almost as cold as the city outside it, lit with an array of cheap candles which smoked too much. The solstice decorations of mistletoe, holly and ivy garlands hung everywhere. There were frescos painted on the walls, which must have been bright and colourful when they were first done. They had faded with time, discoloured by the greasy smoke of those same candles, cracking in places so the faces of the gods they represented were hardly recognisable anymore. The temple had belonged to one god many years ago. He was little more than a shadow himself now, lost behind those who had come later. Now there were too many images of gods to count. Various artists had tried to add the newcomers up to a point, with varying amounts of success and skill. Perhaps they had lost the will to go on.

As the Church Imperial had made it its mission to slaughter all the gods right across the continent, it must have been difficult to keep up. A human being could only paint so fast. But the Temple of Lost Gods had felt the need to at least try. If only for their memory to go on.

Countless dead gods gazed down on her now. Their eyes seemed to follow her in the candlelight, and she wondered if they recognised what she carried inside her mind. Or sensed in her still some traces of the place she had been, where no mortal was meant to tread, and from which no god was meant to escape. The place to which they had all been exiled.

You didn't actually kill a god. That was impossible. But they could be stripped of all divine power and exiled to a place beyond reality, to the Nether, where they ended up lost in the wandering ways.

No other god had ever made it back, except Eninn.

And only because of you, he reminded her fondly, his voice no more than a whisper in her mind.

She glanced up at the vaulted ceiling high above them, painted dark blue with small golden stars dotted on it. Great soaring pillars like slender trees reached up to support the roof, carved with patterns of leaves and vines, hiding stone birds and other creatures—so lifelike that she thought they might move at any second. It was beautiful. A fading beauty, true, like an old woman trying to cling to her youth. There was something tragic about it, that air of regret.

'It happened late last night.' The vicar made his way down the aisle, fingers brushing against each of the columns like a lover's caress. 'I thought I saw a light, so I came back to check. A candle left unattended could burn down the whole place and take half the Rookery with it.' Lyta knew that only too well. Her own house not far from here had been destroyed in a fire. That hadn't been a stray candle though. That had been entirely deliberate. Halfway up the length of the temple, the vicar paused. 'But I hadn't got much further than this when I . . . I don't know. I heard something, footsteps and laughter maybe, and I thought it was just children. They get in here sometimes, up to mischief. And then . . . It all went dark.' He brought his hand up to his head and winced. 'I think someone knocked me out. I only woke up when one of the custodians found me. There was blood. So much blood. And that's when we found it.'

Turning left, he led her through a small oak door and down a bare stone staircase. It curled around on itself, down and down into the depths of the temple crypts. It was even colder down here, bitterly so, the kind of cold that ate into the bones. Their footsteps echoed strangely, and Lyta could have sworn that there was someone following them.

It sent a shiver up her spine, but she kept going, trying to shake off the feeling that those gods were still watching her. They couldn't be. It wasn't possible.

'We found it like this,' said the Vicar of the Seven Churches in a voice of misery.

It could have been an ordinary storeroom, if a whirlwind had been through it. The candles burning there were flickering stubs now and must have been lit when the alarm was first raised, but they still showed the place clearly enough. Like how the inner door had been forced open, boxes and cases strewn everywhere and the various reliquaries smashed. There were bits of gold, gems and pearls scattered across the flagstones, abandoned in favour of what the reliquaries had held. Some of them anyway. There were relics here too, she realised—bits of bone, hair and . . . was that a tooth? The place had been destroyed.

'How many relics were down here?' Lyta asked, unable to keep the shock from her voice. The gods honoured here might be lost, but that didn't mean their relics didn't deserve at least a little respect. None whatsoever had been shown.

'Twenty, that I know of by name,' the vicar said, and his voice trembled again. 'But more, a lot more. There was no inventory. I've been trying to familiarise myself with them, with what remains of them, but . . . The ladies who maintain the temple will know.'

Ah yes, Lyta thought. There were always ladies who ran places like these, changed candles, sorted flowers, cleaned up, decorated it for festivals like the Winter Solstice, polished everything to within an inch of its life. Including him perhaps.

'They aren't even very powerful relics, just—just all we had left of those lost deities. Things they touched or blessed, their treasures, bones of their Aspects or Champions, things which—' His voice broke and he turned away from her.

Lyta gave him the moment he needed. She continued to examine the scene before her. The relic thieves she knew tended to be religious themselves, in search of the divine. Respectful. Careful. None of them would treat their intended targets in such a way. Most thieves would take the reliquaries too. The amount of precious metal and gems could not be ignored.

Whoever had done this, however, hadn't cared. It seemed more like vandalism than theft and that might be what had shaken the vicar so much.

'Vicar?' she began and then felt awkward. 'What is your name? I can't call you vicar.'

He blinked his mournful eyes in confusion. 'Most people do. Or Prester, which is the actual title. I'm Alaric. Alaric Hayden.'

'Are you from Amberes, Alaric?' she asked. She didn't know the name Hayden, but that didn't mean much. There were new people in and out of the city all the time, from all over the world.

'My family live near Anchor Gate.'

Ah, she thought, the nicer end of the city. Not quite Falconbrook but not far from it. New money. Probably a third son of a merchant family then, with no talent for the family business, farmed out to one of the temples to keep him out of trouble. She knew he'd sounded too well spoken and seemed far too shaken by simple burglary and vandalism to be from around here.

'Right then, Alaric,' she said. 'Looks like some kind of relic thieves have been in, that's for sure. Not our local ones.' Du Lac and his lot would never treat relics like this. Say what you liked about them, they knew what they were handling and treated them with respect. Besides, they usually stole to order. But if this lot had been searching for something, it looked like they'd lost their temper and trashed the place instead. She bent down to pick up a gnarled tooth. It could have come from a boar.

That belonged to Moccus, said Eninn. *Or, rather, one of his people. He was a pig god. Some of his Chosen would grow boar's teeth like that and they had the most awful little eyes.*

Lyta shut down the voice in her mind firmly. She didn't want to think about what the followers of Moccus, the Pig God, would look like right now. She had no idea who that even was, but she trusted Eninn to be right. So she was definitely holding a distorted human tooth. Great. She held it out to Alaric who cupped his reverential hands around it, muttering a prayer, or an apology. She couldn't tell. Perhaps he didn't know either. It could have been both.

There was nothing left in it, her god told her solemnly. *No power, as such. Probably why they left it behind. If there was a single item here with any significant power, the thieves took it with them.*

Alaric slipped the tooth into an unbroken box he'd found somewhere among the debris and then looked around vaguely, as if searching for somewhere to put it. Finally, he settled on the surface of the one shelf which hadn't been torn down off the wall. He fussed over it, making sure it was straight. The only thing in the room that was.

'Do you know what they actually took?' she asked as gently as she could of this almost broken man.

But Alaric wasn't listening. He dropped to his knees and began to pick up some of the other pieces while repeating prayer after prayer, as if saving one relic had finally spurred him into action. Tears fell among the destruction and Lyta's heart lurched for him.

He believed. He really believed. Even in a place where there were no gods left.

'Prester Alaric?' a voice called from behind them, echoing down the steps. A woman's voice, older and only a bit shaky. Less shaky than Alaric's anyway.

The vicar didn't answer and Lyta sighed. She didn't want any part in this. What had Kit got her into? Why was Kit even involved?

'We're down here,' she called out and saw Alaric flinch as her voice rebounded off the walls. He didn't stop in his prayers though or his frantic searching.

An older woman bustled down into the crypt, carrying a lantern which gave a great deal more light than the miserable candles.

'There now,' she said. 'I've called on the charity committee and the mother's guild and— Oh, you're young Kit's sister, aren't you? Lyta?'

Something punched all the air out of Lyta's body. She knew this woman. She hadn't thought about her in years. In all honesty, she'd assumed she was dead.

'Auntie Florrie?'

The woman laughed, lines wrinkling the edges of her eyes. 'Aye, my love. That's what you all called me back in the day, wasn't it? The little ones still do. It's good to see you, Lyta. Happy Solstice.'

Florrie Stone had been one of the few who had ever been any help to the two of them after their mother died. She'd even helped nurse Rhea towards the end. Lyta remembered those arms holding her close while she wept. But that was Florrie Stone. She cared for all the lost children of Amberes—the Saint of the Rookery.

'Happy Solstice,' Lyta echoed because she didn't know what else to say.

'Kit said you'd help, that you have experience of things like this. And that you have connections to the palace no less.' Florrie wore the kind of expression that in Lyta's experience people usually wore when they thought about her brother.

Kit had a talent with people, with making them adore him. Especially matronly old women who thought he needed to find a nice partner and settle down. Or who needed some heavy lifting done and perhaps something fetched off a high shelf. 'We didn't know where else to turn. The watch aren't interested. "Where's the crime?" they said. Can you imagine? Knocking out our vicar and doing the gods know what in here? As if that's not a crime?'

Oh yes, Lyta very much could imagine the reaction of the city watch had been exactly that. Temples tended to deal with things themselves, and the watch dealt with mundane civic matters. They avoided anything too complicated. This was Amberes. The different strata of the city tried not to get tangled up in others' business. The criminals dealt with the criminals, the aldermen with the aldermen, nobility with nobility and the temples . . . well . . .

She could also picture Kit saying she had experience of things like this, the little bastard. The grin he would have worn. Of course she had experience of theft—mainly with committing it. She was going to make him suffer for this.

Eninn had a good laugh at her expense as well. He was almost as fond of Kit as she was. And as fond of getting her into situations like this.

If it was anyone else, she'd have said Kit was out to con them, but that wasn't his style at all. Straight as an arrow, that was Kit.

Florrie gently squeezed the vicar's shoulder and he paused in his prayers, raising his red-rimmed eyes.

'I saw Druon's hand, Florrie,' he whispered. 'A shrivelled hand, reaching for me. It held a candle with a golden wick. The stench of its smoke . . .' He shuddered and then opened his eyes wide. 'Was it a vision, do you think? His days have just begun, the darkest nights before the new dawn. What does he want of me? Druon, of all gods.'

The old woman glanced up at Lyta and shook her head in despair at such fancy. Druon was a lost god of Amberes, the oldest one, and the Winter Solstice had once been his festival, although Lyta knew little more about him than that. No one did. He had a lot of names but none of them had helped when the Church Imperial marched in and chopped him to pieces. They'd thrown him in the river and now he was little more than scary stories to keep children in line. *Behave or Druon will come for you.* A tale for the darkest nights.

Florrie tutted solemnly but not unkindly. 'Come on now, my pet, you need to rest. We'll gather what we can and have it all ready for you to bless again come Vespers. My girls are here to help. They've all come. And Lyta will make sense of this for us. Won't you?'

Lyta froze, not wanting to make any promises.

That didn't seem to matter to Florrie, who clearly had already made up her mind. She shooed Prester Alaric up out of the crypt, turning him over to another pair of middle-aged women who bustled around him efficiently. *Girls indeed*, thought Lyta. There was a host of them who clustered proprietorially around the temple in a desire to do some good and most of them were now gathered beneath all those fading frescos waiting for her to finish up.

'Florrie?' Lyta asked, lingering beside the steps to the crypt and watching the women fuss over the vicar. 'What happened to him?'

'A nasty blow to the head. I'm not sure if he was knocked out or if he just fell over himself and hit it on the way down. Blood everywhere, there was, but that's head wounds for you. We found him out cold in the nave.' She rested her hands on her hips and surveyed the damage. 'Kit said you'd help.'

She fixed Lyta with another of those determined looks and Lyta knew she was not going to get much choice in this. She had faced down an evil duchess, a sadistic magister of the Church Imperial and a jealous king, yet she had never felt quite so nailed to the spot.

No one crossed Florrie Stone, especially not here in the heart of the Rookery.

'You don't think it's the usual relic thieves either?'

'Nothing much of value here to thieve, love.' Florrie shook her head. All the same, she looked fit to slap someone about in a very definitive manner. 'And our local lads know better. They're relics of *dead* gods, all lost to the Nether and the wandering ways. Someone new has been stealing relics, true, but only the ones with power in them. There's always a risk in all the temples, that's why we lock up. No one thought this would happen to us. Temple of the *Lost* Gods, remember? Moccus, Vessuna, Tamfana, and the like. We don't even have names for some of the really old ones. And if they were regular thieves, they've left far more valuable things here in monetary value alone.' Lyta thought of the jewelled reliquaries scattered about down there. She chewed on her lower lip as she made her decision.

'I'll need a list of what's missing,' she said. 'Someone will know something. Someone always does. I'll take my leave.'

As she started down the aisle, Alaric pulled away from his attendants, his expression flustered as he hastened towards her again.

'Don't you want to see the body?'

Lyta froze in her escape.

Body? No one had mentioned a body.

The Vicar of the Seven Churches had been in shock, but she'd put it down to the relics being raided or the blow to his head. Florrie didn't have that excuse.

'What body?' she asked, as calmly as she could.

Florrie rolled her eyes up to the ceiling above. 'That boy,' she muttered to herself, clearly in reference to Alaric. It was also obviously not the first time she'd said something of that kind. 'Go and rest now, Prester. Lucielle will take care of you.' She gave a rather pointed glare at an ashen-faced woman a few years older than Lyta who carefully hustled him away.

'Well, he did get knocked out,' Lyta reminded her. There was no need to be uncharitable here. Not in a temple. Gods were still listening. Maybe only one, but that one was hers.

'More than once. Landed on his head as a babe a few times, I suspect. No wonder his family wants shot of him . . . well, no matter. He's ours now and we're keeping him. Luce will get him patched up, but he wouldn't hear of it until you came. Yes, yes . . . The body, yes . . . We found a body, up there behind the altar no less. Put it in the vestry, out of the way.'

'You moved it?'

'Well, I wasn't going to leave it in the middle of my temple,' Florrie replied with no small amount of indignation. 'Blood gets in between the tiles, you know, and no amount of scrubbing—'

'Florrie, why didn't you tell the watch about that?' Lyta snapped, getting back to the matter at hand. Moving the body was the surest way to get rid of any sort of clue as to what might have actually happened, even Lyta knew that, but it was too late now.

Maybe Alaric wasn't the only one in shock. Or maybe Florrie and those who ran the temple were hoping to make the body disappear so as not to invite any more trouble. But then, why ask Lyta here?

Of course, Florrie hadn't asked her here. Alaric had. Interesting.

Florrie snorted. 'Like I said earlier, what's the watch going to do? Tramp blood and dirt all over the place, get in our way and come out with sweet bugger all? They didn't want to know. Not about this, not about him. We're just the Rookery, Lyta. You know that as well as I do.'

Eninn growled something about her not being far off in her assessment which, frankly, was no help at all. He might have no power left to him after their jaunt to the Nether and back, but he was still an annoying little sod when he had a mind to be.

And as he was residing in her mind, that was acutely irritating indeed.

Lyta clawed for some remnants of patience. 'Why don't we start again? Kit said you needed help because someone had broken into the temple. No one mentioned a body. Who is it?'

Florrie shrugged. 'No idea. Come on then, I'll show you.'

'Right, and send someone to the palace to fetch help.'

The woman looked aghast. 'The palace? Well, of course, one of my girls can go but who's going to come *here* from the palace?'

Lyta sighed heavily. This was going to be awkward no matter which way you looked at it. But she didn't know what else to do.

Sylvian had duties, and vows, and a thousand other things tying him to the queen. Responsibilities that held on to him far more securely than she ever could. She knew it. He was the one operating under some kind of delusion.

But he had promised. If she ever needed him when she was about the queen's business in Amberes . . .

If she ever needed him, full stop.

He'd better bloody come.

CHAPTER TWO

Sylvian

The Rookery was quieter than usual which made Sylvian instantly suspicious. He could still read the currents of this place. Some things were too deeply ingrained to ignore. As Sylvian approached the Temple of Lost Gods—deliberately taking his time, because he wasn't actually at Lyta's beck and call no matter what she thought—he noticed that there were a lot of the usual women who clustered around the place, all of them busy with something or other. The remains of the first solstice bonfire was a black scar on the ground outside, stark against the snow. As he stepped foot inside, every eye turned on him, assessing, judging.

Clearly they were finding him wanting, but he had learned long ago not to give a damn what anyone around here thought of him. Amberes hadn't been his home in a long time. And the Rookery was still little more than a slum, no better than the wharfs or the warehouse district. He might have been dragged up through its gutters, but he had left it far behind him.

He held his head high and pulled the invisible mantle of royal bodyguard around him, donning the persona he knew disguised all he had once been from everyone else.

Everyone except Lyta anyway.

He found her outside the vestry, right at the far end of the temple, leaning against the wall by a little wooden door. Waiting. Lithe and beautiful, her fox-like hair escaping the plait she had tried to tame it with, contrasting with the dark-green cloak like threads of rose gold.

When her blue eyes met his, something in his chest inflated, leaving him breathless. Gods, he missed her. Every day, every minute they weren't together. Like part of him had been torn away.

He could still picture her face when he'd asked her to marry him, the way her eyes welled up with panic, the step she took back, right on the verge of outright flight. He'd been so sure, so utterly sure, she'd say yes. Why wouldn't she say yes? He was offering her a home, security, devotion . . . everything she could want.

But oh no, not Lyta Cornellis.

On his finger Ystara's ring shivered in response to his emotions and he closed his hand into a fist. He didn't need the goddess to tell him how he felt about Lyta. But he couldn't stop her either.

Since Ystara and Eninn had made their deal to save Lyta's life, since he had begged for their help, he had become the champion of the Goddess of Love, bound even more securely to the defence of the queen, the goddess's Aspect on this earth. How, he didn't know. Beatriz had tried to explain it to him but he didn't understand. Not really. Nor why the goddess he was supposed to serve couldn't help him with the woman he loved. Lyta defied even Ystara, it seemed.

But fuck, he wished just once she would have taken his hand and walked the easy path with him. Just once.

A smile flickered over her lips, his Lyta, a brief and heart-breaking smile, and her gaze never wavered from his face. He knew she still loved him. Even if the goddess didn't whisper reassurances whenever he doubted. Which was far too often.

Lyta waited until he climbed the steps and approached her to move, taking a step forward and indicating to the door.

'He's in here. I didn't know what—'

Screw this, Sylvian thought, and pulled her into his arms, kissing her like he was drowning and she was air. Then they were just standing together, far too close, staring awkwardly at each other, silence swallowing them up. Her surprise gave way to passion, and she pulled him to her again, burying one hand in his hair. He tipped her back and she let him, giving him the control he needed, yearned for, even if there would be a catch in that later on. But right in that moment he didn't care. How could he?

Her body fitted perfectly against his, but even if that dream came true it couldn't last. Even if he prayed to his goddess to keep her there forever.

Even Ystara wasn't powerful enough to compel Lyta Cornellis. And his goddess was not fool enough to try. Lyta belonged to the little trickster.

I'm yours, Lyta.

He had said that back in the Scholars' Tower, when he thought his life was about to end. He had meant it with everything that burned in his soul. Much good it had done him. Life had somehow managed to get in the way regardless.

'*Live in the palace? Are you mad?*' she'd replied when he'd tried to explain about the quarters he'd been offered. '*What would I do there? And what about Kit? I can't desert him! Someone has to look after him.*'

That fight had been one of epic proportions, even by their standards. He had said things he really should never have said. So had she. But he couldn't stay away from her. He hadn't a hope.

'Well,' she murmured, her lips brushing his like a sigh as she pulled back. 'That's a greeting.'

Sylvian knew he was an idiot. And if this was a small measure of the retribution she owed him, well . . . perhaps he really was due it.

'I missed you.'

'Clearly.' She almost managed to hide her laughter in that one word and his heart warmed against the winter's cold. Her nimble fingers stroked his jaw and for a moment he thought of kissing her again.

An older woman cleared her throat pointedly, her disapproval plain.

'Sylvian, remember Florrie Stone?' Lyta said, as if they hadn't been wrapped around each other like a pair of teenagers in the grip of true lust. 'She's still in charge here. Florrie, this is Captain Sylvian Chant of the Queen's Bodyguards. Impressive, no?'

There was a slight emphasis on the word 'Queen's'. He didn't miss that either. And *impressive*? Definitely not.

The old woman's face was like the stone she was named for. So she remembered him. Sylvian hadn't forgotten her either. Florrie had been a friend once, to him, to all the wild children of the Rookery. But she'd never forgiven him for what had almost happened to Lyta and Kit. Few people had, aside from Lyta and Kit themselves. And that had taken several near-death experiences.

'Nice to see you again, Florrie,' he said, straightening his uniform to remind her of all it represented. It was a complete lie, but he could always lie with ease. No change there.

Florrie looked him up and down and let out a huff which was the only response he was likely to get, but she stepped back into the vestry, leaving the door clear for them to enter after her. Not a single word of greeting, nothing but that glare which would happily consign him to the Nether given half a chance.

Sylvian was fairly used to this kind of response in Amberes. Not only did he almost land Lyta and Kit in a giant shit-heap of trouble almost fourteen years ago, he had escaped the city and had made something of a name for himself. He'd risen about as high as someone from this quarter could hope to, sworn brother-in-arms to a king, personal bodyguard to him and then to his queen. And more besides. He was the strong right arm of the foreign Crown who claimed their city, the enforcer of its will.

They didn't know the half of it and frankly he'd rather it stayed that way. Let the likes of Florrie Stone loathe him. In saving Lyta and Kit, Ranulf Wray had done an absolute number on Sylvian's reputation here long before he came back with King Francisco. But that had been for the best of causes and he'd made his peace with the old thief. Lyta had forgiven him, so had Kit. They had gone through hell together getting that cursed book and rescuing Ben Alvarez. He didn't care what other people thought. Least of all busybodies from the Rookery, no matter how beloved they were.

'They moved him,' Lyta said, her tone less warm to Florrie now, having sensed the situation. No one could have missed it. If someone had told him seven months ago that Lyta Cornellis would have his back, he would have laughed in their face. But here they were, with a dead body and an elderly woman who probably thought he was a demon in human form.

Some things, he reflected, would never change. Tides came and went, the summer was hot and the winter freezing, and the old women who ran the Rookery would protect their own. And may all the gods help him if he ever hurt Lyta again.

Of course they had moved the body. No one would want to leave a corpse on display in their precious temple. Not a temple like this anyway. Elsewhere there were gods that thrived on things like that, but thankfully, not here in Amberes. Not anymore, anyway. And for that simple fact they were all eternally blessed.

Blood was power, after all.

A memory of Montalbeau shivered its way through the back of his mind, of that room deep underground, the black smoke coiling up around him, digging through his thoughts and memories as it hardened, encasing him in obsidian, while all the time that bitch of a nameless goddess looked on, feeding on fear, horror and despair.

He shook the memory aside. It reared its head far too frequently. He wondered if Lyta still had nightmares about it too, but didn't dare ask.

'Doesn't matter,' he said. 'Show me.'

Florrie removed the heavy, embroidered altar cloth which had been used to cover the body and folded it carefully, all the while avoiding looking at the dead boy. He had been laid out as if for a funeral, on his back, hands folded on his chest, eyes closed.

And he was only a boy. No more than thirteen. Lack of food might have stunted his growth and left his cheeks hollow. Or he might have been small for his age. His clothes were pretty simple, nothing fancy, but not poor quality either. Hand-me-downs, maybe? The type of thing he and Lyta had grown up scrounging for. But they were well-kept and clean. The front of the tunic had been torn apart.

Probably when someone or something had ripped his heart out.

Sylvian sank down on his haunches, balancing on the balls of his feet so he could get a better look. There must have been a lot of blood all around him, wherever he had fallen, but they'd washed that away already. There hadn't been a trace of blood in the main body of the temple. He would have smelled it.

'He's a kid,' Lyta said, her voice shaking slightly. 'Do you know who he is?'

This was to Florrie rather than Sylvian. She shook her head. 'Not from around here, I think. And I know most of them that come here for charity. We feed them, find them jobs, places to stay, to be safe. You both know that. He isn't one of them.'

He had that very fair hair that signified heritage in the far north. The skin tone too, possibly, although death and blood loss were also contributing factors there. Sylvian wasn't sure what could have cut him up like that, opening his chest, wrenching the ribs up and aside. He wanted to say nothing human, but then, given all he'd seen, humans were perfectly capable of the most horrific things—more likely in fact. He thought of those stories from the far north where they had once executed people in a way not entirely dissimilar, creating wings of blood and bone from ribs and innards, all the while keeping the victim alive. Annika's ancestors' work. If this had been the intent, the work had thankfully been left unfinished. The hollow left behind in his chest was like staring into the void.

'So why kill him and just knock the vicar out?' Lyta asked. Her voice sounded thin, echoing, and he knew she was barely holding it together. She didn't show it, but no one could look on something like this and not be moved.

'The vicar?' Sylvian asked, still examining the body. There were marks on the boy's hands: burns, scars, old and new. Interesting. They might signify something. He didn't know what yet.

'Prester Alaric, the Vicar of the Seven Churches. He's new, from near Falconbrook.' *That said it all*, Sylvian thought. Posh boy trying to do good, which was preferable to what the richest denizens of the city usually got up to. Lyta didn't comment any further than that but he knew she'd have opinions. She turned away from the body now, staring at the colourful windows behind them. He wondered if she was trying to suppress tears or vomit. Things like this took people in different ways. 'He was assaulted, knocked out before they rifled through the relics down in the crypts.'

Relic thieves didn't tend to kill as part of their work. Not even the worst of them. Especially not kids. Even assaulting the vicar would be a step outside their usual track. In and out quietly and secretly, and leaving as little trace as possible. If everyone knew a particular relic was missing, the harder it was to shift afterwards, unless they already had a buyer waiting.

This was different. Even given all he had seen in the horrors of war, Sylvian had never seen anything like this.

Something had gone right through the boy from behind, snapping the ribs like twigs and ripping through the flesh with brute force, leaving them like skeletal fingers unfolding from the remains. Scraps of fabric clung to the wound. Charred. Burned perhaps. As if a musket had gone off inside him. But no, that didn't explain it either. None of the possibilities that presented themselves were right.

There weren't any fresh marks anywhere else. No signs that he'd tried to defend himself either.

There were no knife marks around the wound. He hadn't been cut open. The skin was torn and ragged, like the bloody remains of his shirt. Carefully, Sylvian lifted a pathetically thin shoulder and examined the back as best he could. The fabric there, while blood-drenched, was untouched. There was no entry wound. Nothing.

The same thought kept coming back to laugh at him.

It was as if something had ripped itself out, from inside his chest.

Carefully, he lowered the body down again and stared at it.

It sent a chill through him. No one practised blood sacrifice in Amberes these days. Those gods were long dead, and good riddance. But it had a feel of it here in the temple, left there on display.

The face of the goddess in Montalbeau rose in his memory again, laughing at him as he struggled with the shadows, helpless against her, as she swallowed him up and drank down all his terror, feeding on it and making him her own.

He'd been a sacrifice. So had Lyta. All of them in fact. Or at least that had been the intention.

The dark and vicious goddess Iseult had served would have had her people do something like this, he thought. She would have relished it. Sylvian wasn't sure how he knew that, but he did.

By Kyron's helm, this was no good.

'Have you asked your friend if he recognises anything?' he asked Lyta meaningfully. She glanced briefly at Florrie, who was now muttering a litany of prayers, her eyes closed, no doubt horrified by Sylvian's close examination of the corpse. He knew Lyta didn't want anyone finding out about Eninn and neither did he. Their lives were complicated enough.

'I can tell you later, but there's not much.'

And there wasn't much he could do here either, not now. Sylvian's skill lay with the living. Admittedly, mainly with making them *not* living anymore. He was good at that. The dead, once dead, were a mystery to him.

'I can ask the royal physicians to have a look. But I think it's fairly clear what killed him.' He didn't bother to point out the gaping hole in his chest. Lyta would only mock him if he did. Or at least, he wished she would. Right now, her eyes were strained with dismay. Had she expected him to have an answer? 'As to why, I don't know. We'll get a description passed around and see if anything turns up. It's possible that the death and the theft aren't connected, just a horrible coincidence. Not likely, but possible.'

Lyta didn't look disappointed, not exactly. But he felt like he had failed her somehow and he never liked that feeling. He had done it for real far too many times.

She drew in a shaky breath and for a moment he thought she might bolt.

Instead she hunkered down beside him. 'Burn marks on his hands and a few on his clothes. Nothing serious. Some of them have been patched.' She didn't quite touch the blood-soaked fabric, but her hand lingered above it. 'That might be something?'

'Might be. Florrie? Anything to add?' he asked. If he didn't couch the words in gentle tones, he didn't really care. This should have been reported long before any theft, and no one should have moved the body to begin with. They were probably lucky they'd thought to contact Lyta and not carried out an impromptu burial in the graveyard behind the temple without saying a word.

'May the gods bless him and keep him and may his next life be—'

'Quite,' Sylvian said, straightening. Lyta followed suit. 'Lock this room and don't let anyone in. I'll send for a wagon from the palace to pick him up. It won't be long.'

'That's it?' Florrie asked. She didn't sound impressed.

'No. I want a list of what's missing from the crypt and the justiciars will want to talk to your vicar.'

'Yeah, he's not going to be much use,' Lyta interrupted softly. Not unkindly but clear enough. She didn't count the vicar for much.

'All the same. You asked me to come, Lyta. I'm here. Might as well do the whole job. I'll get one of the justiciars onto it. I promise. That's all I can manage for now.'

The boy was dead. There was no one else to kill. Sylvian wasn't going to be a lot of help here.

He stepped out of the vestry and was relieved when Lyta came with him while Florrie stayed behind, covering the body again and then locking up. There were a few other women still milling about, trying to have a good snoop without being seen to do so. Whether at him and Lyta, or the body, he didn't know. He didn't like either option.

'What do you really think?' Lyta asked.

Sylvian rolled his shoulders. This wasn't his field. Francisco had actual people for investigating things like this, his justiciars. The royal physicians could be persuaded to help usually. They were far too eager to get their hands on a fresh corpse to work out what made it tick and what made that ticking stop. The Church Imperial had the Inquisition. Even the city watch had bailiffs who sometimes bothered when enough of a fuss was made by the right people.

'Something nasty happened in there last night. Not just a theft or a murder. Something more.'

Lyta made a sour face. She knew it as well as he did. They could both taste it on the air. It was far too familiar.

Montalbeau.

'The duchess is dead,' Lyta said firmly. She ought to know. She'd killed the bitch. Well, she, Kit and Beatriz had between them. He wasn't entirely sure of the details. Sylvian had been completely snarled up in her dark magic at that stage and no help to anyone. 'He was just a kid.'

'I know,' Sylvian replied and took her hand in his. She was trembling, her skin icy cold, even wrapped up in wool and leather as she was. She needed a pair of good gloves, he thought absently, and tried to rub some warmth back into her fingers. Surprisingly, she let him. The whole city was in the grip of the worst winter in years. It was starting to feel like they were never going to feel warm again, solstice fires notwithstanding. Maybe he'd buy her gloves for the festivities, if she'd take them. But this cold, bone-deep and terrible, he thought, was something else. She remembered Montalbeau as well. 'I'd better get back and report.'

She nodded glumly. Lyta might put on a tough face, and she could endure anything if she had to, but that didn't mean she wasn't affected by things like this.

'Do you have to straight away?' she asked. 'I thought, maybe—'

The stab of guilt was keen.

He grimaced. 'The queen has requested that I—'

Her face fell. She couldn't hide it, no matter how much she tried. 'Oh, sure.'

He didn't need to say anymore, didn't have to explain. But somehow he couldn't stop himself. 'There's this business with the council, the Baron de Marasso is due to arrive and she wants—'

'I understand. Don't worry about it, Syl. We are where we are.'

And there really wasn't a lot more to say than that, was there? Nothing that wouldn't end up in yet another argument.

The queen called and he would answer. That was the way it had to be. His old commander was coming here and he needed to be in attendance when he arrived.

Marasso was one of Francisco's most trusted nobles. The king had nominally given Annika charge of Amberes in his absence, but she was pregnant and her time fast approaching. So now he was sending someone else to step into her shoes. Or on her toes. Or something. A good man, Sylvian knew that. He'd served under him in the army and counted him among the best he had ever known. But still . . .

Of course Francisco had fucked off. Much as he honoured his king, Sylvian knew all too well that Francisco could be thoughtless.

And Lyta, his Lyta, had given up even arguing. Maybe she understood his situation better than he did. Lyta had walked away from him before. Perhaps he deserved it this time as well.

'Lyta,' he murmured, and his hands slid around her body so he could hold her close, just for a moment. 'I wish it didn't have to be like this.'

Francisco's precious, beloved tiny queen was almost nine months pregnant, the size of a rabid boar with a similar temperament, and so the king had found a bloody border dispute in Westphalia to involve himself in and ridden off with all but two of his bodyguards and half his troops. It wasn't even his territory, belonging to some distant cousin or other. But no, he had to go and sort it out, the Soldier King, the Golden Lion of Castile.

'You're her champion,' the king had reminded Sylvian. 'Chosen by the Goddess of Love herself. It's your own fault.'

And off he went.

Once Sylvian had thought there was nothing Annika could do that wasn't made of grace and dignity. She was a scion of a goddess, an Aspect of the divine lady of love, Ystara. Men adored her at first sight and always had. For a time, Sylvian had been among them.

Oh how very wrong every single one of them had been.

No promotion was worth this. No duty, no honour, no vow.

And as for his fault? All he had done was as his king commanded and he was going to be paying for it for the rest of his miserable life. Most of all by being separated from Lyta.

'I could come with you, I guess?' Lyta said, a peace offering, of sorts. 'See what your physicians say?' The wavering grin that found its way on to his face made her glare at him in warning. 'I'm still not moving in there with you. Kit needs me. Besides, they don't want me in there. I'm a thief, remember?' She elbowed him in the ribs.

'Yes, but you're *my* thief,' he replied, hiding the stab of disappointment behind a smile.

*

'Getting into the Rose Palace is admittedly a hell of a lot easier when I'm with you,' Lyta muttered as they passed through the main gates and into the primary courtyard. 'Hardly anyone gave me a suspicious look at all.'

'Didn't give you much trouble before.' Sylvian might have countered with the fact that it would be even easier for her if she had only agreed to marry him when he asked, that this could be her home too. Oh, not the grand royal chambers or anything like that. But there were married quarters in the lower west wing, behind the barracks where he still lived now, and all kinds of staff made their homes there. There were gardens. It was nice.

But he knew the kind of face she'd make, and the cold that would settle between them yet again, so he shut up. He had no idea why she had refused. It didn't make sense. She was a widow now. He'd thought they were all right six months ago. He'd waited an appropriate time for grieving and the like. He'd spoken to the queen about it and she'd given her blessing gladly, as did Ystara. It should have been easy.

But then he'd asked her and Lyta had said 'no', like he'd suggested something obscene. She had looked so horrified at the idea and fuck—it had hurt. It still hurt.

He loved her. Adored her. But no one could hurt him like Lyta.

This time, they didn't head to the palace barracks, or the guards' rooms, and definitely not up to the royal chambers—an area Lyta had once infiltrated far too easily for a bodyguard's comfort—but rather down into the workday rooms of the lower levels, the administrative heart of the city.

Sylvian wasted no time handing out orders, summoning a justiciar and demanding the royal physicians be fetched to oversee the body. The faster they could get things in motion the better.

Fast was a relative term though, as the body arrived before the physician. When the man finally ambled in, he was clearly irritated. *Not my problem*, Sylvian thought and indicated the body, a pitifully small bundle wrapped in funerary rags.

'I need you to tell me what happened to him.'

The physician's scowl deepened. 'Where did this one turn up?'

'*This* one?' Suspicion sharpened Lyta's voice. 'You've seen more than *one* like this?'

'What have you two pitched up with now?' asked General Vasquez as she arrived, her voice bringing Sylvian to attention in an instant. He moved so fast he was sure he heard Lyta snickering at him. Not loud enough for the general to hear. She wasn't suicidal.

Vasquez was a small, neat woman in a formal uniform, who could take on an empire if need be. She certainly ran one. If she was here already on the vague report Sylvian had sent ahead to her, this was serious.

'Found him in the Temple of Lost Gods,' said Lyta. 'Someone knocked out the vicar, ransacked the vault and left this poor kid behind.'

Vasquez's inspection was cursory. She locked eyes with the physician who nodded curtly and her mouth tightened into a hard line.

Not good, Sylvian thought. *Not good at all.*

'Like the other three,' said the royal physician.

'There's another *three*?' Sylvian asked. He didn't want to but the words spilled out.

'All found over the last two days. Each one younger than the last. Grotesque.' Vasquez moved on as if the thought was no longer important. 'Sylvian, the queen demands our presence.'

'Wait,' Lyta interrupted. 'No one is going to follow up on this?'

'Of course someone is,' said the general and turned her cold gaze on Lyta. 'You, Cornellis, find out what you can.' Vasquez waved her hand dismissively. 'I can't think of anyone better placed, can you? Poke around. Do what you do best.'

Lyta sucked in a breath, and Sylvian knew she was about to say something which might end up with her behind bars.

'We'll both do it, general,' he said.

'No, Sylvian,' Vasquez replied. 'The queen will need a report. You've already been gone too long. With me.'

Lyta gave him a helpless look and Sylvian didn't know what to say. He had to go. There wasn't a choice. Not for either of them.

CHAPTER THREE

Kit

Typis Cornellis was busier than ever, with new orders coming in all the time. Since the move to Twelfth Moon Street, and when word got around about the commission from King Francisco, scholars, citizens and nobles alike had started beating a path to the door. Which would have been fine if Kit had another twelve hours in any given day. He would have taken on more staff, but to be honest it took so long to train them up, it would be more trouble than it was worth, and the Worshipful Company of Art and Word only allowed him so many. And rules were rules, as the smug bastard in charge of licences was so fond of saying. Besides which, apprentices couldn't do everything and there were no extra journeymen available. Kit was run ragged.

Jem and Molly were similarly rushed off their feet, because books needed to be bound and above all accounts had to be kept or they wouldn't be doing much of anything anymore, royal contract or not.

It wasn't only the contract for the king. It was everything else as well.

Ben was a scholar rather than a businessman, often lost in his books, his studies or his own mind. Not exactly practical and easily distracted. And that was when the business of House Alvarez could spare him at all. He was still a lord of one of the richest trading houses in the city, a seigneur of the royal court and Andalusian nobility. Beatriz might run things but she didn't allow her little brother to slack off either. Everyone knew him now he was back in

Amberes. And everyone wanted something. Scholars and the like were eager to involve him in various topics of research and Ben welcomed them all, as excited by each new prospect as a child on their name day. Everything was a puzzle to be solved as far as his lover was concerned, even people. Kit didn't know how to deal with that. Any time with Ben felt like it was stolen. For the last month, for example, he had spent every free moment in the Blacksmiths' Guild, fixated on his latest project.

It was . . . *difficult.* That was the problem. Everything was difficult.

Kit drank cheap brandy until he slept like the dead, or worked himself to the bone all through the night. It was easier that way. It blocked out the memories of all that had happened. Of Montalbeau and the Scholars' Tower. Of the duchess.

He still couldn't drown the nightmares.

Lyta wasn't faring much better. He knew that. He heard her sometimes, when she woke herself screaming, or worse, when she didn't, when he warred with himself over going in there and waking her up, because the noises of fear and desperation she made couldn't be blocked out. Or when she couldn't sleep at all, and paced around the little room next to his, or took off into the Amberes night doing the gods alone knew what. But she wasn't about to let him help her. She still thought it was her job to be the one in control, the one saving the day and Kit knew she'd turn his help aside if he offered. He did what he could, but it was not enough.

He'd thought she'd leave as soon as everything had settled, shack up with Sylvian or something, but he had his duties to the palace and she shut down any suggestions she should be there with him. She seemed *aimless* somehow. He didn't know what to do about it. Lyta had always been the one to mind people, whether they liked it or not. And now she was trying to step back, to let him live his life as an adult. He knew she was trying. He wanted to help her, he really did. He just didn't know how.

So Kit carried on, throwing himself into his work and hoping beyond hope that one day she would tell him what she needed, allow him to be there for her, for once. That she would let him in.

Same with Ben really. Because Ben could be as changeable as the weather and Kit wasn't entirely sure anymore where his lover stopped and the gods inside him began. The Ben he had known, the man he had fallen in love with, had perhaps only truly existed between the Scholars' Tower and the Fortress of Montalbeau. But Kit had to believe he was still in there somewhere and sometimes, just sometimes, it was as if the powers of *The Book of Gold* had never touched him.

Those moments were rare. They never lasted long.

It was as if, as well as three remaining gods, Ben carried around an hourglass that was fast running out of sand. Every moment was precious, and Ben worked too hard all the time, as if chasing a solution. And heaven help anyone who brought that up.

So when Ben showed up mid-morning at the printshop, Kit was surprised. And a little apprehensive.

'I wanted to see you,' Ben told him, eyes a touch wary. 'Do you have a moment? Can you talk?'

Ben was dressed in what he considered *work clothes*. When he'd told Kit that, Kit had laughed because they were more formal than anything Kit would wear, except perhaps to the royal court. But the Seigneur of House Alvarez was expected to dress in brocade and fine wool and silks, and a printer was not. And such finery suited Ben.

'Come into the office,' Kit replied. They had argued last night. It had gone from bad to worse.

Ben had that familiar glow in his eyes and the faint touch of gold to his skin, which meant that his gods were stirring. Was he using magic already? Trying to smooth the way, make this less awkward? Kit wasn't sure if he did it on purpose or not, but he didn't like it. Whenever Ben used magic, it made his own skin crawl. But how could he explain that to the man he loved without yet another argument?

And he did love him. Far more than was wise.

Kit stepped inside first, holding the door for Ben, who slipped past him. The scent of sandalwood and cedar drifted after him and Kit couldn't help but inhale deeply, as if he could capture and hold that little piece of his lover. He closed the door firmly, shutting the world outside. His office was a small room off the front of the shop and he was not used to having such privacy, truth be told.

'What's the—?'

As he turned, Ben grabbed him by the shirt, pulling his head down so the Seigneur of House Alvarez could kiss him thoroughly, driving all thoughts of anything else out of Kit's mind. Ben kissed like he meant it, like it was something he was determined to get right. He was a scholar, after all. He studied everything until he perfected it.

'I missed you,' he murmured, his lips still catching against Kit's.

The rush of relief made Kit giddy. 'The feeling's mutual. What brought this on?'

'Do I need a reason?' He pulled back, as if unsure or defensive. Something in his eyes wasn't right, not really. That was not a good sign.

'No,' Kit said, a little too quickly, unwilling to let him go. 'Of course not.' He kissed Ben again, lingering over each movement. The air around them shimmered in that way it did when the gods were at work and Kit tried his best to ignore it. He couldn't avoid the magic that permeated his lover. But he didn't have to like it.

It made him nervous.

Ben broke off the kiss with a sigh, sensing Kit's concerns. His eyes studied Kit and in their hazel depths something else looked out. It was unnerving.

'You all right?' Kit asked tentatively and trailed his hand down the side of Ben's face.

Ben frowned, tried to smile, failed. He leaned in against Kit's palm for a moment. 'Yes, it's just . . .' He stepped back again, shaking his head as if to dislodge something. The gods in his head were always there, ready to interfere. 'They're at it again. I wanted to say I'm sorry. I got caught up in my work last night. And I was . . . I was rude. It was inexcusable.'

Kit let him go, reluctantly. He didn't want to fight. He never wanted to fight. 'Everyone forgets sometimes.'

But Ben shook his head. 'I know, but I'd promised to spend the evening with you and then—'

'It's all right, Ben . . .' Kit began, but Ben swallowed hard, still not finished.

'It isn't though, is it? I was horrible to you. Kyron doesn't know when to stop and he gets away from me sometimes. Just slips out. They all do. I'm sorry Kit.'

It had been Kyron then? It hadn't sounded like Ben, Kit knew that, the things he'd said last night as they parted. That cold, dismissive tone. Kyron, the Warrior . . . yes, that had sounded very much like *him*. But Ben had also sounded very much like a member of the Andalusian aristocracy, of which he was a prominent member. Which worried Kit even more.

He didn't like the nobility. Didn't trust them. Never had.

What on earth was he doing in a relationship with someone like Seigneur Benedictus of House Alvarez? He was such a fool.

Maybe gods were easier to deal with than the aristocracy.

Kit pushed that thought firmly away. It wasn't true. 'Are they getting worse?'

'All the time. Like they're chipping away inside me, trying to . . . I don't know . . . dig their way out, maybe? Or force me to do what they want. Ever since Ystara left them . . . It doesn't matter. Not anymore. That's why I'm here.' To Kit's surprise, he grinned. 'I have a plan.'

That didn't bode well. It was the way he said it. He sounded exactly like Lyta. Or Eninn. Certainly not like himself. 'What kind of plan?'

'You'll see. I wanted to ask a favour of Lyta actually.' He stopped, winced and the colour drained from his face.

'Ben?' Kit caught him as he swayed on his feet. For a moment several different expressions ghosted over his face and then he was Ben again, wide-eyed and breathing hard, fighting for control.

'It's all right.' He twisted his head to one side as if clearing a crick in his neck and ground out the words. 'Just . . . just a disagreement.'

That was one way of putting it. The gods who had squirrelled themselves away inside him when he read *The Book of Gold* were impatient and difficult, and they wanted out. Kit and Ben had thought transcribing the book and printing it would suffice. It hadn't worked. Reading the words had brought Kit to his knees, such was its power. He had hidden the one surviving copy, and they had told no one else of its existence.

'You can't go on like this,' Kit said, as patiently as he could. This was another source of many an argument. But he had to try, for Ben's sake. 'Have you talked to anyone? Beatriz?'

The mention of his sister was probably not the greatest idea. Kit knew as well as anyone what having an older sister determined that they knew what was best for you, all the time, was like. The problem was, they were usually right, though he would never admit that to Lyta.

Ben shook his head. 'She has her own concerns. Her abilities have never recovered following her defeat of the duchess. I don't know why and now our family have taken notice. It's a mess. I'm hiding in the Blacksmiths' Guild for as long as possible.' He was trying to make light of it. Kit wrapped his arms around him, held him close. Ben let out a long breath. It sounded like relief. 'It's going to be fine, Kit. I've found someone to help, an alchemist, and he's brilliant. He read one of my treatises on the divine and came here to seek me out. Can you believe it? We're working on a solution together.'

Kit let out a low laugh at that. 'Should I be jealous of this brilliant man seeking you out?'

Ben frowned. 'Why would you be—? Oh.' He smiled at Kit's fond expression and blushed. 'You're teasing. I'm sorry. I'm never sure.'

Kit gently tilted Ben's face up with a finger under his chin. He really was beautiful and he didn't see it. Beautiful and brilliant, and a little broken sometimes. All Ben really wanted to do was solve puzzles, work out the impossible secrets of the universe, unravel all the knots of divinity. He had been born a Divine Nexus, a lodestone for gods and a storehouse of godly power. That would leave anyone a bit broken.

Kit had never met anyone like him. And had never loved anyone so very much. Ben knew that, surely?

So Kit kissed him again gently, to reassure him. 'No, I'm serious. Well, a bit serious. I trust you. It's everyone else trying to steal you away.'

'Thomas isn't . . .' Ben made a face, taken aback by the suggestion. If Kit had doubted him at all, he wouldn't now. Thomas Charnock. Ben had mentioned letters from him and his arrival in Amberes. Kit hadn't given it much thought. Maybe he should have. It wasn't jealousy, not exactly. But Kit knew he wasn't as clever as half the people Ben associated with, and Ben's own genius dazzled him every day. 'Honestly Kit. He's not my type.'

'And what is your type?'

'That is such a printer question.' An amused smile blossomed on his lips now. 'Do you want me to show you? You can be very demanding, Kit Cornellis. It must be the craftsman in you. Such a perfectionist.'

Kit relented and grinned back at him, relaxing at last. 'So can you, heart.'

By the time Ben left, Kit had completely forgotten that he hadn't actually got an answer as to what the plan was, or what Thomas Charnock the alchemist could do for them. Ben had a way of being far too distracting.

The office seemed very quiet all of a sudden, but Ben's scent of sandalwood and cedar lingered. Kit tried to busy himself with paperwork. The new batch of ink wasn't the right quality. He'd already done a couple of tests with it and he wasn't happy. Too acidic by far, the kind of ink that would eat away at even the best quality cotton-rich paper over time. He needed to report it to the guild—which wasn't going to go down well because they'd been the ones to recommend it—and try to find something else. Or make his own again. That was going to cost. That was one letter he wasn't looking forward to writing. He pushed it aside.

The artist he'd commissioned for the etchings wasn't delivering either and that was going to be another fight he really didn't want to have. He loathed confrontation at the best of times. And the way some of them looked at him, the other members of his guild who were meant to be his brothers and sisters—as if he was an upstart, as if he didn't know what he was doing, as if he had somehow swindled a king to get this job. Many of them were just waiting for him to fail.

Sometimes it felt like failure was the only thing he was close to delivering.

They were certainly no closer to printing Francisco's book. Ben was still trying to come to terms with the effects of *The Book of Gold* on his mind and body, and working on its fresh transcription was difficult as it threw up all kinds of complications. The gods liked to argue, it seemed. And when they did agree on a text, reading it frequently sent Kit into a daze. Ben had set up a study in Beatriz's house because it was quieter and the printshop could be like the centre of the Great Market at times. Kit fretted constantly over Ben which probably hadn't helped either.

He still didn't really know Ben Alvarez. He wasn't the scholar they'd rescued from the Tower, or the man who had gone into Montalbeau either. He was the Seigneur of House Alvarez, and a man who had studied in some of the finest universities in the world. He was beautiful and a Divine Nexus, and fragile.

Kit was terrified of breaking him. Though it seemed as if the gods were already doing that themselves. It was worse all the time, as if Ben was clinging to the end of a thread which was quickly unravelling.

Here he was, thinking about Ben again. About holding him, kissing him, about finding a way to make things work with him and protect him, while the gods gnawed away inside him. Kit sighed and pressed his forehead against the desk, banging it gently as if he could knock some sense into himself.

'Um, Kit?' Jem cleared his throat meaningfully. He didn't sound happy. Jem filled the doorway, his broad shoulders and chest clothed in a work tunic and his hair tied back. He looked nervous and that alone gave Kit pause. Nothing scared Jem. Well, nothing except Molly, his tiny firebrand of a wife. 'Kit, we've got company.'

That didn't sound good either.

'I don't have time right now.' Or the energy, but since when did that matter? He'd already wasted the morning. Well, not wasted.

Not entirely. But he'd got next to no actual work done. 'Can you deal with it?'

'I—I don't think—'

A noise in the main workshop brought Kit to his feet, a crash of something hitting the ground. 'What the—?'

He pushed past Jem, out into the larger room where tall windows threw light across his equipment and saw Petrus Janlow standing by one of the presses, a case of Kit's carefully ordered type spilling over the floor at his feet.

'Oops,' said Janlow with an unrepentant sneer. He kicked some of the pieces away with his boot. Far too expensive a leather to belong on that foot, Kit thought bitterly.

Crossing Janlow had only ever brought him and Lyta misery. Kit might hate the man and everything about him, but he also had a keenly developed sense for self-preservation. There were four other men and women with the gang leader—rough, hard, the worst of the city. He knew them to see and had always tried to pretend he didn't. But they knew him too, clearly.

The moment Kit appeared every eye was on him like a pack of hunting hounds spying a fox.

Great.

Royal printing licence, he reminded himself. Respectable businessman and guild member.

And still Janlow could waltz in here like this and cause chaos whenever he felt like it.

'What do you want?' he growled, grabbing a spare pullers' lever for the presses from where it leaned against the wall. It was the closest thing to a weapon here. Behind him, Jem did the same. They were big men, strong and not afraid of a bit of violence, either of them. But they were also outnumbered and surely outclassed. The other heavies moved their hands to weapons, not so concealed beneath the long cloaks they wore, all the same colour and bearing the same crest as Janlow's.

Janlow's gang. Alderton's employees. Same thing now.

'Well that's no way to greet an old friend, *Kitten*,' Janlow sneered at him. Kit swallowed down the reply that came first into his mind.

This man was no friend of his. He would have gladly seen Kit dead as a boy and had made Lyta's life a misery on more than one occasion. Ranulf had saved them from him, but only just. Using *Kitten* was another dig, one designed to get a response which Kit refused to play into. He knew better.

'You aren't welcome here, Janlow,' Kit said, amazed at how even his voice sounded. 'Best leave now.'

'Or what? You'll call the watch?' He grinned at his companions, as if to say '*And what would they do?*' There was a ripple of laughter, nasty and knowing, but Kit held his ground. 'You're a respectable businessman, Master Cornellis, I know that. I'm sure they'd come running. But so am I these days, so all they'd do is tell us to play nice, isn't that so? And I do want to play nice, Kit. My patron wants a word with you, that's all.'

'Your patron?' He knew the answer, but it didn't mean he was going to say it and give Janlow any form of legitimacy in any of this. 'Or your master?'

Janlow scowled. 'Lord Charles Alderton.'

They all knew full well who was holding Janlow's leash these days. He had no more reason to defer to him either. The nobleman from Albion had almost killed Lyta, and had persuaded Frida to betray them all. If Janlow was the last man in Amberes Kit wanted anything to do with, Alderton ran a close second. And if he ever laid eyes on Frida again . . .

He kept his voice low and steady. 'I have no business with Lord Alderton either. If you'll excuse us, we're busy.'

'A conversation. Won't take long. A proposition, that's all. Hear him out, Kitten. Before anything awful happens to your lovely new premises. It's taken you all this time to get up and running again after the last unpleasantness.'

Anything awful. Great. Janlow had once burned Lyta's house to the ground to make a point. But at least he wasn't demanding money to make sure that his particular brand of something awful didn't happen. A conversation. Fine. He could spare a few words for Lord

Charles Alderton. They probably wouldn't be pleasant ones. But that still didn't mean he was a fool.

'I'm not going anywhere with you.'

'No need. He's right outside in his carriage. Waiting. He doesn't like to wait for long, Kitten.'

Kit raised one eyebrow, firmed his jaw and stared Janlow down.

Call me Kitten one more time, he thought, and tightened his grip on the length of wood.

'Well he can come in here and talk then. Like I said, I'm not going anywhere with you or him.'

Janlow snorted out a laugh. 'Suit yourself. He won't like it though.'

'I don't much care,' Kit told him. 'If he wants to talk, that's my condition. And you lot, out.'

As Janlow and his thugs obeyed, Kit glanced at Jem who gave the impression of having been carved from stone, his eyes blazing with anger. Good. At least there were two of them here.

He was grateful Ben had gone. There was no telling how Kyron, the God of War, would react to a threat like this. He'd try to help, which meant anything could happen. The gods forgot that Ben was mortal and Kit couldn't bear it if Ben got hurt on his account. But he'd seen that flush of rage fill Ben's face too many times when Kyron took control.

'You sure this is a good idea, Kit?' Jem asked.

'No. Not in the slightest. But I'm not sure what else to do. Just watch my back, all right?'

Jem nodded curtly. 'I sent the boys out back, told them to take a break. Molly's already on the way to the watch house. They might not hurry along but she'll make a scene until they do come, believe me.'

Kit did. He absolutely did. Molly could raise an army if she set her mind to it. He trusted the two of them in a way he trusted few other people. When the duchess and the Magister were coming, he'd given the second proof copy of *The Book of Gold* into Jem and Molly's keeping. They'd returned it without even taking a look. When he'd asked why not, Molly fixed him with that implacable expression and said, 'It seems like an awful lot of trouble, that thing. Best left alone.'

She was not wrong.

Alderton swept into the workshop as if he owned it. Everything he wore was quietly understated but clearly the best, tailored to make the most of an already excellent physique.

The exiled lord from Albion cast a dismissive eye around the room—at the cabinets of type, the ink, the presses, the sheets of printed paper hanging up to dry like washing high overhead, scraps of paper scattered everywhere ready to be used as wrappers, padding or to wedge between wobbly bits of type—assessing it, calculating its worth in an instant no doubt, and finding it wanting. His upper lip curled in a way that set Kit's teeth on edge.

Kit tightened his grip on the lever and glared. He knew his worth and that of his workshop. Trust someone like Alderton to be unable to appreciate that.

'Master Cornellis,' said Alderton finally. He cast a glance at Janlow, who followed close behind him. 'Leave us be, Petrus. I will speak to the master printer alone.'

Master printer. That was a concession Kit hadn't expected. Not that he was about to drop his guard.

Jem, Kit noticed, didn't move. He was holding his lever in both hands, his feet hip distance apart, ready for anything. Alderton turned his cool gaze on him but the big bookbinder didn't flinch.

'My partner,' Kit said, careful not to name him. Alderton probably already knew who he was. Lyta was convinced the Albion lordling knew everything that went on in Amberes, and pulled most of the strings as well, but that didn't mean Kit was going to offer anything extra up on a plate.

'Indeed,' Alderton said. He glanced around for a moment, but clearly decided that the typesetter's stool was beneath him. He indicated the proofing desk under the window, a plain wooden table with benches on either side where Kit and Molly would meticulously check the first sheets of any print run for errors. 'Would you join me, Master Cornellis? Kit?'

Kit lifted his chin and took a seat opposite him, still keeping the lever within reach. 'What do you want with us, Lord Alderton?'

No first names for him. If Alderton thought him rude, so be it. There was nothing in his words or tone to give that impression, but this man was not a friend and never would be. He could talk as sweetly as he liked, but Kit knew him for a monster.

Alderton didn't smile. He didn't try to charm Kit or anything like that. His smooth expression didn't quite crack, but there was an urgency in his grey eyes that didn't fit all Lyta had said about him. This was a man who ruined people, who blackmailed the great and the good and destroyed all those who got in his way. As a landlord, he was the worst kind, intent only on profit and not on his tenants' welfare. He'd been known to put people out on the street for any infraction, even for a whim. Because he could.

But right now he was . . . *worried.* More than worried. There was an edge of frantic in his gaze and the set of his mouth. Kit could read people. It was one of his strengths. This was a man on the edge. Not in a dangerous way though. This was a person in need. Afraid.

'I want you to intercede with your sister for me. I need her help.'

For a moment Kit couldn't think of a thing to say in response to that. His eyes grew wide, mouth parting in surprise.

'*Lyta*? You're talking about *Lyta*?'

It was not like he had another sister.

Lord Alderton had the grace to look uncomfortable at making the request. 'I realise the last time we met we did not part on the best of terms.'

'You kidnapped her, threatened her and she only escaped with a knife in her back. She's lucky to be alive.'

Alderton spread his hands between them. Even his nails were spotlessly clean. 'My employees were overzealous. You know how that is, I'm sure. They can get carried away in their eagerness to please. Like your . . . man there.'

Kit's surprise gave way to a dark irritation.

'Jem isn't my employee,' Kit growled. 'As I said, he's my partner.' If this man was trying to approach him as some kind of equal,

Kit was not having that. Especially not if he was implying whatever Kit thought he was implying about Jem. The dark-skinned man was a skilled bookbinder and Kit was damned lucky to have him in the business. Especially after everything that happened earlier in the year. 'Look, if you think I can persuade Lyta to do anything she doesn't want to do, you really don't know her. My sister has a mind of her own, and that mind is very firmly set against you.'

Alderton gave a sigh. He withdrew his hands and reached into the inside of his coat. Kit flinched, expecting a wheellock pistol or at least a knife to emerge and for this to all turn very nasty very quickly.

But instead the lord brought out a small oval bundle, wrapped in wine-coloured velvet. He unfolded the material to reveal a miniature, framed in gold; a portrait of a woman, young and exceedingly beautiful, with hair the colour of honey and a heart-shaped face. She wore a pale pink gown which set her skin aglow. She was little more than a girl, not even twenty if Kit was any judge.

'I know all about headstrong sisters, Master Cornellis. We have that in common. This is Viola, my youngest sister, the only one still unmarried, despite the best efforts of my good lady mother. She has been too indulged in her studies and interests, as a favourite of the royal court. She apparently arrived here by boat from Albion last week, but she never made her way to my house. We had no foreknowledge of her travelling here and it was only when her maid came to us a few days ago, dishevelled and near out of her wits, that I was even aware she was here in Amberes. She has vanished without a trace and I am very much afraid she is in an awful lot of trouble.'

CHAPTER FOUR

Lyta

It was only a brief and stolen time with Sylvian, moments shared over a dead body no less, but that was all she got these days. It was her own fault. She didn't like it but there was nothing else for it. He was sworn to the queen, bound to serve her with divine ties. So when Annika snapped her fingers, he had to go running. Lyta knew that.

He'd offered Lyta a place beside him, a home, a life. And she'd panicked. The thought of being married again, even to Sylvian, the thought of having to live at the beck and call of the queen, or worse, the king if he ever came back . . . She ought to have made a clean break of it then. It would have been fairer to him, to both of them. But she couldn't.

Thirteen years apart hadn't done it. She kept coming back to him. He was an addiction, something she could not quit. A need, like air.

The feeling of his lips against hers lingered, even now, his hands in her hair or stroking the skin of her jawline, and she had to push it right to the back of her mind if she was going to get anything but daydreaming done. It was stupid anyway, to dwell on such things. They had no future together and any dreams of that had been like a mirage, or delusions brought on by stress and exhaustion of all they had gone through six months ago. They'd spent too many years apart. She'd married someone else and lost him. She didn't want the same thing happening to Sylvian. Once, Ranulf had called her his lucky charm, but that wasn't true. Not even when she found him again, when she thought she was rescuing him from Montalbeau. He'd died because of her.

She couldn't risk Sylvian. Not now.

And there was divine power at work in their lives which twisted everything beyond reason. She didn't know what she was feeling half the time and if it was real. Not only was he sworn to the queen, Sylvian was Chosen by Ystara, the Goddess of Love, her champion. And yes, *that* was probably Lyta's fault as well. His life was not his own.

Sylvian was not hers. Not anymore. He belonged to the goddess and through her to the queen. The back of her mind was the best place for him.

Unfortunately the back of her mind was where her small feral god now lived and Eninn found it all hilarious. *You're following him into gainful employment. Whatever are you turning into? It'll be settling down to a respectable court position next. Annika will have both of you leashed. And then Ystara will try to get her claws into you as well. You see if she doesn't.*

That was exactly what she was afraid of. She lived free in Amberes and she was happy with it. Even if it meant she couldn't have Sylvian.

She didn't need this. She didn't need any of this.

'If you don't stop,' she warned Eninn, 'I will find a magic pin and yank you out like a winkle, understand me?'

Don't be shellfish, Lyta, he replied, and her head rang with his howls of laughter as he delighted in his own cleverness and his truly appalling taste in puns. Gods, what was she going to do about him? He was going to drive her demented. She stamped angrily down the street towards the Rookery, furious because she had set herself up for that and she had only herself to blame, trying to ignore him because attention was what he craved.

She didn't know how Ben Alvarez coped with a trio of the bastards in his mind. But then, if he was to be believed, as a Divine Nexus he had been made for something like that, born for it. She had not. She was a thief and nothing more. She didn't want to be anything more.

Just because she hadn't been able to let her god die on his own in the Nether and the wandering ways. Just because she'd been stupid enough to go after him and get him back. He wasn't even a very good god.

I love you too, Eninn murmured in a sing-song echo which bounced around her skull like laughter. *You should eat something. You get so ratty when you're hungry.*

And he wasn't wrong about that either. He knew her better than she knew herself sometimes. Her stomach growled loudly.

'Soon,' she told him. 'I have to see someone first.'

The streets and alleys of the Rookery pressed close together, narrow and winding, a little maze in the middle of Amberes. The smell was worst in summer, but now, in the depths of winter, it was still bad. Street cleaners didn't come down here much. The stooped timber-framed houses hung out over the pathways, almost touching at the top as their own weight pulled them down. Snow had melted into a miserable sludge in the gutters and refrozen.

The Rack of Lamb on Miller's Row might have sounded like somewhere people would take their elderly mother for a nice lunch, but once they saw the sign hanging outside, with a graphic, full-colour depiction of a flayed sheep stretched out for torture, most of those people would have turned tail. They'd have dragged dear mama behind them, and found somewhere else, somewhere nice and safe, up on Meir or in the Old Quarter as quickly as possible. It wasn't far from the Temple of Lost Gods or her old house, dug in deep like a tick in the Rookery, and eternally subject to the moods and dark humour of its landlord, Etienne du Lac.

Lyta used to drink there frequently with Frida. It was a handy staggering distance from her former house on Larch Lane, which still had not been rebuilt because she didn't have the money. And no one else gave a damn since the buildings on either side showed no sign of falling down yet. She could probably have asked General Vasquez for the necessary cash, she supposed. They owed her a wage at least.

But being obviously in possession of a large amount of money in this part of Amberes was never a good idea, even if she promptly spent it on something. Her neighbours would assume there was more and set out to find it, through fair means or foul. And if word went around too widely she was working for the queen, no matter how tangentially, she didn't know what would happen. She had been branded a snitch once in her life and she was never going to allow that to happen again.

She found a table in the corner which wasn't particularly sticky and sat with her back to the wall because she wasn't stupid.

It didn't take Du Lac too long to appear. He was playing at jovial host today, a grubby towel flung over one shoulder and a smile on his face as he handed her a mug of the watered-down ale he pretended was full-strength and wished her a happy Solstice. She didn't take a sip. It was still too early and she wasn't sure her stomach would take it after the morning she'd had. He'd probably pass it off to someone else soon enough.

'Are you after food? Sal and the girls are off until Solstice, but I'm sure—'

Again, her stomach decided this was a terrible idea and threatened to revolt if she ate anything he cooked for her.

'No, thanks. I need some information. Florrie Stone sent me.' It wasn't strictly true, but Florrie would probably back her up anyway. And if she didn't, Lyta would be long gone.

Du Lac sat down opposite her and used the towel to wipe the surface of the table half-heartedly, not as if he actually meant to clean it. 'Information's a lot more expensive than ale, pet. You could pay in kind.'

Lyta raised an eyebrow. The man was twice her age, bald and had a face like a smashed-in turnip, so she sincerely hoped he didn't want what it sounded like.

Seeing her expression, he laughed as if she was a court jester. 'You're not my type, pet. Even leaving aside our ages, or the fact you were married to Ranulf Wray. I meant information in return, that's all.'

She tried not to let him see the sigh of relief. That kiss from Sylvian might have made her desperate, but not *that* desperate. Still, she didn't mean to insult the man.

'I can probably do that,' she replied. 'Depends on what you want. If I don't know, I can keep my eyes and ears open for you.'

It was a fair enough offer and he nodded.

'That goes both ways, doesn't it?' He waved over one of the pot-boys who removed the ale and came back with creamy Byzantine coffees for both of them.

Du Lac sipped his first and made that face she was coming to recognise as the one worn by those who commonly drank the stuff, one of relief and contentment. A moment later she wore it herself.

'It's good,' she said.

'I bought a stove-top *cezve* pot off those boys from Vienna. Costs, but by the gods and all that's holy, it's worth it. Now, what's this about?'

The tavern was almost empty, but she scanned the other figures, huddled in their own corners, studiously ignoring her and Du Lac.

He noticed the glance. Of course. 'No loose lips in here, Lyta. Never have been, or at least, not twice. What are you after?'

She told him about the robbery at the temple and his face grew grim. When she got to the body his eyebrows drew together.

'Not one of us,' he rumbled ominously.

'I didn't think so. Not your style. They trashed the place too. Where's the profit in that?'

Du Lac seemed to settle a little at the assurance and nodded, draining his coffee and calling for another. They sat in silence while it was brought over, waiting until they were ostensibly alone again.

'*Merde*,' the relic thief growled. 'There's definitely someone new on the scene. If any of mine catch them, there'll be hell to pay. You rough someone up, knock out someone who walks in on you . . . that's shoddy, but shit happens. Killing *kids*? No.' He scowled. 'Four of them you say?' He drained the second cup almost as quickly. 'Someone was up to something at the old temple up by the Scaldis Gate three nights ago. Don't know what, but there were reports of people in there mucking about. Rituals or what have you. Time of year for it. Nothing left to steal there, so it might be nothing. There are always nutters around. The Blacksmiths' Guild have their place on lockdown. It looks like someone got in there. Or tried to.'

The Blacksmiths' Guild was notoriously close-lipped, comprising as it did, glass-blowers, swordsmiths and alchemists, as well as all kinds of other artisans who didn't want their trade secrets getting around.

'Is something missing?'

'They don't only have relics of Gloir in there. They collect all sorts and try to figure out how they work. Alchemists think you can tap into godly power with them, or maybe take it out and stick it in something else. Harnessing it or what have you. The *great work*, they call it. All kinds of mad theories. They have old relics there too, ones that should be elsewhere, or that were thought destroyed outright. They do like to poke and prod at stuff, don't they? I've provided some artefacts for them in my time. De Werve and his people pay well.'

Right, well it was information and a lead of sorts. The Blacksmiths' Guild . . .

'Thank you,' she said. 'And what's your price?'

'Haldevar,' he said and it was like a lead weight suddenly dragged Lyta's stomach down to the grubby floor. 'Who killed him, Lyta?'

Haldevar had been a friend, a colleague and one of the few people she'd trusted in Amberes. He had been a partner of her late husband's, a gifted burglar until an injury had put paid to that, and then he'd moved to information-trading and life as a fence, all while running a spice shop up on High Street. He'd been the best. He'd died because someone had thought he had something Lyta had stolen.

That someone was Frida, his sometime lover and Lyta's former partner in crime, her only close friend. Until she'd betrayed Lyta to Alderton anyway.

Haldevar's death had been an accident, Frida claimed, but Lyta didn't believe that for a moment. Even if it had been, the man was still found floating face-down in the Scaldis.

'Well?' asked Du Lac, reminding her that Haldevar had been respected by the entire criminal underworld of this city. What did she owe Frida anyway? The woman had probably put a knife in her back. She'd certainly double-crossed Lyta readily enough.

'If I knew that for certain, they'd be dead already.' But even as she said it the lie hung there awkwardly.

His eyes narrowed as if he could read her thoughts. 'He was a good man and he said good things about you. You, your mam, your da and most of all your brother. Don't make him a liar in death, Lyta.'

Haldevar, like Ranulf, had been as close to family as she had. The mention of her father made Lyta wince. He was a ghost on the edge of her life, a vague recollection of the shape of a man missing from her childhood. Her mother had adored him, no doubt about that, and she and Kit must resemble him because they were nothing like dark-haired, dark-eyed Rhea Cornellis. He'd been a good man too, those who had met him on one of those fleeting instances when he came home had said. But what use was a good man when he vanished like morning mist? Lyta had been too young to remember him as more than a shape, an outline. Kit didn't remember him at all.

Haldevar had been a good man too, yes. Definitely, one of the best. Unfortunately he had terrible taste in girlfriends. But Lyta still couldn't bring herself to say Frida's name. It was a death sentence.

'He ran afoul of a certain lord from Albion. His people did it. And —' Fuck, she might as well admit as much as she could. He'd find out anyway. 'It was because of something I took so . . . I'm not proud of it, Etienne, but there it is. We did a job that went wrong. Badly wrong.'

'The Montalbeau one?'

Eninn's balls! Did everyone know about that? She'd thought it was meant to be secret. A laughable thought in Amberes, where information was a currency as much as gold.

She pushed back Eninn's reply saying she should leave his balls out of it thank you very much and swallowed hard. 'No. Before that.'

Du Lac nodded slowly, fitting some pieces together in his mind. He was smart and very, very dangerous.

He changed the subject so quickly that she knew he'd made a decision and she wasn't sure she wanted to think about what that might be.

'Speaking of Montalbeau, there're rumours about what happened there too. About what she had there, the duchess.'

The blood left Lyta's skin and she didn't try to hide it. She wasn't that good an actress. But she had to warn him even if her voice shook when she did. 'Du Lac, anyone who sets foot in that place is asking for trouble. It's the stuff of nightmares and we were damned lucky to make it out alive. Even if that unholy bitch is dead, don't make the mistake of thinking it's safe now. I'm surprised the king didn't give it the same treatment as the Scholars' Tower.'

If he didn't heed that warning, it wasn't her fault, she reasoned. When the king left it, the Scholars' Tower was no more than ashes and ruins. She wished that he'd done the same to Montalbeau. So long as no one asked her to go back, that was fine with her.

Du Lac snorted. Not dismissive, not exactly, but still, she didn't like it. 'So I've heard. Bad place. And you were at the Tower too, weren't you, when Francisco destroyed it? You get yourself into a lot of trouble, Lyta Cornellis. You ought to take more care.'

She laughed. She couldn't help it. It was a mix of relief and resignation because she feared that he was right. 'That is very true, my friend. Very true indeed.' She started to get up, but Du Lac's fingers closed on her wrist, stopping her. She slid her other hand back to the hilt of the knife she had tucked out of sight, but he looked up at her face with genuine concern.

'Whatever is going on with the temples, they've graduated to dead bodies, Lyta. I'll keep an eye for the relics, you know I will, and any other information that might help you. This is bad for all of us and whoever is messing around with divine power needs to be stopped. But you need to watch your back, understand? There's something bad going on. You can do all sorts with the right kind of relics. They can kill, no doubt about that, but worse as well. Gods are not something to play games with.'

This was a man who knew what he was talking about on that front, and he was clearly in earnest.

'I know that,' she assured him and for once, Eninn stayed silent.

'Some of them are old, Lyta, and they're not as gone as people would like to believe. Some of them reach back here from time to time.'

'I thought no one came back from the Nether,' she said before thinking about the statement.

Du Lac eyed her curiously. 'We don't know. Not really. Some say the barrier between here and there has been damaged. It's thin this time of year to begin with. That's why we light the fires, to drive off those that are unwanted.'

Lyta dropped her gaze to the tabletop, aware of the eerie way he was studying her now. This was a man used to relics, and to the presence of gods. He might not sense Eninn, but then again, he might.

'Damaged how?'

He gave a brief laugh. 'That's the question, isn't it? Something happened not so long ago. Around the time of Montalbeau perhaps?' He read her reaction and she saw the knowing smile broaden. Oh, he was getting information from her all right, whether she wanted to share or not. 'You be careful, you hear? You're wearing a relic around your neck, girl, and you're closer to the Trickster than anyone. But he can't help you against everyone. The Winter Solstice was once Druon's holiest time. Old gods like that . . . Stories say he still walks our streets on the nights of the Winter Solstice. Rich pickings, Amberes.'

Druon again she thought. The bogeyman of Amberes. *Be good or Druon will climb back out of the Scaldis and chop you to pieces.*

'What do you know about a hand?' she asked, remembering Alaric's ramblings.

'A hand? Druon's hand?' He arched his eyebrows. 'Is that what this is about? Now, that was a relic . . . No one's heard word of it in centuries though. The hand of Druon Antigonus, the Giant of the Scaldis, Cissonia's brother. He had other names too and a dark reputation. Nothing could stop the two of them. She ruled the land and he ruled the river. Took a toll whenever anyone passed by—gold, blood, virgins . . . whatever he fancied.

'They said he wore all the gold he collected until it looked like he was made of it, but he was all stone underneath. He was hacked apart and thrown in the Scaldis up by the Steen in the end. Some imperial hero with a magic sword. You know how they love to claim those sorts of stories. But someone kept the hand and made a relic of it, or so I've heard.' The laugh was more of a scoffing snort this time. Du Lac didn't have any more time for the Church Imperial than Lyta did. 'Some people still hear him from the river at night—Druon, that is. Still listen to him and there's some as would welcome him back if they could. The solstice is the time to do that. Like I said, his time. Always was. But old gods mostly want blood and they don't much care who it comes from. There are always zealots out there more than ready to provide it. Then and now. Be careful.'

*

Lyta made her way up the length of Cornmarket Street, dodging a stream of carts and animals going from the docks to the markets. The music of her city, the shouts and bellows, the creaking and grinding, sang out around her. The tower which housed the Temple of Cissonia loomed over her the whole way, rising above the city, behind the Great Market and the elaborate guild houses. She stared at it, the weak winter sun catching on the golden figure which adorned the top of it. It was the highest point in Amberes and the goddess was the patron of the city. The bells the tower housed rang out the hours, and sounded the alarm in times of trouble—fire, attacks, floods, anything really. It was the heart and soul of the city.

Was Cissonia made of gold like her lost brother? No. If so that statue would have been nicked and melted down long ago.

Vasquez had told her to investigate, so some information ought to have been forthcoming. Then again, knowing the general, maybe not. Vasquez only told people what she felt they needed to know. And other than 'There are three others', that was all Lyta had. She needed to find out what was going on before there were any more.

As Lyta reached the bustle of the Great Market, the heart of Amberes, where hawkers cried out like a choir and stallholders haggled for their lives, her stomach was protesting so loudly she was fairly sure everyone could hear even over that noise. And while Du Lac's coffee had staved it off for a while, it couldn't work miracles. If it could, he'd have charged a lot more. In the middle of the market industrious urchins were already building up the new bonfire for tonight, a precarious tower of anything that might potentially burn, and begging for coins for doing it.

The seductive aromas of a pie stall drew her in and she bought a crisp shell of pastry that might conceivably contain chicken, if she was lucky. Or possibly seagull. She didn't want to think too closely about that anyway. It tasted divine, whatever it was and she was still wiping the crumbs from her face when someone called her name. She turned sharply, ready to run in an instant. Some instincts never went away and they had always served her well.

Outside the ostentatious entrance to the Blacksmiths' Guild house, with its decorative portico and columns, topped with the gilded statue of Gloir at the apex, Ben Alvarez was waving at her with far too much enthusiasm for someone of his lofty standing in so public a place. Other people turned to look and she raised her hand half-heartedly. No getting away from him now anyway.

The Alvarez siblings were like bloodhounds with a scent when they wanted something. She knew that better than anyone. Beatriz had only agreed to help them in the first place so long as they brought Ben home to her first. Oh, they were cultured and rich, and so very clever, but that, Lyta had decided, just made them worse.

Ben wanted her now and he wasn't going to let her slip away. Heaving out a sigh, she changed direction, making her way across the heart of the market to meet him. It was not as busy as usual. Midweek in winter always was quieter than any other time of the year. The solstice celebrations would swell the crowds in the city a little, but it was early yet. While Amberes still churned through trade for half the continent, the north and the western islands, there was less by way of actual goods for sale. Weather affected sea trade, and crops had further to travel. The butchers did the best trade of all, but come the turning of the year, even they slowed until spring. This winter was the worst she could remember, and everyone muttered darkly how quickly stocks were dwindling. Every ship that arrived came through dreadful storms and ice floes. There was even talk of the Scaldis freezing over upstream, and that was no good at all, that Druon was stirring, making his displeasure known. Rumour had it that in Londinium the Temesas had frozen so solidly that they were holding great fairs upon its surface, which seemed like the height of idiocy. The one thing certain about ice was that it melted. But what else did anyone expect from Albion, Lyta thought.

Ben grinned broadly as she approached and promptly pulled her into an embrace by way of greeting. He was richly dressed, far from gaunt scholar they had found under the spell of the Magister. Beatriz was feeding him up and probably bringing in tailors from Paris and the Duchy of Milan to dress him in such a fine black velvet trimmed with fur. The cloak alone was worth a small fortune. Ben wore it all like he had thrown it on before running out of his sister's very fine house this morning. Which he probably had.

'I tried to find you earlier, Lyta,' he said with an enthusiasm that did not bode well. 'This is Piers. Lord Stirling, I mean. Piers, this is Lyta Cornellis. I was telling you about her, and her brother.'

Another man, just as richly dressed as Ben but far more aware of it, swept his cape over his shoulder and gave her a courtly bow that might have knocked another woman's common sense from her head. He was dressed in rich wools, dark blues and greys, which highlighted the golden hues of his skin and hair. His eyes were the colour of amber and there was laughter caught in their depths. He was handsome, and by Ystara, he knew it.

No, she thought a second later. *He was pretty*. That was worse.

Sylvian could snap him in two. He wouldn't even break a sweat, her Syl.

'Stirling,' said Lyta, completely and deliberately ignoring the title. She had never trusted a title and nothing she'd experienced in the last six months could convince her otherwise. Kit had the right of it when it came to nobles. Although even he had one notable Alvarez-shaped blind spot.

'Mistress Cornellis,' Stirling said with a smile. It was, admittedly, a good smile, genuine and open, with intelligence behind it. She'd underestimate him at her peril. 'I've just arrived in Amberes from Albion and Seigneur Alvarez was good enough to offer to host me. We corresponded for some time, after his visit to Oxford . . . what was it Ben, seven years ago?'

'Eight,' Ben replied happily basking in the warmth of friendship renewed.

Dear gods he must have been a child, Lyta thought. And Ben an infant. But clearly Ben was happy to see this man again. Lyta had never seen him so carefree, not even with Kit, and that gave her pause.

She studied his face a little more carefully. The strain behind his dark eyes was still there. Was this all an act? Was it for her sake or for Stirling's?

'I thought he'd dropped off the face of the earth until a few months ago,' Stirling went on, without noticing the uncomfortable silence. 'It was so good to hear from you again my friend, and fortuitous for me since I had business here.'

Well, Ben almost *had* dropped off the face of the earth. He'd been lost inside the Scholars' Tower, barely aware of who he was or what he really wanted. And if the Magister had had his way that was where Ben would have stayed; his own Divine Nexus, obedient and subdued, drawing untold gods to him so the Magister could steal their power. What would have become of Ben then didn't bear thinking about.

Lyta glanced at Ben and he had the grace to look a little panicked. So he didn't want his old friend to know what had happened to him. Fair enough. Everyone had secrets.

'What's your business?' she asked Stirling.

'I'm here at the behest of my master, Doctor John Dee, of the royal court of the Virgin Queen, regarding the alchemist Thomas Charnock. Ben knows him, from the Blacksmiths' Guild.'

Ben promptly turned scarlet.

'What are you working on with alchemists, Ben?' She tried to keep the suspicion out of her voice.

'Oh just . . .' There was something disarming about the way he got embarrassed when the subject turned to his work. Like he didn't expect anyone to be interested. Maybe that was why he adored Kit. Kit was always interested, though he admitted to Lyta he often couldn't follow half of it. But he still tried because he loved Ben. 'Charnock sought me out when he arrived here. He heard about my research and he's already made such headway in something similar. We've been honing the theory together, working on a way to . . .' Lyta narrowed her eyes, aware he was skirting around the answer. 'It's a way of balancing . . . um . . . the *genii* and moderating its influence on . . . that is . . . containing . . .'

He stared at her as if he wanted her to pick up on something which she was completely missing. Something he didn't want to say out loud. Not here anyway. *Genii*? What the hell was that? Latin? She stared at him blankly, waiting for clarification. 'My *friends*, you know?'

Oh. *Gods*. He meant the gods.

Friends now, are they? Eninn muttered darkly and Lyta frowned. They hadn't been friendly to him. Ystara had made a deal and seized Sylvian's fate into the bargain. She seemed to have found a way, through Sylvian, the queen and that bloody ring, to slip free from Ben's body where the others were still trapped. But the others—they were the reason Eninn had ended up in the Nether and she'd had to pull him back out.

Ben caught her distant expression.

'I just need a little peace and quiet sometimes,' he told her, misinterpreting her silence. Was that a flash of guilt in his eyes? 'You know?'

Now that was a need she could understand. 'Perhaps I should get you to demonstrate,' she replied and grinned as Eninn spluttered in outrage. If Ben had found some kind of way to quieten the gods inside him that might be worth knowing, if only as a threat.

Eninn had many opinions about that, which he preceded to list. Oh yes, shutting him up once in a while would be a pleasure. Serve him right.

'I'd be happy to,' Ben assured her, clearly delighted with the prospect. 'That's what I wanted to ask you actually. It's quite simple really, just a series of alchemical symbols and the pure metals which, when you combine them in the right way, with a physical object to focus them—I find an amulet works best—'

Stirling laughed and clapped Ben on the back, cutting him off mid-phrase. 'He'll go on for days about it if you let him, Lyta.' The newcomer laughed, speaking of Ben as only an old friend could. 'Gets lost in his work. That's the thing about great minds like Ben.'

Ben's cheeks went scarlet again, his eyes shining at the praise.

Great minds like Ben. The warmth in Stirling's voice didn't seem feigned. There was genuine affection there. How well had they known each other in Oxford? Lyta wondered what Kit would make of that. Nothing good, that was for sure. Kit was still having more than a little difficulty with the fact that the scholar he had fallen in love with was part of one of the richest families of the Andalusian nobility and inadvertently stood for everything Kit had grown up despising. Nor would Kit himself ever fit into that world.

Ben was a good man at heart, Lyta knew that, but he simply didn't understand Kit's objections. The gulf in their backgrounds could not have been wider. Ben clearly adored her brother. And her Kitten was smitten, the rhyme a delight with which she tormented him whenever it got too sickening.

She had tried to stay out of it. She really had. But Kit hadn't even started to deal with the trauma of everything the duchess had put him through, and if Iseult of Montalbeau was mentioned he jumped away like a scalded cat.

Kit and the nobility had never gone together. Now it was even worse. Just when he had fallen in love with one of them. It wasn't fair.

A charming and so-very-pretty old friend turning up now, with the same interests and background as Ben, who thought he was brilliant . . . was very bad news indeed, Lyta thought ominously.

'You're a scholar then?' she asked Stirling, determinedly changing the subject. 'What do you study?'

Amberes didn't have a great university like Oxford, Salamanca or wherever else Ben had apparently studied in his time. It was on Annika's list of things to do for the improvement of the city apparently, but it was going to take years. Centuries even. The queen did not make small plans. But all of that was far down the list behind new fortifications and the citadel the king wanted first.

'Piers is one of the foremost students of alchemy and natural philosophy in the royal court of Albion,' Ben blurted out, as if he couldn't keep the words in anymore. His eyes shone with pride. 'He's here to consult Master Charnock, and he's seeking a new publisher for his own writings. I was telling him about Kit, and you of course, and he's desperate to meet you both.'

Lyta gave Stirling a mirthless smile and raised an eyebrow. '*Desperate*,' she echoed.

But his answering smile was again genuine enough. Not a trace of embarrassment either. He knew she was mocking him but he didn't care. Interesting.

'*Absolutely* desperate.'

At least he was amusing. There was that.

'Well,'—she shrugged her shoulder—'we can't be having that.'

How much had Ben told this friend of his about her and her brother? Had he explained about the variety of gods currently resident in his own head, or the one in hers? Or had he told him about Montalbeau and *The Book of Gold*, which wouldn't be much better really?

This was the last thing she needed, but it was Stirling who spoke before she could find out what he knew.

'Do pardon me, both of you, but I have an appointment with Guildmaster de Werve at the Shrine to Gloir this afternoon. Now I've presented my credentials to his secretary, I'm eager to see the man himself.'

The guilds all kept a guild house up around the market and near the Old Exchange, but they were all for show. Blacksmiths tended to be rather more hands-on with their work and fires, smoke and other noxious fumes—not to mention explosions—were frowned upon in the nicer areas of the city. That was why the Guild Quarter was on the other side from palaces and fine buildings, between the Rookery and the docks. The Glorious Company of Blacksmiths, which included alchemists, bladesmiths, smelters and glass-blowers in their number, had been the main leader in this exodus—or expulsion—from the Old Quarter, and while they might call their headquarters the Shrine to Gloir, it was also a massive complex of workshops, furnaces and warehouses. She was certain that there was an actual shrine in there somewhere. Probably buried under a mountain of equipment or used as storage. Though they worshipped the god of hearth and forge, they were not exactly known for their devoutness. And Gloir had been missing for many years. She glanced at Ben who was wearing a slight frown now. As far as they were concerned, Gloir might still be missing. She doubted Ben had said anything.

They would never have let him back out again if they knew. Ben had to be aware of that. People who followed gods too devoutly tended to guard them jealously. Gloir might have other ideas too. The strain was back in his Ben's eyes, which Kit had said signified an internal struggle or debate; the gods peering out from behind his mask. For a god adored by blacksmiths to walk into their guild and not announce their presence . . . that had to be hard. She knew a god could be tempted, persuaded and indeed tricked. The Magister had beguiled Kyron and Nimyeh to trap Eninn. Gloir had, at best, failed to stop them, and had perhaps not tried so very hard.

Lyta thought of the boy with his burned fingers and the gaping wounds in his chest. Could he have been an apprentice smith? The idea rooted abruptly in her imagination and she couldn't shake it. His clothes indicated that too. He was the right sort of age and build. There had been no sign of an insignia but then with the damage to his chest, there wouldn't be. Du Lac had mentioned selling relics there as well, dangerous ones. Stirling could be her way in. And Ben could help. It was the least he owed her.

'Well, we could go with you, couldn't we, Ben?' she said as sweetly as an innocent. 'You can show me your work, while we wait for Stirling, like you offered?'

For a moment she thought Ben was going to kiss her. It shouldn't have made her feel so guilty. She was just doing her stupid job.

'*Poke around*,' Vasquez had said. '*Do what you do best*.'

She was going to do just that. Perhaps generals should be a little more careful about the orders they gave. And if the Blacksmiths found out and complained . . . well, Vasquez could deal with the repercussions.

CHAPTER FIVE

Lyta

The Blacksmiths' Guild, wedged firmly in the heart of the Guild Quarter, towered over all the other headquarters, workshops and warehouses. It supplied most of the other guilds and surrounding businesses with equipment and skilled workers—the beating heart of the whole place. A position as an apprentice with the Blacksmiths' Guild could secure not only a child's but the whole family's future, and any openings were hotly contested, especially in the poorer areas.

The ramshackle complex of buildings, surrounded by high walls, was as secure as the Old Steen prison itself, and probably more secure than the Rose Palace ever could be. Lyta had been in both, for various reasons, but she'd never set foot through these imposing gates. Ranulf had always maintained that stealing from the blacksmiths, like stealing from the temples, only led to trouble and she was inclined to agree. The Blacksmiths' Guild guarded its secrets well. The guild house overlooking the Great Market was all about show, and would inevitably make a much more tempting target for most thieves anyway. This was where the real work happened and in the Blacksmiths' Guild that meant hard work, both physical and intellectual.

The gates were made of iron of course, with intricate whorls and filigree in between bars as big as her arm, both beautiful and functional. A work of art really. You could say it was showcasing their abilities, or just showing off. They were manned by guards, whose only concern was the guild, dedicated to its protection alone, huge figures as hard as the iron they worked.

Stirling spoke to the one who came out to greet them, a hulking man with a delicate collection of earrings piercing his ears from top to bottom, and hints of elaborate tattoos peeking out at his collar and cuffs. He nodded solemnly and asked them to wait a moment.

Lyta shuffled her feet in the sludge clinging to the street and studied the gates again, and the view beyond them.

Inside, there were inventions and materials that could cause all manner of problems in the city, not to mention secrets the guild members would kill to protect. In the middle of the complex, a tower rose up high, its roof gilded so that it turned red with the setting sun and flared like a beacon with the dawn. Amberes was the City of Towers after all, all the better for keeping an eye on the shipping lanes and the approaches to the city. Somewhere in there was a shrine to Gloir famous for its beauty, though she had never seen it and didn't know anyone who had. Everything else in the Blacksmiths' Guild sprawled out from that, a jumble of buildings, as if everything had been gathered up by a greedy hand and then left huddled together inside the red-brick walls. She could see the guild members on the other side of the gates, going about whatever business they had or socialising in the tree-rimmed garden that greeted visitors. Like Gloir and the guard at the gate with the earrings, some favoured elaborate jewellery and decoration, while others were plain and workmanlike, but they all drifted between what was commonly thought of as masculine and feminine without much heed as to where they had started or where they might finish. That wasn't of any interest here. Beauty, skill, art, ingenuity, however . . . those were prized.

She remembered the glimpse she had seen of their deity in that awful chamber in the Scholars' Tower—neither man nor woman, or any fixed point in between, with a tracery of molten gold beneath their skin and blazing in their eyes. They had been as trapped as the others, but still seemed to hold on to some remnant of compassion as opposed to the blind rage of Kyron the Warrior and the cold calculations of Nimyeh the Wise. If she could have reached any of those gods at that moment for help, it might have been Gloir. But as it was, Gloir, despite their protestations, had not actually lifted a hand to save Eninn.

They talk a good game, Gloir does, Eninn whispered. *But still, don't rely on them. They'll always suit themselves first.*

Isn't that the case for most gods? Lyta thought and he bristled in a nascent huff.

Lyta fell in beside Ben as Stirling greeted a portly man in heavy leathers and a hastily thrown on cloak trimmed with fox fur. She recognised Guildmaster Andras de Werve though she didn't actually know him. She made it her business to recognise all of those who ran with the upper echelons of society. She certainly didn't want them recognising her. At least De Werve had worked for his title, earned it through skill and probably cunning as well. Blacksmiths didn't let just anyone run their guild. He was known as someone fair, if not overly kind, performatively charitable and as honest as any of the other guildmasters. He was an alderman of the city, as high as anyone in Amberes could climb, a member of one of the great families, who even now were jostling for position as Annika formalised positions on the council to help her govern. There was little doubt De Werve would be included. Not as Mayor, though rumour was he wanted the post. Count Ursel had that sewn up as usual. No one expected anything different.

As the two men exchanged greetings, she turned her attention to Ben, pitching her voice as softly as possible.

'What exactly is his business here?'

'He's an alchemist, I told you. But so much more as well. One of the most—'

'Yes, you said all that. Did you tell him about—?' She didn't want to say Montalbeau right out in the open like this. 'About *that* place and what happened?'

'He only just arrived.'

Lyta gave a rumble of doubt. 'Just like that, after all this time?'

'Well, yes. There was a ship in from Albion the other day. Beatriz had a consignment of wool coming in on it. Do you know their wool—?'

Sometimes his innocence was endearing. She intercepted before she could get a lecture on the qualities of the wool that came from Albion.

'Is very good. Yes, I do. And all the more costly thanks to this weather. This isn't about wool, Ben. Isn't it all a bit *convenient,* if you know what I mean? And are we going to have to stand around out here until nightfall?'

Naturally, that was the moment that Stirling and De Werve finished exchanging pleasantries so they heard that last part quite clearly.

Ben took the expression of consternation on the guildmaster's face in his stride. He gave a small bow; that of someone with a far higher station to another who was still respected and honoured. 'Guildmaster, please forgive us. The weather is not something to which I am accustomed and I have been unwell of late. My servant does worry.' He managed to look patient and yet very cold at the same time, the perfect picture of noble endurance. Something seemed to shimmer in the air around him and De Werve nodded slowly, his features changing to show compassion.

Sneaky, Lyta thought. Ben was becoming almost as devious as she was. She wondered which one of the gods had done that for him. Not Kyron whose main approaches to life were destroying things in as violent a way as possible, and generally roaring inarticulately. Nimyeh perhaps, Goddess of Wisdom, or Gloir as this was their place and the smiths their people. The God of the Forge and the Hearth would know how to manipulate them.

Speaking of which, Ben was using magic. She knew he could, in theory, though she had never seen it herself. But she could feel it now. The sensation was like ants on her skin.

What would Kit say to that, she wondered? Nothing good. He had always hated magic to begin with and their experiences in Montalbeau and beyond hadn't done anything to change his mind. Quite the opposite. Was this what they had been bickering about then? Because, given Kit's general mood last night and this morning, she had no doubt they had been arguing.

It's just a nudge, Eninn protested. *Everyone does that.*

You don't, she replied noiselessly. Oh, but he would if he could. She knew that as well. He always had. He just didn't have the power anymore.

She wasn't thrilled to be cast in the role of servant but it meant that De Werve lost all interest in her at once. He was the type.

'Of course, Seigneur Alvarez, please forgive us our inhospitality. As you say, the weather does us no favours. Let us step inside while we continue our discussions. I can have refreshments brought to you and your . . .'—his eyes ran over Lyta, as if bewildered by her very existence—'. . . servant.'

He did not have to sound quite so confused about the concept. Lyta could have been a very good servant if she'd wanted to be. Not that she did. Lyta pursed her lips and stared at the place on his face where she really wanted to plant her fist.

'This way, Lyta,' said Ben in a brisk and business-like tone, and swept from the courtyard and into one of the stark doorways in the bleak corridors beyond.

'You're all very cosy in here,' Lyta muttered, following him closely while carefully memorising the route and anything else that might come in handy at some future date. It was an old habit, but it had never failed her. There were all kinds of workshops here and the noise was a constant. Hammering one minute, shouts the next, something that sounded distinctly like an explosion as they turned the corner.

'It's fine,' Ben assured her gently when she almost jumped out of her own skin. 'Ballistics testing, nothing to worry about. Francisco has them working on weaponry of course.'

'Of course,' she muttered. The thought of what these people could get away with in this place in the name of their craft made her shiver inside. Making war machines for the king would be the least of it. Oh, she could imagine Francisco's face—like a child with an endless collection of new destructive toys.

At the far end of the corridor, Ben opened a narrow door and stopped abruptly.

'Can I help you?' he asked in a crisp, polite voice which didn't bode well. He didn't even sound like Ben, but not exactly like any of his gods either. She wasn't sure who he was in that moment—Lord Alvarez perhaps?

A young woman with a duster in hand froze where she was, reaching up to the shelves to clean. 'I—I beg your forgiveness, master,' she stammered. A pretty girl, caught in her work in a place where they preferred servants to be invisible. It always set Lyta's teeth on edge. There was no need for him to take that tone with her. Not like the Ben she knew at all. 'I didn't think you were here today. And Mistress Lanval does want us to get ahead with the cleaning.'

Ben shook his head and cast a despairing glance at Lyta, his expression clearing again. 'I have asked them not to bother in here. It disturbs everything.'

He ushered the stray cleaner out and closed the door firmly behind her. Then he sighed. 'Enough,' he murmured and from the distant expression Lyta knew he wasn't talking to her. 'There's no harm done. She's just doing her job.'

'Ben?' Lyta asked, cautiously.

'It's Kyron, concerned with security,' he said with a self-deprecating smile. 'I've tried to tell him . . . Well, it doesn't matter.'

The room was not much bigger than an accountant's office in the Exchange, long and thin, with solid workbenches fitted to the wall on either side and high windows all along the left-hand wall letting in the light.

Everything was carefully locked away, she realised, not a sign of his work anywhere in view. So much for trust in this guild.

'Ben, I need to find out about the apprentices here,' she told him, now they were alone. 'If anyone is missing or—'

He was already fishing something out of a strongbox. 'First, try this on. It's what I was talking about earlier. Tell me what you think.'

He slipped a chain around her neck. From it hung a tear-drop-shaped pendant. It wasn't a lot different from the pendant she habitually wore anyway, just heavier. But the metal was . . . strange.

Lyta run her fingertips over it. The metal crackled beneath her touch, dark, almost like iron. In it she could see threads of gold and silver, and something else: a spiderweb of tiny fractures which rippled as they caught the light. She lifted it up to peer at it more closely and saw symbols there, shapes which swam in and out of focus. Familiar somehow, like she'd seen them long ago, or in a dream. Light flared in the depths of those lines, moving, circling. Almost hypnotic.

She was sure she knew those symbols. From Montalbeau perhaps, or the Book, or maybe dancing like ghosts across Ben's skin?

'What is it?' she asked. It was a question for both Ben and Eninn.

But neither of them answered. Ben was watching her, waiting, as if expecting some kind of reaction. Studying her with those other eyes again. Nimyeh, she thought, and Gloir as well, watching her like she was a specimen in a jar. What they expected to see, she didn't know, but they were both there, peering at her through him. She hated the sensation. And Eninn—

There was no sign of Eninn at all.

Her hands closed convulsively on the chain as she tried to rip it free. Ben's hands locked on hers, holding the amulet in place. Kyron was there in that instant, his abject hatred burning in Ben's eyes. She knew the warrior god loathed Eninn. He'd been the one to hurl her little trickster in the Nether. But this time, Kyron did nothing more than hold her hands on the amulet in a crushing grip so unlike Ben's, stopping her from removing it.

She bared her teeth. Slowly the glow faded until just Ben was left and he carefully unfurled his fingers, releasing her. She snatched her hands back.

'It's all right, Lyta,' he said and pulled out another necklace of almost identical design from beneath his collar. It hung around his own neck and had been there all the time. 'Nothing has happened to them, I swear it. They're . . . subdued, focused. Their power is mine to wield. The combination of metals, the symbols and Master Charnock's help to bring it all together, we have a moment's peace. Control. Balance.'

Balance? *That* had been *balance*?

'I don't know what anyone else has been telling you, Ben, but they are not in the slightest bit subdued.'

'But they can't *do* anything.'

They couldn't? She shuddered. Kyron hadn't been under control. Quite the opposite. Ben had been . . . someone else. Or some*thing* else. A mix of them all, those gods from *The Book of Gold*. She knew they hated Eninn, and for that split second, she'd seen that hatred on full display in his face.

She'd threatened to pull Eninn out of her head. And now . . .

The amulet dangled around her neck like a noose.

'Fuck's sake, get it off me,' she snarled at Ben.

'Of course.' He sounded almost bemused as he plucked it from around her neck. 'He doesn't have any power left, does he? Like a used-up relic. That's interesting. I suppose that's why—' Lyta didn't hear what he supposed. Suddenly Eninn was screaming in her ears.

Lyta! What was that? What happened? Where were you? Lyta, don't leave me like that. What did he do? Lyta! It was like the Nether, like being back there alone.

'It's all right,' she shouted out loud, because there wasn't any other way to make herself heard. 'I'm here, we're safe. It's okay.' She could barely catch her breath for the panic coursing along her veins, squeezing the air from her lungs. He was still a child. Everyone forgot that. He was forever a child and he still had nightmares about the Nether. So did she. In-between all the other bad dreams.

Ben's hand brushed against her shoulder and a pulse of something calming ran through her.

'And you can stop that and all.' She jerked free. 'Whichever one of you it is. I don't care. Leave us alone.'

'It's fine, Lyta,' Ben said, his voice so gentle and caring, the Ben she knew, the man her brother loved. 'It's safe. It's just me.'

She wasn't sure that was any better.

'I don't want your magic, Ben. You're messing around with things you don't understand.'

But Ben was stubborn too. 'How else are we going to come to understand them? I thought perhaps, as we share a similar situation, you might help me.'

'Help you? With what?'

'Testing the extent to which—'

'I'm not your test subject, Ben Alvarez. Don't do that again. And make sure you warn someone before sticking one of those on them.'

Lyta's hand wound around the pendant representing Eninn that belonged around her neck, not quite a disc, the edges uneven, pierced by an off-centre hole. A *relic*, Du Lac had called it, and maybe it was. She had never considered that possibility. Its cool and certain touch was a comfort. It didn't hum and squirm under her touch. It was only a piece of metal and Ranulf had given it to her. It was part of her. And there was nothing weird about it at all.

'There aren't many people like us, Lyta,' Ben said. 'It's not being an Aspect. We don't channel divine power like Beatriz. Nor do we serve its will like Sylvian. They're part of us. We're different.'

'And they're going to remain that way,' she told him firmly. 'Part of us. Not a thing to be used, manipulated or turned on and off. Or Eninn is, anyway. Why couldn't I hear him? Your lot were very much on display.'

The way they had been watching her, almost enjoying the show, just tormenting Eninn—was that what this was about?

'That's an interesting question,' Ben said. 'Perhaps he's so very much weaker than them. He always was, of course. And now he has almost no power at all. Not since the Tower. It's interesting. An anomaly.'

He turned around to grab one of his many notebooks, pen and ink. Already using her as his test subject she realised, despite her objections. She instantly rebelled.

'I'm not like you, Ben Alvarez. Not in any way. I'm not a Nexus or whatever—'

He didn't so much as glance back at her, but started scrawling in the book as he replied. 'But that's why I want your help. I think you became one, Lyta. Or else the possibility was always there, hidden inside you because otherwise . . . Divine Nexuses are created through bloodlines, like Aspects. If only we knew more about your parents.'

She slammed her hand down on his desk, making him jump. 'Who has been putting these ideas in your head?' Finally, he stopped writing and looked up at her, with a hint of concern. 'Does Beatriz know? Does Kit?'

It was the wrong thing to say. She saw that in the anger flare in his face the moment she said it. And it wasn't Kyron this time. Just a lord of a noble house, who had been threatened with his big sister and his boyfriend.

'I *do* have ideas of my own, you know? I *used* to be famous for it.'

Before the Scholars' Tower, before the Magister. That was why the bastard had been so desperate to control Ben, wasn't it? For his mind as much as his abilities. For that love of solving impossible puzzles and all the mysteries that brain of his could unravel. Perhaps all Ben wanted was to prove that he still could think for himself. That his ideas weren't being fed to him by the gods in his head. That his mind was still his own.

She could understand that much. No one wanted to be controlled. Or dismissed.

His voice was chilly, but his eyes even colder. He'd been hoping she'd be impressed. And she was the only person who he'd thought might understand. Damn it. He'd wanted a connection and she'd told him no.

'But why, Ben?' She softened her voice, but she was still shaking, and Eninn's fear thundered in her heart. He'd thought he'd lost her, that he was back in that dreadful place, alone and powerless. She'd felt it all and it was terrible, a world of horror and betrayal, of loss.

'Why? Because I want a normal life, Lyta. I need to find a way to free the gods from my head, I promised them that and I *am* working on it. And if I don't, I'm scared I'll lose myself. They're always there, always gnawing away at me, at what makes me . . . well, *me*. I have to solve this. We're running out of time.' She felt a pang of sympathy. How could she not? 'Besides, I want to be able to spend a night with Kit, once in a while—'

'Things I really don't need to hear about, Ben,' she warned him. That was her brother's sex life, he was talking about, after all.

He threw up his hands in despair, a painfully elegant gesture. 'Well there's nothing else to hear, is there? Every time we've tried anything more than—' At her glare, Ben narrowed his hazel eyes and ploughed on. 'I start getting helpful suggestions on positions from Gloir, or a story from Kyron about how some of his warriors had sex with each other before battle in tribute to him, or . . . general *encouragement*. And once I got a half-hour lecture on sexual diseases from Nimyeh. Do you wonder that I want to shut them up? So I can take a breath. And think. And feel.'

Lyta's face flushed. The idea of trying to do anything with such an audience . . . At least Eninn had the good grace to make himself scarce when she and Syl found a moment together. She didn't ask where he went. She just knew she was alone. She couldn't imagine trying to lead any kind of life under those circumstances.

'I'm sorry,' she whispered. 'I didn't know.' And Kit wouldn't have told her either. No wonder he was so frustrated all the time. He was probably blaming himself. That was his way.

'Sometimes, we manage,' Ben said, despondently. 'But, let's say there have been a lot of cold baths.'

She decided to try a different tack and get off this subject.

'Warn a person, Ben. It's—it's frightening to just lose him like that. He's part of me. You know? He always has been.' She tightened her grip on the pendant and felt that faint, answering pulse from the cool metal.

Ben's stare intensified, and with it came the sensation of being studied again. She could see the ripple of light beneath his skin, the ghosts of the same symbols which marked the pendants he had made. No wonder they unsettled Kit. And Ben too, if he was really aware of the full extent of it. She'd be driven to distraction.

'You gave me the idea,' he said, without quite meeting her eyes. 'With your pendant, and Sylvian with Ystara's ring. That was how Ystara escaped, through that connection. That bond. Thomas—that is, Master Charnock—realised it and I thought you—'

Charnock again. She didn't like the way everything kept swinging around to him.

'How much have you been telling people about us, Ben?'

She didn't like the thought of that either. First Stirling, now Charnock.

A knock on the door interrupted them and when Ben answered, a young girl was standing there, an apprentice. Eight maybe? Blonde and bright, with enormous blue-green eyes.

'Master Charnock sent me to see if you were free, Master Alvarez?'

'Yes, of course, Clémence,' he said. 'Lyta? Coming? You'll want to meet Master Charnock and see him at work.'

Did she? This was the one who was pouring these ideas in Ben's head about controlling gods. Maybe she should.

Ben was already out the door talking to the girl, Clémence, so what other choice did she have? Leave? Sit here and wait? She needed to have this out with him and find out what else he was up to. Eninn was still shivering in the corner of her mind and that was unsettling enough.

As they left, they passed the cleaner again, dusting one of the windowsills and not doing a particularly good job of it. Lyta wondered if she was waiting until Ben had gone so she could get back into the workroom and finish up.

Clémence turned out to be quite the chatterbox. She knew everything. People always underestimated children. Lyta remembered that from her own grubby childhood. But children listened and they saw and they remembered. And she had wanted information on the apprentices. This was her chance.

'Must be a cushy number here,' Lyta suggested, as they descended the stairs to the lower levels. 'Everyone wants to join this guild.'

'The temple set it up for us,' Clémence told her. 'After Pa died. Me and my brother. We have food on the table and a roof over our heads and good work to do. He's learning to be a jeweller on account of his fingers being tiny. I'm one of Master Charnock's apprentices. Picked me out special.'

She was proud of her position here, rightly so. An orphan from the docks or the Rookery made good. Well it had to work out one day.

'No one would want to leave that, would they?' Lyta asked her.

The girl shrugged. 'Some do. Some people are never happy. Not even when they get the really good jobs.'

'Who ran out on a good job? That doesn't sound like a good idea.'

'Ugh, Caspar Hondt. And Jules Sabbe.' She said their names like they were the most irritating boys imaginable. Perhaps they were.

'Recently?' At least she had some names to check.

'Oh, weeks ago. But Caspar was fierce homesick and Jules didn't want to be here in the first place. But no one else. Although . . . well, Mathius didn't come back yesterday, but he will.'

She pushed open the large oaken doors and jumped down the steps on the far side. Like any child.

'Apprentices,' said Ben, as if he'd given Lyta a gift.

'She's very young.'

'One of the youngest,' said a carrying voice from the other side of the large chamber which opened out before them. 'And one of the most helpful too. A real talent. Our Clémence has a great future ahead of her. Like Ben here.' At the far side of it a man was hunched over his books, scrawling away at a piece of parchment. He swivelled around on his stool, blinking at them, owl-like, wearing a broad smile.

He looked like he was part of this jumbled, chaotic room, a man dressed in haphazard clothes with ink stains on his fingers. Behind the desk at which he worked the shelves rose to the ceiling and each one was a jumble of books, papers and objects great and small. And gathered together on the middle one, within easy reach . . . relics, Lyta realised. A tug in her chest told her Eninn saw them too, recognised the power locked inside them. A long blue feather, a box made of polished ebony, a golden coin, a carved horse . . .

They shouldn't be here, Eninn murmured uneasily. *What is he doing with them?*

Lyta didn't have a chance to ask what he meant. She knew he was still shaken after Ben's trick with the amulet, but now he sounded angry as well. On edge.

'Whose are they?' she whispered as quietly as she dared.

I don't know. All different divinities. Some from far away. Lyta, I don't like this . . .

'I know. Neither do I.'

The girl was already digging through another random pile of flotsam, pulling out a wide flat piece of shining black stone like a dish or a tray—obsidian, Lyta realised with a twinge of alarm. For a moment all she could see were the warriors enslaved to the duchess, the black sheen of their obsidian armour, the way it had crawled up around Ranulf, stealing his freedom and his life. A shudder of alarm ran through her and she tried to keep it locked deep inside her. She wasn't sure if she succeeded, but Ben and Charnock didn't appear to notice and Clémence was already at work.

The girl unstopped a vial and poured out a liquid metal. It shone like silver and moved like it was molten, but there was no sign of heat. Nothing should move like that. Eninn shivered again, repulsed, and as Lyta came closer she was sure the liquid shivered in response, as if reaching out to him. She took a cautious step back. Just in case.

'It's living silver,' said the alchemist, and she had the distinct feeling he had been watching her rather too closely. 'It represents transformation, eternal change. It is an ever-changing metal, a study in opposites, which binds as it purifies. It exists in a liminal state, between forms. And it is a perfect conduit for our purposes.'

A conduit? What did that mean?

Silver shouldn't do that, Eninn whispered, and Lyta was inclined to agree. Nothing should do that.

'Is it . . . is it dangerous?' she asked aloud.

The little girl laughed out loud at the suggestion and an unexpected blush filled Lyta's cheeks.

'No, it just moves,' Clémence said. 'Like honey or melted wax.'

And yet you could burn yourself with hot wax all too easily, Lyta thought, and if you rammed your hand into a hive after honey, you were going to get stung.

The alchemist reached out a welcoming hand. 'Thomas Charnock,' he said. The accent was from Albion, but he sounded more like one of the sailors and dockworkers than the lord Lyta was expecting.

He hadn't learned their language from scholars and the nobility then. And he didn't have that polished sheen of Lord Stirling. 'And don't worry, lass. We hardly ever blow things up in here. That's De Werve and his gunpowder projects in the east wing.'

'And what's your project?' she asked, trying not to let her gaze linger on the relics on display, though she made a mental note of each one. She'd ask Du Lac about them, see where they had come from and if they had been stolen.

'Us?' He winked at Clémence who giggled again, before settling herself and her flat dish of living silver down on the floor in the middle of an elaborate chalk circle. 'We are alchemists. We study the lore of silver, the words of gold, and the truth of the divine. We talk to the gods, learn their secrets and then we use them to mankind's advantage. Benedictus and I are going to unlock wonders together. Will you join us, Lyta Cornellis?'

CHAPTER SIX

Sylvian

'Do you want to explain yourself, Captain Chant? I'm having a busy enough day without finding my bodyguard missing.'

Annika was seated on a chair that might as well be a throne, in her private audience chamber, with her swollen ankles propped up on a footstool. Her even more swollen belly was front and centre and there was absolutely no way he was able to avoid looking at it, or accept the responsibility for it that had been thrust upon him. Nor indeed his *actual* responsibility for it.

'Your majesty,' he began, as he went down on one knee. It was safer down there. 'It was a matter of some urgency. I had to go immediately.'

Behind her, otherwise still as a statue, Juárez winced and Sylvian realised he had probably given the wrong answer. He was used to that.

'I know. I heard.' Annika sounded peevish. He wondered if her back was at her again. Or if there were stomach cramps. Either was possible and neither boded well. She ought to be in her bed, but she wouldn't stay there. The royal physicians were despairing. But the king had left her in charge of Amberes. She took duty very seriously, even if it conflicted with her primary duty to produce an heir. Besides, no one could actually tell her what to do, so that was that.

And if she didn't take charge here, who would? One of the many nobles and such sniffing around for scraps in the absence of her husband? No, that would not do at all. Annika was not going to be pushed to one side. Not even by her much-desired pregnancy. Not until it was absolutely necessary.

Her time was drawing close. He wondered what it must be like, to have that much control over everything and then to see it shrinking away right before your eyes because your primary obligation outweighed everything else. Including your own freedom. She had to give Francisco a baby. That was why they had ended up in this mess to begin with.

'So, explain what took you away from me, bodyguard?' she asked when he said nothing else.

He expected her to tell him to stand up, but she didn't so he was forced to stay on his knees.

Where she liked him, a dark voice murmured away in the back of his mind. It almost sounded like Lyta. Annika had enchanted and charmed every man she met as long as Sylvian had known her, but it didn't seem to work on him quite the way it used to. Perhaps that was Ystara's influence. Or Lyta's.

'There was a murder and a robbery at the Temple of Lost Gods. I was asked to help discover what had happened.'

'By Lyta Cornellis.'

'Yes, majesty. The Vicar of the Seven Churches had asked her to come.'

Annika pinched the bridge of her nose and closed her eyes. 'Of course he did. Divine Ystara forbade the good people of this ridiculous city should resort to the watch or the justiciars.' She sighed and made another brief gesture with her elegant hand, indicating he should stand. 'At least Lyta is one of ours. Vasquez? Would you care to explain what's happening now?'

Ours? Sylvian wondered if anyone had told Lyta that. And what her reaction would be.

The general took a seat at the secretary's table. Where had the man gone? She had obviously sent him off on some task or another, which meant she didn't want anyone but Sylvian, Vasquez and Juárez to hear about this.

'I've instructed Mistress Cornellis to investigate. It seemed . . .'—Vasquez cast a scathing glance over Sylvian before returning her attention to the queen—'. . . *expedient.* She can go places we can't. This city is still wary of you, Majesty. She belongs here.'

'If there's something to be found, Lyta will find it,' Sylvian said and caught a flicker of something in Annika's eyes. Jealousy? The queen hid it immediately. But he was sure he'd seen it. Carefully, he bowed his head again. 'I was always going to come back, your majesty.' He said it as gently as he could. He wasn't sure if she believed him, but the ring on his finger was like a brand. It marked him as her champion, as hers.

They were bound together now, the two of them, inexorably tied by blood and by divine will. Ystara had decreed it—her price for helping Lyta, her demand on him as her Chosen. As long as Annika carried the child—his child, though no one could ever know that—he had to protect her. If he, or the ring he wore, were absent for too long . . .

He still remembered all too clearly the feeling when he'd taken leave, months ago now, and the frantic summons back when the queen had collapsed. He'd known before the messenger arrived at the printshop door, waking up suddenly at Lyta's side, with his heart thundering, covered in sweat, with Ystara's ring burning into his finger as if made of acid. It had taken a week for the queen to recover. A common complication, the royal physicians had said. Nothing to worry about. But the queen and Sylvian had known there was more to it than that. Her pregnancy was no commonplace thing. She was an Aspect and such pregnancies were dangerous. It could cost the queen her life. Beatriz had made sure they both understood that. He had not made the same mistake again.

If the queen lost the baby she would lose everything, and if the father of the child, the true father and her champion, was not by her side until the birth, protecting her, helping her, supporting her, then her life could be forfeit. Sylvian had begged her to talk to Beatriz about it. If anyone knew the truth of this, it was the Lady of House Alvarez. Not least because of Beatriz's abilities as a healer.

But Annika had refused. She couldn't risk word spreading any further, she said. The vultures of Francisco's court were already circling, seeking weaknesses, closing in on her. So too were the aldermen of Amberes.

And so here he was, trapped in the palace rather than making a life with Lyta.

Which was why Lyta thought he had chosen his duty over her.

It wasn't true. He had put his life on the line to help her rescue Ben. He had defied the king and almost died for it. She was the one who had managed to talk quickly enough to get them out of it and he still wasn't entirely sure how she had managed that. No one was, but he had his suspicions. No one had yet fully explained what had happened to her when she vanished and came back with Ennin's voice in the back of her mind.

'What did you find?' Annika asked, completely ignoring his words. When he stared at her blankly, she frowned. 'At the temple, Sylvian. Apart from Lyta.' There was a warning in the last three words.

He'd stolen some moments, that was all. Annika wasn't happy about that.

Sylvian kept his voice carefully even. 'Very little. I've had the body brought back here and the royal physicians are examining him to see what they can determine.'

'We're following up on that, your majesty,' said Vasquez, focused on her reading. She paused and passed something else to the queen. Annika glanced over it and nodded before handing it back. 'We need no more dark magic in Amberes.'

And it certainly had an air of dark magic. Dead children in temples, stolen relics . . . none of it was good. Those who would attract the attention of the divine in such ways were rarely content with one act. They got progressively worse. They had seen that in the French campaign, and in Gravenenga.

And in Montalbeau.

'Lyta will find something,' Sylvian said. Might as well give her the credit. She'd take it anyway. And he didn't doubt she'd turn something up. She always did.

'Yes, have her report to you as soon as she knows anything else. Take charge of her, Sylvian. And this time do it properly.'

'Me?' Sylvian blurted out in horror. Francisco had tried to put him in charge of Lyta once. It had not ended well. The thought that Annika would give him that role again was stranger still.

'Yes, Captain Chant,' said Annika, as if talking to an idiot. 'I think you're best placed. You should spend more time with her anyway. There have been . . .'—she gave a sigh and her eyes flicked to the floor—'unsavoury rumours abroad. And here in our court. About you.' About Annika. About them. She didn't need to say it out loud. In fact, it was safer not to. It didn't bode well. The queen waved a hand dismissively when he opened his mouth to reply, and the words never came out. What could he say anyway? If only Lyta had agreed to marry him. It would have solved that problem. Maybe. 'And what about this matter with Ursel, Vasquez?'

Sylvian stepped back, taking his position to the left of the room, facing Juárez, who was very carefully avoiding eye contact. Probably so he didn't laugh. Take charge of Lyta indeed. He was going to lose body parts.

Count Lancel Ursel had been the Mayor of Amberes under the Duchess of Montalbeau. And now, as Annika was in the act of overseeing the reformation of the city council, the aldermen were all vying for position. Having clashed with the duchess on numerous occasions, he was still in with a chance of keeping the role. But nothing was certain.

'He's waiting outside,' Vasquez replied. 'There's been a theft, he says, from his private office in the Exchange and would speak with you. However, the rest of the aldermen are gathered as well, awaiting your decision on the new council. To see one on his own and not the rest would invite speculation.'

'What else do we know at this time?'

Sylvian made eye contact with Juárez, asking the question and his compatriot nodded briefly. Ursel had been robbed then. That was not good. He was one of the most powerful men in the city and not to be crossed lightly. Whoever had done it was either very brave, or didn't care about the consequences.

Vasquez shook her head. 'Very little. The guards were asleep on duty. If they were mine, they'd be on charges. Ursel won't say what was taken. No sign of ransom or blackmail. Not yet.'

Annika sighed as if this was all so very tiresome. 'One thing at a time then. Sylvian, you can interrogate Ursel.'

'What?' He wasn't a politician. Besides, *interrogate* meant something in Francisco's court and they all knew it.

'*What, your majesty*,' Juárez corrected him, but it was more from reflex than anything else. He shifted uneasily.

'We cannot *interrogate* the alderman, majesty,' the general replied carefully. 'Especially not at this delicate stage of negotiations regarding the council.'

Annika sighed again, this time somewhat petulantly. '*Interview* him then. Find out about the theft he reported. You'd think he'd be delighted we're taking an interest.' She sifted idly through some of the papers perched on her bump before handing most of them back. 'Moving on,' she said, her voice lightening again. 'You should both know that the Baron de Marasso has arrived, sent by my beloved husband to aid me. He waits outside for an audience.'

That caught the attention of both Sylvian and Juárez. Marasso was already here in Amberes? Sylvian would have been happy to ride out and meet him. Any number of the royal guard would have. He deserved that honour at least. The Baron de Marasso had been Francisco's right hand, back in the Burgundian wars, a soldier to the core, and the men around him adored him. Both Sylvian and Juárez had served under him at one time or another. And gladly.

'Juan Alvarez de Marasso is a hero of the kingdoms, your majesty,' said Juárez, who was no more immune to hero worship than Sylvian was. 'A master tactician. You could do far worse than have him by your side until the king returns.'

Annika's face transformed to stone. The ring prickled on Sylvian's finger and he curled his hand into a fist. Something was wrong. Vasquez had gone very quiet too, Sylvian realised. He frowned at Juárez, who seemed as confused as he was. It ought to be good news.

So why was she upset? He could ascribe it to her condition, perhaps but he knew better than that. Annika was a politician to the core.

Carefully, she found her voice. 'The baron has always been loyal to my husband above all else. And I'm sure he will serve me just as well. But he comes from Valladolid, and he's as much a creature of the court as any of them. He'll be seeking status and power, and all the other virtues of position he can gather. They are all the same.' Her eyes fixed on Sylvian again. 'He is an Alvarez by blood, a cousin to Beatriz and Benedictus. Perhaps we can remind House Alvarez of where their loyalties lie and what they owe us. Another task for you then, Sylvian. They are your friends. See to it.'

Did she doubt House Alvarez now? No, that wasn't possible. Perhaps it was just Annika baulking at someone else having a say in her court? She did so like to be in control.

A messenger arrived with more papers and Vasquez took them, shooing the boy out. She sorted through them quickly on the secretary's desk.

'Majesty?' The general held out a scroll. It was thick and ornate, various ribbons and seals adorning it.

Annika lifted her chin, her expression betraying her confusion. She took the scroll and opened it deftly, her eyes scanning over the contents, missing nothing.

'Shit!' she said at last.

It was like hearing an angel throw up. All three of them stared at her in shock and she held out the scroll to Sylvian.

He froze. Why him? Why would she . . .? He took it in a hesitant grip.

As he read it, every other concern fell away into a gaping pit of horror.

'The Church Imperial has sent an *inquisitor* to Amberes?'

At Vasquez's sound of disbelief, Sylvian passed it to her, relieved to get it out of his hands.

'They want an investigation into what happened to the Magister of the Scholars' Tower,' Vasquez added, scanning through it. 'It would not be wise to allow such a thing to take place. I'm sure we would all agree on that. What are they doing? It's not an edict of grace, at least not yet, but it's the first step.'

That was the last thing that anyone wanted. Especially Sylvian as he keenly remembered the moment he had taken the bastard's head off with the very sword he still carried. His throat went dry. An inquisitor would want to interview him, and Lyta. And more than interview them. An edict of grace gave those guilty of crimes against the August Imperator a month to confess and throw themselves at the mercy of the inquisitors. *Mercy* being a relative term. The word 'interrogate' hung over them now, with all the same implications. If they caught Lyta . . . if they caught either of them, but especially Lyta, with Eninn lodged inside her . . .

Panic seized his heart and squeezed tight.

'What do you intend to say, your majesty?' He managed to force out the question, already knowing he didn't entirely want an answer. But he needed to know. He had to. Lyta was in danger now. Lyta, Kit and both the Alvarezes.

Something else to remind them where their loyalties lay, he thought bitterly. All of them. A carrot and a stick, all in one.

But Lyta . . . dear gods, Lyta might do anything. There was no telling. He loved her still, loved her with all his heart, but the woman was unpredictable at the best of times. He needed to get her to safety, right now. He had to warn her.

Annika rolled her shoulders as if they were stiff and sore, but all the same she drew herself up in all her royal dignity. 'I shall reply that we are delighted that he has come to our fair city and that the Imperial Temple here will no doubt be greatly honoured to host him. I will be further overjoyed to grant him an audience when time allows, but given my condition that cannot be guaranteed. I'm sure he'll understand. I'm only a weak and frail woman, after all.' She paused, thinking of how to use this to her advantage, and *there* was the Annika of House of Vasa Sylvian knew once more, shining through. If anyone could find a way, it would be his queen.

'Perhaps the Baron will take on the Inquisitor. Everyone might enjoy a more direct approach and he's known for that. We shall see.

In the meantime, as my beloved husband might say, this Inquisitor can rot in his precious temple until he fucks off again. I may rephrase the last part. I need to think. The last thing I want is yet another power attempting to undermine me here. No word of this is to go beyond this room, general, captains, until we have a plan. Understand? No one must know.'

No one? Not even Lyta?

The gleam in Annika's eye answered that before Sylvian could ask it. He'd have to get Lyta to safety without telling her why. And not telling Lyta something was a sure-fire seed of another fight. Another round of chaos. But the queen had given the order. And she knew.

'Isn't this dangerous, your majesty? I thought we decided—'

'*We*?' she said and her voice chilling. '*We* didn't decide anything, *Chant*.' No one moved. No one dared. The mantle of queen slipped away again until there was just a young woman with far too much on her shoulders. 'You must be more careful, Sylvian. There have already been rumours. Dangerous rumours. Francisco's wretched cousins and the rest of the court and . . . We must tread carefully, you and I. I think, having your lady closer is wise at this time, no matter what her reputation. Perhaps because of it. In fact . . .'—her hand strayed absently across her belly, a maternal gesture which wasn't lost on him—'perhaps we should insist Mistress Cornellis take quarters here in the palace. She is *my* servant, after all. And I would be most put out if anything were to happen to her.' She arched a perfect eyebrow, fixing him with *that* look, one he had grown to dread. 'Or perhaps Sylvian, it would be more palatable if you made your own offer to her again? With more vigour this time? It is Ystara's will, after all. And above all earthly women, you belong to *her*.'

Ystara's will. Ystara's Chosen. That was the problem at the heart of this, and the reason Lyta had refused him in the first place. Part of it.

The queen was the rest.

Sylvian tried to picture it—making the offer again, her completely predictable reaction, the whole sorry thing unfolding in his mind and making him want to curl up and die on the floor right here and now.

Being the Chosen of the Goddess of Love hadn't helped him then and it wouldn't help him now. Lyta had made her feelings perfectly clear. He would be ignoring her wishes, and that never ended well. What was Annika thinking?

He recalled Lyta's face when he'd asked her, when he'd thought it was all going to be hearts and roses, and it turned out to be . . . well, definitely *not* that. But when had he and Lyta ever had anything like that? Gods' graces, how was he going to explain all this? Because if she ever guessed a fragment of what was being said in this room, she'd never forgive him. She'd run. She'd run so far and so fast he might never find her again. Or else, she'd do something . . . *spectacularly* foolish. And for Lyta that really meant something. He knew that better than anyone. And no doubt Eninn would help her. If only to defy his sister-goddess.

But the queen was right. Their position here was precarious, and if such a threat to one of her people became public knowledge it would do them no favours. If an inquisitor of the Church Imperial could sweep into Amberes and demand one of her servants be handed over to their mercy like that—or worse, just take her—Annika's authority, such as it was in this city, and in the many kingdoms they ruled, would be destroyed.

And no doubt Francisco would make his own displeasure known in as bloody a way as possible.

Vasquez carefully took the scroll back and added it to one of the neat piles, burying it under several others, carefully out of sight.

Annika watched her and then nodded, satisfied, as if everything had been sorted out and packed away as neatly. 'First, I must see the Baron de Marasso. Ursel and the others will have to wait. Show him in, Sylvian.'

An inquisitor in Amberes. Sylvian had to push down another wave of panic. Annika would protect Lyta, wouldn't she? She had to. Gods, what was he going to do?

'Chant,' Juárez murmured a warning. 'The queen gave an order.' Sylvian snapped to attention again and moved before panic could get the better of him again. He pushed it down inside him, where it would churn and boil until later. Because he had to. His duty was everything. His will was bound by his vows. Bound to serve, no matter what he wanted. The queen would always come first.

That was what Lyta had said. And she was right.

The first anteroom to the private audience chamber held but one person, the Baron de Marasso, a handsome older man with a distinct resemblance to Beatriz and Ben Alvarez, although while the siblings were slight and elegant, he looked like a hawk about to strike. His complexion was darker, after more years spent in the open. He wore splendid clothes straight from the Valladolid court, dark velvets and brocade trimmed with fur, and his black hair shot with silver. He was still broad-shouldered and strong, having kept his physique in trim. An old soldier, no doubt about it and Sylvian was struck by a wave of recognition and relief at the very sight of him. The baron would deal with the Church Imperial. He lived for that. They were the enemy of Francisco's collected kingdoms of Castile, León, Aragón and the Brabantine, and on the battlefield Marasso had been the king's champion time and again.

More than that, Sylvian knew in his heart of hearts, Marasso had saved him. When he'd been only a conscript in the army intent on throwing his life away at the first opportunity, the baron had seen something in him and hauled him out of the front lines before he could be slaughtered. He had been the one to tell him if death was what he wanted, he should make it count for something more. He'd taught Sylvian the sword, trained him thoroughly, ruthlessly, alongside the other selected few from among his *tercio* to fight with everything in them, creating elite warriors with skill and determination. Few generals drilled their own men, let alone trained them one-on-one, but Marasso did. He was tough but always fair, even bordering on kind. He had initiated most of the bodyguards who ended up serving Francisco.

Kneeling in the rain, in a ruined castle in the aftermath of the bloodiest battle of the war, Sylvian had bared his arms to the king, and his knife. Francisco had carved vows of fealty and obedience into Sylvian's skin. Almost to the bones.

Marasso had looked on with approval. He'd made his own marks there before when Sylvian had been his man. And now he'd given him up to a greater cause. With pride. With delight. With purpose.

The memory shuddered through Sylvian and punched the breath from his lungs.

'Chant?' the baron exclaimed. 'Sylvian Chant? It *is* you!' Before Sylvian had a chance to say a word, Marasso embraced him like the father he'd never known, slapping his back and then pushing him back to arm's-length so he could examine him in uniform. 'Gods and goddesses, boy, how are you still alive? I thought Francisco would have got you killed by this stage.'

The delight in the nobleman's face was palpable as he held Sylvian in front of him, both hands on his shoulders in a grip like iron. The rush of relief that welled up in Sylvian's chest took him by surprise. Marasso was here. It was going to be all right. He'd fix everything.

'No, I'm . . . I'm his bodyguard. That is, the queen's bodyguard now. Lord Baron, I'm to escort you to her.'

'Of course, of course, but what a delight to see you. When was it last? Not since that fiasco with Alva in Napoli? You pulled me out of that mess, no doubt about it. I always knew you'd go far. Francisco doesn't know what he has in you, boy, leaving you here. Or maybe he does? Who else would protect the queen half as well as you?' He laughed, delighted, and clapped Sylvian on the back again. 'Ah, but I'd take you back into my service in a heartbeat if he'd let you go.'

Francisco knew exactly what Sylvian was. And so did Annika, Sylvian thought grimly, though he couldn't let that show. He couldn't see the queen ever letting him go. And if the king did, it would be to the sword, no doubt.

But he bowed, accepting the compliment. The praise was an exaggeration. He simply wouldn't have been able to live with himself if the old man had died on his watch.

'You are too kind, my lord.'

Marasso shook his head. 'Well, we will have to catch up later, you and I, but I should not keep our beloved queen waiting, especially not in her delicate condition. I believe you know my cousin, Lady Beatriz? I dine with her this evening. You should join us.'

It was another dismissal, Sylvian knew that, even if it was couched in a friendly invitation, albeit to someone else's house. These were the currents of court and of the hierarchy of command to which they both were accustomed. Friendship and respect was one thing, but duty overrode all.

'If you will it, my lord,' Sylvian said, and neatly let himself fade into the background as Marasso swept into the audience chamber to face the queen.

The man had been like a father to him once, a warrior he was proud to fight alongside, happy to follow into the teeth of death. Before Francisco, he would have marched after Marasso anywhere.

Baron de Marasso being here would mean extra protection for Annika. He would defend her here in Amberes in ways Sylvian never could. Politically, socially, all of that, but the problem was, he was used to being in command. And Annika did not take well to people attempting to control her. In that, she and Lyta were more alike than either would like to admit.

'Dear baron,' Annika said, her voice pitched in that charming way which worked wonders with most men. 'What an honour to receive you in *our* court.'

It wasn't quite as charming as she might have thought. Even Sylvian could see that she was annoyed and Marasso surely would as well. The emphasis on 'our' would not have gone unnoticed. But Sylvian knew now that he could see past Annika's glamours where others could not thanks to Ystara's ring. The baron seemed delighted with the greeting. Maybe her magic was working after all.

'I bring word from the king, your majesty—his most devoted greetings.' He handed a letter to Vasquez, who took it without comment and gave it straight to Annika unopened. Such was the way of things. A message directly from Francisco was for her alone. Divinities help the fool who opened it. 'He bid me to be of every service to you as you navigate the court, to help you as your time approaches, and to guard your welfare as he would himself.'

Annika's whole demeanour remained as cold as the icy country from which she came. She was a foreigner in Francisco's court, something she was never allowed to forget. At least here in Amberes they were all foreigners. No wonder she hadn't wanted to return to Valladolid where a sea of people far more manipulative than Marasso would encircle her and cut her off from power. They would make her a prisoner and a puppet. The length of the journey and the dangers she and the child might encounter on the way were, Sylvian knew, a convenient excuse. But that didn't mean she was safe here either. Not now.

Annika scanned the letter in a cursory manner and smiled. It was not her real smile.

'You are too kind, my lord, and you are most welcome,' she said at last. 'There are a number of matters where someone of your experience can help us. General, if you will detail our issues to the baron?'

Vasquez rose and led him away, already launching into a description of the message received from the Church Imperial. From the tightening of Marasso's shoulders, that obviously went down as well as could be expected and by the time they had reached the other side of the room, he was radiating indignation. The door closed behind them and Annika sank back in her chair with relief.

That was when Sylvian realised that she had got rid of his mentor very quickly, far more quickly than was politically wise. Dark hollows like bruises ringed her pale eyes and Sylvian's ribs tightened in a vice, a warning from the goddess who had chosen him.

'Your majesty? Are you all right?'

This time the smile was her own, but that was even more of a worry. It looked broken.

'Yes, yes, just tired. And my head is aching. I think I should retire. It has been a long day. Sylvian, please reschedule the meetings with the aldermen. I'll talk to them about the council appointments tomorrow. That at least can wait.' She levered herself to her feet and made for the door to her private quarters, pausing only to stretch her back, her hands pressed hard into the base of her spine.

'Will I send for your physician?' Juárez asked, concerned. 'Or a healer? Lady Beatriz will come, you know? We have but to ask.'

'Another Alvarez?' she replied, her voice genuinely exhausted. 'No, not yet, Luca. I'm not in so dire a state as that. I will have a letter ready to dispatch back to the king shortly. Get one of the messengers for me.'

She missed him, Francisco. Pined for him. A surge of something like sympathy filled Sylvian, but more than simply that; pity for her, anger at Francisco for putting her through this, and for sending Marasso to take charge when he knew his wife well enough to know how she would take that. She didn't trust Beatriz Alvarez, perhaps even less now Marasso was here nipping at her heels.

And now he had to go and threaten Beatriz on her behalf as well, while still making sure that if the queen needed her the Lady of House Alvarez would come to her aid.

And he still had to find Lyta.

'Talk to Ursel first, Sylvian,' said the queen. 'Then Beatriz. And then bring Lyta back here.'

Annika had given him a litany of orders, he thought. The clock was ticking, time slipping through his fingers. But still he set about dutifully following each and every one. He would have to leave Lyta until last because the moment he confronted her with these demands, he knew in his heart of hearts, she'd refuse.

Or worse, she'd take off on her own, leaving mayhem and destruction in her wake.

*

In the outer chamber, Lancel Ursel kept apart from the other petitioners, nearest the door. He was pacing back and forth, his narrow face a picture of focus and concern. When he saw Sylvian, he stiffened, wiping his expression clear, the consummate politician.

'Captain Chant,' he said. 'Is her majesty quite well?'

'Yes, my lord, as hale and hearty as ever, but tired. She asked me to have a word with you, if that would be convenient?'

Ursel hid the horror of that concept poorly. Of course, Sylvian belatedly recalled, with Francisco, *having a word* with someone often involved blood, violence or a not-entirely-accidental fall out of a window. 'No, I—I'm sure that isn't—No.'

So he definitely had something to hide. Lots of something probably. Rumour had it he was slippery as an eel when it came to political dealings or trade. But now he was just scared. Interesting.

Sylvian kept his own tone calm and even, but implacable. 'It was not technically a request, my lord. More an instruction. It's relating to the unpleasantness at your office at the Exchange?'

Ursel breathed again, the colour rushing back into his face as understanding caught up with him. Relief. What had he thought? That Sylvian was there to execute him on the spot? Very interesting.

Sylvian knew he had a reputation—they all did, Francisco's men—but even here in Amberes? What were the aldermen up to if Ursel reacted like this? And was Ursel himself involved?

Instead of gracing Ursel with another word, Sylvian faced the rest of the gathered company, waiting until they fell silent and watchful.

'The queen has retired, gentlemen,' he said addressing the room. 'Her condition is trying and she must think of her health above all else. General Vasquez and the royal secretary will deal with your petitions and place them before her majesty at the earliest convenience. The Baron de Marasso will also be engaged in the business of the formation of a new council from this time on. That is all.'

There was a general roar of dismay and disappointment, not particularly vehement. The aldermen milled about, muttering to each other as they waited to speak to the royal secretary, Cortez. So this was where he had been, placating them all while they waited in vain.

Sylvian caught the secretary's eye who gave him a curt nod. He didn't look thrilled at the prospect before him now. Dealing with the aldermen was not something to be wished on the unwary.

'You have her ear, do you not?' Ursel asked Sylvian. He was standing a little too close, his voice carefully pitched so as not to carry.

'I am her bodyguard, but I have no influence on her majesty, sir.'

'Oh, come now,' he began, suddenly all smarmy and slick. He definitely wanted something then, and saw Sylvian as a way to get it. Gods, Sylvian hated his kind. No wonder the queen wanted to smother any possible rumours about the two of them. It was too great a risk already. The aldermen were known to pick at any thread offered and blackmail was a time-honoured tradition here.

'Do you have something you wish to say to me after all, sir?' He wished Ursel would get to the point. It would be so much easier. 'Best spit it out.'

The tone quelled him again. Ursel cleared his throat awkwardly.

'As you know there was a disturbance at the Exchange the other night, Captain Chant. The queen wanted information on what was taken, but it is . . . it is a delicate matter. With all the unrest in the city, the guild workers being difficult, the thefts and the like, I wondered if you and I —man to man, that is —could . . .'

Sylvian stared at Ursel's panicky eyes until he trailed off.

'Walk with me,' he said to the foremost alderman in the city, as if he had all the authority here. Which, he realised, he did. He had Annika's authority and she had the king's. He needed to remember that. 'Perhaps some fresh air would help us speak frankly.'

A dozen pairs of eyes watched them leave the room and Sylvian didn't like that feeling at all. Who else was watching them? And what did they want?

He was a bodyguard, not a politician. So why did it suddenly feel like he was being forced into a new and entirely unsuitable role?

CHAPTER SEVEN

Lyta

Lyta wasn't sure what to expect in the alchemist's workroom. *The lore of silver, the words of gold and the truth of the divine.* She really didn't like the sound of that.

Was this safe? Was it really possible to talk to lost gods?

Your guess is as good as mine, said Eninn, which Lyta didn't find comforting. *If they're reaching into the Nether, that can't be good.*

'I reached it. You came back with me,' she murmured under her breath.

Yes, but we didn't have a choice. They're doing this deliberately. And using relics to do it. And words of gold? Doesn't that sound like a certain book to you?

'You don't know that.'

She could picture his expression the moment she spoke, telling her to wise up and face the reality in front of her. And he had a point. Du Lac said the alchemists wanted relics. And someone had been stealing them. If only she knew what had been taken. And Ben knew more about *The Book of Gold* than anyone. He *was* the book. But would he be foolish enough to share that knowledge with an alchemist he barely knew?

As she watched him talking animatedly to the other man, all sparkling enthusiasm and driven by the desire to solve his problems in one fell swoop, she feared that he would. That he had.

Where else would he have learned to make those wretched amulets? Ben's blind ambition in pursuit of the unknown and unfettered trust in others had landed him in trouble before.

The little girl sat perfectly still, staring into the black dish of living silver while Charnock circled her, burning some mix of herbs. There was verbena in that mix and something floral. Lyta didn't know what exactly. She knew that underlying smell though. It lingered in the corners of the dodgier ends of the city and Janlow's bars reeked of it. It came from the east and Haldevar had told her never to go near the stuff.

'*It messes with your head, pet. Makes you feel good at first, then see stuff, and then you can't get enough of it. No one needs that.*'

Lyta cast a nervous glance at Ben, but he was busy with one of those amulets which he had brought with him.

'Ready?' Charnock asked him.

'It's only going to last a little while. The shield won't be perfect so don't push too hard, all right?'

'I have every faith in you, Ben,' said the alchemist, taking the piece from him. Not an actual answer to what Ben had said, Lyta thought. But Charnock was ready to go ahead with his experiment no matter what. That was obvious. 'Ready Clémence?'

The girl hung the amulet around her neck.

'Stay back,' Ben told Lyta. 'Whatever happens, don't get too close to the circle.'

'Is it dangerous?'

Clémence was just a kid and no matter how engaged she seemed to be in doing this, Lyta didn't want to see anyone exploited or put at risk. Why not have an adult do this? Unease clawed at the base of her throat. She could do it. True, she didn't *want* to, but better her than a kid. There had to be other apprentices and journeymen. Hells, even other alchemists.

'It's a summoning. He's done a thousand of them. You'll be safe if you stay back here and stay quiet. Clémence is well versed in the ritual, and that's important. We wouldn't want anyone to panic and upset everything. It's a great privilege for us to be here, Lyta, to see Master Charnock at work.'

A great privilege? She didn't even try to keep the disbelief and disgust off her face.

'It's your work that makes this possible for more than a moment, Ben,' said the alchemist. Ben beamed with sudden pride. Gods, was he so in need of praise? She ought to warn Kit about that. 'Your amulets stabilise the connection so we can truly communicate, focus the divine power into something manageable. Before it was but a fleeting thing, or too overwhelming for safety. Now we can form a connection and sever it at will.'

'A connection with what?' Lyta hissed. 'And why a child?'

'Children are more open to possibilities,' said Charnock. 'More malleable and they rebound much more quickly. Of course, if too young, there are other complications. The full force of the divine on an unformed mind would wipe it like a chalkboard.'

Lyta glanced at Ben who looked unsettled now. Well, too bad. She wanted answers and if that insulted this man so be it.

'Well, we wouldn't want that.'

The alchemist laughed. 'Not at all. But those who can truly connect with the divine are few and far between.' Few and far between? There were two of them right here, but she didn't want to announce that either. Charnock knew about Ben. Why wasn't he sitting there in a circle like a sacrificial lamb? Because he was the Seigneur of House bloody Alvarez probably. And Clémence was just a poor kid from Amberes. 'There are specific bloodlines with innate talents. We were beyond fortunate to find Clémence. It's quite safe. You'll see.'

Lyta opened her mouth to give a response but Ben threw her that look, that Kit-patented look which begged her, pleaded with her, not to fuck this up for him. She knew it well, but she hadn't been aware that her brother was now giving out lessons.

Ben needed this. For some reason, he craved this man's approval. And she had already upset him once today. She didn't want to make it worse. She'd never hear the end of it from Kit for one thing.

'All right then,' she murmured. She pushed her stool as far back against the wall as it would go and sat on it, tucking her feet up under her, shoulders pressed to the stone. She would wait then, wait and watch. And if she thought Clémence was in danger . . .

She'd wanted to find out what was going on in here. Now it seemed she had a front-row seat. And she didn't like it.

Ben was fidgeting, restless. She might even say he was nervous, and that put her on edge as well. He suddenly didn't seem so sure of this work, or his part in this. Not like before. Was it fear of something happening to the kid if his amulet didn't work, or fear of failing in front of Master Thomas Charnock? She wanted to think that it was the former, but she couldn't discount the latter either. Ben clearly idolised the man.

Once Charnock had finished burning whatever it was he was burning and the air hung heavy with the scented smoke, he unstopped a jar of oil for Clémence, who rubbed it into her hands. The scent of roses grew stronger, cutting through the smoke. Expensive stuff. Haldevar had often bemoaned the cost of pure rose oil. Carefully replacing the stopper, the girl set it down and picked up the shining black tray again, placing it carefully on her knees so the living silver pooled in the centre and finally fell still.

'Ready, Master Charnock,' she said solemnly, the childishness gone now. She was a guild member, an apprentice to an alchemist. That meant something around here. Childhood was a luxury.

Charnock met Lyta's gaze and smiled, as if he knew something she didn't. Quite a lot of things, she would have thought. But she didn't like the implication.

He bent down and added a series of symbols to the edge of the circle around himself and Clémence, his blunt piece of chalk scratching away at the flagstones.

'This circle is now sealed,' he said in solemn, echoing tones which carried all the formality of ritual. 'Great ones, who have stood in the congregation of lesser gods, and judged all who have passed beyond and would return, we call to you across the veil. We put our trust in you.'

As if caught in a dream, Clémence held her rose-oil-drenched hands over the dish while Charnock drew a black-handled knife from his belt. He moved it in a complicated series of gestures through the air—the kind of theatrical nonsense that impressed the gullible at the market—and then slashed it across both of her palms.

Blood splattered down on the obsidian, mingling with liquid silver.

Lyta was on her feet with a cry, but Ben's hand closed on her upper arm, pulling her back down. His strength was far greater than normal and she couldn't pull free. The glow of the divine filled his face, drenching it in otherness.

'*Do not interrupt.*' Gloir's voice was musical, the tone not to be argued with. '*This is the great work. This is all that we strive towards.*'

'But he just—'

'*Don't!*' and this time it was Kyron's growl. Ben's hand tightened like a manacle.

The girl inhaled sharply, her whole body going rigid while the surface of the silver began to tremble. Ripples spread out from the centre, like someone had thrown a stone in a still pool. Clémence clenched her teeth and her eyes went wide and unseeing as her breath came in fitful starts. She convulsed, her body shuddering as if she was taking a fit, but she kept her arms stretched out, palms up, cupping her own blood like an offering until it overflowed from her fingertips.

And then she went completely still, red blood dripping into the silver. Her breath evened out, her face gentled and she looked around her as if seeing this room for the first time.

'Ben, what the hell is going on?' Lyta snapped.

He stared at her for a long moment as if he loathed her. It wasn't Ben, not anymore. '*Blood binds,*' the god said with Ben's voice. She wasn't sure which one. She didn't care. '*Silver wakes. Blood ties. Silver breaks.*'

Eninn snarled inside her skull as the gods faced each other. They had betrayed him. But he had betrayed them first. The lost gods of Amberes despised each other.

And Lyta didn't blame them.

When Ben replied, his voice was very quiet and still. Gloir again. '*She is safe, We give our word. The amulet will protect her, and the circle will protect us. Charnock will reach further than ever before. A fit offering. The power we will gain from this is immeasurable. This relic is powerful and old.*'

What relic? That was hardly the issue, was it?

'He cut her.'

'*And we will heal her. She feels no pain. Trust us, Lyta.*'

But Lyta didn't trust them. Not one of them. Perhaps not even Benedictus Alvarez right now.

Charnock lifted his voice again, circling the girl in the opposite direction.

'Hail to you, Lord of the Crossings. Blessings shine on this day. We give you tokens and offerings, trophies of your enemies, the marks of their passing. Come forth and speak to us here and now, within the circle which holds the edge of the veil. The veil is at its thinnest, here in this your city, your place. This is your time. Come to us without fear or ill-intent. I offer this token.'

He picked up a small but thick gold coin, so worn the faces were almost smooth, and tossed it into the tray. He's taken it from the shelf, Lyta realised. A relic. Was that what Gloir had meant?

The ground shook beneath them, a rumbling which transferred itself to the walls. Lyta tensed, ready for disaster. She could still make it to the door if she sprinted. She might even be able to pull Ben out with her. But it would mean leaving that little girl there, bleeding.

'What's happening?' Lyta murmured warily.

'*Don't move, Cornellis,*' Kyron said, his voice quite unlike Ben's. '*Don't draw attention. It is not safe here.*' The warrior god sent out something like a growl from the depths of Ben's chest and Lyta scowled.

The air sweetened, sickly and cloying, heavy with verbena, roses and the coppery tang of blood. A heat haze shimmered around the circle. The hairs on the back of Lyta's neck and all along her arms rose in alarm.

Everything blurred as if a fever swept through her. She was back there, floating in that empty place, adrift in the void where she'd flung herself in pursuit of Eninn. She was lost again, helpless, in the place where the gods went to die. But this time, there was no way back. There never would be. She was lost forever in the Nether. The wandering ways stretched out before her in that lightless, endless place.

She tried to breathe, but there was no air. Only the stench of roses, verbena and blood. So much blood. She was choking on it. Drowning in it.

Ben's grip on her weakened. He was feeling it too, he had to be. But he didn't let go. Eninn leaned closer in her mind, as if he was trying to wrap his protection around her, even if he no longer had the power to do so. And now he sounded worried.

They're reaching into the Nether and it calls us back. Lyta, we shouldn't be here. Not you, not Ben, none of us.

'*It is the great work, cousin,*' Nimyeh told him in scathing tones, as if talking to a troublesome child. They could hear each other now and communicate. That rarely ended well. '*There is knowledge here to be had freely. And power too.*' Ben wore a smug expression which didn't belong on his face. '*Charnock can free us all. He has given his word. All it takes is time to perfect the process. Do not interfere and all will be well. He will help you as well. Don't you long to be free again?*'

Power. Lyta remembered all too well the last time the gods in Ben had made a deal like that. It had almost cost Eninn and herself their lives, and Ben his freedom. But it seemed they never learned. Oh, she was going to have words with Ben after this.

'Speak to us,' Charnock intoned. 'I bid you come forth.'

The air was boiling and freezing. Something was drawing nearer. Something terrible.

'No,' Lyta whispered, her voice not quite her own. It wasn't Eninn either. It was . . . this was wrong. All of this was wrong. The sense of dread which swept over her was like drowning in syrup. 'Stop.'

Clémence's eyes filled with the golden light of the divine, glinting like that coin in its bath of living silver. The same light rippled under her skin and Eninn recoiled. Beside her, Ben and all his gods did the same.

'*I am here,*' said the girl, but it wasn't her voice. It was deep and resonated as if reverberating through Lyta's chest instead of in her ears. '*I see you, child.*'

From somewhere far away she could hear the roar of a bronze battle horn like the old warriors used to carry ahead of their armies, held aloft, a deep-throated wail rumbling through her.

Old, powerful, terrifying . . .

Charnock froze, his whole body rigid with anticipation.

'Great lord,' his voice trembled, 'We humbly seek your wisdom. We would make this connection fast and sure—'

His voice choked and he froze as if a fist had closed around his throat.

'*Impossible*,' the voice told him. '*It is impossible, foolish man. Blood of my blood is the only thing that will do that and that is not willingly given. Speak, little cousins. For you have knowledge of it. Find your voices. I know you are there.*'

The pull within Lyta grew stronger as if something was being dragged from her. Eninn clung on by his fingernails. She wrapped her will around him and held him close. They had to stop this. They had to.

Ben stood shakily, clutching an amulet in his painfully tight fist. 'They choose not to speak,' he said. 'They remember you. You have no place here anymore.'

Ignoring Ben completely, the girl who was no longer a girl stared only at Lyta. She had no amulet to protect her. In the back of her mind Eninn writhed like a fish on a hook, desperate to stay hidden. She had never felt him afraid like this. Not even when his brothers and sister had trapped him and flung him through the tear into the void.

'*I know you*,' said that ancient lost god, the one of which all the others were scared. '*I know what you have usurped. It is mine, Trickster. It will always be mine. I will take it back.*'

They were all staring at her now—Ben, Charnock and Clémence.

Lyta swallowed hard before forcing out the words with what little bravado she could still muster. 'I think you have the wrong person.'

'*You know this place, human child. You remember. You stood here. I will follow in your footsteps. I can see the way clearly now. I will find you. You call to me. I would not have come but for your call.*'

Enough! she wanted to scream but her voice was stuck in her throat again. They didn't know what they were doing, did they? They certainly had no idea what they had summoned.

No one would call on that sort of power willingly.

Clémence's blood-drenched hands were white as bone clenched on the edges of the tray as if she would pull it apart as easily as honeycomb. In its pool of blood and silver, the coin trembled. The living metal rose like a crown around it, twisting in the air, and the obsidian paled beneath it, changing, glowing with a strange inner light. Her face was luminous as well, but underneath, her features were lined with agony. The thing inside Clémence and the girl herself were not the same.

'You have to stop this,' Lyta tried to tell them. No one was listening.

'*I will take back what was mine*,' said the dark voice. '*You will serve. All of you. To Amberes, all things return.*'

The amulet hanging around the girl's neck flared, its light suddenly intense, and the material of her tunic began to smoulder. The air reeked of burnt fabric, skin and hair.

'Enough,' Ben barked, dropping his own amulet. His voice was a thunderclap. Behind it came the full force of the three gods combined. Even then, the spell surrounding the girl held, burning up inside her. She gasped for breath, her eyes widening, the expression her own for a moment, but then the alien consciousness was back. Tears like molten gold spilled down her face, leaving burning tracks.

'*You will serve, all of you. Remember.*' The voice was a long drawn-out hiss now and those golden eyes never broke their gaze on Lyta.

Ben took three steps, crossed the chalk circle and with a swift and fluid movement, kicked the tray out of the girl's hands. She fell forward with a desperate cry and he dropped to his knees, wrapping his arms around her, holding her tightly. 'Thomas, enough,' he yelled, his voice fierce and filled with command. This was the Ben Lyta knew, the one who would never allow harm to come to another. 'Stop this. You have to close the connection. Now.'

For a moment Charnock just stared, like he was dazed or uncomprehending, as if words no longer had meaning. Then he flinched, taking in the splattering of silver still writhing like a living creature in the circle, the coin rolling into the corner, and Ben curled around the little girl, his skin glowing, dancing with symbols and words no one could hope to translate. The scholar trembled from head to foot with the effort of warding off whatever was coming through, his clenched jaw a hard line.

'Depart in peace,' Charnock commanded, finally finding his voice again. 'Go with our gratitude and release this vessel, restoring her to strength and health. Guard her against snares and wild animals, the falls of the unwary, and bless where she walks.'

He rattled off the words but even as he finished, Clémence shook like a leaf in the wind. The old god was not going.

It wasn't working, whatever it was. 'Ben, you have to do something,' Charnock hissed.

Ben opened his mouth and the voices of the gods spilled out from his glowing lips. It was music and nightmares twisted together and Lyta clapped her hands over her ears. Clémence arched in his arms and let out a strangled cry.

Abruptly, she went limp in his arms. The tray clattered to the ground, no longer obsidian but transformed to bronze.

Ben lifted Clémence carefully, pulling the necklace clear of her neck. He dropped it to the flagstones. As it hit them, the metal shattered like glass. Clémence drew in a ragged breath and then opened her eyes, blinking as if waking from sleep.

Charnock slumped to his knees.

'That was . . . *magnificent,*' he murmured, his eyes triumphant.

CHAPTER EIGHT

Lyta

Clémence held her hands out dutifully while Ben spoke to her—words Lyta didn't understand. The cuts closed where he brushed his fingertips to them. She didn't seem upset or in any pain now, but Lyta still watched them with suspicion. Ben's gods were difficult at the best of times, selfish and self-absorbed. She and Eninn knew that better than anyone else. They'd let this stupid ritual go too far.

So had Charnock and Ben.

What had Nimyeh said? Charnock would free them. Clearly they had given up Kit's translation of *The Book of Gold* doing that job and had moved on to someone new. Perhaps Ben had as well.

Ben helped the girl to her feet and she chatted away excitedly, asking questions about what had happened. She didn't seem to remember anything thankfully. Finally Charnock told her it was time to go and attend to other chores.

'Ask the cleaning staff to send someone,' he told her.

Clémence skipped off, Ben following her out of the room like some kind of hen making sure its chick was all right.

Lyta didn't move as if her feet were rooted to the spot.

'May I help you, Mistress Cornellis? You have questions?' Charnock asked in his smooth, calm voice. The man who looked like his head had been beaten like a drum was gone now and the alchemist was back. *Master Charnock*, she thought, and scowled.

'You might say that.'

How many children worked for him in this way? How many of them had been left for dead in a temple or a ruin or a laneway somewhere in Amberes? She knew that was a leap but she couldn't shake the thought. Did he even understand the risk he took reaching into the Nether like that? Messing around with the lost gods? If Eninn and the others were afraid of what he had contacted, how dangerous was it?

Because she had felt its power. And it remembered her, knew her. That could not be good.

None of those questions would make their way out of her mouth. They seethed in her throat like eels, choking her.

'Is she the only one?' she managed at last.

'Who can do that? Yes. Remarkable, isn't she? A true treasure. We were so lucky to find her. She has bloodlines stretching back to the very earliest gods of Amberes I think. I can't prove it of course. There are no records, but—'

'She could have died.'

For a moment he stared at her, as if she had said something unearthly or sublimely ridiculous.

'I assure you,' he replied at last, 'I would never have allowed anything to happen to her. And as you saw, neither would Ben. Clémence is *unique*. Her youth and vitality make her perfect for this and she—'

'*She's* just a child.' Lyta bit out the words, her gaze boring into his.

His face hardened at her obvious disgust. 'She's an apprentice to this guild. None of them are children once they sign their papers. It's the way of things in here. Do you think she'd be safer working with De Werve's gunpowder, or Lynan's war machines? What about the glass-blowers? Have you seen the injuries that can happen when molten glass explodes? Or when a child her age mishandles a lathe? Ah, but they have such tiny fingers, don't they? Skilful.'

Lyta folded her arms. Apprentices weren't children anymore. She'd heard Kit say similar things about his guild, but at least he took care of the boys in his charge. That was supposed to be the deal, wasn't it? Just because it might be worse, didn't make any of this all right. 'I don't think you're making the point you think you're making.'

His gaze turned glacial.

'Then please take it up with the guildmaster, but he will tell you the same thing. No progress can happen without risk. Clémence was perfectly safe, as were we all. You saw that. Even now Ben is probably off making sure she's being fed and spoilt by the kitchen staff. He does that, you know.'

Yes, because he knows this is wrong as well, deep down. He might not say it, not if he wanted to keep in with his new friend, not if his gods wanted Charnock to find them a way out, but he knew it. Ystara had escaped and now the others wanted the same thing. And Ben had all but admitted that was all he wanted too. Time to be himself again, to prove himself, to be with Kit. Oh, she was going to have words with him. And then Kit. And then with Beatriz, and see how he liked that.

The problem was, Charnock wasn't entirely wrong either. Out on the streets in Amberes, Lyta knew what might happen to kids the same age as Clémence. It certainly didn't end with a huge meal and being spoilt by anyone. Not in a good way. They were much better off apprenticed to a guild. Any guild.

She forced herself to calm, to breathe evenly.

'Where did you even learn to do that?'

'In Albion. At the house of Doctor John Dee. A harsh master, proud and difficult, but he is a magus. *The* magus, in fact. I still have my souvenirs and my scars. I had to leave—professional jealousy is a terrible thing, especially from one soon superseded by those he taught—but it turned out even better here. I'm the master now. And this city . . . this city of lost gods . . . There were more gods in Amberes than anywhere else at one point, did you know that? They gathered here to make a stand against the God-Emperor of Caput Mundi. They've left traces of themselves everywhere.'

And now he was telling her the history of her own city. Excellent.

'Traces?' she asked, suspicious of what that might mean.

He waved his hand at the shelves behind him. 'You know, relics, bloodlines, echoes.' He stared at her and for a moment she thought he'd reach out to touch her. He was close enough. She hadn't even noticed him advancing on her. He moved so slowly and carefully he barely seemed to move at all and then he was right there. Sneaky. If he lifted his hand he could brush his fingertips against her pendant or her face.

Then she'd have to snap his wrist. It wouldn't be pretty.

She stood her ground. Neither of them moved, but he studied her far too intently, as if searching for something inside her.

'You heard him, didn't you? You and that little thing in the back of your mind. Ben isn't the only one, I know that. And while he's special—a Divine Nexus, no less—you're something else. You've *been* there. I saw it in your eyes, the moment he spoke to you. There's a story about an old banished god who left his children behind him,' he murmured. His voice was musical, almost hypnotic. She could see how people fell under his spell. 'He could call to them, talk to them, even from the Nether. And they were going to lead him back. He made them from alabaster and rose gold.'

Lyta flinched. She couldn't help herself. That phrase . . . a memory sparked and it was all nightmare.

A knock behind them broke the spell. Charnock's knowing eyes grew suddenly round with alarm as Lord Stirling appeared with De Werve in tow.

'*You*,' said Charnock in disbelief, Lyta and stories about old gods forgotten now. 'What are you doing here?'

Stirling fixed him with an aristocratic gaze so full of loathing it made Lyta want to shrink back into the shadows. 'This man is a charlatan, Guildmaster de Werve,' he said as if denouncing a villain in a mummer's play. 'He's wanted by the authorities in Albion on numerous charges.'

De Werve cleared his throat meaningfully. The accusation was clearly no surprise. Perhaps Stirling had been making it to him for some time now. Probably since he got here. 'That's as maybe, Lord Stirling, but as I explained, this is not Albion. And we have found his work to be more than satisfactory.'

'Stolen work,' Stirling replied grimly. 'And he will steal again, from anyone foolish enough to work with him. I have proof.'

'What's the meaning of this, Piers?' Ben asked, arriving back only to encounter this display, utterly confounded by the turn of events.

Charnock shook his head. 'Stirling is a bitter and failed rival, my lords,' he said. 'That's all.'

Stirling waved the papers he held in the air. 'I have letters from—'

'And I'm sure they're very convincing.' Charnock advanced on De Werve. 'They probably even look real. He's *always* very convincing is our Lord Stirling. The Queen of Albion relies on that. You're aware of the importance of the work we're doing here, guildmaster. Real work with practical applications, groundbreaking alchemy. There are risks, no doubt about it, but all great work comes with risk. That's the way of it, is it not? Are you going to let the baseless accusations of one foreign nobleman with a grudge stop us?'

'Of course not,' said De Werve. 'The work is the most important thing. Even you must admit that, Lord Stirling. Master Charnock has delivered on his promises and he stays here, under our protection. You have established his presence, as you requested. But we will not be willing to cast aside a member of our guild, particularly not one with such results to his name. Not to a foreign power from whom he has sought shelter.'

Stirling took a step back as if he'd been punched in the guts while Charnock preened himself.

'You're making a grave mistake,' Stirling said.

'If this is so, present your case to Queen Annika,' Charnock sneered. 'See if she will bow to Elizabeth's whim. Or do you not have permission to do that? Do you fear what will be discovered if you did?'

And he laughed, a darkly mocking sound.

'We should go,' said Ben, his hands closing on his friend's arm to pull him away. But it was like trying to move stone. Anger simmered under his voice. 'Piers, really, *now*—'

'Where is she, Charnock?' Stirling snarled. 'What have you done with Viola?'

The ersatz innocence on Charnock's thin face was not convincing. Nor was it meant to be. He was loving this. Oh Stirling might be every inch the lordling, and Lyta was no more fond of the nobility than her brother but right now, anger was getting the better of him and he was about to do something rash. Charnock knew it too.

'With *whom*?' Charnock asked, the derision of it rubbing salt into the wound.

Stirling lurched forward, hands out ready to strangle the man and Ben wasn't able to hold him back. If he assaulted Charnock in front of witnesses, here in the heart of the guild, there would be trouble. Charnock knew that. He was counting on it. Stirling was doing his work for him. They'd have him up on civic charges at the least, and locked up in Old Steen no matter whose court he served.

The rulers of Castile, Aragón and León had no love for Albion. Neither did the council of Amberes. They would relish making an example of him.

Lyta wasn't having that. She could see when a man's buttons were being deliberately pushed. Stirling's distress was not feigned. Whoever Viola was, he'd come here intent on finding her.

Lyta slipped between them, catching Stirling's shoulders and shoving him back firmly, stopping him in his tracks. She felt something of Eninn behind that movement, a force a little greater than she should have been able to manage. Her god was unnerved too, especially by all that they had seen here, but enough was enough. Stirling was so surprised at being manhandled by a mere woman, that he stumbled and Ben caught his arm again in a stronger grip which carried a hint of Kyron around it like an odour, holding on to him this time.

'Not here.' Lyta stood firm, blocking his way. 'Not now.'

Something in her voice did it, his reaction apparent in his shocked expression. What that might be, she wasn't sure, but it came from the lingering atmosphere in Charnock's workroom, and she didn't like it. Gods of old, she needed to get out of here. And fast.

Gods of old, Eninn murmured darkly. *Quite.* He had no power, no presence of his own. It couldn't have come from him, not directly. He was as shaken as she was. What Charnock did here felt like a threat to them both, and she and her feral god were in agreement here and now. They wanted out.

'Come now, Lord Stirling,' De Werve was saying, still trying to calm the situation, the consummate politician. 'We are brethren in the craft, all of us. This is unseemly.' He and Ben managed to usher Stirling away and Lyta was left standing there, with the uncomfortable sensation of Charnock's gaze locked on her back.

'Impressive,' said the alchemist. 'Like I said, there's more to you than meets the eye, Mistress Cornellis, isn't there?'

At least she had an escape route now. And an excuse. She couldn't wait to get out of there.

'Not really. Just a gutter rat from Amberes, me. No one of consequence.'

Charnock grinned. 'Well, as a gutter rat from Londinium, like recognises like. You have an affinity for the great work and a connection to the divine of your own. That's why Ben brought you here, isn't it? He has an instinct, I tell you, a way of seeking out the right people. And he was right about you. It recognised you, that god from the beyond. Knew you. Like you called him forth just by being here, better than any relic I've ever used.' Lyta shook her head. She didn't want to hear any of this, didn't want to be true, but most of all didn't want to admit it to the likes of him. 'I think we will meet again, Mistress Cornellis. In fact, I'm counting on it.' His voice softened, melting to charm and invitation. 'I can show you wonders, Lyta.'

She thought of that glimpse into the Nether and shuddered. Horrors, more like. Was this what he'd said to Ben too?

'I've seen your wonders. I don't need to see more. Who's Viola?'

If the abrupt question startled him, he didn't show it.

'Viola? Just a girl who thought herself more important than she was. Far too clever for her own good. *No one of consequence*.' He tilted his head to the side, mimicking her. 'Why not ask Piers Stirling? While you're at it, ask him where he goes after dark and who he's really after? And what he's willing to do to find her.'

And that told Lyta everything she would ever need to know about Thomas Charnock.

He laughed as she walked away. It was a deeply unpleasant sound.

*

Outside in the courtyard, Ben had managed to get Stirling to at least calm down enough that he wasn't going to cause an out and out scene right there in the guild. Neither of them looked happy now. She'd never seen a friendship sour so quickly.

'I'll report them to the queen.' Stirling didn't specify which queen, Lyta noticed. 'They don't understand the danger.'

'Who are you looking for?' she asked bluntly, catching Stirling off step and unprepared.

'What?'

'You're looking for someone. You asked him where she was? Viola? Who is she?'

'I—I can't—It's none of your business.' He spluttered a bit and Lyta caught a glimpse of panic in his eyes. So he hadn't meant to say that about Viola, whoever she was, not even to Charnock probably, but especially not where he could be overheard. What was he hiding? And if this was a matter of the court of Albion, why hadn't he approached Annika first? Because she would say no? Or because it would embarrass the Virgin Queen?

Later, she promised herself. If it was important, she could get it out of him later. Until then, he was a liability.

'Dear gods, get a hold of yourself,' she told him. 'Maybe we can help you. Maybe we can't. But you certainly can't help yourself right now. Let's get out of here and we'll talk. All right? All of us.'

'A good idea,' said Ben. He was trying to be the voice of reason here. But something still burned in his eyes. Maybe he wanted to get Stirling away from here before his supposed friend ruined everything for him. 'I can't believe you did that. I vouched for you. Why didn't you tell me you were planning to confront Thomas? Come on, now. Before they kick you out for good. And me with you.'

'That's not going to happen,' Lyta couldn't stop the sharp note entering her voice and didn't care. 'You're the golden boy in here right now, aren't you?'

Ben flinched, as if she'd actually reached out and pinched him. 'Lyta, I can explain . . .'

He didn't though. His voice trailed off as he saw and correctly read the expression in her face. He and Charnock were doing something dangerous, far more dangerous than they realised, and that girl Clémence was at the heart of it. Lyta thought of the boy in the temple and the other bodies the physician had mentioned. It might not be connected but something in her mind was tangling them together and she really didn't like it.

Charnock had been way too interested in her as well. That never led anywhere good. He knew far too much already. How many apprentices did he have access to?

'How much, exactly, have you told that man about me, Ben Alvarez? And this one, for that matter?' She flicked a dismissive hand at Stirling. '*My* business is my own, and I don't like it shared.'

Lyta poured every ounce of Amberes menace into her voice and the Seigneur of House Alvarez quailed in front of her. He thought they were friends, or had done right up to this second. He was her brother's lover. But that didn't mean she belonged to him, or that he could run his mouth off about her private affairs to all and sundry. He had no say over her life. She wasn't going to give that power to the queen, let alone House Alvarez.

He'd forgotten who and what she was. Lyta wasn't having that.

'I'm sorry,' he said, and almost sounded like he meant it. 'But it was important. And I thought—I thought it might help.'

'I don't need help. You, on the other hand . . . you very much do. Have you told Beatriz what you're up to in there? All this *great work* business? No, I didn't think so. Did you tell Kit? You'd better not have told that bastard Charnock anything about Kit, do you hear me?'

If he'd put Kit in danger, gods help her—three against one or not—she'd end him.

CHAPTER NINE

Kit

Kit hadn't known what to do about Alderton's request, and he had no idea where Lyta was now. She'd headed off that morning to find out what had happened at the Temple of Lost Gods and it was late into the afternoon now. She could be anywhere. Amberes was her playground, hers and Eninn's. True to her word, Lyta was determined to let him live his own life. The problem was that meant he never knew where she might be because she was no longer haunting him. Besides, he wasn't entirely sure he wanted to help Lord Charles Alderton.

But the thought of a sheltered young woman like Viola missing in Amberes, and the obvious concern in the man's whole demeanour, wouldn't leave him. Eventually Kit closed the workshop early and sent his workers home. No one complained. Why would they? The drying lines were all filled with sheets printed today. The city watch notices banning bonfires in built-up areas could be printed tomorrow. No one was going to pay any attention to them anyway.

He locked up and made his way up along the banks of the frozen canal towards Beatriz's house on Crescent Street in the hope she or Ben might have some ideas on what to do.

Or possibly just in the hope that he'd see Ben.

Beatriz was at the heart of a flurry of activity, with two artists of the new school presenting their commissions to her, unfortunately at the same time due to some kind of mishap. Neither of them was happy to see the other and Kit hung back, watching the creative equivalent of a pissing contest, commenting on each other's garish paintings with veiled contempt.

Eventually even the usually placid Beatriz grew impatient with them, and paid both in full before dismissing them.

'Hello Kit,' she murmured as she watched them both march for the front gate as if now in contention to see who reached it first. It might have been comical in other circumstances. 'Are you here for dinner?'

He hadn't thought about dinner. She often hosted lavish affairs, and had politicians, trade partners and artisans gathered on any given evening. It hadn't occurred to him when he started over here that she might be preparing one of her soirees.

'I know we weren't invited . . .' he replied, suddenly awkward. 'I can come back tomorrow.'

She smiled at him fondly. 'Of course you are. You're always welcome here. Forgive me, I have so much to do and my manners are lacking. And Ben is hardly ever here at the moment.'

He was hardly ever at the workshop either, Kit thought glumly. It was one of the reasons they had argued last night. He spent so much time on his countless other projects. And Beatriz felt it too, he realised.

'You sound tired.' He held out his arm to escort her back into the upper parlour with its two blazing fires and heavy curtains drawn against the chill of winter. He was fond of Beatriz, despite the fact she had scared him half to death when they first met. But as he came to know her, to understand her open and giving nature, which remained the same in spite of the vast divine power she had once embodied, he had found that their friendship was as important to him as his relationship with Ben. 'Have you been overdoing it?'

She leaned in close against him. 'No more than usual. We have too many visitors, that's all. And there is much to do.'

It was hard not to love Beatriz. She was all that was gentle and good in the world. She treated people as friends from the first and for the most part garnered loyalty and devotion from everyone. The magical nature which permeated her presence, her natural ability to heal and comfort with little more than a touch, and the vast wealth which she shared widely meant that the great and the lowly of the city knew her, respected her and vied constantly for her attention. Whether it was the nobility who courted her as the Lady of House Alvarez, or the merchant class who sought her investments as well as her advice, or the artistic community who craved her patronage, or the poor who relied on her charity, they all came to her eventually.

And Beatriz made time for each and every one.

Even if it meant draining herself to do it.

Once he got used to it, standing in her presence, Kit had decided, was like standing in a ray of sunlight. She improved the world just by being in it.

He deliberately tried not to think about what she'd done to Iseult of Montalbeau, or how he had helped her do it. Beatriz had died and returned from the beyond. It had changed her. How could it not?

She had not been the same since. Even he noticed that. Her strength was diminished and she tired far more easily than before. Ben had commented on it but had only said his sister was a force of nature who would not be reasoned with. Ben feared she had burned herself out, or the gods had found other channels with which to manifest themselves in Ben, Annika and Lyta, taking with them the power that had once flowed so easily through her. Kit couldn't tell if she missed it or not. Beatriz was a pool of deep water, with only the faintest ripples on the surface to betray her inner thoughts and feelings.

'Visitors?' Kit asked. She didn't sound thrilled about the idea, which was also unlike her.

'My cousin, the Baron de Marasso, will be here shortly.' She sighed, sinking into her favourite chair in a flurry of velvet. 'Our family is . . . *concerned* about my life, it seems. They wrote me a letter and now Juan arrives . . . He's quartered in the palace, thank goodness, because I don't know where I would have put him. This house is too small for him.' Kit winced at the thought. It was the biggest house he had ever been in. Beatriz saw his reaction and smiled fondly. 'Hopefully his arrival is but a coincidence. Juan is a favourite of the king, one of his former generals, and Francisco has sent him here to advise Annika.' Kit tried to imaging how well the queen was likely to take that and made a face. 'Quite,' Beatriz laughed, reading his expression effortlessly. 'And a friend of Ben's from Oxford is staying with us. Ben turned up with him out of the blue, so excited to see him I couldn't say no. Marasso dines with us all this evening. I can't imagine them having much in common. How do you feel about joining us?'

Kit let out a brief laugh of his own. 'Do you want me to keep the peace? Wouldn't Sylvian be a better choice?' He meant it as a joke, but Beatriz didn't laugh this time.

'I can always count on you, Kit,' she murmured, ringing a bell for refreshments. 'And Sylvian is too busy these days, I fear.'

Kit glanced down at his clothes, repaired once too often. The only really good clothes he owned were carefully tucked away in the wardrobe at home and the only time he had worn them was to visit the palace and receive his papers from the king. It had been all of half an hour and he had taken them off as soon as he got back home.

'I'm not dressed for—'

'Since when has that mattered here? No, you're fine, my dearest Kit. Ben is going to come back smelling of chemicals or covered in soot, or worse. If he even manages to come back in time. Or his alchemist friend will be rambling about his discoveries and theories which no one else will be able to understand. I've seen it all before. You just wait.'

'And the baron?'

'I haven't seen him in ten years. He's a war hero so there may be stories. I'd hoped he and Sylvian would get along anyway. But . . .'

She sighed. Sylvian was always tied up with his work for the queen, Kit knew all about that from Lyta.

'There's still time to run away,' he told her.

Beatriz smiled at the thought, but that was when one of her servants appeared to tell her that the baron had arrived.

'Too late,' she sighed. 'Ready to help keep the peace?'

Keeping the peace in House Alvarez? Was that his job now? Well, he had offered.

The Baron de Marasso swept into the room and embraced Beatriz with what looked like genuine familial affection.

'It has been far too long,' he murmured to her, his voice a soft rumble. 'And you are even more beautiful. Your father would be so proud, my dear.'

Beatriz flushed, completely caught off guard. Not what she had expected. Not in the slightest. She had been braced for confrontation, Kit was sure of that.

Marasso gave Kit an appraising look. 'And this is?'

'Master Christopher Cornellis,' Beatriz told him. 'A family friend. He is the king's own printer here in Amberes.'

That was when the baron smiled, at the word 'king', and Kit felt himself instantly judged. He sketched an adequate bow and kept his ink-stained hands behind his back. Just like that Marasso put him from his mind.

'And where is your brother, my dear? I haven't seen him since he was a boy. I have heard great things about his scholarly endeavours. Still buried in his books then?'

A clatter downstairs told them of fresh arrivals and raised voices couldn't help but announce Lyta, Ben and another, all arguing loudly.

Wonderful, thought Kit as Beatriz paled. Lyta could always make a grand entrance at the most inopportune moment.

'Shall I go and see to that?' he asked and she gave him a nod, regaining her considerable charm.

'Yes Kit. My thanks. Please, take a seat, Baron. What would you like to drink? Let's not stand on ceremony. We are family after all.'

As Kit left the room, the voices rose from below again and he paused, steeling himself. Unfortunately that gave him time to hear, from behind him, the baron's jovial question.

'Taken a lover at last, Beatriz? Handsome specimen for a bit of Amberes rough. Does he have a sister?'

For a moment he thought about defending Beatriz's honour. Maybe even his own. But what could he say? *Wrong Alvarez*?

That would clearly be even worse. They were nobility. And he was no more than a bit of Amberes rough. He fled.

Downstairs, in the normally pretty little courtyard which was now snowbound and bare, he found Lyta, Ben and a handsome fair-haired man, all at each other's throats.

'Ben, you have to see reason here. He's dangerous. I have proof. We have to do something.' The accent made Kit pause. Another one from Albion. The last thing he needed. He thought of Alderton and his stomach sank.

'You should have taken it to the queen if you suspect foul play. Why didn't you?' Ben spat back at him. Ben, of all people! He barely raised his voice most of the time.

'Who's dangerous?' Kit asked as he joined his sister. She had her arms folded in front of her and that familiar glare that could only mean trouble. Lyta was angry too. No, worse. Lyta was livid. Seething.

'Ben's new workmate, one Thomas Charnock, an alchemist. They're all alchemists these days apparently.'

'I'm *not* an alchemist,' Ben replied curtly, as if she had called him something much worse. Maybe she had on their way here.

Lyta narrowed her eyes. 'Let's not get into what *you* are right now.'

Sweet gods of old, Kit thought, dismayed as the animosity between them hit him full force, *what happened*?

'This is all getting blown out of proportion,' Ben tried again, visibly reining in his anger, reverting to that calm and even voice he used when he was trying to make peace. Frankly, it drove Kit up the wall sometimes and it definitely was not going to work on his sister. 'No one was harmed. I know you haven't seen anything like that before, Lyta, and it must seem strange but—'

The urge to protect the man he loved had Kit putting himself between the two of them before Lyta could do anything drastic. No one condescended to her.

'Will all of you calm down and tell me what happened?' he said.

Everyone ignored that request. Of course.

'I'm leaving,' Lyta snapped.

'Beatriz wants us to stay for dinner. Their cousin is here.'

'Cousin?' Ben asked, suddenly wary. 'Which cousin?'

'The Baron de Marasso.'

For a moment Kit thought Ben would break out into a string of curses that no well-brought-up scholar should know, let alone the Seigneur of a noble house. Just for a moment his gaze snagged on Kit's and he winced—guilt, grief or simply regret? Kit couldn't tell—but then Ben seemed to pull that mask over his face, the one which locked every emotion deep inside him. It held nothing of the man Kit loved. The shock of that was like a bucket of cold water.

Ben stepped away, deliberately distancing himself from Kit and Lyta.

'I need to go to my sister. Lord Stirling, will you accompany me? You are a guest in our house, after all, and a member of the royal court of Albion. No doubt, the Baron will be honoured to make your acquaintance. Master Cornellis, it was good of you to come, but there's no need to stay now. Goodnight.'

Ben had shut him out. Completely. It was like a different man had taken his place. He swept by Kit without a glance, as if he barely knew him. Kit could only stare after him.

What was that?

Lyta growled under her breath.

'We should just go,' he said, and tried to ignore the sick feeling in his stomach.

'What about *Beatriz wants us to stay for dinner*?' she mimicked him ruthlessly.

'I know, but I think I've lost my appetite. How about you?'

'Oh I lost mine hours ago.'

'Lyta, *what happened*?'

Lyta sighed in exasperation. 'Ever had one of those days? Everything happened. Absolutely everything. Come on, let's go home. I'm done.'

He had to tell her. He was about to make her day even worse. 'We had a visitor—Alderton.'

Her whole body stiffened. It always did whenever that particular lord from Albion was mentioned.

'What did he want?' Lyta's eyes went from irritated to blazing with outright hatred.

'He wants your help. His sister has gone missing.'

'His sister?'

'Viola.'

At the sound of the girl's name Lyta let out a groan and sagged back against the wall.

'Viola Alderton,' she echoed and closed her eyes in despair. 'Oh, of course. It just had to be *her*, didn't it?'

CHAPTER TEN

Lyta

The cold was settling in again by the time they left Beatriz's house, misting their breath in front of them as they walked along the dark, empty streets. In the heart of winter, most people went to bed early, saving fuel. Only the rich like Beatriz Alvarez and her ilk dined late by candlelight. Even the taverns were quiet. No one wanted to be out in the streets. If they weren't already in their beds, they were huddled around the fire. It was only the last night of the solstice that they would celebrate, and then the streets would be alive until dawn, ready to welcome the sun and drive back the darkness. But that was still three days away.

Kit walked alongside Lyta, faded red scarf wrapped around his neck. Lyta had carefully repaired that old thing so many times she wasn't sure how much of it was still the one their mother had made for him. He gave her a look when he noticed her staring.

'What have I missed then?' he asked gruffly.

Ah yes, matters in hand then. 'Alderton's sister is missing and Stirling knows her from Albion. He came here looking for her, but didn't want to raise the alarm. The moment he arrived at the guild though, he was throwing accusations around the place about Ben's mentor, Charnock. And as for him, he's . . . he's . . .' She didn't have words that went far enough for what she thought he was, or time to list out all the possibilities. 'He's dangerous, and as he knows Viola Alderton too, those accusations could well be fair. He taunted Stirling about her. So, all the alarm bells are ringing, you know? And Ben and that Charnock are up to something *shady*, involving the gods. Your boyfriend's been telling him all our business. I think we're already involved more deeply than we want to be and I don't know what in.'

Lyta sighed, trying to speed up in order to keep off the cold. Kit slightly lengthened his stride, irritatingly unruffled by her change of pace. 'And the dead kid at the temple might be a Blacksmiths' Guild apprentice. Or at least I think so. There are a few missing. Maybe not missing, but unaccounted for. But I only have a little girl's word for that. And she's under Charnock's spell and all.'

'The dead kid at the temple?' he halted, his voice stretched thin by concern. '*What dead kid*?'

She filled him in on what she had found at the Temple of Lost Gods, and at the guild, and watched his expression harden. Apprentices had nothing, were pretty much entirely dependent on their masters and Kit had been one himself once upon a time. If their masters didn't look after them no one would. The guild system relied on that one truth—that a master took care of an apprentice above all else.

Charnock saw them as members of the guild, earning their keep and learning their trade. There were pay offs for that, she understood as much. But at the same time, they were only kids.

And Charnock had sliced her little hands open without a moment's hesitation.

'Is that why you went to the guild with Ben?' Kit asked.

'Seemed like a good idea. Stirling was going there anyway. Turns out he was meeting De Werve to warn him about Charnock. Or trying to anyway. They don't want to listen. Charnock has them all wound around his little finger now.' She let out a long sigh. 'It's not good, Kit. Not good at all.'

Kit nodded uneasily. 'Ben told me all about Charnock. He sent letters of introduction ahead, sought him out and Ben was flattered by his interest. He's something of a rising star. He knows all about gods, Aspects and the nature of a Nexus. Apparently he's amazing. A genius.' He didn't sound happy about that, and she didn't blame him. She didn't trust Charnock, but more, she didn't like him either. Or his effect on Ben.

'Ben is not the best judge of character. He likes you.'

As a joke it was not her finest, especially not in this situation. Kit scowled at her.

'Dead children, stolen relics and a voice talking about following you back from the Nether,' her brother said, summing up all her problems. 'Add to that a missing aristocrat and a couple of alchemists far too interested in all our business. And Ben . . . Ben means well, but he forgets how dangerous all the knowledge in his head can be. He wants nothing more than to solve puzzles. We know that, but maybe some things shouldn't be solved.' He let out a long sigh of his own as they rounded the corner onto Twelfth Moon Street. 'You're right. This isn't good.'

'It never is, Kit. Gods and Aspects and aristocracy . . . When we get involved with the likes of them, it never is.'

*

Twelfth Moon Street was a good area, a place of business and heavily regulated by the city watch. A nice part of town. It lay just off the Meir, too close to the Rookery to be expensive, but not really part of it. It wasn't far from Kit's old shop on Book Alley so supplies were easy to come by. Residents here liked their peace and quiet. That was good for business. Lyta knew it was one of the reasons Kit had seized on it as a location, that gnawing need for acceptance. Ben had wanted to move him up to the more prestigious Lombard's Street, right by the Rose Palace where the Golden Angel Press was located, but that hadn't been an option. Kit had tried to tell him as much at the time.

Even so, Twelfth Moon Street had shops they couldn't afford to buy things from, and studios for artists who thought a printshop was a step up from a pigsty. But it also was peaceful and quiet and lent an air of respectability to the business, king's warrant and all.

Lyta hadn't thought about the risk of an attack in the street in all the months since they had moved here. There hadn't been a need. Not even in the middle of the night. Twelfth Moon Street was safe, well-covered by the watch and no one would even dream of being attacked here.

So it came out of nowhere.

They were huge, six of them, each of them masked and wielding clubs and coshes. Not a blade in sight, Lyta realised, not that it was much of a relief right now. Clever really. If stopped they couldn't be arrested for carrying prohibited weapons. A club was just a stick, even if it was as thick as her arm. But they could do a hell of a lot of damage with what they had. Especially with their builds.

'Cornellis?' the first one growled.

Anyone else might ask what they wanted or even denied all knowledge of the name. Lyta opted for something else entirely.

'Kit! Run!' she yelled. But it was already too late. Besides which, her brother wasn't the kind to run from a fight. Never had been.

One lunged at her and Kit was there, knocking the man aside, but not before a club slammed into his side. He grunted and staggered back before rounding on them again, trying to put himself between the brutes and his sister. Lyta grabbed at one of the weapons, ripping it out of an unsuspecting hand and launching a kick to the guts that sent the attacker sprawling to the ground. But there were far too many of them and they didn't wait politely one by one either. This was street fighting, Amberes-style. It was brutal and hard, and it was fast.

Kit was already pinned by three of them, desperately trying to tear himself free to help her. And as Lyta tried to duck again, a solid weight caught her under the solar plexus, knocking all the fight out of her and a hand closed around her throat. The grip was powerful and implacable. He squeezed until she saw sparks dance in front of her eyes as her breath ran out.

'Enough,' the man told her. 'Give it back, thief.'

'What?' Lyta tried to say, but the word was little more than a gasp.

If she only knew what the bastard was talking about. And if he'd only stop choking her. Her confusion must have shown. He shook her like a rat, lifting her off the ground until she was kicking helplessly. She'd pass out in a second and then they could carry her off in peace. Perhaps that was the plan. If they didn't accidentally kill her first. The fucker had a scarf wrapped around his face and a hood pulled up, but the dim light flashed on the collections of earrings he wore. Even as her eyesight blurred and her mind reeled, she recognised them from somewhere. Panic didn't give her a second to work out where.

They were after something. Something stolen. Problem was she hadn't taken anything. Not in ages. She'd been trying to be good. Kit had made her promise. Besides Sylvian was watching. She worked for the gods-blasted queen!

'Let her go!' Kit's voice sounded so far away. Shadows were fighting with the flickering lights on the edge of her vision now and this was all about to go even more badly wrong. She knew it.

'Take her back with us,' said one of the others. 'We don't have time for this. The masters have ways to loosen her lying tongue.'

A sound like an explosion cracked through the night. Lyta slammed into the cobbles, but at least she could breathe again, drawing in a great gulp of air, which was more than she could say for her captor as he fell beside her. Half his face was missing, a mass of blood. The noise burst around them again and the remaining thugs scattered. Beside her, blood turned the grubby snow scarlet.

A pistol. Someone had a pistol.

Lyta tried to push herself up on shaking arms, her whole body protesting. If someone was carrying a weapon like that out in the open in Amberes, things were very bad indeed.

Hardly anyone could afford the bloody things to start with. They were the preserve of the royal armoury, nobility or assassins.

With a wild stab of hope she tried to focus on her saviour, coming towards her from the other end of the street. Sylvian? No, this figure moved differently. They walked calmly up the middle of the road, refilling the wheellock pistol with gunpowder and shot as they came, and winding back the mechanism, every movement deliberate and practised. They paused to take aim again with an expert eye, even in the darkness.

'Stay down Lyta,' said Frida. 'I've got them.' She fired again, the burst of noise and light making Lyta drop, hands over her ears.

There was a thud as Frida's next target hit the ground somewhere by the junction with New Street and sprawled there, unmoving.

How many was that? Two? The others had fled.

'Fucking amateurs!' Frida muttered, lowering her weapon and glancing down at Lyta. 'Who are they? What did you do this time?'

Frida? What the fuck was Frida doing here? Kit had warned her—

Kit! She scrambled around to where he lay, groaning and thankfully very much alive, but clearly having taken the brunt of the attack. He rolled onto his side and spat out blood into the scuffled and muddy slush beneath them. He wiped his face in the red scarf.

Great, that would stain.

'Are you all right?' Lyta gasped, her throat and chest aching with the effort.

'Yeah. Wonderful.' He dragged himself upright, and then paused, his eyes barely focused. He shook his head and squeezed his eyelids tightly together. 'Just give me a second.'

He'd walked away from worse than this, she reminded herself. Much worse.

Frida stood there in the snow, gazing down at the two of them and cocked her head to one side.

'And I thought the boss was overreacting.'

Once she had been Lyta's dearest friend. Now . . . now Lyta wasn't sure what she was exactly.

'The boss?' Lyta echoed, her tongue thick and unwieldy in her mouth.

'Lord Alderton told me to watch over you. Glad I did now.'

'We don't need—' she started.

'Yeah, right.' Frida interrupted, her tone scathing. 'That was a friendly dance invitation, was it? Who have you pissed off now, Lyta?'

She held out a gloved hand, which Lyta pointedly ignored as she dragged herself up and helped Kit. He rose slowly, carefully, and she knew that meant he was hurt and trying desperately not to show it. You never showed weakness to an enemy.

And whatever she was now, Frida was not a friend.

'Just you?' Lyta asked. 'Where's Janlow and his mob?'

'Searching for his lordship's sister. That's where everyone is these days. And I don't work with Janlow, you know?'

'Certainly looked like you did to me.'

'Enough.' Frida sighed in frustration. Or guilt. 'Let's get you two home and looked at. That's a nasty gash, Kit.'

Kit brought his hand up to his head and it came away bloody, which focused Lyta's attention on him again. Head wounds bled, but she could clean it up. He'd be fine.

'We can get ourselves home.'

'Lyta, be reasonable,' Frida began.

'Why your boss thinks I can help him, or even that I would, I don't know.'

'Because we haven't been able to find her, that's why. You can get places we can't.'

'What sort of places?'

'The Blacksmiths' Guild for one thing, as you proved today. And look at what happened. They all had the right build, didn't they?'

Frida was not wrong. Lyta remembered the ones guarding the gates and the walls of the compound, especially the one with all those earrings.

Carefully Lyta dropped to her knees beside the nearest body and pulled down the mask to reveal the broken face. It was messy, but the ear on the left side was still intact. Earrings, yes. Gold and silver, some set with beautiful stones. And tattoos crawling up the side of his throat, almost lost under the blood. There wasn't much left of his face to recognise, but she'd seen enough. She hurriedly searched his pockets but there wasn't much there. A little coin, some nails and . . . She looked at his hands—strong, thick, the fingernails short and blackened.

'Smith?' said Frida with a knowing smile.

Lyta glared at her as she released the man. She didn't deign to answer. 'He thought I'd taken something.'

'From the Blacksmiths' Guild? What was it?'

'Nothing,' Lyta replied. Frida cast her a dubious glance but that was the problem. She had taken nothing.

All she'd done was watch an alchemical ritual and she hadn't been able to get away from that fast enough. She didn't have a scrap of evidence they were involved with the dead kids or the stolen relics. Charnock's reaction to the mention of Viola's name had been evidence he knew her—*Far too clever for her own good too.*

Gods, his words grated now. Was that what he thought of Lyta too? What did they think she'd taken? That would have been useful to know in between the threats and violence. Earrings was a dreadful enforcer. Whoever had sent him ought to be ashamed of themselves.

She glared at Frida. 'None of your business, is it?'

'Leave it, Lyta,' Kit's voice rumbled, a gentle warning. 'Let's get home.'

He was right. She couldn't stay out here and he needed seeing to. Besides, Frida wasn't worth her time.

Even if she had saved them.

'Tell your boss to leave us be. If I find anything out about his sister, I'll send word. But otherwise'—she pointed a finger at Frida—'I don't want to see you anywhere near us.'

It might have been more convincing if her hand hadn't been shaking.

'Lyta!' Another voice brought their attention to the corner where the Meir became Palace Street. The hiss of steel being drawn married with the rapid crunch of footsteps in snow as a man in the formal uniform of the royal bodyguards sprinted towards them.

Earlier would have been better, Lyta thought. A lot better.

By the time Sylvian arrived beside her, his mouth a hard line and every nerve ready to fight, Frida was gone.

'You missed all the fun,' said Kit bitterly, twisting to work out where he was hurt and how bad it might be.

Sylvian took in their injuries, which were thankfully minor, and the bodies still sprawled on the street, whose injuries were about as far from minor as you could get. 'What on earth happened to the two of you? Was that Frida?'

He sheathed his sword in a fluid motion, grabbed Lyta's shoulders and shook her gently to get her attention like he thought this was her fault.

To be fair, it usually was. But still.

His hands stayed on her shoulders, strong and warm even through the layers of her clothes. And Eninn help her, all Lyta wanted to do was fold up and let those arms catch her. She couldn't though, not now. Because if she gave in to that temptation she was pretty sure she'd collapse and she needed to stay strong for Kit.

'Let's get inside,' she muttered. 'It's bloody freezing out here.'

For once he didn't argue. That was, she decided, a minor miracle. Eninn should be proud. Or maybe it was Ystara's doing. Who could say?

Sylvian looked so solemn, she didn't have the nerve to point it out to him. But then, finding her and Kit surrounded by corpses probably didn't help his mood. She let him lead the way.

'The—the bodies?' Kit asked, trailing behind them. Lyta glanced back and saw him stagger, just a little. She darted back and slipped under his arm.

'Sylvian,' she snapped and he came to Kit's other side, supporting him effortlessly.

'I'll sort it out, fetch the watch if someone hasn't already called them. But for now, Lyta's right. Let's get you inside.'

Lyta's right. Not a phrase she expected to often hear pass his lips.

What was he even doing here this late? It couldn't be good.

What was wrong now?

CHAPTER ELEVEN

Sylvian

The conversation with Ursel had been concerning. Sylvian didn't like to think of how much else the alderman was leaving out because this all sounded about as bad as it could get. Yes, someone had stolen something from him, something old and powerful and very dangerous indeed. It wasn't meant to be there. It wasn't even meant to exist and how the Ursel family had got hold of it, Sylvian wasn't going to begin to guess at. But they had owned it, and it had served them well.

A relic of power, of Cissonia herself, the goddess of trade and prosperity, the patron goddess of Amberes—no wonder the man and all his forebears were rich.

And now it was gone.

Another relic. No dead body this time so there was that to be thankful for, he supposed.

He wrote a note to Vasquez. He ought to have gone back to the queen and informed her, but it was already late and he didn't want to disturb her again. She'd looked worn-out when she dismissed them all. And visiting her now, when the court was at revels or already heading to their own—or someone else's—bed would be like handing out pamphlets connecting the two of them and stirring up another hornets' nest of rumours.

Besides, he had orders. Find Lyta. Bring her to the palace. And he had good reason to obey. There was an inquisitor in Amberes. Time was of the essence.

Inquisitors investigated crimes against the Church Imperial, hunted down gods and conducted all the religious vendettas their Divine Emperor required. He'd seen their work in various campaigns with Francisco and some things he couldn't wipe out of his memory. Torture, immolation, brutal executions . . . nothing was off-limits. And few but Francisco stood against them.

Lyta had been involved in the death of a magister, and Lyta had a god in her head. If they knew that . . . Even the queen might not be able to protect her. Especially not if the Church Imperial had already taken her into custody.

Royal authority meant nothing if not enforced. All Amberes would see that. The whole continent.

The king might rage and promise retribution, but it would be far too late. For Lyta, for him, for all of them. He'd headed straight for Kit's printshop, but they weren't there. Then he'd gone to Beatriz's house to find he'd just missed them.

It had taken some time to extricate himself there because Marasso had been working his way through Beatriz's wine cellar and wanted better company than Ben and his scholar friend, who were barely talking to each other.

'I'm still on duty, my lord,' he said. 'Forgive me.'

Marasso started telling Beatriz about the time the two of them had been caught in a skirmish and Sylvian stood there awkwardly while he was praised to the skies for something he remembered somewhat differently—a bloodbath, nothing to be proud of—but the baron told a good tale and it sounded almost like an adventure instead. If you pretended it had happened to someone else and didn't call to mind the faces of those who hadn't made it out the other side.

'Do forgive me,' Sylvian interrupted when Marasso paused for breath. 'I need to talk to Lyta rather urgently.'

The old man gave him a knowing look. 'Who is she, this Lyta? Your beloved?'

Sylvian shifted awkwardly. That didn't seem like a big enough word for what Lyta was to him.

'Lyta Cornellis,' Ben supplied, before Sylvian could formulate an appropriate answer. 'You met her brother earlier. Christopher?' Since when did Ben call Kit *Christopher*? He sounded so oddly formal it put Sylvian's nerves further on edge. 'They went home, Sylvian. They weren't able to stay due to other commitments. You might still be able to catch them.'

He needed to hurry up and find her, get her to the palace and . . . deal with it then. Why did it feel like he was running out of time?

'Oh, the printer,' Marasso interrupted his thoughts. 'You never answered me, Beatriz. What on earth are you doing consorting with tradesmen?'

The tone was abruptly less pleasant. Blame the wine, Sylvian thought, but that didn't help.

Beatriz glowered at him. Her patience with this visit was waning fast. 'I head a *trade* organisation, Juan. It's where our money comes from.'

He rolled his eyes. Few nobles, in Sylvian's experience, liked to admit they were involved in trade. Money appeared out of thin air, it seemed, a blessing from the gods. 'That will have to stop when you wed.'

There was a long, arctic silence.

'When I *what*?'

'Wed. Marriage.' He waved a hand heavy with rings idly. 'I thought Aunt Teresita wrote to you. We had a meeting back home. The elders of the family. They are highly concerned about the reports we received, about your *abilities*, my dear girl. Don't worry, I'll arrange everything.'

Ben sat up a bit straighter, appalled, and his friend leaned in, intrigued.

Beatriz's voice went very precise, an instant danger sign. 'I read Teresita's letter. I wrote a reply. I am not powerless. I am making a recovery. And I am not planning to wed anyone as yet. When I do, I will arrange it as I see fit, cousin.'

Marasso, however, didn't read the room. He carried on, his tone still jovial. 'You need to get with an heir, my dear girl. It's your duty as an Alvarez. The bloodline and all that. There is a time to advance and a time to retreat. A fact of life. We understand the risk but there is no greater duty. Now, it's time to move to the next phase—that of wife and mother. It's a matter of your own protection as well. You're here on your own in this city.'

She gestured the room. 'Hardly alone, Juan. And I am hardly helpless either. This isn't a matter for debate. There are inherent dangers in what you suggest.'

'The family feels very strongly about it, child.' He ploughed on in that paternalistic tone that was never a good idea in Sylvian's experience. Not with any woman he had ever met. He tried to signal as much with his eyes. Marasso didn't notice. All his attention was fixed on Beatriz, as if he could browbeat her into submission. Why not? It had always worked in the army. 'Very strongly. Not to undermine you, sweet girl, but you're not getting any younger and that recent unpleasantness with the Duchess of Montalbeau had . . .' He glanced towards Ben who ducked his head in guilt—no question where Marasso had heard about that then—and then noticed Stirling. He checked himself, remembering the lord from Albion was there as well. 'It had a detrimental effect, didn't it? Anyway, a good marriage—'

'Enough,' she said, her voice a knife's edge. 'I will hear no more of this nonsense. I am fine as I am.' What Marasso was suggesting was a dangerous plan, Sylvian knew that better than anyone. Aspects rarely had children and the risk to their lives during preganacy was great. Look at Annika. Beatriz was right to be appalled. Her family were looking at her as no more than breeding stock. He knew the aristocracy did that, but he'd never seen it stated in so blatant a way before.

Marasso tried to gentle his voice. He really did. 'If you already had someone, it would be a different matter. A beloved. Not your printer though. We must think of the family line, and any marriage is as much a matter of familial alliances, isn't it? A handsome fellow I'm sure, but really . . .' He poured himself yet another glass of wine, a deep red, like blood. 'Although his sister must be very beautiful. Is she?' Sylvian didn't know what his expression was like in that moment, but Marasso laughed knowingly at whatever he saw scrawled on Sylvian's face. 'Well, I never thought I'd see *that*, Chant. She must be special indeed.'

'She is, sir,' he said as curtly as he could while not actively insulting his superior, but at least it was a change of subject. He owed Beatriz that much and he could handle being the target of a drunken man with too many opinions. 'Very special.'

And then it hit the old man—the realisation Sylvian was hoping to avoid.

'Wait, she isn't the *one*, is she? From all those years ago?' He peered at Sylvian and beamed with delight. 'It *is* her, isn't it? Well, good for you, boy. After all this time. Ystara be praised. You see, Beatriz? Love finds a way, doesn't it? It will for you as well. Surely the Lady of Love will protect you and deliver you a healthy child to carry on the line. I'll find the perfect husband for you.' As if he was picking a stud for his favourite mare.

Enough, Sylvian thought. Love was not finding a way. Love was causing too many complications. And what Marasso was talking about wasn't love. It was politics and power. The ring on his finger had gone cold. Ystara was not pleased and any second she might demand he do something about it. The goddess liked Beatriz and probably had plans for her as well. Ystara gained power from love, not from forced marriages or alliances based on filial duty and trade advantages. 'If I may, Lady Beatriz, I must leave. I still have duties to attend to this night for the queen.'

He needed to find Lyta, before something happened. Why did it feel like something was going to happen? The Inquisitor wasn't even here yet. And yet the feeling persisted, gnawing away inside him. That somewhere out there, Lyta was in trouble, that she needed him . . .

But Marasso answered before Beatriz had a chance, stepping into her role in her own house. 'Of course, Sylvian. Our beloved queen really does work you to the bone, doesn't she?' Sylvian couldn't help himself. He winced and saw Marasso notice that too. The baron smirked and Sylvian swallowed hard. Had that been a dig? If so he had given far too much away. But Marasso was already laughing. 'Dismissed. Who am I to come between a man and his . . . what's the word . . . *lady*?'

Sylvian really didn't like that tone. You could infer anything from a tone like that. And the last woman mentioned had not been Lyta, but the queen. He had said he had duties this night for the queen. He could kick himself. He drew in a very careful breath and bowed. Marasso was drunk, that was all. Bringing up Beatriz's marriage prospects like that, making all those insinuations in front of a stranger . . . He'd probably be mortified in the morning, though he'd never apologise. And Sylvian wouldn't expect him to. He was the commander.

'Lady Beatriz,' Sylvian drew the formality of his role around himself like a shield. 'The queen sends her regards and thanks you for your friendship.' He couldn't share what else the queen had said about loyalty and her veiled threats. Not with Marasso here. Not now. But he could give Beatriz the respect she was due in her own house, and hand her back the power here.

Beatriz, wearing a mask of cool indifference, bowed her head graciously. 'We are most honoured. Tell her that I will be happy to attend her at any time if needed.'

'You're close to the queen, are you not, Sylvian?' Marasso cut in again. He wasn't letting it go. Ystara pricked against Sylvian's skin. Furious now. He could clearly feel that and he had the sensitivity of a brick.

Beatriz stiffened, alarmed, and Ben squirmed in his seat. Stirling sat back, watching them with interest. He couldn't know the undercurrents of this, could he? But he was certainly paying attention now.

Sylvian chose his words with care. 'I have the honour of protecting her, at his majesty's command.'

Marasso didn't seem to notice. Or if he did, he didn't care. 'His majesty has given some . . . *interesting* commands, has he not? And he honoured you in other ways too.' He nodded at the ring Sylvian wore, the royal ring of the Vasa, Ystara's ring, which marked him as the queen's champion.

'Careful cousin,' Beatriz murmured. She fully understood the risk of the things he was implying.

Marasso shot her a quelling glare. 'Of what, cousin? Rumours are only rumours.'

'Rumours are dangerous, for all of us. The House of Alvarez does not indulge in rumours.' She stood, which forced the baron, Ben and Stirling to stand as well, breaking the conversation. 'I should retire. And Sylvian should be going. We have delayed you in your duty too long.'

He bowed, grateful to her for her intervention, and followed her from the room. She paused in the hallway, and reached out to take his hand. Her hand lingered over the ring.

'Forgive him,' she whispered, though whether to Sylvian or the goddess, he didn't know. 'He drinks to forget, I think. He has seen too much in Francisco's service.'

They all had, Sylvian thought, but couldn't bring himself to say it. It was not an excuse. Not really. Not for those insinuations. But it seemed to placate Ystara at least. The outrage faded and the tug in his chest was back, the need to find Lyta. Now.

'I understand, my lady. And we should say no more of this. I hold the baron in the highest honour. He saved me, you know. Long before I saved him.'

She gave a soft laugh. 'Not the way he tells it. Do remind the queen I am at her service and that I am here if she should need me. At any hour.'

It was a gracious offer, especially since Annika was too busy throwing out threats. But Beatriz was kind and patient. Sylvian valued that in her. He always would. He had seen too little of kindness in his life.

'I shall. And I will assure her of your friendship. She will be most relieved. Thank you.'

She smiled briefly and then paused, a little embarrassed perhaps. 'But my cousin has a point. If my family desires to see me wed, they are not likely to give up easily. There was already a letter, it's true. And now he's here. He's the blunt instrument of their will, of course, but an effective one. They'll try others. I should take matters into my own hands, divine Ystara willing. Intercede with her for me, will you, my friend? I don't have the strength I once wielded and should they confirm that . . .' she sighed, shaking her head.

'Since the duchess?' he asked.

She gave a wavering smile. 'It was . . . it was a trial. And I was lucky.' She had died. He knew that much. Iseult of Montalbeau had killed her to steal her magic. He still didn't understand how Eninn and Ystara, and whoever else had been involved, had managed to bring her back. But she had been changed in the process, she had admitted as much, and did not have the same strength as before.

Beatriz seemed to shake aside the thoughts like a bad dream. 'Your comrade in arms, Captain Juárez? He is . . . he's from a good family, is he not?'

Juárez? Sylvian frowned, bewildered at the change of subject. 'Well, yes, I think so. His father is a minor lord from just north of Seville. Not as exalted as an Alvarez, my lady.'

She sighed, but that same smile flickered over her lips. 'He's a good man, though?'

'The best.' In that at least, he had no doubt at all. He trusted Juárez with his life, and had done more than once.

'Good to know,' she murmured, which left him even more confused. 'I met him once. And he wrote to me afterwards. It was … chivalrous. I might have need of a good man. And sooner than I would have thought.'

'Beatriz, if you need help, you know I'll be there in an instant. I owe you—'

She gave a startled laugh. '*You*? Dear gods, Sylvian, Lyta would murder me.' Sylvian recoiled. He hadn't meant that! But Beatriz just shook her head as if amused. 'Not to mention what your goddess would do if I interfere with *her* plans. I have encountered her power already and I don't want to anger her. No, don't worry, darling man. Ask your goddess to aid me. She'll listen to you.' Would she? Sylvian wasn't so sure. She certainly hadn't thus far. 'Goodnight, dear heart. Commend me to Captain Juárez, if you will. Tell him . . . tell him

I have a matter I would discuss. Yes, that's for the best, I think. Now, hadn't you better go and find Lyta?'

Sylvian took his leave and headed out into the night. He didn't know what Beatriz was up to nor what her interest in Juárez was either. A good man? Yes, he was. But she was the Lady of House Alvarez.

The baron had spoken of finding her a husband and Beatriz had said she'd do that for herself. It wasn't Sylvian's place to intervene but this would only end badly. He knew it. Beatriz was not someone to cross and neither was the old man. Kit might be only a printer from Amberes, but Juárez was a minor lord's lesser son and probably not a lot better in the eyes of House Alvarez back home in Andalusia. He didn't want to see Juárez caught up in the same sort of mess he was.

Ystara however had plans of her own. She always did. And through him and the queen, her power was growing. Beatriz knew the gods better than anyone else. Perhaps she was counting on that. She was an avowed mistress when it came to making deals. Maybe even with the divine.

Sylvian made his way briskly through night-time Amberes, unafraid of any attack or danger. Only once had he been caught unawares, by Janlow and his gang, and that would never happen again. He scanned the streets ahead and around him, but no one moved and that put his teeth on edge. He only knew he needed to find Lyta now. Before anything else happened, get her back to the palace before he explained about the Inquisitor. A drumming insistence in the back of his mind warned him he was running out of time. Maybe Ystara knew something he didn't. He hated the feeling.

The city had been quiet of late. The cold kept everyone indoors, besides those who kept the streets in order after dark. No one was keen to be out causing trouble at the risk of freezing off body parts. Besides, he was a royal bodyguard, blessed with the right to bear arms in the city streets and able to fight his way out of just about everything.

So he was completely unprepared when he reached the corner of Twelfth Moon Street and walked straight into yet another scene of mayhem and violence with Lyta right at its heart. Because of course she was. She always was!

His first thought, the one that sent his heart into his throat so quickly it almost choked him, was that the Inquisitor had wasted no time and gone right after her. But they didn't look like the Praetorians who accompanied an inquisitor. If they had been, the outcome would be very different already. The fact he was too late to be of any help was a minor blow to his pride. He could take that.

But he *was* too late. There were bodies strewn around and Kit was the worse for wear.

Frida had cast him a single glance, given a smile that might have been a sneer, and was gone.

'They were from the Blacksmiths' Guild,' Lyta told him, as he helped Kit inside and closed the door behind them. Not Imperial soldiers. That was one thing. That alone let him breathe. Lyta tried to find what little healing ointments and bandages she had scattered around upstairs. Going back to Beatriz would be an option, if he could persuade Kit to move, but that wasn't happening either. He wished he could. She could deal with the full force of two stubborn and injured Cornellises. She was probably the only one strong enough to do that. But Marasso might still be there, and Sylvian didn't want to give him anymore amusement than he'd already had on their account. Or cause Beatriz more grief. He ought to make Lyta leave for the palace now, whoever she thought had attacked her. But he knew exactly what she'd say to that.

Sylvian kept catching glimpses of the marks on her neck, the red blotches that were going to be bruises soon enough. He would have been too late to save her, he knew that. She might have been dead right now.

If Frida hadn't been there.

Frida *Fucking* Elwynn of all people.

Outside, the city watch arrived and Sylvian briefed them rapidly. It didn't take long. The dead men, he thought, could be blacksmiths, which would confirm Lyta's suspicions. This was not good. Not good at all. The Blacksmiths' Guild was the most powerful in the city.

De Werve sat on the council and had done for years. He had been Mayor three or four times and had inherited his seat as alderman from his father. His wife was a Rockox by birth, his sons and daughters riddled through the great families. The queen liked the old bastard for the love of all the lost gods and was thinking of making him Mayor yet again, if only to quash Ursel's ambitions. Many people admired him, respected him and relied on him as well. Like Ursel and De Moy and the others, the notables among the aldermen of the council, the trade families of Amberes, De Werve was important to peace in the city.

Ursel had mentioned disquiet among the aldermen, rumours of something afoot. He didn't know what, but he wasn't happy with the turn things were taking.

But why would blacksmiths attack Lyta?

Sylvian locked the door of the printshop. He needed to tell Kit to talk to his own guild, to make sure that he was protected. This could send the whole city sliding into chaos. Guilds did not go to war against each other.

But until the council was reconvened, there wasn't really any central body other than the queen to conduct city business and keep the peace. Royal guards in the streets would make things difficult in Amberes and if one guild turned on another . . .

What were the blacksmiths thinking? And why did they want Lyta?

Thieves didn't have guilds. Was the idea to knock Kit out and then take her wherever they wanted to take her? It made his stomach twist with unexpected anxiety.

He needed to talk to her. He needed to know what had happened and to tell her the queen wanted her to move to the safety of the palace. The problem was he didn't know how to even broach the subject, or how she would react to Annika's demands.

In the room above the workshop, Lyta was still trying to persuade Kit to let her check his injuries. Sylvian set to work on the fire. After the house on Larch Lane burned down, Lyta refused to leave it banked and unattended, which meant it had to be lit from scratch. She had it all laid out and ready, but even with his field skills, it took time.

Lyta didn't say a word. Sylvian glanced back to see her head tilted back, trying to work the pain from her shoulders and neck, before she turned her attention to Kit's cuts again. Looking after her little brother, as always, whether he wanted her to or not. They'd hurt her, the bastards. He was glad they were dead, the ones that were. If he'd been there the pile of bodies would have been a damned sight higher.

'What happened with the blacksmiths?' He tried to keep the concerned tone out of his voice but failed. The flames caught finally, and he fed more tinder into the fire. 'What would they want with you?' He paused, realising who he was talking to. He cast a suspicious glance over his shoulder and saw her staring back at him, pale and wan. 'What did you steal from them, Lyta?'

'Nothing.' She snarled that one single word. A warning.

He knew better than to trust that answer. 'Really?'

Her glower deepened. '*Really*, but they thought I did. Said to give something back, but I swear to you, Sylvian, I took nothing. I think they're involved in the murder in the Temple of Lost Gods. That kid, the one we found there, I think he was an apprentice. Du Lac said they're always buying up relics, so why not steal what they can't buy? I went to the guild headquarters with Ben and his friend, to see what I could find out but . . .'

Sylvian sat back on his heels. Gods, she'd been busy. How did she manage to get into so much shit so quickly? It was like an art. 'Lord Stirling? I met him at Beatriz's.'

Lyta snorted. 'There are two of them in fact, both from Albion—Stirling and Charnock. Ben's mates with Stirling and working with Charnock. Right at the heart of it. And knowing what we know about him, that's not a good thing. Those men hate each other and the problem seems to boil down to Viola Alderton, who is missing. You see the issue?'

Alderton? This lurched from bad to worse, with Albion at its heart. What next?

'Do you think they know what happened to her?' Kit asked.

'Stirling seems to think Charnock does.' Her temper was visibly growing shorter by the second. 'He's a nasty piece of work, Kit. You want to warn Ben off him. If you can.'

'If I can,' he echoed glumly. 'Ben's his own person, Lyta. I don't think warning him off is going to do what you think it will.' Kit drew in a long thoughtful breath. 'And it adds another layer of problems. If I tell my guildmaster what happened here tonight, he'll be honour-bound to raise it with the aldermen.'

'Your guild ought to be protecting you,' she told him sharply. 'If you won't do it, I will. They need to raise it. Make sure nothing like that—'

Kit interrupted her curtly, because Sylvian could imagine the humiliation if Lyta of all people went to report this to her brother's guild. 'If they get involved, especially now as they all jockey for position on the new council, something like this could kick off a guild war in Amberes, Lyta. No one wants that.'

That was an understatement but Lyta wouldn't see it like that, not when Kit was involved. Even now, she was barely holding herself together with the fear that something could have happened to him. And Kit was not taking this renewed protectiveness well. Sylvian could sense trouble brewing anew. He cleared his throat meaningfully, which got their attention.

'Let me get this right. Two feuding alchemists are here in Amberes, both connected with the Alvarez family, at the same time that their cousin, the Baron de Marasso, has been sent here by the king and is finding his place at court?' Never mind trying to pick a husband for his cousin against her will. 'And now, Lord Alderton's sister, also linked to both of these men, is missing?'

What chaos from Albion had arrived in his city?

'Alderton wants Lyta to help him find her,' Kit went on and Lyta gave another bitter snort. No question what she thought of that proposition then. 'I did warn him. But . . . she's just a girl, Lyta. She was so young in the picture he showed me.'

No wonder Alderton had gone to Kit rather than Lyta or him.

'We don't want anything to do with the Aldertons, Kit,' Lyta said.

'On that we agree, but—' Kit hissed as she dabbed ungently at the cut on his head. He grabbed the cloth from her. 'Give me that. I'll do it myself.'

Sylvian, who had been at the wrong end of Lyta's supposed healing ministrations once or twice, could sympathise. The fact that she relinquished the cloth and sat back, letting him do it, spoke volumes about her new determination to let Kit look after himself. They all knew she was trying. It must gall her that she still managed to bring this trouble down on him.

And now she was itching for a fight. Frustration did that to her. Sylvian knew she was trying to be strong for Kit, trying to keep his spirits up, but she wouldn't be able to do that forever. She was crumbling, barely holding herself together with guilt.

The fire was almost merry now. At least something in the room was.

Alchemists and relics and dead children. And now a missing noblewoman from Albion. Marasso and the Alvarez clan somehow mixed up in it. And the guilds. Vasquez was going to love all this. And as for Annika . . .

'Why didn't Alderton go to the queen?' he asked.

'They're not exactly on good terms after all the business with your ring, are they?' Kit said. 'Alderton and the queen.'

'And Stirling?'

Lyta shrugged. 'A loss of face for Albion maybe? I don't think Viola Alderton or Lord Stirling are meant to be here at all, and Charnock knew it. Taunted him about it.'

The Queen of Castile, León and Aragón would not be inclined to help any noble of Albion, that was certain. They were old enemies.

Kit pushed himself out of the chair, and went to the little kitchen off the main living area, emerging with a bottle of brandy and some earthenware mugs, pouring one for each of them.

They drank the brandy, which burned its way down their throats. Sylvian told them about the queen's command that Lyta come to the palace, although not about the Inquisitor, not yet. It was all dangerous enough right now and if he spooked her, there was no telling what

Lyta might do. Especially in this mood when she was trying to be strong for Kit, to protect her brother, the primary and all-consuming goal of her life. Tread carefully, he told himself. She was upset, frustrated and worried.

She made an exasperated noise. 'You can send in a report. The queen can wait. I can't leave Kit now.'

Kit scowled. 'I can watch out for myself, Lyta. We discussed this.'

And what a fun conversation that must have been. Sylvian could tell that. He could read Lyta like a book.

Before she could launch irrevocably into a fight with Kit, Sylvian interrupted, deciding it was better to take the brunt of this himself. Give her a target before she said something stupid and upset her brother. Because she would. And then she'd torment herself about that as well. 'You work for her. That involves doing what she says, I believe.'

'Oh, you do, do you?' Lyta folded her arms defiantly. 'I never agreed to that.'

'Yes, you did,' he told her as firmly as possible. 'You might not have meant it, but you did.'

'She knows who I am and what I do, Syl. If she wants unquestioning obedience, well . . . she has *you*, doesn't she?'

He pinched the bridge of his nose and counted silently to keep his temper. It was getting harder. He knew what Lyta meant in all its agonising permutations. 'Then come and tell her yourself. Resign if you must, but do it in person.' And once he had her safe, he could work out what to do next. Lock her up probably. He wasn't proud of it, but it might be the only way. She was never going to forgive him. 'Kit, you need to talk to your guild. Make sure they have your protection in order and—'

He hadn't reckoned with how stubborn Kit could be either. They were notorious for it, the Cornellises.

'It won't work, Syl. Like I said, what are they going to do? The Blacksmiths will deny everything. Besides most of my guild don't like me very much. Got above my station, didn't I? De Werve will claim they were after a thief and everyone knows Lyta's reputation. They'll say it was regrettable and that'll be that. I got in the way.'

A wince of frustrated guilt traced across Lyta's face. *Regrettable* . . . That was a word for it. He knew she regretted everything she had brought down on Kit's head. And she had done that all her life.

She was trying to protect him, even now. She had promised to step back and let him live his life. But that was going wrong too. Because not protecting her little brother, even when he was twice her size now, was something Lyta just couldn't do.

'That doesn't matter,' she cut in. She still wanted to make sure that Kit was safe. That was all Lyta ever wanted. 'Sylvian's right.'

'Of course I am,' Sylvian muttered.

Lyta's jaw tightened. He could see her bristling, the fight swinging around to him again. Because if they had a fight now, if they argued, and one or the other of them stormed off, they wouldn't have to talk about the queen, or about her coming in with him. Or anything else. Oh he knew Lyta Cornellis far too well.

'Well it makes a change,' she told him and smiled. No, not a smile. It was a smirk designed to dig into every bruise she had ever given him.

He had spent the better part of the evening running after her, trying to find her. And when he had she was knee-deep in trouble. Again. Because trouble followed Lyta Cornellis everywhere and every time he had to pull her out of it, he was terrified it would be the last time. That he'd lose her. He didn't quite snap, but the misery came out in a rush of utter resentment he couldn't stop. 'A change would be nice, Lyta. But here we are *again*, with people coming after us because of *you*.'

And he still hadn't told her the worst of it. Who else was coming. Why. An inquisitor. Gods and goddesses help them—an inquisitor was coming.

She had the gall to look insulted. 'Me? I haven't *done* anything.'

'Really? Why do I find that impossible to believe? Oh yes, bitter experience.'

Kit pushed back the chair, letting it scrape loudly across the floorboards which shut them both up for a moment. He stood, towering over the two of them, the brandy bottle clutched in his hand. He was exhausted. Fed up. Sylvian knew the feeling.

'I'm going to bed,' said Kit. 'If you're going to fight or—' He waved his free hand at them descriptively. 'Or *whatever*, try to be quiet about it.'

He left the two of them staring at each other, awkward and unmoving.

Whatever?

Lyta broke first. She almost wilted where she stood, but sank into his chair instead, her head in her hands. Because now Kit was gone she didn't have to be strong anymore.

Anger evaporated, replaced by concern.

'Are you all right?' Sylvian was at her side and on his knees in moments. He took her shaking hands in his, smoothing his fingertips over her skin. She was so cold.

'No,' she sighed. 'I'm exhausted and I hurt.'

'Where?'

'*Everywhere*, Syl. *Everywhere*. Shouldn't you be back in the palace? I thought you weren't meant to be away from her for longer than a flaming gnat's fart.'

Another jibe. Another attempt to push him away. She was entirely predictable in the aftermath of any kind of disaster, wasn't she?

Sylvian sighed as another shard of guilt struck deep inside him. Because Lyta wasn't wrong. He should be with the queen. He hated that. 'She wants you to come to the palace for your safety. Please, Lyta, I'll explain everything, but you have to come with me.'

Lyta glanced to the door Kit had vanished through, stricken. 'Now?'

Sylvian relented with a sigh.

'I think tomorrow might be preferable at this stage. It's late and it's dangerous out there. Besides, you aren't really fit for it now, are you?' He took in her haggard appearance. She was going to bruise badly. She was lucky nothing was broken. He didn't know what Annika would make of her when she turned up black and blue. He had been sent to find her and bring her to safety and all this had happened because he'd taken too long. He'd known somehow. Something in the back of his mind had been screaming it at him. Perhaps it was

Ystara. Perhaps it was his own instincts, or whatever scraps of a bond still clung on between the two of them.

It had been a warning, that was all. It had to be. It happened all the time in Amberes. If some of the guild enforcers wanted to send a message they had many ways, but this was the most effective. And thieves didn't have guild protection. She was better known than she thought, especially around the Rookery and the Guild Quarter.

Lyta had wriggled her way into the Blacksmiths' Guild and if something had gone missing who else would they think to blame?

And again, the threat of an inquisitor nagged at him. What if it wasn't blacksmiths, no matter what Lyta thought?

'Off to the palace again. And here I am without a thing to wear,' she muttered. It was a peace offering, of sorts. It was all he was going to get.

Sylvian reached out to cup her face, lifting her chin. Lyta, to his surprise, let him, seeming relieved at his touch. He ran the pad of his thumb along the line of her high cheekbone and this time she didn't flinch.

'It could have been worse,' he told her. 'You've had much worse than this.' He hated the thought of it, the memories. All the times he couldn't protect her, all the things that had gone wrong in the past. He couldn't bear to let it happen again. 'What did you do, heart?'

'Nothing, I promise,' she sounded in earnest. 'Went into their stronghold with Ben, that was all. I wanted to find out about the apprentices. Found out too bloody much about what they're up to in there. Charnock has found some way to talk to lost gods and I think Ben is helping him. And his gods—they're far too bloody eager, the bastards. I guess we know where the missing relics are ending up. Charnock had a whole shelf of them, powerful ones, Eninn said. They used a coin to reach through to something old and awful from the Nether—a coin and a child, and a ritual. And blood. It's never good when they use blood.'

'A coin?' Sylvian's shoulders tightened. Her eyes focused on him keenly like she was expecting the worst.

'Yes? A coin. Why?'

'The relic of Cissonia that was stolen from Count Ursel was a coin. An old one. Something he should never have had, I think. Might explain his family fortune if it's actually got divine power.'

Lyta sighed. 'Oh, it had power all right. A relic of Cissonia, the last real divinity of any power left in this city. That must have been how he made the connection, but it wasn't Cissonia we were talking to. That voice . . . it said it knew me, Syl.'

Her eyes were very wide, the colours shifting in the firelight, but he thought he caught a ghost of Eninn in their depths. Once again he wondered where she stopped and the Trickster began. Deliberately, he changed the subject back again.

'Stealing relics from the Temple of Lost Gods is bad enough, but the mayor too? Is De Werve involved?'

'I don't know. He thinks the sun shines out of Charnock's arse, I can tell you that. If it advances him, maybe. I don't know. The aldermen are all devious little bastards, but Charnock? He's something else. He knew, Sylvian, knew about Eninn and me, knew about Ben and the gods from *The Book of Gold*. We need to talk to Ben. He's close to Charnock. Too close. I'm sure he's been telling the bastard a lot of things we don't want known. Perhaps if we can get Ben to talk to us we can piece it all together. And make Stirling tell us what he knows about Viola Alderton, what he thinks Charnock did to her or . . .' She closed her eyes again and leaned into his touch a little more, squeezing her eyes tightly closed as if trying to make herself focus. She was ready to collapse. He could feel that. But here she was, still spinning plans within plans as she went down.

None of which involved returning to the palace, he noticed.

'They can wait,' he told her. 'You are exhausted. You should sleep.'

'I can't. There's too much. If they're coming after me for something I didn't do, I can't sit here waiting. And I need to find out who killed those kids. Before there's another death.'

Of course, she was thinking about the kids. They didn't have anyone else. She wasn't just trying to hold it all together for Kit this time. She had been flat out since early this morning and Lyta was not going to stop any time soon, not with vulnerable lives on the line.

If she knew an inquisitor was coming to Amberes she might never sleep again. He would stand watch over her tonight, he told himself. He'd keep her safe. Tomorrow would be soon enough. The queen could wait.

He offered up a small prayer of appeasement and protection to Ystara all the same, to watch over Annika and the baby, to forgive him this one time.

His decision made, Sylvian gathered her in his arms.

'What are you doing?' she protested.

'Taking you to bed,' he said simply and she went perfectly still, suddenly aware and watchful with that fox-like attentiveness he knew so well. She was almost vibrating with it. She stood warily, as if ready to bolt.

'To—to bed?'

He gave her an arch look. 'Are you going prudish on me now?'

'But you . . . the queen . . . and your vows. Don't you have to go back?'

She was so close, her mouth only an inch away. And Sylvian lost his mind.

He kissed her, taking his time, parting her lips with his tongue and revelling in the sensation. Gods, he had missed her. His body ached for her. She was everything, all he dreamed of, and those dreams seemed to be sent by his goddess herself to torment him. Yes, he was sworn to protect the queen, bound to her by fate and divine will. But he *wanted* Lyta. He would always want Lyta. Every fibre of his being was pulled tight as a wire with that desire.

For a moment he feared she'd tell him no. Then she kissed him back.

His mind whirled and Lyta clung to him, body to body, pulling him closer, her hands on his face, on the back of his neck, in his hair. She moaned, deep in her throat, a sound of surrender and pleasure all in one.

And then reality seemed to catch up with her again. She pulled back enough to focus on his face. Her eyes were so blue, sparkling with the hint of tears.

He knew what she was going to say, what she was thinking. He just knew.

'Don't, Lyta,' he whispered, a prayer, an entreaty, his lips still brushing against hers. 'Please, don't.'

'It's a mistake.' Her voice was very small. A bit desperate. 'You belong—'

'No. I don't. *We* are not a mistake.'

It seemed like the longest breath a woman had ever taken, but Lyta breathed in and then out again, weighing up everything, or possibly like him, not able to think rationally at all.

'All right,' she replied, her voice wavering as she spoke and her arms snaked around his neck. 'To bed. But not to sleep. Not yet.'

'I wouldn't dream of it.' He couldn't keep the laugh from infecting his voice this time and she smiled. She actually smiled. He pushed aside thoughts of the morning, of the future, and of the dangers descending on them from his mind and filled it instead with her. For a moment, just a moment, Sylvian thought everything might be all right again.

He was, as everyone so often told him, a fool. But he was her fool most of all.

Hadn't he said so himself, on his knees, expecting to die at any moment?

'I'm yours Lyta.'

Liar.

He pushed that stray thought away and kissed her again, filling himself with the sensation of her, the taste of her, the wonder. She pulled him after her as she made for the bedroom, the door taking far too long to locate and open. He kicked it shut behind them. It was only a few strides to the bed and that was all he was conscious of. Lyta, in his arms, a bed. Silence. Safety.

They shed their clothes with desperate hands, and then he touched her skin, dusted with a constellation of freckles and smooth as silk. All his thoughts of his queen or his vows or anything else fled as Lyta drew him down with her.

CHAPTER TWELVE

Lyta

Sylvian's touch on her bare skin wasn't a dream. It was real, something longed for past bearing. Her body melted beneath his questing fingers and she tried to pull him closer, flesh to flesh. She couldn't get close enough to him, even though she knew it would all end in tears. He was a fire, one in which she would gladly burn forever.

Did he know that? Did he realise?

He had been lost to her for thirteen years and she had thought that she hated him. She had convinced herself of the fact, because she had to in order to survive.

But it had been a lie.

Lyta had refused to marry him. She had to. But she ought to have told him they couldn't be together, that it was for his own good. That she didn't want him and what they had shared had been a mistake. That he had his duty and she wouldn't or couldn't share him with that. That she wouldn't take his scraps of attention.

Another lie. All she did was lie to him. She didn't want to do that anymore. She would take whatever she could, and gladly.

His lips brushed against her collarbone, his tongue dipping into the hollow above it and at the base of her arching neck. His teeth grazed her so gently, teasing her, tormenting her. He laughed when she shuddered against him, that deep and knowing rumble which was infuriating and intoxicating all at the same time.

Stolen moments, she told herself. That was all they had. Stolen moments.

But she was a thief, after all, blessed by the Trickster God of Thieves. So stolen moments it would have to be.

'Why does the queen want me in the palace?' she asked him, because if he was distracted as she was he might let the truth slip out.

'For your safety.'

It couldn't just be that. What did a queen care about her safety? Sylvian's mouth traced a line along her jaw while his hands slid up her sides. His touch was so careful, so delicate, like he was afraid to break her.

'For reasons of her own.'

'She always has reasons of her own. But that doesn't mean it isn't to protect you as well.'

'What aren't you telling me, Sylvian?'

There was definitely something. She knew it because she never told him everything either. She needed to protect him, just as she had to protect Kit. Everyone she loved . . . they were always in danger because of her. It had been Kit this evening. They could have killed him in attacking her. It wouldn't have been the first time either. She'd got Ranulf killed. She'd almost lost Sylvian to Janlow and his gang, and again when Iseult tried to enslave him. Perhaps she had lost him, to Ystara and Annika instead, but at least he was still alive. She couldn't bear it if she brought the same level of destruction down on him as she had on her husband. That was why she couldn't consider marrying him. Gods how she wanted him . . . But look what had happened before. He didn't deserve that, not Sylvian. She had to keep him safe and he would never understand why. Sylvian thought he was so strong. But Ranulf had been strong, and cunning, and oh so skilful. He'd thought he knew everything. And in the end . . .

Sylvian brought his mouth back to her lips again and froze.

'Lyta?' he whispered, a sound of disquiet. She opened her eyes to find him watching her, concerned.

'What?'

'You're crying.'

She was? Confused, she brought her hand up to her eyes and her fingers came away wet. 'I am?'

'If it's too much, or too soon, or . . . Did I hurt you?' He drew back even as he asked it, but there wasn't a trace of irritation on his face. Just worry. Gods, she didn't deserve the scraps she got of him. 'I'm sorry. I shouldn't have. If you don't want to—'

'But I do,' she told him, holding his face and pulling him to her again. She shouldn't say it. She tried to stop herself but it all came spilling out anyway. 'You must know I want to. We've wasted far too long, Sylvian. Don't make me beg, Captain Chant. It's humiliating. You're mine, remember? That's what you said.'

The smile that flickered over his lips was still unsure, but he leaned in again and Lyta captured his mouth with hers. She kissed him like she might lose him forever. Which, she knew, she might. At any second.

'I am yours,' he assured her and set himself to proving it to her.

If only for a moment, Lyta thought and felt the sting of those treacherous tears again.

And then she couldn't think, couldn't even form words as Sylvian's body moved against her and within her, pushing her to the brink of ecstasy. She called out his name as she came and felt him shudder inside her, dragged over the edge alongside her. She clung to him, gasping for air, one hand tangled in his hair while the other pressed to the small of his back, where it bowed against her. Holding on to him as tightly as she could.

Because she knew, come morning, he would slip out of her grasp yet again. And she would have to let him go.

*

A noise woke Lyta in the night. For a moment she thought it might be Sylvian trying to be quiet as he put his uniform back on in the dark before slipping away like a ghost of what might have been. But then she realised his body was still pressed against the length of her, his arms loosely wrapped around her, holding her close. His chest rose in the steady rhythm of deep sleep, and when she twisted towards him, he pulled her a little closer and muttered something about staying put.

But the noise that had woken her came again. It wasn't Sylvian. Someone was moving around in the workshop downstairs, and it didn't sound like Kit either. She'd know the sound of her brother anywhere. And while Kit got up with the dawn, there wasn't a hint of light outside.

'Sylvian?' she whispered and tried to shake him awake. He muttered something unintelligible and rolled over, taking half the blankets with him. Grabbing his shoulder, she shook him again, harder this time, but still he didn't wake up.

Something was wrong, terribly wrong, because Sylvian woke, with a frightening clarity, if a floorboard creaked when it shouldn't. She couldn't wake him. He slept like someone enchanted. Lyta pulled on her discarded clothes, moving soundlessly, barefoot across the room and opened the bedroom door.

There was no one out there. Kit's door was firmly shut and from beyond it she could hear him snoring away.

Both of them useless then. Great.

It's magic, Eninn told her softly, as if even tucked away in her mind the little god was wary of speaking too loudly and giving them both away. *I can't help them, just you. And I don't know how long I can hold it off.*

Oh yes, she'd got that. A spell of some kind was keeping Kit and Sylvian asleep, but not her, thanks to Eninn. Downstairs she could see an eerie, flickering light, moving around the workshop.

Shit.

Someone was searching the workshop. And then she realised, she had no idea where Kit had hidden *The Book of Gold*, but this was obviously the first place anyone was going to look, wasn't it? Someone who knew he had it to begin with anyway, who knew that Kit had made two copies. And there weren't many people with that knowledge.

Only one copy remained of the two created when Ben had tried to spill all of that knowledge out without a thought as to what it might reveal. The notes from which Kit had printed the proofs had been burned by the Magister. The first copy had been destroyed when the duchess died. But the other one, the one Kit had told Jem to hide when the city was attacked . . .

Jem had come back after it all calmed down, and Kit had said '*Don't worry about it, Lyta. I've got it. It's safe.*'

Ben knew about the copy. Ben Alvarez . . .

The movement downstairs shifted subtly. It sounded like someone going through the store cupboards now. It was only a matter of time until they came up here and started searching the private rooms. And they would expect everyone to be asleep, and vulnerable.

Sylvian and Kit were not going to wake up while that bloody spell was active, whatever it was. She wrapped her hand around her pendant, squeezing it for luck, and crept down the stairs. She needed to see who this thief was who dared try this in her home. She needed to find a way to wake the others.

Lyta! Look out!

She hadn't even made it to the bottom when Eninn's shout rang through her head, almost making her jump out of her skin. A pair of hands came through the gap in the steps from underneath her, grabbing her ankles and jerking them back. She went down face first into the workshop, the world tumbling around her. With barely a second to recover, she rolled as best she could, avoiding a much worse fall onto the stone floor.

The noise should have woken the dead but upstairs, given there was no sound from them, the men slept on. Lyta cursed loudly as she righted herself and spun around, looking for her attacker.

'I don't know what you think you're doing in here, but you have broken into the wrong place,' she said, with a lot more bravado than she felt right now.

The workshop looked empty, but she knew it wasn't.

On top of one of Kit's precious printing presses sat a withered hand, severed at the wrist. It must have belonged to a huge man long ago, but now it was grey and shrunken, the brittle nails yellow. The fingers curled up and it held a lit candle which gave out an unearthly, watery light, its flame an unnatural silver.

A hand of glory, Eninn said. *A very old one.*

Lyta knew about the hand of glory. All thieves did. It was a thief's myth, a legendary spell, the hand of an executed convict, mummified and used to cast an enchantment of sleep over all within a building, leaving its user, and those they chose, free to steal as they wished. She had never seen one. Not even Ranulf had. In fact, he'd been the one to tell her they weren't real.

The candle was the only source of light but she knew this room as well as the palm of her own hand. She scrabbled on the table behind her, found a type tray her brother had left there, and with a silent apology to him, she hurled it across the room.

Pieces of metal scattered everywhere like birdseed but the tray itself flew true, clattering into the hand and knocking it to the ground.

The candle went out, plunging the room into darkness.

For a moment she felt a wild thrill of triumph, and them something slammed into her side, taking her off her feet and down in a heap.

The smell hit her next. And gods, what a smell. It rolled over her like hot tar, clinging and choking and . . . smothering. She gagged as something made of rot and decay, of filth and shit, rolled over her. Her vision burned, tears starting in her eyes as if she'd walked right into the thick stench of a tannery.

A pair of hands grabbed her throat and tightened. Not this again! Kicking and struggling, she tried to break free, her nails tearing into the short cloak the figure was wearing, thick wool, still damp from the snow, and heavy. So heavy as it fell around her, suffocating her, holding her down and stealing her breath.

Lyta grabbed her pendant, reached for Eninn with a prayer for help, and then realised that there was nothing but the cloak covering her now. As she tore it away, it came to pieces in her hands, sticky and foul, disintegrating to smears like rotten vegetation in her hands. Gagging, Lyta rolled back to her feet and tried to stand, still fighting the urge to vomit.

She wiped her streaming eyes with her sleeves.

There was a boy standing in front of her. Glowing. The air around him shimmered with a haze and she knew where that dreadful stench had come from. His very presence was creating it.

He might have been ten, or a little older. Slowly he lifted his hand, stretching it out to her. For a moment she thought she heard dogs growling and the sharp tang of urine rose around her.

'*Lyta Cornellis,'* he said and his voice was like an unearthly music. It dulled her senses, blurring her mind and consciousness. Her throat tightened again and her stomach roiled. '*Come with me. We have need of you.*'

'That's not going to happen,' she told him, trying to will herself to move.

'*This is not a matter of choice, but of command. You will come.*'

'Who are you? Why do you want me?'

The child smiled, but it was not the smile of a child. No, this was old and knowing, and mocking. And she knew what it was.

'*I am Voseh, lost for a thousand years,*' he said proudly. '*I am decay and the end of all things. I am the tangle of despair. No one can stand against me. Kneel and accept your fate.*'

The end of all things . . . Her hand rose to her pendant, not to hold it this time, but to take it off. Voseh wanted her to take it off . . .

He's lying, Lyta, Eninn whispered, his voice a much-needed breeze clearing the miasma. *You have to listen. You have to think. You still have a choice. If he's the end, then who ended him? If he was lost who brought him back?*

Who brought him back? Oh she had a very good idea of that.

A force made of stench and rot and all things foul closed around her again, crushing her, bringing her to a ball on the ground, writhing with pain. A small hand pressed against her forehead and suddenly it felt like his fingers were drilling directly into her brain, a golden line of command.

'*You will obey.*'

It was is if the sludge of a cesspit rose around her and closed over her head. Of course she would obey. She had no choice. That knowledge filtered through her body like water trickling through rock. She would obey, and she would get up and go with this glowing, god-possessed child. There was nothing else she could do.

'*Better,*' an ancient voice sneered from his lips. '*Much better. Obedience suits you. Now bring me the relic and the book and come with me.*'

The book? But she didn't know where *The Book of Gold* was. She hesitated and felt that familiar tug at the back of her mind. Eninn, it was Eninn, trying to pull her free of this enchantment.

She reached out and closed her hand around the pendant, squeezing tight, warring with the need to tear it off and the need to cling to it for dear life.

'Lyta!' Sylvian's voice was a roar from far away, like distant waves on cliffs. Bells rang in her head which really couldn't be good. She'd been beaten up already once this evening, and the tumble down the stairs wouldn't have helped and now this . . . this . . . *miserable thieving bastard* was trying to control her. How *dare* he?

The thunder overhead grew louder, nearer. She could breathe again and the terrible weight pressing down on her was gone.

'*Ah*,' said Voseh, his glowing eyes alighting on the pendant, realisation of something eldritch and ancient filling them. He recognised Eninn then and for a moment Lyta got the impression he was almost amused. '*Let me deal with that for you, child. Set you free of this feral godling. It will take but a moment. Give up your relic and your false god. He has no power left to hold you so. He has no power at all.*'

He grabbed the pendant, almost tearing the chain off her neck.

Eninn's immediate reaction speared right through her, a spark of rage which turned the little pendant white-hot.

Get off her! She's mine! Panic came with the thought, rising through her and with it a flood of emotions that weren't hers. *Need and love and desperation, she was all he had, all he had left and he couldn't lose her because . . . because . . .*

Voseh shied back with a curse, nursing his hand, eyes and mouth wide in shock. The pendant, when it came back to rest against her chest, was as cold as ice.

A relic, Du Lac had called it. And it was hers. Hers and Ennin's.

Voseh was trying to push Eninn from her, first directly and then by stealing the pendant which had always tied her to him.

And then what would he have done with her? She had felt the force he exerted on her, the control slipping from her fingers like water. She would have gone with him wherever he told her to go, would have done whatever he said.

She wrapped her hand more tightly around her pendant again and gave Eninn another little prayer of thanks as she struggled to breathe.

'*We'll make you pay for this, thief!*' Voseh snarled, and Lyta knew he wasn't talking to her. She was nothing to him and all his rage was directed at Eninn. The small figure vanished and the frozen night filled the workshop. Lyta fell back again, her vision blurring. Thunder sounded all around her, the earth shaking, the ground . . . no, it was footsteps, men rushing towards her and she was falling again, down onto the flagstones as a wolf-like figure bounded by her in pursuit of the god-possessed child. The door slammed in the wind.

'Lyta?' It was Kit, dropping to his knees beside her. 'Lyta, are you all right? Who was that?'

'Sylvian?' His name dragged on the inside of her throat like barbs. It felt like she'd swallowed acid and every breath made her want to throw up again. 'Where's—?'

'Gone after him. Lyta, talk to me. What happened?'

Kit had a lantern, a small nightlight burning inside it. She'd seen it in his room, but she didn't like to ask too many questions about why he kept it burning. Its glow was bright and steady, and real, so real. Now she was grateful, as she looked up into his worried face.

'A boy . . . a god . . . Voseh? I don't know . . . Looking for something. He wanted me to get the book and go with him. And I would have. I couldn't— It was only Eninn who—'

'The book?' He didn't ask which book, she thought, but clearly he knew full well what she meant. And Voseh hadn't just been after the book. He had tried to compel her to remove her pendant. Her hand tightened around the little scrap of metal again. Was that what the blacksmiths had wanted too? But she hadn't stolen this. It was hers. It was real, as was Eninn, and he was still protecting her. Even now, with no power of his own.

'He tried to take this from me—I don't know—to part me from Eninn, I think. He wanted me to go with him. And I think—I think if I did—' She tried to slow her racing heart, calm her breathing. It wasn't working. 'I think it would have been a very bad idea.'

Her brother smoothed his large hand over her head. He was trembling. 'No shit. But—but why didn't we hear anything? You could have been taken—you could have been *killed* and I was asleep up there, out for the count. What happened?'

'A hand of glory,' she croaked and waved in the direction where she had last seen it.

Kit frowned in that way he did when he didn't want to believe her tall tales but he straightened and went over to investigate anyway. She knew the moment he found it.

'What the *fuck* is that?'

Lyta tried to stand up and her legs gave out before she even made it halfway. She flopped down onto the flagstones again. 'Told you.'

Kit stared at it for a long moment then went to fetch a hemp sack and bundled the thing inside, trying not to touch it directly.

I could have lost you, Eninn whispered. His voice was faint.

'But you didn't,' she tried to tell him, still failing to pick herself up off the floor. In the end she gave up and slumped there. Getting up could wait. She folded her mind and her will around her god instead. 'It's all right. If it hadn't been for you—'

I was useless, powerless, exactly like he said.

'No,' she murmured, exhaustion welling up around her and this time she was ready to give in to it. But Eninn needed her. He needed reassurance. He really was a child at heart. 'You saved me. You aren't powerless. You have me. We have each other.'

'I could have lost you, Lyta.' Was that Eninn or Kit? She wasn't sure.

'I'm harder to get rid of than that. I'm a . . . what's it called? When a god chooses a mortal to fight their battles?'

'A paladin. Chosen. Like Sylvian.' That definitely sounded like Kit.

Lyta thought about that for a moment and then laughed. It hurt to laugh. 'Maybe not that then. But something like it. Eninn's paladin . . .'

The world blurred around her again and her head filled with sparks of light. Golden light which flared in the darkness as it smothered her.

The door slammed open again, bringing freezing night, whirling snow, and a furious Sylvian Chant.

'They got away. I've never seen anyone move so fast. And the snow's coming down hard now. I can't see a bloody thing out there. Damn it, Lyta, what were you thinking? Why didn't you wake me?'

She almost laughed again. She would have if she could have found the breath or some way to use it that didn't hurt. What had Voseh done to her? It felt like her insides had been scraped out.

She held out her hand to him and the lamplight caught on golden sparks of light tangled around her fingers. She stared at them and they blurred, dissolving into her skin, eating away at her mind and will, at her bond with Eninn. Voseh's spell or enchantment, she supposed, or whatever it was he had tried to bind her with. It still lingered.

Lyta, this isn't good. You need help. Eninn this time. Eninn and not Kit. Maybe. Why was it so hard to tell them apart?

Sylvian's arms around her felt so good. 'Lyta? Talk to me? Just me.' She was almost able to focus on him. Almost.

'I need Beatriz,' she told Sylvian and everything finally went black, which was, she realised with her last conscious thought, such a relief.

CHAPTER THIRTEEN

Lyta

Amberes was starting to stir, the early risers beginning their day, but the moon lit the way. Cissonia's bell rang out some hour, but she had no idea what it was. The chimes seemed to go on forever, reverberating through Lyta's head, laughing at her, taunting her. She had taken on a god, even if it was an old dead one housed in the body of a child. What kind of idiot was she?

Charnock must have sent it. Who else could have? He thought she had stolen something, but what? Or maybe he wanted *her* now. *Her* and the book.

Sylvian had carried her, refusing to put her down even once, which was just as well because she'd only have fallen over, something she did not want to admit to, not even to herself. Every time she tried to close her eyes again one of them, Kit or Syl had been there, waking her up and making her talk to them. It was still the middle of the night, for the love of all the gods, so surely she was entitled to some sleep?

But apparently not if her brother and her sometime lover were to be believed.

And Beatriz was even worse.

Wrapped in a silken robe that cost more than anything Lyta had ever seen, she swept into the parlour like an empress.

'Dear gods, what happened? No, don't explain, it will take too long. Let me see. Did she pass out?'

'A little. We tried to keep her awake, but she took a blow to the head and . . .'

'Several blows to the head,' Kit interjected. He was worrying his hands together like their mother used to when she fussed over one of them but didn't quite know what to do. Strange how Lyta remembered that now, in this instant. Rhea belonged in the past, and that past could be a painful place to visit. 'We were attacked going home, and then someone broke into the workshop. He did something to her. Something magical.'

Beatriz's hands were already on Lyta's face, her magic testing and probing and trying to help. And gods, it stung. Eninn didn't like it either.

'I'm fine, really. I need to sleep.'

'You most certainly do not,' the Lady of House Alvarez snapped at her.

'Well, that was uncalled for,' Lyta chided, aware that her words were slurring a little, but to her relief, Beatriz smiled ever so briefly.

'Insolence is a good sign. Apologies, but you cannot sleep right now. When my work is done, I will have the most peaceful bedroom prepared for you and then you can sleep to your heart's content.'

Peace. She could do with a bit of peace and the beds here were comfy. She remembered that. She also remembered what she and Sylvian had done in one of them—not a lot of sleeping—the night after they escaped Montalbeau and lost Ranulf.

Sudden grief made her throat tighten and with it that now familiar guilt. Was this what she had been feeling earlier? When she had made love to him after crying her eyes out? Before Voseh? Her stomach clenched and she tried to suppress the urge to vomit.

Beatriz, naturally, saw it all.

'He's gone now as are all his filthy little webs. You have concussion though, and bruising to your throat, and your ribs, although I don't think magic caused that. Divinities, Lyta, what have you been doing tonight?'

The urge to say having sex with Sylvian, just to see the horror on his face in all its awesome glory, was powerful, but she pushed it down. 'I was attacked. Twice. Don't underestimate Voseh. That little bastard threw me down the stairs.'

'Well, you do incite that urge in people,' Beatriz murmured, as if it was entirely understandable. 'Voseh,' she mused and shook her head slowly. 'I've never heard of him. Ben might know something, but whether that knowledge would help us . . . Lie still now. I'll do as much as I can, but you need to cooperate with me, Lyta.'

'Easier said than done,' Kit muttered. 'Lyta doesn't cooperate with anyone.'

'I will remember that,' she told him, the threat ringing in her words. She didn't have to put up with his cheek as well.

'You're sounding more like yourself already,' her brother replied, and grinned at her. It shouldn't have been the relief it was. If Kit could grin, then maybe she was going to be all right. Or maybe he trusted Beatriz.

Maybe they both did.

Sylvian, on the other hand, was still a ghastly shade of grey. Lyta reached out her hand for him and he took it, wrapping his strong grip around her fingers and holding her oh so gently. Like she was fragile. Or precious.

She couldn't think like this. Reality was going to catch up with the two of them very soon, and there would be more than enough heartbreak to go around. Was that what she had been feeling earlier rather than grief? Knowledge that she would lose him? And that itself was a form of grief too.

'Beatriz?' Ben's voice came from the hallway outside and Kit's head came up like a hound scenting its quarry. 'What's happening?'

When he appeared, Ben was still rubbing sleep from his eyes but looked far more himself than he had earlier in the day.

'Lyta was attacked,' Kit said, a little too hurriedly.

'We both were,' Lyta corrected him pointedly. Let him try to wriggle out of that.

'You were attacked *twice*,' her brother growled.

'What happened?' Ben's voice was suddenly stern.

Without warning, Kit upended the sack he carried on the table and the hand of glory thudded onto the polished surface.

Both Alvarez siblings physically recoiled.

Now she looked at it, Lyta could feel a wave of . . . something coming off it. Malice perhaps, like it was reaching out, seeking someone or something.

It was a hand, she reminded herself. Of course it was reaching out. That was what they did.

'*I saw a hand*,' Prester Alaric had said. '*Reaching for me*.'

'Ben, deal with that monstrosity,' Beatriz snapped, pushing Lyta back down as she tried to move, though whether to retreat or head towards the ugly thing she didn't know. 'Get it out of my sight. Lyta stay still and let me help. Now.'

There was no arguing with her, not when someone needed her help. Lyta knew that as well as anyone. She lay back and let the warmth beneath Beatriz's hands sweep through her, carrying with it the glow of summer evenings, rich as honey. The pain ebbed away when faced with her magic. Without pausing she reached out to Kit as well and, somewhat reluctantly, he took her hand and let her heal him.

There, in the light that Beatriz always brought with her, Lyta felt like nothing could touch her. Not even that ghastly hand.

'Thank you, Beatriz,' she murmured. 'We never thank you enough.'

Beatriz smiled. 'Now I *know* you hit your head. No need for thanks, Lyta. Just rest.'

The throbbing headache pressing at the inside of her head faded and she drew in a normal breath again, squeezing Sylvian's fingers with more strength now to let him know she was all right. He gazed into her eyes for a long moment and then released her, standing up as he pulled that invisible mantle of royal bodyguard around himself again. Crisis over, she thought. Everything must go back to normal. Which meant—

'I need to report this,' he told her. He was leaving. Of course he was. She tried to quell the disappointment and failed.

'The queen isn't going to care about what happens to me.'

'Yes, she will. Now more than ever, we need to consider your safety. She sent me to protect you and I've done a piss-poor job so far.' Protect her from what? The queen couldn't have known a god was going to attack her. Lyta was about to ask Sylvian, but with a wince that told her he'd let something unintentionally slip, he pressed on. 'Besides, we need to tell her about that.' He waved his arm towards the table where Ben was circling the hand of glory, as if it might bite.

And it might, Lyta thought bitterly. Or bring something else here with even bigger teeth.

'It's remarkable,' Ben said thoughtful. 'The threads of power emanating from it are so strong. I've never seen anything like it. It has an aftertaste of the divine about it, doesn't it, Bea? Like acid or . . . Where's Piers? He should see this. He'll have thoughts. Maybe he's seen something—'

'Do you understand what *out of my sight* means, Ben?' Beatriz barked at her brother and he backed up like she'd lashed out physically.

In the end, she sent a servant to knock on Stirling's guestroom door, but before they could return, a noise came from out by the main entrance. Hushed voices of the doorkeeper and a couple of Beatriz's other retainers rose through the courtyard, and then Stirling himself appeared, wearing a heavy cloak and gloves.

Lyta only caught a glimpse beneath it, before he pulled it closed again, despite the warmth of Beatriz's house. He wasn't wearing his finery now. He was dressed in a plain tunic, with what looked like the symbol of the Blacksmiths' Guild, the uniform of the servants and apprentices who worked there. It was a momentary glance, but Lyta was sure.

'Good gods, what are you all doing up at this hour?' he asked, as if bemused. His blonde hair was in disarray, and his cheeks pink from the cold.

Ask him where he goes, Charnock had challenged her and Lyta wondered what else was missing from the Blacksmiths' Guild now. Was she going to get the blame for that too?

'Where were you?' asked Ben, an edge of suspicion blunting his voice.

'Out. I—I couldn't sleep. I thought I'd . . .' He frowned, clearly not wanting to answer. Not really. In the face of their suspicious glares, he backed down. Deciding he couldn't hide what he was wearing, he handed the cloak to a servant and smoothed down his hair. A little self-consciously, Lyta thought. 'I went looking for Mistress Alderton, that's all.'

Surprisingly it was Kit who replied. 'Viola Alderton? Half of the underworld of Amberes is searching for her, half the watch as well. Her brother is raising hell. What made you think you could find her?'

'Because I know her,' Stirling said. 'A lot better than her brother does. And a lot better than the criminals of this city, begging your pardon, Mistress Cornellis.'

Lyta gave him a thin and meaningless smile. She wasn't sure how she felt about being seen as the representative of the entire criminal underworld of her city. But then, she was aware that her mood was hardly the best after everything that had happened to her in the last twenty-four hours. She'd had enough of everyone for one night.

'You came here following her, didn't you?' Lyta raised an eyebrow and waited. He had said as much to Charnock, but at the same time, Lyta had a sense there was more to it.

Stirling shifted, uncomfortably under her glare once more. She might have taken a few too many hits to the head tonight, but he was a terrible actor all of sudden. 'I hold Mistress Alderton in the highest esteem. She is highly educated and possessed of a remarkable mind. If she had been born a man, her family would have . . . She's still welcome at court, a favourite of the queen. Charles on the other hand . . . well, they don't call it exile, but why else would he be here in Amberes?'

'Piers, don't change the subject.' Ben's tone rippled with admonishment, and a strange undercurrent of command. It wasn't the gods, not exactly, but it was certainly something magical, almost like Voseh had used on her. His skin had taken on that golden sheen, remnants of *The Book of God*, a hint of his magic or the gods inside him.

When he spoke again, his voice seemed even more powerful. 'I think we need some truth from you, don't you? Why are you here?'

Ben could use the divine magic in him when he set his mind to it, and if the gods cooperated. Kit had told her what he did when the printshop was under attack, and in the Scholars' Tower to defeat the Magister. Kit had never trusted magic, not even when Ben wielded it. Perhaps *especially* not when Ben wielded it.

'Did you break into the Blacksmiths' Guild?' her brother cut in, his patience at an end. He'd seen what Stirling was wearing too then. Kit didn't miss much. And what other reason was there for a disguise like that? 'Are you the reason they came after Lyta?'

Lyta counted herself a good judge of people and either Stirling was entirely taken by surprise by that question or his playacting abilities had returned full force. If so he ought to be on the stage. They loved the theatre in Albion, didn't they? 'Who came after Lyta?'

Kit took another step forward, his shoulders squaring, his form filling the room with sudden threat. 'A group of guild enforcers making free use of rather a lot of cudgels. And that isn't the worst of it. The Blacksmiths' Guild think she stole something. Was it you?'

Stirling backed up, confused and looking for an excuse to bolt. 'I have no idea what you're talking about. If you would excuse me—'

'I don't think so,' Sylvian murmured dangerously. He'd managed to slide around to cut off any chance of escape. 'Where were you?' His free hand toyed with the hilt of his belt knife. With a sigh, Lyta pushed herself up to sit. It gave her a fraction more dignity, especially with the men in her life vastly overstepping the bounds of what she needed them to do. It was her job to look after them. She could look after herself.

Most of the time.

Stirling had been poking around the Blacksmiths' Guild again. And something had been stolen. Something valuable enough to send the heavies after it.

Lyta didn't know why she did it, but it was time to save Stirling from the others. Perhaps it was pity. 'He was searching Charnock's workshop for a relic.' He froze, staring at her, snared. 'Something already gone, I presume, or you'd be far away with it by now. And whatever it is, they think *I* took it, so it was gone long before you got in there. Did Viola Alderton make off with it? Perhaps you had better explain what you're doing in Amberes, Stirling. What you're *really* doing here? And you might want to tell us what that thing is as well.'

His eyes followed her pointing finger and latched on to the hand of glory in an instant. The look of abject horror on his face told Lyta two things: it wasn't his, but he knew exactly what it was.

'Where did *that* come from?'

Interesting, Lyta thought. 'The god-possessed child who attacked me left it behind. It wasn't the first time they've used it either, I think. They've been stealing relics far too easily. That's what knocked out the vicar in the Temple of Lost Gods, I imagine Syl. He probably hit his head as he passed out. Look, something is going on in this city, something I don't entirely understand, and I hate that. Suddenly you're here, you and Charnock—who has a handy line in summoning gods by the way—both of you tangling yourselves in Ben's life, because Ben can be a gullible idiot. Oh don't *start*, Kit, it's true—*we* don't trust easily. We've learned that the hard way. So spill.'

She watched the expressions which flickered over Stirling's features, as fast as flowing water, playing out emotions that he wasn't even bothering to hide anymore. Eninn was with her. She could feel him, as if he was leaning over her shoulder, glaring at the man from Albion much in the same way she was, blurring into her.

They both knew a trickster when they saw one.

'Very well,' said Stirling. 'I will tell you as much as I can, but you are not going to like it. Viola came to find Thomas Charnock and retrieve something he stole from Albion. I followed. Viola has vanished. I believe Charnock realised she was here and did . . . did something.' Ben made a noise of protest but Stirling pushed on, ignoring him. 'He is dangerous. I don't know what he has promised you, Ben, or the Blacksmiths' Guild, but the end result will be terrible indeed. He can reach the gods on the other side of the veil, and encase them in a human form, for a time at least. It does not last. The divine always tears itself out eventually, unless it is held there by a bloodline bond or some other means. God and human cannot long inhabit the same vessel.' He stared at Ben for far too long a moment until Ben dropped his gaze to the ground. 'Present company excepted.' Stirling glanced at Lyta, and his expression flickered. He knew, she thought. Just like Charnock had known. She didn't know if Ben had told him as well, or if he was able to sense divinity. Some people could. They were usually priests or acolytes, but honestly, she had no idea what Stirling really was.

'Viola is from one such bloodline,' he continued. 'She is an Aspect like Lady Beatriz, a divine-given high priestess of our Lady Rhiannon, sovereign goddess, the Shining Queen of Albion. Viola had the keeping of our most powerful relic and Charnock stole it from her. We didn't realise until it was too late and she took off after him to retrieve it before anyone could stop her. Believe me, if we had known, she would never have left our shores.'

'Viola Alderton?' Lyta asked, bemused. 'Are you sure you have the right person?' If Viola was from a divine bloodline the same went for her brother and, to be honest, Lyta didn't see it.

Stirling nodded. 'The queen is beside herself. Her sovereignty hangs in the balance. We cannot rely on the authorities here. If Francisco found out . . . if Church Imperial found out . . .' He sighed with the weight of those possibilities. 'Albion's enemies, within and without, would fall on us like wolves and there would be war, a war which would spread here and across the continent. Without Viola and the relic . . . if anything happens to her . . .'

'But it's just a relic,' Kit said. 'Why would Viola risk so much for a relic?'

'*It is not just a relic,*' Ben replied, his voice suddenly filled with those otherly tones. Kit flinched back from him but Ben didn't appear to notice. '*It is more. Far more. This is no mortal theft, is it, Lord Stirling?*' The air rippled with the divine and they did not sound happy.

Stirling drew in a breath again and then pulled himself up to his full height, his hands clenching into fists at his side. He looked like a prince from a story, Lyta thought, a tragic one, all determined nobility, clinging to a dignity he couldn't quite grasp anymore. He was desperate.

'Please, Ben, for the sake of our friendship . . . please, all of you, I need your help. I will do whatever it takes. I have to find Viola and retrieve that relic. And, more importantly, the goddess who hides within it. Help me return our lady, Rhiannon, to her people. *That's* who Charnock stole. The Royal Goddess of Albion.'

CHAPTER FOURTEEN

Lyta

Another lost goddess. Missing, stolen, dead . . . who knew? The last thing any of them needed was another bloody goddess in their lives.

'*Lies*,' Ben said, his voice wavering in that same unsettling undertone again, Gloir's voice perhaps. Lyta wasn't entirely sure. '*How dare Rhiannon's servants interfere in our work?*'

Kit stepped closer to Ben and took his arm, the touch so gentle and brief Lyta wasn't sure that anyone else would have noticed. But Ben stopped speaking, his breath catching in his throat, and then he gave the briefest nod. And Kit, her Kit, frowned back at him but didn't move away, holding on to the scholar like he might a jar of naphtha. He wasn't happy about the way the gods flowed through him. Not now. Not at any time, but especially not now.

Ben leaned against Kit and the glow that had started to swell inside him again seemed to subside a little.

Foreign gods and goddesses are always trouble, Eninn murmured. *And someone who can steal a goddess is dangerous indeed. She must have been well hidden indeed for none of us to sense her. Like Cissonia in her bell, locked away perhaps.*

Stealing a goddess—that was the type of thing the Church Imperial would do, Lyta thought. None of them needed another power like that in the world. And that wasn't even including what Francisco would do if he thought Albion was interfering in the affairs of his many kingdoms, or straying on to his territory. Kyron, the God of

Warriors and Warfare, would know that. He could probably sniff out even the hint of a war in the making and revel in it.

But Ben had been suppressing the gods inside him, forcing them to be silent and bending them to his will. That's what he believed anyway.

Or maybe the gods had decided he didn't need to be distracted and had hidden it from him. She could believe either option right now.

'*We could have told him that Charnock's dangerous,*' Lyta replied carefully within the confines of her own mind. '*And we met the man. Be quiet. I don't know how much Stirling actually knows about us, but I'd rather not give more away. I don't trust him any more than Charnock. Did you hear his voice when he spoke about Viola and Rhiannon?*'

The voice of a believer, a zealot.

She wasn't sure how clearly that all got across to Eninn but her little god quietened down and she sensed his agreement.

There was a long and painful silence.

'I think,' said Beatriz with that kind of firm and self-assured voice which always seemed to come out of the mouths of people who could make anything better if given enough time and the smallest amount of general cooperation, 'that we should all have something to break our fast, drink some mint tea or coffee, and take a breath or two. It is far too late to return to bed anyway. Piers? Can you tell cook that we will be eating earlier than usual. Give her my apologies and tell her I will make it up to her.'

If Stirling was surprised at being asked to pass messages to Beatriz's staff he didn't show it. He gave her an elegant bow and left the room. Possibly grateful to be gone.

And just like that Beatriz had given them a moment of breathing space.

'I can't imagine Francisco will like any of this,' Lyta said quickly. 'Not them being over here, mucking about. Not any of them.' Sylvian's expression told her he agreed completely. She'd been half-hoping he'd laugh it off and say the king wouldn't care. But they both knew that would be wishful thinking. 'But . . . we have to help. Charnock's—'

'My friend and colleague!' Ben protested.

'Up to his neck in this, obviously,' Lyta finished pointedly. Ben's face fell in dismay. 'Think Ben. He's dangerous and you know it, no matter how much you don't want it to be true. We can't leave him with the power of a royal goddess in his hands.'

'Perhaps we should just *ask* Thomas. I'm sure there's an explanation.'

Poor Ben, she thought, torn between his old friend and his new one. He wanted to believe the best of everyone. He'd learned nothing.

'Ask then, but carefully. If this man is as dangerous as Stirling makes out, and from what I saw I have no reason to think he isn't, *Ben* . . .' He made to protest again. Her glare was warning enough to quell that. 'If he really conned an Aspect and stole her goddess, what do you think he has planned for you and your friends, Seigneur Alvarez?' Ben opened his mouth again, but stopped. She swore for a moment she saw tears in his eyes along with the anger. Then he nodded glumly. Well, at least he was trying to think now.

Kit rubbed his shoulders and whispered something, drawing him into a gentle embrace. Ben closed his eyes, letting his head fall back on her brother's shoulder. Thank the gods for Kit, Lyta thought. Maybe he could make Ben see sense. 'Right then, something to eat while we can is always a plan. And then we need to work out what to do next.'

'We go to the palace as instructed,' Sylvian said, flexing his hand. 'We report it all to the queen. No more delays, Lyta. We've wasted enough time.'

'Wasted?' She arched an eyebrow at him.

He at least had the grace to look embarrassed. Good. 'You know what I mean.'

'Well excuse me if my getting the crap beaten out of me has held you up, Captain Chant.'

'She gets ratty when she's hungry,' Kit chimed in, not helping at all.

She turned on her brother, even angrier to find herself proving his point. 'And you get—'

'Enough,' Beatriz said, and when the Lady of House Alvarez used that tone, people listened. Everyone fell silent. 'We eat. We gather together what we know. We make a plan. Lyta?'

She rolled her eyes. 'Fine.'

*

Lyta had for some time been fully convinced that Beatriz's cook was some kind of wonder worker, or an Aspect of some forgotten god of the feast, or at the very least a fae creature trapped in her service. But she didn't want to ask too many questions in case the older woman, who ruled the kitchens here like some kind of ladle-wielding empress, would take offence and vanish into the wilds or the hollow hills never to be seen again. And who would eat all her utterly perfect sweet pastries then? She even made coffee, strong, rich and laced with cream and sugar. It was even better than the Venetian café in the Great Market or Du Lac's. Who she bribed to get the beans was anyone's guess.

Lyta was on her fourth mug, and her fifth almond pastry, when the sound of a mailed fist on the outer gates stopped the muted conversation. The city outside was still silent and dawn was barely staining the sky so the sound travelled.

'What now?' Kit sighed. Because it was always something else. And that something else was always more trouble.

'No plan for us,' Lyta muttered, grabbing another pastry just in case. 'When has there ever been time to make a plan? They only fall apart anyway.'

A few moments later the door to the dining room opened and admitted Juárez. At the sight of him, Sylvian surged to his feet, all formal attention and royal guard, his eyes fixed on the middle distance.

Lyta had not forgotten that Sylvian was meant to be back at the palace last night, and that she was meant to be with him, not here eating sweet pastries and drinking the finest coffee in the whole city. He hadn't let her. He seemed uncommonly anxious about her safety and she didn't like it. Try as she might to ease his mind, he kept insisting they ought to leave. He'd tried. He'd really tried. But she'd told him to wait. She hadn't had the heart to tell him she wasn't going. If she did, he might try to throw her over his shoulder and carry her there and that was bound to end poorly.

Especially as now, he had backup.

She shot him a suspicious glance, but Sylvian didn't react.

'You need to come with me now, both of you,' Juárez said without preamble. It was a bark of command, but not one she had to obey. Eninn's mockery would be unbearable. And that would be before Kit got in on the act.

She stayed firmly in her seat and bit into the pastry.

It was Beatriz who fixed the Andalusian officer with a stern look that even the queen would be hard pressed to imitate. Juárez didn't stand a chance.

'Are you impugning my hospitality, Captain? Sit down, if it please you. Join us.'

Juárez froze, and then gave an awkward bow. She outranked him socially and politically as well. Vastly. And he knew all about her. Probably more than Lyta since they were both creatures of the same court, albeit different ends of it. Like most of the men from Francisco's court Juárez seemed to regard Beatriz as some combination of a holy woman and a queen in her own right. He probably didn't know the extent of her power. Lyta had seen her resurrect herself to destroy the Duchess of Montalbeau. One crossed Lady Alvarez at their own peril.

But it wasn't about Beatriz this time. Juárez might be uncomfortable about crossing her, perhaps even devastated that he might have insulted her from the expression he wore, but the problem he had come here to lay on their shoulders was so much worse.

'My deepest apologies, Lady Beatriz. This is an urgent matter. Another body has been discovered.'

All good humour evaporated from the room in that instant.

'Where?' Lyta asked, the back of her neck prickling with alarm. Her stomach twisted and suddenly all those sweet pastries turned out to have been a really bad idea.

'It's the same as the boy you found in the Temple of Lost Gods. And the others. A theft gone wrong, they believe. The queen has directed us to investigate it without delay.' He hesitated, still not saying where. His eyes flickered to Sylvian, then back to her. 'In the Imperial Temple.'

'The Imperial Temple,' Sylvian echoed him. He didn't elaborate but Juárez nodded solemnly, equally concerned.

'I know,' he said. 'But we have no choice. They asked for you by name. You and Lyta. They know you were at the Temple of Lost Gods. They know about the other bodies. She can't send anyone else. It would be deemed a grave insult and relations are sour enough already. Sylvian, be on your guard.'

*

The Imperial Temple was the stronghold of the Church Imperial in Amberes. The Church had no power within the city walls—on that the king, the aldermen and previously the duchess had agreed—but all gods were traditionally welcome here, so they couldn't exactly turn them away. No Scholars' Tower though, and no legions or militia, no power beyond their own temple complex and no interference in city matters. Definitely no Praetorian Guards, their elite military troops. Even the Patricians who they guarded were discouraged from entering Amberes. And those who populated the temple weren't encouraged to set foot outside the extremely high austere gates.

Following the death of the Magister, Francisco had torn down the Scholars' Tower on the road to Luttich, and scattered the rubble. It had been a message. He'd taken what remained of the library there, and any treasures he had found first though. Francisco was nothing if not practical in matters like that. No one referred to it as *looting*, but it was what it was. The spoils of war perhaps. He'd killed any number of Imperial troops that day. And priests too. Oh he had been in a rage. A murderous rage.

Sylvian had barely escaped with his life and Lyta had danced on a knife's edge to save him. She still remembered the look on Francisco's face far too clearly. It was something else to have nightmares about, as if she was lacking subject matter at this stage.

The high priest of the Imperial Temple in Amberes had knelt in the rain, acolytes arrayed behind him, outside his own gates, and everyone had thought Francisco would kill him then and there. What was one more beheaded Imperial just then? But Francisco had let him alone. Public opinion had softened somewhat. Frater Caelinus was a good man, the local people said, firm but kind, and devout too. Help could always be sought in his temple, and with very little cost to those who sought it. Some kind of honey trap, Lyta always thought, or perhaps a propaganda tool in a heretical city. If not exactly forgiven or forgotten, the Imperial Temple carried on as before, quietly, privately, behind closed doors.

Lyta had never set foot in this particular temple before and had no wish to do so now. It lay not far from the New Gate, along the side of the other end of the Falconbrook canal, all in all a very strategic location. Property in Amberes was all about the location and the advantages it could give, especially regarding the canals and the gates. Nevertheless the entrance to the temple faced the outer walls, its back turned on the city in which it was based. It was the traditional orientation of all Imperial temples, all attention fixed on Caput Mundi, the centre of the Imperial world. But Amberes noticed the slight, and remembered.

The temple had its own high walls, its narrow windows barred and, the people said, it had no interest in anything beyond itself. Or at least that was what the Imperials wanted them to believe. Every thief in Amberes agreed it wasn't worth the trouble which robbing it would cause, even if it had been less of a challenge. Everyone knew it was a miserable, loveless place, without beauty or riches anyway. Acolytes took vows of poverty and obedience and were thoroughly miserable even on the best of days, their heads bowed, their eyes downcast.

And yet, Lyta remembered the riches the Magister surrounded himself with, those jewels and sumptuous robes, and she wondered how true that was. How much was a show? There, and here as well.

That said, there wasn't much to indicate any riches as she, Sylvian and Juárez stood at the temple gates with the small force of men who Juárez had brought with him, in the biting cold of the winter's morning.

'Tell me again why we're here?' she asked. Juárez glared at her. 'Yes, yes, I know—the body, the queen, all that. But why *us*?' She leaned in close to whisper to him. He carried a scent of cloves and cedarwood, and something else earthy. 'Syl and I are not exactly their favourite people, remember?'

'They asked for you.'

'That does not fill me with joy and confidence either.'

'Don't worry,' he sighed, as if schooling himself to patience. 'We won't let anything happen to you. There are no Imperial militia allowed within the walls of Amberes. Acolytes are forbidden weapons and they aren't even allowed to leave their compound without escorts now. The king has not forgotten. Neither has the queen. None of us will. They know this.'

Lyta rolled her shoulders, tried to stretch to work out that damned knot in her neck which was still lingering. 'Good for them. I don't want to make the mistake of trusting anyone even remotely connected with Caput Mundi.'

'We are definitely not going to do that,' Sylvian said, in a surprisingly composed voice. What he had to be calm about, she had no idea. He was the one who had actually decapitated the Magister in the Scholars' Tower. They would love to get their hands on him to make an example of, she was sure of that, either to make him fight to the death in the arena for their pleasure or to drag him through the streets of Caput Mundi until the city itself tore him apart. But he looked so composed. His professional face, she decided. It was unnerving. 'Don't wander off. No adventures Lyta.'

Something small inside her wanted to reach out and thread her fingers through his, to hold him for a moment and feel the warmth of his skin against hers again. Something she could never admit to, or let have its way. Anyway, the gloves he had insisted she borrow hampered her.

Eninn's mind against hers was a reassurance she wasn't aware of needing before last night. Lyta had always relied on herself alone.

She took care of Kit and made sure they were both safe. She wasn't used to people looking out for her. Not even her god.

'All right,' she told him. 'No adventures.'

'Lyta,' Sylvian said after a wary pause. 'There's something I didn't tell you.'

'Just one thing, huh?' She didn't bother disguising the suspicion. No one ever told her everything. Not even Sylvian. Perhaps especially not Sylvian.

'It's the other reason we wanted you to come back to the palace. The queen received a letter. There's an inquisitor here.'

For a moment all she could do was stare at him in disbelief. 'And you didn't *tell* me until *now*?'

Sylvian didn't bother to hide the guilt. 'I didn't want to scare you.'

'Scare me?' Right, because she scared so easily. Lyta narrowed her eyes.

His reply was halting, hesitant. 'You . . . tend to . . . to do things without thinking if you're cornered. I wanted to get you to safety first.'

She indicated the temple with a nod. 'That went well then.'

He didn't trust her. He'd thought she'd go off on one, do something stupid, like confront the bastard or worse. And now . . . *now* she was going to have to face him anyway. *Knowing* that Sylvian thought she couldn't be trusted. This went from bad to worse. How could he not have warned her until *now*?

'We should have gone to the palace last night,' he muttered. 'They would have told you everything.'

In her heart of hearts, Lyta was afraid that he was right. She would have panicked. She would have done something stupid. She usually did.

Lyta swallowed down the reply that sprang first to mind and pulled the hood of the cloak closer around her face. It belonged to Beatriz and it was warm and heavy, the finest quality, and a scant comfort. She didn't deserve something so fine, but it might hide her face. She could hope.

A god in the body of a child had tried to kidnap her last night. And a group of blacksmiths had tried the same thing a little earlier.

What was standing in front of the gates of the Imperial Temple waiting to find out if there was an inquisitor in there waiting for her compared to that?

The magic of House Alvarez probably still hung about her. She wondered if the Inquisitor would be able to sense it. Or anything else that lingered in these halls. Maybe it would mask Eninn. Maybe it would protect them. Gods, she had to hope for something.

Just a minor miracle. Was that too much to ask?

Lyta had entered the chapel in the Scholars' Tower, and grinned in the face of the statue of the August God. She'd stolen some of his offering of fruit which had been a phenomenally bad idea. She wasn't touching anything this time around, not if she could help it.

They had been invited this time, she reminded herself. That had to count for something. Asked for. Which was a lot less comforting. And she was here with two royal bodyguards and a squad of soldiers too, on the orders of the queen and at the invitation of the high priest. Still, she tried to make herself as inconspicuous as possible.

The gates opened on silent, well-oiled hinges and they were ushered inside by dark-robed acolytes with closed-off expressions. Wary, every single one of them, and probably with good reason. They knew what had happened to the Scholars' Tower.

And they knew what the king would do to them if it all went to shit.

Lyta desperately hoped that prospect was in the forefront of everyone's mind right now.

The walls rose high as cliffs around them. In the middle was a statue of a man in ancient Imperial military garb, holding his hand aloft in blessing. He was handsome, but then he always was, their God-Emperor. Eternally young and powerful, fed on the power of so many other deities, the August Imperator gazed down at Lyta and Eninn flinched.

What is it? she thought frantically. Trying to hold him still in her mind was like grappling with a greased eel. *What's wrong?*

He's here. Lyta, he can see me. The August One is here!

CHAPTER FIFTEEN

Lyta

The face of the August Imperator gazed down at her, his eyes cold and empty, his mouth a hard line. A statue, just a statue. But Lyta could feel him now as well, his attention on her, boring into her, the way she had felt Voseh last night, burrowing into her mind and her heart, prying open her soul. Searching for Eninn, trying to figure him, and her, out. Not yet to pull them apart as the God of the End of All Things had tried to do. But she feared he could, easily. Voseh's power had been but a trickle of water to this torrent.

Shit, not good. Not good at all.

This should not be possible. Not here in Amberes. The August One had no power here. It was not allowed.

And yet, she could feel him. She couldn't avoid it.

Rather than the Imperator's statue in the Scholars' Tower, Lyta was reminded of the statue in the depths of Montalbeau, the duchess's nameless goddess, drinking down their nightmares and feeding on their pain. It felt alive, watchful and malevolent. That divine presence threaded through the whole temple complex, like strands of a web. She could feel that now as well, Eninn making it all clear to her even as he thrashed around, showing her the full horror of it and trying to persuade her to run. But she couldn't. To run now was to reveal everything and she was not going to do that.

She needed her god to get a bloody grip.

Lyta must have tensed though because Sylvian stepped closer. 'All right?' She shook her head but didn't say a word. She couldn't. The urge to start screaming was powerful and she didn't trust herself not to give in if she opened her mouth. He frowned, uneasy. Not afraid. Not her Sylvian. But he knew something was wrong. 'Stay with me. We can leave if you—'

'Captain Juárez?' An elderly man hurried forward from the nearest doorway in the sheer walls. Lyta felt the pressure on her shrink back and it was a courtyard again, surrounded by faceless buildings. Nothing grand or impressive about this place, apart from that wretched statue which wasn't so much grand as terrifying. She managed to breathe again and focused instead on the high priest. 'Thank you so much for coming. Please thank her majesty for her gracious help. We simply didn't know what to do.'

Eninn's voice filled her head, fast and panicked still, words falling over each other to reach her. *Because they don't know who did it and they don't want to be blamed, and if they did know, they'd be too busy flaying that person alive to bother with us, but if he knows we're here then sooner or later they're going to notice too and then . . .*

Lyta clenched her trembling hands into fists and pushed Eninn right to the back of her mind. That wasn't fair, perhaps. It was easy to forget that whatever else Eninn was, he was a child—a god, a thief, a rascal, a trickster, but forever a child. And he was terrified right now.

Later, she would deal with him. Comfort him, reassure him, something. Whatever you did when your god was having a panic attack and rapidly losing all control of himself.

He was caught in a nightmare. She knew that, understood it. The feeling was far too familiar.

'It's going to be all right,' she murmured, below hearing, just for him. Because saying it out loud made it real, didn't it? Made it true? She had to believe that.

Juárez was speaking in that calm and reasonable voice she had noticed Sylvian also used when he needed people to do what he wanted. Perhaps they all used it. That and the *I can kill you without thinking about it* tone that often went with it. She couldn't hear exactly what he said, but the old man in the robes listened to him as if all his prayers had been answered.

'They respect soldiers,' Sylvian murmured to her in what she supposed he thought was reassurance. 'They admire strength. They serve a soldier god, after all. Their Imperator is a warrior, like Kyron.' Lyta cast him a horrified glance. She seriously hoped he wasn't like Kyron because their God of War was a heartless bastard, with no concern for anyone but himself. Sylvian nodded as he caught her meaning. 'Let Juárez handle it. He has experience with them.'

'With killing them?' She probably shouldn't sound quite so hopeful.

'Sometimes. Now, quiet. We don't want to cause trouble, do we?'

Definitely not. She tried to move a little closer to him all the same and ignored the hint of a smirk that tugged at his lips. He'd remind her of this later. She knew that. But right now she didn't care.

She didn't miss the way Sylvian, and all the royal troops with him, never stopped scanning their surroundings, taking everything in, counting people, checking for any hint of danger. It was an unexpected comfort. She was doing the same thing, although her aim was to try to work out escape routes and contingency plans. Most of them involved flinging herself from the walls, and she'd take her chance with the drop if it came down to it. If she could get to the roof of the main building she was pretty sure Amberes would provide a way out. It might not be pretty, and it might involve jumping for her life, but the city pressed close enough. She could do it.

Calm, she told herself as much as Eninn. *Stay calm. We were invited. They need our help. And if anything happens to us in here, Francisco is going to go to war with the whole Church Imperial.*

Not for her, not for his troops either. She wasn't so foolish as to believe that. But if the Church crossed him in this, if they used this as some kind of trap, if they destroyed something that was his, if they broke their word to him . . . He wasn't someone to cross.

What had Sylvian said of him once? He didn't like anyone taking anything that he thought belonged to him. That went for his men as well. And his wife. She could recall his expression as he prepared to kill Sylvian. That was how he thought of people, as things he owned.

And he thinks that about me too probably, remembering the way the king had looked at her. It wasn't a comfortable thought.

One false move here, she suddenly realised, and the whole continent could be plunged into war. It wouldn't take much to escalate, especially if Francisco started slaughtering random Imperials himself. Other kingdoms would take sides. Perhaps they were only waiting for the opportunity. Which side would depend on the advantage it might give them. The high priest of the Church Imperial knew that too.

And with the Sovereign Goddess of Albion missing and the man responsible working here in Amberes, talking to the lost gods, stealing relics . . . Lyta didn't like any of this. War seemed to tremble in the air. Amberes, Albion, Caput Mundi and all of Francisco's combined kingdoms. His own little empire in the making. No wonder he was at odds with the Church. He was almost recreating the greatest acts of the Imperator without the need for divine power. Just a man. The powers that be in Caput Mundi must hate him as much as he hated them.

Sooner or later something had to give. He'd do something. They'd call down a crusade on him like they had on Henry of Albion, and all the hells would be unleashed on Amberes.

'Please, come with me,' said Frater Caelinus. 'It's this way. We don't know when it happened, but sometime after Compline and well before Matins, in the dark of the night. The shrine would have been locked, but when the first acolytes arrived this morning to prepare the offerings, the door was open and . . . well . . . This way, please.'

He didn't tell the royal soldiers to wait outside and though he glanced suspiciously at Lyta, he made no comment as to who she was or why she was there. That unnerved her. They didn't like women much, keeping them as wives and mistresses, servants and whores, which mostly meant they were locked away and not part of daily life, especially in a temple such as this. She wondered if there were any other women here at all and suddenly felt very small and isolated.

Lyta kept her head bowed, her face as covered as possible and walked beside Sylvian.

As she passed through the towering doors, however, she felt it. The fear fell away and she sensed something else. Something calling to her over a great distance.

'Eninn?' she whispered.

I don't know, he replied and she could hear the intrigue mirroring her own. His fear was gone too. *I sense something . . . something new. Other.*

This was not the Imperator. It felt nothing like his touch. This was need, like a hook pulling her forward. Calling her. Desperate for help.

The temple complex was huge, a warren almost as bad as the Scholars' Tower had been. It would be far too easy to get lost in here and hard to find the way out. She counted her steps, kept track of turns and watched for windows and doors, mapping it with her mind out of habit. Focused now. Determined. This felt like a job and she needed to have her every wit about her.

Sylvian had picked up on the change in Lyta as well and if anything, looked even more concerned. Not for her, this time, but because of her.

'Is this *him* or you?' he asked at one point, when they paused for the old priest to unlock another narrow door. He meant Eninn. He had to.

'Both,' she admitted. 'I don't like any of this. It feels like we're underground again and this time there's no way out. Something wants us here, Eninn and me. Something is calling out to us, pulling us in. Like in Montalbeau.' He understood what that meant which was just as well because she didn't want to elaborate. Sylvian's mouth was a hard line now, any remaining humour gone.

The shrine itself opened out around them, tall as a tower, larger than any of the civic buildings. The only bigger space she'd seen was probably Cissonia's shrine and even that was a close-run thing. They were right in the heart of the Imperial Temple now and she had no idea this was hidden away inside. She doubted anyone in Amberes did.

It was beautiful.

Austere, yes, and bare, but still beautiful. Polished marble caught the light that poured through stained glass high above her and dappled the floor like a painter's palette. It was a perfect circle and it felt like she was standing in some kind of globe. Beyond the ring of coloured glass windows, the coffered dome overhead was a grid of sunken squares and in each one, a sculpted face gazed down on them. They were painted in bright colours, each one unique, and she wondered if they were real people. Or once had been, represented here, as tributes, or sacrifices.

In the middle of the dome, more than a hundred feet above her, there was an open circle, an oculus, through which flakes of fresh snow were already falling, landing in the middle of the rotunda, where they melted slowly away on the bright colours of the mosaic of the Imperial eagle. The air was sharp and fresh, and Lyta breathed it in with a dizzy feeling of relief.

That might be the only other way out of here, she thought. You'd need to fly, but it was a way. And that gave her hope. She was shocked to find what a comfort that was right now.

A man was kneeling on the other side of the vast space, head bowed over a crumpled body. He appeared to be praying, murmuring a rapid litany of words which echoed around them in the perfect acoustics of the shrine. Lyta only recognised a few of the Latinate words, the language of Caput Mundi. It almost sounded like birdsong.

Frater Caelinus cleared his throat meaningfully and the voice fell to silence.

'Forgive me, Inquisitor. They're here.'

Fuck, Lyta thought, and that spike of fear came back.

The praying man glanced over his shoulder and got to his feet with an elegant grace, pushing back his cowl to reveal a heartbreakingly handsome face, which could have been carved from the same marble as the statue of the August One. The resemblance was almost uncanny and even as Lyta felt her mouth open in surprise, she felt Eninn shrink back further.

His hair was short, in the Imperial style, and he was completely clean-shaven, with high cheekbones and a strong jaw, broad-shouldered beneath the black uniform of an inquisitor, form-fitting leather rather than robes. No mere cleric, this man. He could fight, and he would win. Inquisitors were members of the Praetorian, the elite warriors of the Church Imperial, and the Patricians, the highest level of their society, devoted to their God-Emperor above all else.

When he smiled, however, it was an expression of relief and welcome. More than that, it felt like sunlight fell through the oculus high above them instead of snow. He walked towards them and held his hand out in greeting.

'Captain Juárez, I believe,' he said in a deep modulated voice which felt like honey against Lyta's senses. She felt herself relax at the sound of that voice, a voice to be trusted, to be believed. Gods, she thought, that voice could get people to do anything. 'I am Tiberius Octavius Aurelianus,' he said and shook Juárez's hand as if he was a visiting dignitary. 'First Prefect of the Praetorian Inquisitors. My honour to you and your king.'

She had never heard a voice that was quite so dangerous, and never seen a face so designed to make a person want to love the bearer.

'Inquisitor,' Juárez replied formally, clearly already briefed on this man. She wasn't sure how he managed to maintain his air of indifferent respect, but she admired him all the more for it. 'Her majesty the queen sends her greetings and has bid us aid you in this difficult time.'

Tiberius's beautiful face took on a solemn cast again. 'Indeed. More difficult for this poor child than for us, I fear.' He stepped back, gesturing to the body sprawled on the floor, a pool of blood still spread wide around it like a scarlet lake. They hadn't moved the body, Lyta noted. They knew better. Interesting.

The priest began to offer up another series of prayers, muttering them to himself, and a few of his attendants joined in. Meanwhile the Inquisitor studied the arrivals carefully.

Oh, he was dangerous. Too clever by half. His eyes alighted on Lyta and she saw the recognition there. He knew her, or at least knew of her, who she was, what she'd done and perhaps even who hid inside her. She did not like this at all.

His eyes were pale, like ice. Maybe blue, maybe grey: it might depend on the light, or even his mood. Who was to say? She didn't want to look for too long, that was for certain. She didn't want his attention on her at all, but it was far too late now.

'What happened?' Sylvian asked, dragging all attention to the body, and to himself. She could have kissed him right there and then. 'Do you know who it is or how they got in here?'

Tiberius frowned briefly. 'No. The acolytes opened the doors this morning—the shrine is always locked overnight so the spirit of our August Imperator may fill it in order to bless us with his presence—and there the child lay. Broken.' He glanced up to the oculus. 'It is possible she fell. But that does not explain all the injuries. I'm not certain what could. And I have seen many dead bodies, as I believe you have, Captain Chant.'

The look between the two men said it all. Of course Sylvian had seen dead bodies, and the Inquisitor knew it. The Magister's for instance, and that was of particular interest to them both right now. But Lyta stared past them, at the small form sprawled on the marble, and she felt it again, that call, that plea. Someone needed help. Desperately.

Not the child. No, they were beyond help now.

A thousand questions crowded Lyta's head and she couldn't help herself. She had to know, had to see if it was the same as at the Temple of Lost Gods. She stepped forward, approaching the body to examine it. Other injuries, he'd said and you couldn't miss them. The chest had been torn open, like the boy in the Temple of Lost Gods. The girl . . . it was a girl this time, Lyta thought, as something hitched in her chest.

And then she dragged her gaze up to the child's face. It was still and pale, devoid of life and humour. But she knew it. Knew *her*.

Clémence.

She jumped back so fast she slammed into Sylvian who caught her in careful arms. 'What is it?'

'She was at the guild, yesterday,' she blurted out before she thought better of it. 'With Charnock.'

'What guild?' Juárez asked, his tone sharp.

Lyta cast a wary glance towards the Inquisitor and the priest who had moved off a little way and appeared to be in discussion about something. 'The Blacksmiths. Sweet gods of old, she's Charnock's apprentice.'

And she had been so very alive.

Now . . .

Lyta wanted to throw up. No, she was definitely going to throw up. She had seen death before, up close and personal. She'd even caused it. She had stood watch over the bodies of people she knew and loved, but this . . .

Someone had ripped her heart out of her bird-thin chest. Or something had simply *clawed* its way out.

There was no sign of an amulet, no evidence of Ben's work, but there were marks on her hands: not cuts or scars . . . burn marks . . .

'We'll bring her back to the palace, and the royal physicians can do their work,' Sylvian was saying. Like this child was no more than a piece of meat. Lyta felt the surge of outrage start, but . . . but he was doing his job. If he lost his temper, nothing good would come of this. Sylvian had a will of iron when it came to his duty. She knew that better than anyone. 'If you'll get a detailed report from the Imperials?' he went on and Juárez nodded in agreement, making his way over to Tiberius and Caelinus and asking his questions in a firm but respectful tone.

Sylvian waited until they were alone. Guards still fanned out around them, awkward and uncomfortable, a couple of them positively nauseated.

'Are you sure it's her, Lyta?'

'Of course I'm sure. I spoke to her. She took part in Charnock's ritual. He called her special. A treasure.'

'When did you last see her?'

That was the worst thing. She didn't want to say it but she couldn't keep it from Sylvian, not now. 'With Ben. She left with Ben. Gods, Sylvian, what if—?'

But when she tried to say it, she couldn't.

His face was grim as stone. Sylvian had seen more corpses than she could imagine. Men, women and yes, children too. He was a soldier before he was a royal bodyguard, and had fought on the front in the worst of Francisco's wars.

She needed to pull herself together right now. She was deep in enemy territory and had blurted out that she knew the corpse they had found in their holiest place, in front of an Imperial inquisitor no less. He might be handsome and charming, but she knew so much better than that.

And now . . . now . . . She stared at the girl again and found herself fighting to breathe. She was forgetting something, something important.

She was meant to be somewhere else, looking for someone else. Not Clémence. The pull returned, twice as strong now.

'Lyta, try to breathe,' Sylvian said. That didn't help. She wanted to tell him, or possibly just to slap him as hard as she could. 'What's wrong?'

There's something else here, she wanted to say. *Something that needs us, Eninn and me* . . . But she couldn't find the words. She could see Sylvian's growing concern in his eyes, the desire to march her out of the temple before she did something really stupid.

Because honestly? There was a very real risk of it. The need to do *something* was fluttering in her chest like a bird in a cage. And she never could stand to be caged.

'Mistress Cornellis,' said Tiberius, his soft and musical voice vibrating through her body. His oh-so-dangerous voice. She'd been right about that. 'Are you feeling quite well? Lyta?'

No, no she wasn't at all well. Her heart was hammering as if it would tear itself out through her ribs like one of those godlings, and he knew her name, she realised. *The Inquisitor knew her name.* She drew in another shaking breath and realised she was missing something important. They all were.

This was about a thief rather than a murderer. Juárez had said as much when he came to get them—a theft gone wrong. The murderer was far away.

And thieves belonged to Eninn.

She found her voice, far more steady than she would have expected. 'What has been stolen? What relic is missing?'

Tiberius's mouth lifted in amusement and her heart shrank inside her. She didn't like that look. Not at all. He knew something she didn't and he relished that thought. He was playing with her. He had been expecting that question, hadn't he?

'Nothing was stolen, Mistress Cornellis,' he replied. 'Not from us. It would take a far greater thief to steal from this temple. We have the would-be thief, she who dared to intrude here with designs on our treasures. And very shortly we are going to pass our final judgement on her.'

CHAPTER SIXTEEN

Kit

Ben had commandeered part of the cellar in the house on Crescent Street, an area beneath the kitchens, brick-lined and vaulted. It was probably the oldest part of the building and if Kit listened really carefully, he was pretty sure he could hear the canal water on the other side of the wall. That or sewers. In Amberes they were the same thing anyway, the older canals covered over and abandoned to effluent. He was plagued with the unpleasant thought that if the wall gave they might drown before they could get out, trapped in the vaulted ceiling, surrounded by rank water and shit.

It was also bitterly cold. No heating down here. His breath misted in front of his face. The area had been cleared and a number of lanterns had been brought in, which would have given the room something approaching a welcoming glow, if they didn't mostly illuminate the wooden table in the middle on which they had placed the hand of glory.

It made Kit's skin crawl.

Stirling had gone into quite a lot of detail about it. A creation of magic, or alchemy, or something in between. A dozen theories as to how or what was needed. And Ben added the rest, a relentless stream of information. They circled the table, peering at it. A mystery to solve, another puzzle, the kind of thing Ben had always been fascinated with—Stirling was a kindred spirit in that regard. Kit folded his arms across his chest and watched them, failing to hide his distaste.

'Where do you even go about getting one?' he had asked, like a naive fool, unprepared for the answer. Or rather, the lecture.

'You make it yourself.' Stirling spoke as if referring to nothing more than a tool or piece of equipment as commonplace as a mallet or an awl. 'You have to get the body of a murderer, one that's been hung in a gibbet by the roadside preferably. Few people are going to care what happens to someone like that. So you get the body, or dig it up once it's buried and cut off the left hand. Has to be the left. *Sinister*, you see?'

'That's just a coincidence,' Ben cut in, a little sharp suddenly. 'A trick of language. And a superstition. There's nothing wrong with being left-handed, Piers.'

Kit was left-handed. He was glad to hear Ben say it and wondered if that was actually for his benefit. He hoped so. That said, when Ben was in this frame of mind he might not even remember that Kit was left-handed. Or that he existed.

He was wearing one of those amulets Lyta said he'd been making. To focus the gods inside of him, she'd said, to let him use their power, though she didn't seem sure about it at all. It changed him. Even Kit could see that. While Kit understood his reasoning—better than Lyta perhaps—he was still uncomfortable with the idea. Ben had no idea of what the repercussions might be.

And naturally, being Ben, he just dived right in. He'd done the same when faced with *The Book of Gold*, walked right up to it and started reading. It had almost got them both killed.

Maybe it was being down here, or maybe it was the presence of the hand. But Kit hated this. Every fucking second of it.

'Anyway,' Stirling went on as he took out a stylus and used it to turn the hand to one side, testing the stiffness of the fingers. 'Then you pickle the hand in salt and urine, some people say horse dung, to preserve it, and then hang it out on an oak in the sun for as many of the dog days as you can until it dries.'

'Dog days?' Kit didn't understand why anyone would want to do any of this, let alone how.

'The longest, hottest days of the summer,' Ben explained. 'Some theories call for the door of a temple as well, to soak up divine power. To steal it, as it's the hand of a thief. There's all kinds of lore surrounding thieves, Eninn's lore I suppose. We should ask Lyta.' Kit shot him a warning glare but Ben carried on as if he hadn't mentioned her. 'Other writings say the whole process has to be done in midwinter, during the dark days. Some use living silver as the metal exists between states, holding the hand between life and death. The lore of silver demands the blood of a sacrifice, *blood binds, silver wakes . . .*'

'An old rhyme that one,' Stirling finished. '*Blood ties, silver breaks.* Any child knows that.'

Kit didn't. He only knew the first two words.

'Are you all right?' Ben asked him in an undertone. 'You've gone a bit green.'

'I'm fine.' He really wasn't. The way they talked about this thing and the process to make one . . . like they were excited, like they wanted to . . . Even Ben . . .

Especially Ben.

Blood binds . . .

Kit could almost hear the echo of the duchess, the words she'd spoken, and he could feel her knife digging into the flesh of his arm to mark him, bind him. His stomach churned and he had to force himself to breathe through his mouth for a moment or two in case the smell of the hand undid him.

It reeked of dead things and vile magic and everything unpleasant. Why couldn't they smell that? Couldn't they sense the power coming off it? It made something in his chest tighten and twist, something hollow. It felt like it was reaching for him and made him think of Montalbeau, of the labyrinth beneath the fortress, of Iseult.

He really didn't want to think of Iseult. He had nightmares enough.

Kit took another step back as Stirling leaned in closer. Had they played with so many poisons and potions in their alchemical studies that they didn't have a sense of smell left? Or just no sense at all. From what—admittedly little—he knew of alchemy mostly it involved melting things or blowing them up.

He'd like to see that thing blow up.

'Whatever the minutiae of the process,' said Stirling, 'it elicits a transformation, from one state to another, trapping it between life and death, and from that comes power to command states. Charnock argues it's the earliest form of alchemy. He wanted the queen to give him access to Brân the Blessed's head in the White Tower, which was preserved through a similar process. She refused, thank the gods. The head is far too precious.' Stirling gave up on the stylus and pulled at one of the brittle and yellowed fingernails as if trying to pry it off. The whole hand rocked ominously until he stopped. 'Interesting. It's tougher than it looks. I wonder, did they bake it in an oven? Does it smell of verbena to you, Ben? Maybe if we burn some of the outer dermis—'

'Gods,' Kit groaned, unable to stop himself as another wave of nausea struck. 'No one has ever told either of you "no" once in all your overprivileged lives, have they? Please don't!' He could only imagine the stench, and that was enough for his stomach to start preparing the rest of him to vomit. He was already backing up to find a corner.

'I don't think we should,' Ben said. Perhaps it was for Kit's benefit, but somehow he doubted it. 'Not without some more knowledge of what that might do. Too risky.'

Stirling let out a soft laugh, one knowing and almost seductive, with his honeyed gaze locked on Ben. 'You never used to be averse to a bit of risk, Ben.'

Ben cast Kit an apologetic grimace which made him feel a thousand times worse. Stirling knew Ben in ways Kit could never hope to. And Kit had the distinct impression that if Kit hadn't been here Ben might be all in for whatever Stirling suggested.

'No burning anything,' Ben replied adamantly, his attention back on the hand. 'It's big, for a human hand, isn't it? And there's a sense of . . . I don't know. Otherness.' He frowned at it like it was deliberately hiding something from him. 'Divinity perhaps? Is it really the hand of a god?'

'What happens to the rest of the body?' Kit asked, trying to change the subject and instantly regretted it when Stirling gave him a positively gleeful grin.

'Whatever you want. You can render the fat down, mix it with various ingredients and make the candle.' He wiggled his perfect golden eyebrows. Gods, he was enjoying this far too much. 'They say whoever lights it controls the magic, determines who it will affect. Should we give it a try and see what happens?'

Kit looked at the half-burned stub of the candle held by the hand, made from human fat—of course, Stirling wanted to light the infernal thing.

He couldn't let them do that. 'It made Sylvian and I sleep like the dead, Lyta said, and knocked out Prester Alaric. Whoever's behind it, they used it so they could carry out burglary without being disturbed. Who knows where they've been with it and what they've done?'

The hand of a dead god, his mind supplied unhelpfully. No, it couldn't be. Could it? But Ben was rarely wrong.

He tried to make himself study it the way the two scholars did.

What was the wick made of? Hair? No, he wasn't going to ask. He didn't want to know any more. The fact that it was almost the colour of his own hair didn't help. His skin itched and suddenly his stomach twisted inside him as if it was trying to eat itself.

Kit stumbled towards the darkest corner he could find. He didn't care what was there or what he might step on along the way. He needed to get away from that thing.

He bent over, retching without actually bringing anything up, his eyes burning as he gasped for air.

After a few seconds a cool hand pressed against his back, the long fingers soothing in a way no one else could.

'All right?' Ben murmured. 'Can I get you anything? Some water? Do you want to go back upstairs?'

Kit drew in a deep breath and tried to steady himself. 'No, I'll be fine. Sorry.' He straightened, facing his lover. The concern etched on Ben's face in the lamplight gave him a haunted edge. But at least he looked like Ben again.

'We could ask *them*. Find out for sure.' He glanced over his shoulder at Stirling who had gone back to poking at the horrible thing.

Kit swallowed hard. Was Ben asking his permission to let loose the gods in his head? He hated the idea of Ben using them to find out anything, let alone about something like that. He remembered too clearly the way they swallowed Ben's consciousness up with their power. And the way he had rambled and raved while trying to write the contents of the book down. Kit had thought that he'd lost him then and never wanted to go through that again.

But he couldn't stand in Ben's way either. He knew Ben needed to prove himself. He shared that trait. Both of them had lived their lives with someone looking over their shoulders, waiting to pick up the pieces. At least Kit had the printshop to show that he didn't need Lyta's watchfulness. Ben only had this. And Beatriz, generous and caring as she might be, still governed a large part of his life. He needed trust. He needed to show the world that he wasn't just her little brother. Oh Kit knew the feeling too well.

And now they needed to know what this thing was, and where it had come from, to find out what it could do and who had tried to use it against Lyta. Because Lyta might not think she needed protection, but Kit knew better than that.

'I can't stop you,' Kit told him grudgingly. He didn't mean it to sound like that, but the words were out before he could stop them. Ben flinched back from him, obvious hurt in his dark eyes. 'I don't mean . . . Damn it, Ben. It's dangerous. That's all I mean. Are you sure you're up to it?'

And that was the wrong thing too. Benedictus Alvarez wasn't a coward and he wasn't weak. He wanted to be accepted for who he was, for what he knew and could do, for his learning and intelligence. Kit knew that. But he was so easily hurt, he'd been through so much and all Kit wanted to do was protect him too.

He just kept doing it wrong.

A steely glint of determination had entered Ben's face and Kit knew he'd made a mistake. Ben didn't want to be coddled any more than Kit did. Lyta had been trying to step back and let Kit live his life. But he wasn't sure Beatriz was doing the same for Ben.

'Everything is dangerous in some way,' Ben murmured and reached out to touch Kit's face. His fingertips were gentle, almost painfully so, lingering before he turned away. 'And I'm not sickly, you know? Or a child. I won't break. This is my field of study, Kit.' Ben pulled off the heavy amulet he'd been wearing over his head and set it down on the nearby bench. The voice that came out of him next was a world away in difference. Commanding and annoyed, and Kit knew he'd really messed up this time. Nimyeh, Kyron and Gloir, but Ben too, all mingled together. 'Piers, fetch the silver and some antimony. There's a barrel of salt over there. What else do we need?'

They bent together over a case, pulling out jars and containers and muttering things that Kit didn't have a hope of understanding. All the same, he stayed and watched. He didn't want Ben to do this, any of this, but he had the feeling he had just said something very wrong, and to leave now would compound the problem.

He didn't like this one bit, but Ben was already miles ahead of him and doing it anyway. He was drawing something on the table in chalk, surrounding the hand with sigils and a circle, swirling lines which made Kit's vision blur as he tried to study them. He remembered some from *The Book of Gold* and their effect now was the same.

'Ben, I don't think this—'

'Try not to think, Kit. It's not your strongest attribute,' Ben snapped, echoing Nimyeh's tones, and this time it was Kit who flinched. 'The silver.' For a moment neither of them moved and Ben almost growled. 'Do I have to do it myself?'

Kit and Stirling frowned at each other, taken aback by the abrupt change. It was like another person had replaced him, the Seigneur of House Alvarez perhaps. A shiver ran down Kit's spine.

'Ben?' Kit murmured. 'Are you—?'

'I know what I'm doing. It's fine.' Each word was clearly pronounced, but at the same time sounded like it was ground out between clenched teeth. He didn't sound fine. 'I thought you were an alchemist, Piers. And what did you just say about risk? Living silver is a way of reaching the divine. It will show us if there is divinity present and perhaps even wake it.'

'Blood,' Stirling responded, his tone speculative. 'That might be more effective, don't you think? We need answers. Blood and silver would definitely rouse it.'

Ben hesitated and something flickered in his face again. He studied the alchemist closely, and glanced at Kit before shaking his head. 'Blood and silver? That's a recipe for a sacrifice. No. No blood for now. Too much too soon. Let's take this a step at a time.'

As Ben took the jar, the silvery liquid inside surged towards him like it was truly living, reacting no doubt to the gods active in him. He put it down inside the circle next to the hand, taking a deep breath which made his shoulders heave. The metal settled again in the confines of the circle, cut off from his power.

Ben began to glow.

It was something Kit would never get used to, the wonder of it, the beauty, and the horror. Because he knew, on some instinctive level, he was watching Ben ceasing to be Ben anymore. Or perhaps the Ben he knew was the mask, and now he removed it and became something else. Words slid across his skin, twirled around his outstretched fingers and voices seemed to come from all around them, out of the shadows and the darkest corners of the undercroft.

Stirling started, seeking the source in the corners of the room, but Kit didn't bother. He knew those voices far too well. Slowly, Stirling's gaze was drawn back to Ben, and he wore an expression of wonder.

'Ben, are you doing this?'

Ben almost sounded smug, like a child who had a better toy than his friend. 'I told you it was possible, didn't I? Back in Oxford? I couldn't tell you how I knew. And I didn't know for sure, just the tales of my bloodline, of Aspects and their children. But now, look . . .'

The voices grew louder as the light increased. Each one grew distinct. Kit could even pick them out. He knew them better than anyone. He'd listened to them while trying to look after Ben, when he'd been delirious, tried to reason with them, to plead with them. Tried to get them to let Ben go. All in vain.

Kyron was a low, guttural rumble. Gloir's voice was a choir. And Nimyeh, the voice of the ages.

'I saw Viola channel one goddess, admittedly our most powerful one, but this . . .' Stirling exclaimed in obvious delight. 'You told me it was possible but I didn't imagine, you might— Where did you find them? Where did they—?' Realisation filled his face as he caught up. '*The Book of Gold.* I didn't realise it when you told me about it but— Ben, you genius! You didn't hide the book. You *are* the book.'

Ben's face flushed a little, pride and joy at finally being able to share it with someone who understood the deep implications. Not fear the change in him like Kit did. The thought made Kit wince. He didn't mean to doubt Ben, but he couldn't believe any of this was good for him. And clearly he had told Stirling far more than the rest of them suspected. How would Lyta and Sylvian take that? But in many ways, Kit thought, it was Ben's secret to tell. Stirling was right, Ben was *The Book of Gold* now. Ystara had found her way out and Lyta had Eninn, but the others still crowded beneath his skin.

'For now,' said Ben. 'The risk is great and balancing them is difficult. They have needs and desires as well. That's why I made these.' He closed his hand on the amulet again, the light fading slowly and Kit saw relief flood his face. He was exhausted, worn-out and it made Kit's heart ache for the gentle scholar he loved. When he took a step forward, Ben shook his head, stopping him. 'We aren't done yet. I'm fine, Kit. Don't worry. It contains them, helps me focus. But it's a secret, Piers. It has to be. I am trusting you, my friend, with my . . . with *our* greatest secret. Now let me examine this and see what they can tell us.' He dropped the amulet again, spread his hands wide, and the same glow filled the space around the hand of glory.

For a moment nothing seemed to happen. Then the ground underneath them began to tremble.

'*This isn't possible*,' Ben murmured. He remained intent on the hand of glory though. The murmuring voices grew louder, and whatever they were saying didn't make sense. Ben was glowing brighter than the lanterns now and his hands shook. Kit edged towards him. He didn't like this, none of it. Any moment might see Ben buckling under the strain. '*It's old. Very old. And definitely not human. We know it. We know it well.*'

We, thought Kit. It was never good when Ben used '*we*'. And that voice—that strange, multi-layered voice . . .

In the middle of the table, the liquid silver in the jar surged like an ocean in a storm reacting to all the divine power in the room, reaching out for it. Living silver indeed, infecting all around it with life, with vitality. And the hand of glory . . . the hand . . . moved.

No, it was a trick of the light. It had to be. That thing was dead. Well and truly dead.

'Ben, you need to stop,' Kit said. 'Something's wrong.'

'*No, we can't stop now. Just . . . just give us a moment. What is it? I can feel it, like it's reaching out.*' He stepped back from the pendant and left it abandoned on the table, opening himself and the gods inside him completely to whatever power the hand still contained.

The light grew brighter still and Kit had to shield his eyes. The hand itself was aglow now, shimmering light under the wizened skin, like it was . . . growing, swelling, changing.

Ben touched the hand. A shudder ran through him, a bone-deep rattle and he let out a gasp of alarm.

Kit reached out to grab Ben's shoulder, to pull him away. Away from what though, that was the question. The hand? The things he'd written in chalk? The jar? Or maybe all of it and whatever weird interaction it had produced.

But as his hand closed on Ben, something sparked up his arm like lightning and he saw the figure of a man—*huge, armoured, towering over him. He held a sword in one hand and his expression was murderous. Kit fell back, clinging to something cold and hard, something that fitted in the palm of his hand. A coin, a heavy gold coin that was his by right. It meant something, that coin: a tithe, a tax owed to him by all who came here and crossed the river. And this man, this upstart from another place wanted it. The water of the Scaldis swirled around him, cold and dragging him under and the blade came down on his arm, severing it at the wrist. The blade rose again, and fell. Blood turned the river black.*

Kit screamed, but no sound came out.

'I see it now. I see—' He heard Ben's voice, breathy and fragmented through the roar of water and the long plaintive cries of the bronze horns which shuddered through him. 'I see him. Not a man. Not *just* a man. Dear gods, what did they do? I see him. They killed him—sacrificed him. They sacrificed a god, for Amberes.'

He pulled himself free of Kit's hands. The cellar was dark and cold again, and Ben's eyes were not his own. They weren't the eyes of the gods inside him either. They were the eyes of something new, bright and golden, blazing with violence. When they latched on to Kit, there was recognition there. He smiled someone else's smile.

'*Rose gold*,' Ben said, so clearly, Kit could almost feel the hand tangling in his hair once more, dragging his head up, those tendrils of terrible intent plunging into his mind to remake it. '*That was what I left behind. Rose gold and alabaster. I remember now. I remember . . . I remember you.*'

'*What* are you?' Kit gasped.

That slow almost lazy smile spread over Ben's face, not an expression Kit had ever seen there before. Certainly not Ben's. Someone else. Some*thing* else. '*I can tell you. I can tell you anything, truths unnumbered. Whatever you need to know. For a price, blood of my blood. All the secrets of the world . . .*'

The light beneath Ben's skin was incandescent. He was a column of fire, far too bright to look at with eyes unshaded. Kit heard Stirling cry out something—a plea, or a question perhaps—but there wasn't time to pay any attention to him. Nor did he care to.

Kit flung himself forward blindly, wrapping his arms around Ben and pulling him back from the table. There was a crash as they collided with it instead, sent it over, scattering all the elements of this horrible ritual, but that didn't matter either. He needed to get Ben away from it. Nothing else mattered. He tried to find Ben's face, framing it with his hands and opened his eyes a crack to the blaze of divine glory coming from the man he loved. Ben was channelling something else, not the gods within him but something far more powerful, something ancient and terrible.

Had the hand done this? Kit didn't know how but then again he didn't know anything about how the cursed thing worked. He'd had a bad feeling about it from the start.

'Ben, Ben please listen to me . . .'

But Ben couldn't hear him.

'*You cannot be here!*' That sounded like Gloir. The voice didn't come from Ben's mouth this time, but spiralled around them like echoes, as if those ancient gods had been pushed out of him by this new power and were no more than ghosts. '*You cannot steal him from us. He is all we have.*' Kit had a feeling they weren't talking to him though, but to whatever else had spoken through Ben. They were fighting for possession of Ben. For their lives.

'*What have you done, Cornellis?*' Kyron's voice snarled, and Ben's face seemed to twist into his, a violent and vengeful god forcing himself back into Ben's mind. He spat out Kit's surname like a curse. '*You did this. What have you brought here?*'

Him? They were blaming him?

'I don't know what you mean,' he answered. He was never going to be comfortable talking to them, let alone pleading with them, but it was the only way to help Ben. 'I didn't bring anyone here. You're going to hurt Ben. He can't take this. You had an agreement.'

'*When we were safe,*' Nimyeh cried. '*He was to keep us safe. He was to set us free. He has done neither of these things. The great work was meant to free us, to find us new lives, new bodies. Why should we care what happens to him? We should take him and use him until he's wrung out. There should be progress instead of darkness and sleep and treachery.*'

The changes he had seen in Ben . . . even when wearing the amulet, the way his eyes shifted . . . it wasn't holding them back, was it? They were already using him, wringing him out. They had lied to him. But they had done that all along.

'No one has betrayed you!'

'*Then what is this, Cornellis?*'

His voice came out in a desperate whimper. 'A mistake! It's a mistake. Don't make it worse. Please! You'll kill him and then what will happen to you?'

The trembling in the ground went still, and the world around them shivered to take on a fearful watchfulness.

Kit tried to breathe. He had to force the air into his lungs. He let Ben go, spreading his hands wide as a gesture of peace. He had managed to reason with them before. He had to do the same now. 'Listen to me. You have to calm down. You have to listen. You're scared. You're not thinking.'

Ben fell back beneath him, scowling but no longer struggling. The glow was brighter, his eyes full of molten gold. '*We are scared of nothing*,' Kyron snarled.

'But you are. Scared of being trapped again. Scared of losing Ben, of losing the one connection you have to the world. But you can't keep trying to control him.'

'*He is not the only one who can help us. Promises have been made and will fall due. I will be reborn as a prince, with an empire to inherit. Nimyeh will be free to walk to earth, teaching willing ears. Gloir will take back their guild and rule this city.*'

Kit stared, despite the blinding light of the gods, horrified. What promises? Who could do such things for them?

'Kit?' It was Stirling. 'I have to know the truth.' Kit'd almost forgotten that the man from Albion was there. Watching all of this. Listening and taking it all in. 'I'm sorry,' he said as he grabbed Kit's arm and wrenched it away from Ben. The movement was sudden and brutal.

He was stronger than Kit would have thought, his grip like iron and his expression implacable, a world away from the scholar he portrayed himself to be. The struggle was horribly brief and Kit found himself on his knees, staring at the hand of glory where it had fallen to the ground. The hand seemed to reach for him and Kit tried to pull free. But he couldn't.

'What are you doing, Piers?' That sounded like Ben. Just for a second. But Kit didn't get a chance to see if he was all right.

Stirling dragged Kit's arm out over the hand. 'Forgive me,' he said. 'I need answers and I'm running out of time.'

Stirling's knife slashed through the skin of Kit's arm and blood splattered down onto the hand. The moment Stirling released Kit, he hurled the vial holding the living silver at it. The glass burst apart, shards flying everywhere.

'Where is she?' Stirling shouted to the old god who had tried to possess Ben moments earlier, the god whose hand he now drenched in blood and living silver. 'You said you'd tell him anything. I compel you with the blood you demanded and living silver. I demand an answer. Lead me to my lady. Where is she?'

'*Let him go!*' Ben snarled. It was a command steeped in divine magic and even Kit felt it seize them both. Stirling was flung away from Kit like a cat's plaything.

Ben reached out, his fingers so pale in the unearthly light, like they were a weapon, as if he was using it to claw through Stirling's mind.

'*What have you done, Piers?*'

It didn't even sound like just one of the gods now. Enraged. Betrayed. But Ben was definitely in charge, as he had been in the Magister's tower, enraged at the threat to Kit.

'Ben . . . Ben, please,' Stirling raised his hands as if he could stop the man approaching or drive back the power of the divine gathered under Ben's skin. 'You need to ask him where she is. I have to find Rhiannon, do you understand?'

Kit cast a glance around, desperate, and saw the shards of glass still covered in the silver pooling on the ground. The hand lay beyond it, the skin smooth now rather than wizened, his blood staining it red.

Blood brings power and blood binds. Blood is power.

Even as he watched his blood sank into the flesh of the severed hand, vanishing and leaving not a mark against the flawless skin. Like alabaster, holding the candle with its wick of red hair.

Rose gold and alabaster.

The same words the Magister had once plucked out of the depths of his mind.

Something snagged in his chest, a hook, deep inside him. And there was another voice, something distant and faint, but so clear, like the sound of bronze horns in the stillness before a battle.

For a moment, Kit felt like he was hanging in the air, suspended, lost. Arms wrapped around him, cradled him, strong hands, sure hands. Hands like his own. And that voice . . . he knew that voice . . .

It haunted his nightmares, the ones that weren't full of Iseult of Montalbeau. And though it used the same words, said his name in the same way, it wasn't her voice he heard. It was something else. Old.

Old dreams, old nightmares, from long, long ago. Something else wrapped itself around him.

That golden light in Ben's eyes set its attention on Kit now. '*What are you?*' he asked. Not *who*, Kit realised. The same thing Kit had asked to no avail. *What.*

'It's me,' he tried to say, forcing the words around the lump in his throat. There was something else, in that empty space around him, wrapping itself all around him and pressing in. He gasped and felt an invisible noose tighten around him. It wasn't Ben, or the gods inside him. But they weren't doing anything to stop it either. They couldn't. It was strong and ancient, and endless. 'Ben . . . Ben please . . . help me.'

But Ben wasn't listening. The golden glare bore into Kit for a moment longer and then turned on Stirling.

'*What did you do to him, Piers?*'

'Where is Viola?' Stirling yelled, his panic evident. He didn't care about Kit, or Ben, not now. Only his goddess and the woman he thought had her mattered. 'Answer me. Please.'

'*Viola?*' Ben laughed and it wasn't the usual gentle sound. '*Kit doesn't know anything about your goddess or her Aspect. Release him. He's just a printer. He's no one.*'

No one, Kit thought and a wave of misery speared through him. He was no one. That was what he'd heard in Ben's voice when Ben dismissed him before going to see his cousin. Ben was a Divine Nexus, the Seigneur of House Alvarez. And Kit was no one. Hadn't he said as much himself, months ago? Ben had told him it didn't matter.

Well, it mattered now.

'I'm not holding him,' Stirling protested. 'That power knows him. It can speak through him. Make him tell me.'

Ben's voice dropped to a low, dangerous hiss. '*He is mine. And you hurt him.*'

Stirling dropped to his knees. 'What are you doing? Ben, think! They'll burn through you, wipe you away.'

The light in Ben's eyes flared even brighter and Kit realised that it was already too late. Ben was gone. The gods stared out.

'*Then we burn*,' they snarled. '*This is the Nexus, your secret fire, the philosopher's stone. Do you not recognise the very thing you have sought, Lord Stirling? Let us show you the great work, alchemist. Why are you here?*'

He pressed his fingertips to Stirling's forehead. The alchemist's eyes grew wide in horror and he tried to cry out. It was only a thin and strangled noise. Agony flooded his features but he couldn't even scream.

'Ben!' Kit yelled. 'Stop!'

Ben snatched his hand back as if burned. Stirling dropped like a stone and went still. Ben rounded on Kit, the gods fully in control. That could not be good. Kit had never seen him like this. Not in the worst throes of what they had put him through as he tried to write out the contents of *The Book of Gold*. Nor when he had tried to defend Kit in the room above the old printshop. Not even when he had judged the Magister in the tower. It had always been Ben, at the heart of it.

Now . . . now there was no sign of him at all. Not a trace.

'*You*,' they said. '*You think to command us? We remember you. You were banished. Brabo slaughtered you and gave you to the river and Amberes was born. We watched. We were free of you. How have you returned?*'

They thought he was that old god. Was that what had driven them over the edge? That or Stirling? He had to reach Ben. He still had to be there somewhere.

'Ben? I'm *Kit*. Remember? Kit Cornellis?'

But he remembered—memories that were not his own. *The river rushing over him, the blood from his severed wrist, the coin falling with his hand . . . They stood there, let it happen, betrayed him, sacrificed him . . .*

Kit struggled back to himself as that otherness swept through him, the knowledge of something he couldn't know, the sensation of something other and ancient, and so very strong. Was this what Ben felt when they tried to take over? If so, Kit finally understood why he wanted to get rid of them. Oh yes, now he understood.

Ben was brilliant and beautiful, a mere candle which the power of these limitless beings would consume. And he knew. Ben knew. He knew that it was only a matter of time. They intruded more and more each day and eventually there would be nothing of his lover left. It was already happening. Kit could see it himself.

Something linked to that hand was trying to take him in the same way. Something even more powerful. And the gods would fight back. But the first casualty would be Ben.

Kit had to stop this. He had to. It had started with the hand and the spell Ben cast. Whatever was reaching out to control him was all to do with the hand of glory.

What had Ben said about the silver? That it was a way of reaching the divine. Did that mean it could stop it too? Blood and silver . . .

Blood binds, silver wakes, blood ties, silver breaks. Kit threw himself towards the broken jar and the hand of glory, amid the ruins of Ben's spell, and grabbed the largest shard of glass. The blood flowing from his arm slicked its surface as he fumbled with it. There was living silver all over it too, but he didn't care. This had started with the hand and the silver. It needed to stop now, before Ben was gone forever. Or he was. It was already in his mind and in his memories. He couldn't let it get any further.

And if he didn't do something now he was afraid Ben would be lost.

Kit brought the point down into the hand of glory's palm, skewering it. The rest of the glass bit into his own hand, drawing more blood and leaving a burning line behind it.

Blood and silver was a sacrifice. And he had to make it. This had to be stopped.

Everything went still. So still. It was only when his screaming lungs forced him to gasp for air that he realised he'd been holding his breath.

Had it worked? How was he supposed to know about any of this? His job was to print words on paper, to compose lines of text, to create books and pamphlets. That was all. Not this. Not any of this.

'*You are mine, Christopher Cornellis,*' the voice whispered, the impossible voice, an echo of Iseult's married with something else entirely, soft as a sigh right beside his ear. '*Always mine.*' And then, finally, it faded.

The hand of glory twitched, speared through with bloody glass and living silver, and then shrivelled up again, the skin tightening on sinews and bones, all that borrowed vitality gone.

Strength left Kit at the same time and he slumped down onto the cold stone, breathing hard, his hand and arm in agony. All was dark and silent and for a moment he thought maybe he was dead and that was almost a relief.

'Kit? Ben? Gods, Kit, what happened?' Beatriz's voice broke the silence in the undercroft. 'Felipe, help him. Ben, what on earth did you do?'

Her servant hauled Kit upright and slid under his arm to support him. Kit slumped against him, grateful for his strength. There was blood everywhere, far too much of it. It ran down his fingers in a flood, splattering on the ground. It brought him back to Old Steen and the horror of that torture room.

Stirling was trying to pull himself to his feet, shaken, broken and afraid, staring past them in dismay and defeat. At Ben.

And Ben Alvarez, the man Kit loved, was glaring at his supposed friend as if he wanted to murder him, his eyes not entirely his own. Not anymore.

The gods glared out of him, stronger than ever before.

'Ben?' Kit whispered, a strange and broken sound, but as his voice whispered back from the walls and ceiling, Ben frowned, glancing from Stirling to Kit, and the rage drained out of him, replaced with horror of what had happened. Of what could have happened.

'Get out,' he hissed. 'All of you. Get out.'

CHAPTER SEVENTEEN

Kit

Beatriz fussed over him, healing his hand and frowning all the while, but Kit couldn't answer her questions. What had happened? What had they been trying to do in the first place?

He didn't know. That was the problem. They had all gone down there for entirely different reasons. Whatever had happened, had all gone wrong, no doubt about that.

And he didn't want to think about it, what he had seen and felt.

'You'll have to ask Ben,' he said at last.

'Oh I fully intend to. What was he messing around with down there? Him and Stirling and those wretched gods. Don't they think we have enough mundane problems to deal with, without borrowing more from *them*? I know you care about him, Kit, but my little brother is so self-absorbed sometimes.' And Ben was going to hear all about it from her, Kit had no doubt. It wouldn't help. It really wouldn't help. He didn't know how to tell her that. Perhaps he was too cowardly to try. She pressed her hand firmly against his face and stared into his eyes for a long moment. Her voice gentled. 'Are you sure you're all right?'

'I think . . . I think I need to go home,' he told her. 'It's for the best right now. He's . . . he's angry. I messed up whatever he was trying to do with the hand of glory and there's a problem with the gods. I think I'm just making it worse.'

She gave a little growl under her breath. 'There is always a problem with the gods. Especially those three. They're like children, only far more troublesome. Very well.' She sighed and released him. 'I'll talk to him, once he's done sulking in his room. And I need to see that Piers is all right as well. He looked traumatised. Felipe will see you home. No arguing,' she cut in when he had been about to do that very thing. 'You're hurt and I don't know what happened, but not a word. He will be accompanying you.'

Fine, he thought. Felipe could walk him home. He had work to do anyway. Too much work. And Lyta and Ben and all this madness was rising up again to interfere with that. It always did.

At least Felipe didn't ask a million questions while they walked. He never spoke a word. The shop on Twelfth Moon Street wasn't far, a pleasant stroll towards the Johannesport end of the canal. Or at least it would have been if the canal wasn't frozen over and the wind so cold that it felt like that shard of glass was slicing into his skin again. It reminded him of Iseult carving her sigils into his arms, making him her creature, and with that thought, the shivers that ran through him were not just from the cold.

When he reached his door, the hum of activity inside was a relief. It was warm and welcoming and he could hear his apprentices calling out to each other. The busy printshop was like a familiar song. He'd set the galleys for the notices yesterday, all ready for printing. It seemed like a lifetime ago. Type pieces rattled as they were returned to their place. Someone was singing a tune slightly off key as they worked, someone else laughed and it felt like the real world again, at last. His world. He stopped outside.

'I'll let her know you're safe,' Felipe said. 'Will I pass a message to my lady's brother?'

Not my lord, Kit thought. But then, Felipe didn't answer to anyone but Beatriz, did he? And clearly he knew enough about the relationship between Kit and Ben to offer. If that was still a thing after today.

'No I—No, there's no need.' He wouldn't have known what to say anyway.

What are you? Ben had asked as if he didn't know Kit at all, didn't recognise him. And he'd used those words, the words the Magister had used—*rose gold and alabaster.*

And the other voice. He had distinctly heard that voice: *'You are mine, Christopher Cornellis.'*

No it couldn't be. It was a nightmare, his mind bringing back that trauma and tormenting him with it. That was all. But it hadn't been *her* voice. It had been something else, ageless, endless.

He just wanted to get inside and lose himself in his work. He just wanted to hide. He was safe here. He had to be.

Maybe tomorrow, when things had calmed down, he'd try to talk to Ben. Or the next day. He didn't have the first clue what he should say.

You're endangering yourself.

You're walking down a dangerous path which you don't understand.

He couldn't imagine that going down well. Ben wanted to prove himself somehow, prove his work. In Charnock he had someone who believed in him. Kit just wished he would listen to someone else. It didn't have to be him. *Anyone* else. It was like this alchemist had cast some kind of spell over him, but Kit feared the source of that was actually Ben's own ambition. Kit understood it, sort of. He'd clawed his own way to a better life and was determined to cling to it. He'd almost lost everything six months ago, and now he needed his respectability even more. So he could understand Ben's need to prove himself. It was a cold sort of thought that would not loosen its claws. Ben had too many questions and he needed the answers, whether he really wanted to hear them or not. So did Kit.

And maybe the gods inside him were not helping. When did they ever help? What had Kyron said about promises that had been made? Had that been Ben? Or someone else?

The thought sent a chill through him.

'Keep safe, Master Cornellis,' said Felipe with a bow. And then he was gone.

Kit watched until he was out of sight and then stepped inside to meet an onslaught of greetings, questions and requests.

His hand still ached. Beatriz had healed it but it was an uncomfortable reminder of the worst period of his life. Iseult had always called him 'Christopher'. She had always claimed him as hers.

But that voice had not sounded like her.

Someone was playing with his nightmares, taunting him, making him remember his helplessness and misery, perhaps in an effort to reduce him to that state again. And then what? He had felt it reach inside him.

Kit shuddered, tucking his hand in against his chest and holding it close. The same arm that she had first carved her mark into. Why had Stirling gone for that one? That was the past. He was free. She couldn't touch him now. She was dead. He had to remember that. She was gone.

So what had he really heard in that cellar? Who had been speaking to him?

He tried to focus on the various matters of the printshop, on the bills and the orders for fresh paper, and the contract with the city aldermen to print official notices, which, while less fulfilling than the beautiful books he was known for, would pay more quickly and in greater overall sums. *No skating on the canals* was the latest ordinance. Like the people of Amberes were going to pay attention to that. And then there were a host of building regulations which seemed to be revised every month or so. Probably when someone in the civic offices was bored.

It was well after dinner—which had been some cold meat and cheese eaten hastily at his desk, brought to him by Jem who was not about to let him go without because he'd forgotten to eat again—when the others started to leave, and he heard the voice outside in the workshop. Recognised it too. His heart sank.

Lord Stirling.

The last person he wanted to see right now.

He pushed himself to his feet and made for the door, ready to tell the alchemist to fuck off. But as he laid eyes on him, on the relieved expression the other man wore on his wretched face, Kit found he couldn't do it.

Even though Stirling had sliced him open and tried to call on that eldritch power for his own ends.

'You *are* here, thank the goddess,' said Stirling, taking off his cloak and gloves and glancing around vaguely for somewhere to put them, like he could find anywhere clean enough.

'In here,' Kit said. 'You're getting in the way of the work.'

Which wasn't entirely true. The boys were already packing up, but at least in here he could shut the door and his employees wouldn't have front-row seats to whatever this was. Thanks to Lyta they were already far too aware that the Cornellis name wasn't always so respectable, and were constantly eager for more gossip.

That wasn't entirely fair. Lyta was trying. It was just life had a habit of turning on them both.

Like now. Like this.

He waited until Stirling was in the office itself and closed the door firmly behind him. There was barely room for both of them, but that didn't matter. The others would think he was a business customer anyway.

'You have a commission from the king himself, I believe,' Stirling began. 'And the city fathers. The reputation your imprint has been building is—'

Kit wasn't listening to this. None of it. He didn't owe Stirling a moment of politeness.

'*What* do you want?'

Stirling tightened his jaw and then seemed to come to a decision. 'Master Cornellis. I should not have . . . but I . . .' He frowned and then ploughed on. 'I must know. How did you know to do that, back at the Alvarez's house?'

'Do what?'

'Pierce the hand with silver to break the connection. Only a high-ranking alchemist ought to be aware of—'

Kit flexed his hand as the ghost of the pain shot through it again. 'So that's a thing?'

'Oh yes. A *secret thing*. The power of living silver is that of transformation and the reverse which—'

'Blood binds,' Kit said flatly, really not in the mood for another lecture on the wonders of alchemy. '*Silver wakes, blood ties, silver breaks*. A rhyme for children. I heard you back there. I got lucky. You cut me to get your answers—much good it did you—made a sacrifice with my blood. I don't think we have anything to talk about. So, are you finished?'

He was not. Clearly.

Stirling laid his cloak across Kit's chair, as it was the only one in the room, and then placed his gloves neatly on top of it. It left them both standing there, facing each other, as if in a prelude to a boxing match or a back-alley brawl. Either was possible. Kit was broader and clearly stronger, but he still wasn't sure he'd win if it came to it. There was something in Stirling's demeanour which told him not to underestimate this lordling from Albion.

'*Lucky*,' Stirling's mouth played with the word. 'That's a thing as well. I hear you and your sister are known for it.'

'I think we'd both argue about that. Nothing in our lives has ever been particularly lucky.'

If you didn't count lucky to still be alive, he added mentally. No need to say that out loud. He suspected Stirling knew that much.

Kit folded his arms over his chest and tried to loom. Hopefully Stirling would get the hint and go away.

He didn't. That would be too easy. He fell back on formalities.

'You have a lovely workshop, Master Cornellis,' he said in that slick voice, his mask firmly in place. 'I've visited most of the printers in Fleet Street, you know? In Londinium, I mean—those who were taught by Caxton and De Worde and continue their traditions. Who is your compositor?'

'I am. I'm everything here. The boys help but they're still training up. We're still a new business. Galen will be a journeyman soon and that'll help. You didn't come to discuss the finer points of printing, or to compare notes between here and your home.'

Stirling flushed all of a sudden. 'I came . . . I came to apologise.'

That couldn't have been easy to say. 'Apologise?'

Kit wasn't entirely sure if he was expressing disbelief or telling him to get on with it. That didn't really matter. Stirling swallowed hard, his throat working in a way that caught Kit's attention far too easily.

'Yes I—I didn't know. Not about what the hand would do to Ben. Or you.'

'I'm fine.' He didn't feel fine, not really. He felt wrung-out and lost. He wanted someone to hold him and tell him it would all be all right.

He wanted Ben, but he still remembered the way Ben had told them both to get out. 'What is it? The hand. Not human anyway. Not . . .' He shuddered. He couldn't help himself.

'Ben thinks it's the hand of one of the lost gods. All that remains of his body. He says it's the most powerful relic he's ever seen.' That figured. No one was going to dispute that.

'He told you that?'

Stirling flushed again, shifted awkwardly. 'Ah . . . no. I overheard him and Lady Beatriz arguing about it. It was somewhat difficult not to.'

So now Ben and Beatriz were arguing. Wonderful. But given what had happened, hardly surprising.

'It recognised you, didn't it, Kit?' That brought the horror of it back like a cannonball to Kit's guts.

'No,' Kit said firmly. He didn't know what had happened back there, but he didn't want anyone thinking that he had any kind of connection with that . . . that *thing*.

'Ben said it did, that it reached out through you, or through him—he's really not clear which.'

'You gave it my blood, Stirling.'

He shook his head. 'Much good it did, as you said. I learned nothing.'

'I hope you learned *not* to do that again,' Kit muttered darkly.

Stirling ignored the jibe. 'You severed the connection it was building, based on no more than a children's rhyme. That was inspired.'

Kit hated that word. It led to questions about where inspiration came from and he didn't like any of the possible answers. The human mind could think and reason and solve problems by itself. It didn't need help from some random divinity who happened to take an interest if it suited them.

'What do you want?' he asked again. Outside in the workshop a door closed—the last of the boys going home, he guessed. About time. Now if he could get rid of Stirling it would all be much easier.

'Kit—I can call you Kit, can't I? And you should call me Piers. All my friends do.' He stepped forward, right up to Kit and reached out.

Kit flinched back but not quickly enough. Stirling's hand pressed to his face and he seemed to freeze there beneath that touch. He couldn't help it.

Something shivered against his skin, that familiar sense of otherness that Kit normally associated with Ben. Stirling's fingers were as gentle as Ben's, but his touch a lot more knowing. A muscle jumped in Kit's jaw and the other man smiled.

'What are you?' Kit had to stop this, but he was thrown by the sudden intimacy. He didn't know what to do. People didn't act this way with him, especially not handsome lords from other countries. He didn't like it. He didn't trust it. It felt like magic, though he couldn't tell. Stirling didn't glow, didn't have the divine in his blood. But he was bewitching.

'I want to know you. To know your secrets.'

The urge to lean in, to open his mouth, to kiss him, to tell him everything . . . Kit shuddered as he fought it off.

'I don't have secrets.'

'Oh, I think you do. All craftsmen have secrets. And you have an affinity for the great work. Printers do, you know? Perhaps it's because you're already halfway there. You take ideas from the air and make them solid. You mix metals—lead, tin and antimony—and create words on paper. That's a kind of alchemy too.' The hand slipped down to his jaw, his neck and Stirling's voice was music. 'There's treasure in the books you produce. But you more than anyone else, I think . . . You had a vision back there. What did you see?'

Kit took a decisive step back, not that there was a lot of room in his office for a retreat. It was self-defence. He had to turn this around as fast as possible. 'You're the one with secrets. Endless secrets. And magic too.'

'I have what little my goddess gifted me. No more than charm. I need her back, Kit. I will do anything to find her. Anything.'

Kit flexed his hand, the ghost of pain creeping up his arm. No shit. 'I can't help you with that.'

'But you did. And you will. I know you will.'

Shaking his head, Kit opened the door to the office. 'I think it's time you left, *Piers*. There's nothing I can help you with here.'

'What about Ben? You want to protect him, I understand that. He's fallen under Charnock's sway. You must have seen it. He's dangerous, Kit, and you know it.'

That was too much. For all his fears about Ben and what was happening to him, Kit loved him.

'*Dangerous*? Have you *met* Ben?'

That wasn't strictly true. He knew exactly how dangerous Ben Alvarez was, both with and without divine power. And yes, he worried about the effect Charnock was having on him too. But he didn't need Piers, Lord bloody Stirling, pointing it out. Not with all the implications attached to his words either. That somehow he should side with Stirling, turn against Ben, betray him. He would never do that.

'He's not wrong though, is he?' Ben's voice came from the other side of the workshop. He stood in the shadows by the font cabinets, his eyes still slightly aglow. It might have been a trick of the lanterns. But it might not.

Stirling turned sharply, guilt written all over his handsome face. And not a little fear. 'Ben! I didn't . . . I should . . . I should be going then.'

'Yes,' Ben replied coldly. The voice was his own this time, but it sounded so different, the voice of the Lord of House Alvarez, a voice that Kit hardly knew and did not like. 'You should. I think you've caused enough trouble. You and Viola Alderton.'

'I'll find lodgings with the—'

Ben cut him off. 'I really don't care. Just go.'

Stirling glanced back to Kit, his eyes trying to communicate something. That apology he had promised which had never actually happened perhaps? Or a plea for his continued discretion? 'We will talk again,' he said finally.

'I doubt it,' Kit replied, glad to see the back of him. The door banged behind him and the wave of cold air which had entered the printshop was still better than the atmosphere between Kit and the man he loved. The man he barely recognised right now.

They were alone but they had never felt so far apart.

'What is it?' Kit asked, unable to leave the brittle silence to fester. 'What's wrong?'

He knew he sounded defensive. He couldn't help it. He'd been standing there, with Stirling touching his face far more intimately than anyone but Ben had done before. He could still feel the ghosts of his fingertips.

Ben was staring at him, examining him from head to foot, as if trying to commit him to memory like one of those texts he pored over.

'You were hurt,' he said at last. 'Your hand.'

Kit lifted it up, showed it to him, the unmarked palm. 'Beatriz dealt with it.'

'Yes, she told me. She's very good at cleaning up after me.'

Kit could imagine the scolding Ben had been through, and the humiliation of it too. He sighed. 'It wasn't you. It was him.' He didn't know where this was going but he didn't like it and he was tired and fed up.

'Not entirely. I could have . . . I lost control, Kit. The gods, they were so strong, so angry and I . . . I couldn't stop them. I didn't want to. I was angry too. But it wasn't . . . it wasn't me. I mean, it was but also . . . I . . . I was lost in them.'

Kit crossed to Ben and pulled him into his arms. 'I'm fine. *We're* fine. I don't know what happened back there, but we're all right, Ben. Both of us. Aren't we?'

Ben wilted against him and drew in a shaking breath. 'I'm nothing but trouble. I know that. I'm sorry. I could have hurt you. Really hurt you.'

'You have nothing to apologise for, heart,' Kit replied, thinking instantly of Stirling, and all that he'd implied. And of that touch and all it had promised. He pushed that away.

'Really? What about going at the hand of glory without a thought to what it might be and what it might do? I opened us all up to it.'

The hand—he really didn't want to think about the hand again. And yet that voice, that presence lurked on the edge of everything now. 'The hand was . . . awful. I could feel it in my head, or trying to get in there. I saw the moment it was cut off. It tried to show me . . .'

Ben stiffened in his arms. 'Show you what?'

'I don't know. The god it came from. How he died. A warrior with a sword cut off his hand. There was a coin and he fell in the river and . . . He spoke to me, said I was his. He sounded like . . . not like the duchess but . . .' Frustrated with himself, he gave a groan of exasperation. 'It doesn't matter. It was because Stirling gave it my blood, had to be. I stabbed it with some glass and it went away. That's got to count for something.' He tried to make it light. It didn't work.

Ben gave a brittle laugh. 'It had its claws in you before Stirling betrayed us. The glass didn't stop it. The silver did. But it had your blood too, and that's . . . that's not good. Blood sacrifice isn't something to be taken lightly.'

'I didn't do a blood sacrifice.'

Ben sighed heavily, clearly struggling to keep hold of his patience. 'But you did, my love. It had your blood twice, first from Stirling to get an answer it probably didn't even know, and then from you and that worries me far more. If I hadn't been out of control you wouldn't have had to. I'm going to send it to the Temple of Lost Gods. I think that's the best place for it, don't you?'

'Where did it come from?'

Ben blinked, as if Kit had completely changed the subject in the middle of the conversation. 'I don't know, but they can put it somewhere safe, I'm sure. This has all gone too far. All of it. I'm going to take care of it. I'm going to put things right. And as for Stirling . . . I thought he was my friend but he was just using me, wasn't he? To get to Charnock? Why was he here, Kit?'

Fingertips on his skin. 'To . . . to apologise.'

'Oh, *was* he? I wouldn't count on that. Not really.' Ben just gave a dismissive huff and leaned in again, pressing the side of his face to Kit's shoulder for a moment. 'Be careful of him, heart. He'll use anyone to get what he wants. He only cares about finding Viola Alderton. I see that now. I'm sorry, Kit. I should never have dragged you into this.'

'But you didn't. If anything, remember, Lyta and I—'

Ben stepped back, putting his fingers on Kit's lips to silence him. They felt cold. Too cold. And the bleak expression would have stolen anything Kit could have thought of saying anyway.

But he had to say something. 'Ben? Why are *you* here?'

Ben stared at him for another long moment and then leaned in closer, resting his head against Kit's chest, which meant Kit could no longer see his face.

'Something like that was always going to happen. I could have hurt you. I *would* have hurt you. I didn't know who you were in those moments. The gods saw you as a threat. I don't know why. Some connection with that old god and what you saw. Something reaching through me to you, or . . . I don't know. But they were angry and afraid. Whoever that lost god was, they hate him. And he hates them. I . . . I wasn't even aware that I could stop them. I certainly didn't try. I placed you in danger, Kit.'

'I think you'll find that's my sister's job.' He tried desperately to turn it into a joke. He had to. He was starting to panic now. What was Ben trying to say? Everything about this conversation was setting alarm bells ringing like Cissonia's own.

Ben took one shuddering breath and jerked back, gazing up at Kit. Then it all spilled out. 'You don't know the real me, do you? Not really. I don't. Who I was before the Scholars' Tower, who I am now, who I am going to eventually become. None of us know. The gods inside me aren't going anywhere. If anything, their hold is only getting stronger. I lose moments and more, much more. I find myself talking to Charnock without a clue what we were saying, or working on the amulets with no idea what I'm doing. I almost think I'm going to dissolve into them one day, and lose myself entirely. It was like that today. I couldn't control them, couldn't stop them. There was nothing I could do to protect you . . . and I didn't even think that I should . . .' He shook his head again and his eyes glittered like broken glass.

'What do you mean?'

Ben stared up into his face, and again Kit got the impression that he was trying to commit everything about him to that remarkable memory. Kit didn't like that one bit.

This is wrong, something inside him was screaming. Everything about this. And this time there were no gods involved, no alchemical rituals, no ancient hands . . .

It was all falling apart. Right in front of him. Just like he'd always known it would. His throat tightened to a jagged wire as Ben said those fateful words, the words, Kit realised, he had been dreading all along.

'I don't think we should see each other anymore, Kit. I have to let you go, before something awful happens. Before I hurt you.' Kit opened his mouth to argue, but Ben pressed his fingers to his lips to silence him again, cold as ice, trembling. Not like the warmth of Stirling's touch. But there was no magic here, no guile. All Kit wanted was to keep them there, to keep Ben there. Even when he knew he couldn't. Not anymore. He grabbed Ben's wrist. It was impossibly frail beneath his workman's fingers, slender and beautiful. Ben's bones were bird-like and elegant, like everything about him. He pressed his lips against Ben's fingers and Ben sucked in a helpless breath before he spoke again. The words came out in a rush, as if, should he fail to say them now, he would never be able to.

'Please understand. This is for the best. I love you Kit, but I can't risk hurting you again.'

He moved his fingers down to Kit's chest, to feel the rhythm of his thundering heart. Helpless, Kit let him, unable to hold him back, unable to let him go, his fingers still clenched around Ben's wrist, his arm trapped between their bodies. Ben's free hand closed on the back of Kit's neck, pulling him down so their lips came together—a brief and bruising kiss which tasted of salt tears.

And then Ben was gone.

The door banged behind him, and Kit sagged back against the compositor's stone, stunned, the place where his heart had been left hollow and bleeding.

CHAPTER EIGHTEEN

Sylvian

They thought Lyta had stolen from them. First the Blacksmiths and now the Imperial Temple. And to be brutally honest, Sylvian would never have been able to swear on his, or her, life that she hadn't. Lyta was capable of anything. She would happily lie to his face if she thought it was necessary. Lyta was nothing if not pragmatic. The Inquisitor smiled at her, triumphant, and Lyta . . . his indomitable Lyta, was glaring back at him, as if daring him to make an accusation out loud.

Fuck, Sylvian thought, was this how it ended? Here, in enemy territory in the heart of his own city, cut to pieces trying to save Lyta? He drew in a breath and felt the glow inside him, the shiver of Ystara's ring on his finger, and realised that yes, if that was the case, he would accept it. But not without a fight.

Though his first instinct was to draw his weapons and slaughter anyone in his way while he got Lyta out of the Imperial Temple—or tried to—Sylvian locked eyes with Juárez and paused. Juárez knew him, could read him, and always had his back. A brief shake of the head was all the direction he got. Sylvian was far too close to this situation, he knew that. All his instincts screamed at him to get Lyta to safety. They should never have come here. What was Annika thinking sending them here?

That said, what else could she do when the temple requested their help in a matter like this? To refuse to send the very people she had charged with investigating this would be the gravest insult, one the

Church Imperial would never forgive. And they would find out the lie if she pretended it was someone else. They always did.

They asked for you by name, Juárez had said. *You and Lyta. They know you were at the Temple of Lost Gods.*

But that could be part of their trap. Or a way to goad him into doing something foolish. Or to lure Lyta here and then accuse her of theft which would lead to the same bloody end.

Nevertheless, he recognised the way Juárez's hand fell into position and loosened his own sword in the scabbard. He was ready if this went sideways. But it hadn't quite got there yet.

Wait, his brother-in-arms was telling him. *I have your back. But wait.*

If the Inquisitor thought he was burning Lyta, there would be bloodshed here today. It was as simple as that. She was under the queen's protection. Even if she hadn't been, he'd die before he let an inquisitor take her.

He'd made that mistake with the Magister. Never again.

But right now, Sylvian had to let Juárez's cooler mind take charge.

'You have a prisoner?' Juárez asked Tiberius in a remarkably calm and measured voice. 'Do you think she committed this murder?'

The Inquisitor finally tore his gaze away from Lyta and rounded on the royal bodyguards. If he was upset not to get the reaction he had clearly been craving, he didn't show it. 'Perhaps, perhaps not.'

'Nevertheless, we should take her in for questioning,' Juárez replied smoothly. 'As part of this investigation. The queen will demand it.'

Tiberius smiled broadly. 'No need, my friend. The body is yours but not her. This is an Imperial matter and the attempted theft happened in our temple, on our land, as it were. This is my jurisdiction. The king's justiciars need not trouble themselves, and nor should you.'

He sounded so reasonable. It was like a charm he wove around them, that fluid voice, so believable and trustworthy, so logical. Sylvian felt it grate up against every instinct he had.

He wasn't the only one.

'Technically all land in Amberes belongs to the king,' Lyta interrupted. 'So actually—'

'And this mysterious thief of yours may have information we need,' Sylvian went on before Lyta could '*so actually*' them all right out of here, never to be allowed to return. Or worse. Praetorians didn't like to be argued with, especially not by a woman.

Tiberius sighed and shook his head as if it broke his heart to say what came next. 'You may interview her, if you must, but I think she will tell you nothing. We have barely been able to get a single coherent word from her since we first found her. Perhaps she can no longer speak. Trials are a trial, after all.' He laughed at his own bad joke and seemed surprised they didn't all join in. 'But she can scream. We have established that much.' He smiled again, that cold and horrifying smile. Sylvian didn't give him the satisfaction of a reaction to that either. He was stone. He had to be. All the way through.

'All the same,' said Lyta, unexpectedly. 'We would be most interested in seeing the thief. Call it professional courtesy.' And then she smiled. A dazzling smile. Sylvian frowned, hardly recognising her in that second. It was as if someone else stood there, someone with mismatched eyes, reckless and wild. What was she playing at? Was she *flirting* with the Inquisitor?

Tiberius eyed her speculatively. 'Very well,' he said at last. 'Come with me, but I warn you, she is not helpful. In fact she can be downright dangerous. You'll see, Mistress Cornellis. But perhaps, from what we've heard of you, you can be her confessor. One thief to another.'

'Yes,' said Lyta. 'I would be honoured, if she needs a confessor. Thieves don't really go in for that sort of thing though.' She sounded giddy, wrong. This was going from bad to worse. What was she doing? And why was she playing along with him? She had got what she wanted, no matter how dangerous. Somehow, he could feel it. She had won. But this was no game.

Was it professional pride, he wondered? Or did Eninn have a claim on whoever this thief was as well? Anything was possible. He was the God of Thieves. Ever since they had stepped inside the temple, she'd had that jitteriness which he thought signified her god's presence and he felt Ystara stir again, reaching out to him, warning him. His goddess liked this no more than he did and any threat to his love unsettled them both. It was like he could see Eninn underneath her skin. He hoped no one else could. Especially here.

That would not help them at all. All he had to do was get her out of here safely. That was his priority now. His only priority. He should never have agreed. He should never have let her come. Not that he had ever had a choice.

Juárez gave brief directions to two of his men to secure the girl's pitifully small body. Sylvian looked away, unwilling to watch. The three of them followed Tiberius from the shrine and across the huge courtyard to a building abutting the high walls. The stairs inside wound in a tight spiral, leading downwards two or three floors before Tiberius stopped and stepped into a room which held two robed acolytes, heads bent in prayer, and a cage.

It was a brutal thing, that cage—heavy iron, studded with spikes on the inside so that the woman huddled awkwardly in the corner, with nowhere to hide and no safe space left to her. She was dressed only in the remains of a shift dress and her dark blonde hair hung in straggly lengths around her gaunt face. Her eyes were closed and blue-black bruises ringed them.

'Well, Mistress Cornellis?' Tiberius asked. 'You share a god, do you not?'

Lyta muttered something obscene under her breath and took a step forward, completely unafraid. The determination on her face was unnerving.

The air fizzed with expectation and threat, that sense of the divine, the numinous which he found so unsettling no matter how often he felt it. It was everywhere. In Lyta, in the temple, here in this room . . .

'Sylvian,' Juárez murmured, on the edge of hearing. 'This is an extraordinarily bad idea. The longer we're here . . .'

The more trouble they could cause. Or rather Lyta could. Besides, even he could see the glimpses of Eninn in Lyta leaking out now. Whatever was going on here, the little god was more and more obvious. And if the Inquisitor realised that . . .

'I agree. But try telling Lyta.' Try telling Lyta anything when she was in a mood like this. This was what he had feared from the first moment the queen had mentioned an inquisitor. That Lyta would take offence, that she'd want to prove that no one scared her. That she would do something like this. Or Eninn would. He wasn't sure which was worse.

'He's playing with her, Sylvian. If we need to fight our way out—'

'I know. It won't come to that, but if it does . . . We just grab Lyta and run, all right?'

Juárez nodded as if he only half believed that would be possible, and fell back, holding the way out for them if it came to it.

Lyta crouched down before the woman. 'What happened?' she asked softly and the air seemed to shiver around her. Like something was coalescing.

Sylvian had never thought much about the nature of her relationship with Eninn. It wasn't everyone who could carry a god inside them. They were rare beings and now it seemed he knew two of them. Ben was a Divine Nexus. What did that make Lyta? Eninn was just one god, but Lyta had travelled to the Nether to drag him back from the wandering ways. That had to change someone. He hadn't considered how much until now.

Short-sighted of him. He'd been too concerned with his own problems, and the goddess who had made him part of her plans without so much as a by-your-leave. He was an idiot, but what else was new? He was an idiot to be here, and an idiot to let Lyta be here under any circumstances. Idiocy, it seemed, was his default position.

The woman looked up, searching Lyta's face. She had blue eyes, Sylvian noticed, much paler than Lyta's, like icy water. Her lips moved but he didn't understand what she said.

Lyta frowned, listening intently. Then she reached out her hand through the bars.

The woman seized Lyta's arm and pulled her hard, slamming her against the bars. There was a crack as her head hit the metal. Lyta gave a gasp of pain, the air was forced from her body. Sylvian was beside her a moment later, ready to pull her clear, while the caged woman pressed up against her, only the bars separating them, words falling like water from her mouth, none of which made any sense.

Another language, but not one he knew. Lyta seemed dazed, but not actually afraid. It was more akin to amazement.

Lyta said something in reply, whispering in that strange language, a language she didn't know and couldn't possibly understand, let alone speak. The woman's pale eyes widened, and filled with sudden tears. Gratitude, Sylvian realised. It was gratitude.

The Inquisitor flung open the cage door, grabbing the flail that hung on his belt. It came down hard against the prisoner's back, tearing through fabric and flesh. The impact shuddered through her and into Lyta who cried out desperately, jerking back against Sylvian. It wasn't the first time they'd beaten their prisoner either, Sylvian could see now. Her back was ragged with tattered skin and blood, fresh and dried. She screamed, loud and desperate, releasing Lyta as she did so.

As she fell back, Lyta scrambled away and Sylvian dragged her up and behind him. She wasn't hurt. Not physically. That was all he could tell. But she was breathing heavily and shaking like a leaf in a gale.

'Are you all right?'

'Yes.' She barked out the word. 'We need to leave. Now.'

That wasn't like her either. His Lyta would want to intervene, to put a stop to this. Instead, she grabbed his arm and pulled him back with her towards Juárez and the door. 'Sylvian. Now!'

But he couldn't move. He'd seen such violence before but somehow this time . . .

'*You can't do anything. Leave. Get to safety while you can.*'

He wasn't even sure who said that—Lyta, Ystara, Eninn or something else entirely? Did it matter? It wasn't wrong.

Finally, the woman slumped down and the Inquisitor stood over her, watching coldly, examining the ragged rise and fall of her abused back as she struggled to breathe. He seemed to be waiting for her to move again, but she didn't. She curled in on herself, and they could hear a soft sob. Nothing more.

'What did I tell you?' he said, his voice still smooth and liquid as oil. 'I know you understand me, woman. Confess your crimes and it will be quick. I'll use the blade and free you. Give yourself to the

August Imperator. If not, the fire will be slow. They can't help you. No one can. It's your choice.'

He slammed the cage door with the finality of the grave.

The cage had mounts on either side of it, Sylvian realised. He'd seen this kind of thing before. They'd fought the Church Imperial in Napoli, driven them back in a tide of battle and sacked their temples. And the things they left behind . . . He knew what they did to heretics. To anyone they wanted rid of really.

The lower half of the cage was charred and black with soot. When they tired of this game, the Inquisitor would order it lifted up into the courtyard and set a fire underneath it. They would all gather to watch, from the lowliest novice to the Inquisitor himself. If she confessed to whatever they wanted from her, they would take her from it and give her a soldier's death by the blade. If not . . .

They could use the smoke to choke her, or keep the flames blazing. The iron around her would heat up and slowly, so slowly, she'd die. She'd scream until her voice broke and still they'd make it last.

He needed to get Lyta out of here. He needed to warn Annika and send word to Francisco. This man was a Patrician, the First Prefect of the Praetorian Inquisitors, higher than anyone else from Caput Mundi for hundreds of miles. If the Magister had been a prince of the Church, what did that make Tiberius Octavius Aurelianus? And what was he doing here in Amberes? He should never have been allowed inside its walls. They needed to expel him as soon as possible.

He was the type of person who would burn not only a woman but a whole city if he thought it just. A whole kingdom.

'*Get out*,' the voice murmured again, on the edge of his hearing. Not quite there. Not quite real.

'Enough,' Sylvian said softly, trying to make it sound dismissive. He needed to made their departure as commonplace as possible. The voice was right. They needed to get out of here now. 'The woman clearly has nothing to say. You ought to put her to the sword rather than make her suffer like this. It's what you're planning to do anyway. Torture never reveals anything useful or reliable.'

An acolyte took the flail from the Inquisitor and handed him a wet towel with which to wipe away the blood from his hands. He let it fall to the cell floor when finished.

'It's called atonement, Captain Chant. Perhaps you've heard of it? An act of shriving, and it will set her free of that which taxes her. You should try it someday.' Tiberius smiled, baring all his teeth, and Sylvian decided that though handsome his face lacked something—a fist probably, right in the middle of it. 'Or perhaps not. One day, I'm certain, you will come to understand. We will be happy to help you. One soldier to another.'

Oh, he was sure they would. He had killed a prince of the Church, a Patrician. He didn't regret that for a moment. He'd be happy to do it again.

And like the Magister, Inquisitor Tiberius would happily burn the world for his God-Emperor, that was clear. This woman was just another victim. Not even a very important one. They didn't care if she confessed or swore fealty to their god. They would probably do it regardless. One way or the other. She was only a woman.

And so was Lyta.

He felt Ystara growl under his skin. People thought the Goddess of Love was kind and gentle. She was far from it, especially when crossed, or when those she cared for were threatened. No one understood that.

In that instant, Sylvian would have torn the man limb from limb if he could. And Tiberius knew it. He also knew that he was in no danger at all. That there was nothing Sylvian could do here, in his place of power.

But the Magister had thought that as well.

Lyta tugged Sylvian's arm again. 'We need to go,' she said, her voice very quiet and very calm. Worryingly so. Since when was Lyta the voice of reason? 'The queen . . . she'll want to know about the victim, the child . . . Clémence. We need to inform the guild as well.'

She deliberately ignored the cage. Was she remembering when the Magister had captured her in the Scholars' Tower? This could have been her fate. She'd just been a thief then as well, like this woman. Fuck, Sylvian was glad he'd killed the bastard and would happily repeat the whole dance here and now. Every instinct in him longed to deal out death.

'What was she trying to steal?' Juárez asked, finding his voice at last. It was raw with disgust he didn't bother to hide.

'Mistress Cornellis? Did she tell you?' asked the Inquisitor. Lyta shook her head, eyes hard as stones. 'We found her trying to steal Brabo's sword,' Tiberius went on. 'An ancient relic of Amberes and the Church, a relic with great power. You should know it, Captain Chant. Even your name echoes he who wielded it: Silvius Brabo.'

Sylvian kept his face fixed and impassive. He'd never heard the name or anything about a relic, and had no interest in such distractions. His name was nothing. He had no family to give him a name. It came from a whim in one of the temples no doubt, or a list in a council office, kept for picking names for orphans who pitched up with nothing and no one to vouch for them. He had never cared enough to find out.

Tiberius studied his face a moment longer and then shrugged, almost in disappointment. 'This woman was standing over the child holding the gladius, a relic she had taken from our temple. The child was already dead. That is enough.'

'She isn't a murderess,' Lyta said then, suddenly fierce again. 'She had nothing to do with that child's death. She couldn't have.'

'How so?'

'Clémence wasn't stabbed. Not with some old sword, not with a knife either. Nothing human killed that girl. You know that.'

'Nothing human,' Tiberius murmured, studying her face. 'Something divine perhaps?' That hungry glint entered his eyes again. 'Interesting. How do you know that?'

'She isn't the first.'

'So we heard. That's why you are here, after all. Your queen has you investigating. What god would dare enter *our* shrine uninvited, though? The shrine of the Imperator Eternal? That would be folly indeed. We kill gods, Lyta.' He paused meaningfully and grinned at her as if they shared a secret.

Lyta's expression didn't even twitch as she matched his gaze. Sylvian felt a rush of pride. She really was magnificent when she was at her stubborn, belligerent best. And so very dangerous. 'No one can kill a god.'

Tiberius smiled. 'As good as. They're gone and it takes quite the miracle to bring them back again, doesn't it?'

Lyta said nothing at first but her shoulders tightened. 'We're talking about a child. Not a god.'

'Are we?'

'I don't know,' Lyta replied. There was not a hint of a lie in her answer: 'This sword you mentioned, what is it?'

'Our most treasured artefact. Maybe that was why she wanted it? We'll never know if she will not speak.'

'Torture isn't going to drag it out of her either.'

'So it seems.' He leaned in closer, towering over Lyta and Sylvian straightened, hand sliding over his shoulder to his sword hilt, meaningfully. But Lyta didn't back down either, her glare murderous. 'What did she tell you, Lyta? Who is she and what is she hiding?'

'I didn't understand her either.'

Tiberius's expression branded her a liar.

Lyta gave Sylvian a nod. They were done here. He thanked all the gods, regardless of who they were.

They left in silence, rejoining their guards at the main gate.

'Farewell, Captains, Mistress Cornellis,' said the Inquisitor as the gates closed between them. 'I feel certain we will meet again soon.'

Lyta's shoulders tightened as she walked away from him as fast as she could, like her life depended on it. Now, finally, she seemed to have regained some sense of self-preservation. Sylvian lengthened his stride to keep up with her as they got outside and swung around the side of the building. Somewhere behind them, that poor woman was waiting for her own death, all of it dependent on the whim of that sadistic bastard. And there was nothing they could do.

At the corner of Palace Street, his hand on Lyta's shoulder stopped her without any effort at all, no more than a touch. She spun around and buried her face in his chest. Surprised, Sylvian brought his arms around her and held her close, not able to say a word. He didn't know what to say. This was not like Lyta. Not at all. She always had a smart reply, a caustic comment, or something.

'We've got to get her out of there,' she whispered at last. 'She spoke to me, Sylvian. She gave me this.' Her fist uncurled to reveal a carved figure of a horse, old and worn, that kind of butter-yellow bone like old teeth. 'I saw it in the Blacksmiths' Guild. Charnock had it. And I saw her there too, in Ben's workroom, pretending to be a cleaner. She was looking for it even then. She must have stolen it back. It's what they thought I took, I suppose. We were there at the same time.'

She handed it over to him, a small thing that nestled in the palm of his hand, almost abstract in design, but still, very clearly, a horse at full gallop, mane and tail streaming behind it.

'Is this a relic?' he asked. It felt strangely warm in his hand, and the ring shivered strangely so close to it. Lyta nodded wordlessly. She made no move to take it back. Sylvian put it carefully away in the pouch at his belt. 'You did understand her then? What did she say to you?'

'Something is reaching out from the Nether. It's killing the children, using them to search for things like this. Gods can sense the power held in relics, even those that belong to other gods. Eninn sensed the Imperator in there and it terrified him. But the moment he knew she was there, we had to find her. She begged, Sylvian. Do you know what it takes for a goddess to beg? She begged us to get this to safety. Charnock wants it for his ritual, for the thing he contacted, to feed it. It wants her power. It wants all relics of power, and most of all, it wants the horse or that sword. There's more power in them than anything else in Amberes. Except maybe the book.'

'Why didn't we understand her?'

'Because she wasn't speaking our language. Or any language we'd know. No more than a few words, anyway. She spoke with Eninn rather than me, god to god, but he translated. We have to give that to Stirling, to keep it safe. She said he'd know what to do. But we have to get her out. Sylvian, she's Viola Alderton. She's also the Goddess of Albion, Rhiannon. And one way or the other, they're going to kill her.'

CHAPTER NINETEEN

Lyta

The palace was not quite the last place Lyta wanted to be. That was back in that room in the Imperial Temple with a doomed goddess whispering into her mind. A goddess who had called her there through Eninn, who had trusted them with her last relic and her only hope.

No, Lyta didn't want to be in the Rose Palace, but with the Inquisitor here in Amberes, knowing who and what she was, that was where people kept insisting she had to be. It had been hours. Far too long for Viola Alderton. And for Lyta herself.

She was here for her own protection, everyone kept saying. She didn't like the sound of that. She had responsibilities. There was Kit. She had always been the one who looked after him. Even when he didn't want her to. She always would. She had already brought trouble down on his head. What if someone decided to attack him again?

She needed to help Rhiannon, find Stirling.

The blacksmiths wanted her. So did Voseh, the God of Decay. And now so did Tiberius Octavius Aurelianus, First Prefect of the Praetorian Inquisitors. She had no doubt about that.

The palace might be the safest place to be right now.

So long as I get to walk out again, she reminded herself. It wasn't like the Rose Palace was Old Steen. She could get out of here in a heartbeat. She had done it before.

But right now she needed to take stock, catch her breath. Make a plan. She desperately needed a plan.

She had to talk to Alderton too and she wasn't sure what she could say to him.

Found your sister. She's a goddess and she might be insane now. Oh and she's currently being tortured and is probably going to be burned alive. Sorry!

She could not see that going well.

And then there was Eninn.

He had always been cocky and full of wild bravado. That was how she knew him and she was well aware that that was the way he rubbed off on her, the gift he gave her—quick wits, self-confidence, a resolve to never give up. The only time she had ever seen him defeated was when he had been flung through the Nether and she had rescued him. But even then, he'd been resigned.

Now he was almost hysterical. She couldn't make sense of him. Coming face to face with the presence of the Imperator in the temple grounds had been bad enough. Feeling the insidious way his power threaded through everything there had chilled her to the core. But seeing Rhiannon trapped in that cage, beaten and almost broken . . .

She thought he would be outraged, incensed and wrathful. But that wasn't it at all.

He couldn't get away quickly enough. If a goddess of such power could be trapped and broken, what chance did he have?

Rhiannon had drawn her in there and Eninn hadn't been able to stop her. She had beguiled him as well.

'Beware of a god,' Rhiannon had told her. 'Even one that loves you. Especially one that loves you. They will steal your life from you. That's the danger all Aspects face, that one day we will wake up and we will be no more, and only the divine will remain.'

If Eninn could have made her fling that bone horse into the canal as they passed he would have. She'd never taken him for a coward but now . . . now she didn't know.

He'd forsaken his brother and sister gods, that was what everyone said. That was why they had wanted revenge so badly they had allied with the Magister to exile him and steal his power. He didn't even know Rhiannon. Why would he care about helping her?

She was from somewhere else, far away. She could deal with her own problems.

'She can't though. She's helpless, isn't she?' Lyta reached out to him warily. He didn't want to debate this, let alone listen to reason. He refused to reply.

Fabulous, she thought. *Just amazing*. Perhaps Ben could shed some light on it. She'd have to ask. He at least would try to understand. He might be able to convince his little menagerie to help, to explain, rather than sulking like a brat. But when it came to Charnock, Lyta wasn't exactly sure where Benedictus Alvarez stood anymore.

And then there was Stirling. Rhiannon wanted him to have the horse relic. Lyta was going to have to tell him she'd found his missing goddess. Oh that was going to go down so well with everyone—that while in Amberes a noblewoman of Albion, possessed of their most beloved goddess, had been captured, tortured and killed by the Church. Sylvian was right. It might start a war. It would probably start a war. Albion would take on Caput Mundi and the whole continent would be crushed between them. *A holy war*, she thought. And what would the gods do then? What sides would they take? And in a war between gods, humans always suffered most. History was written in mortal blood after all, not the divine.

And Amberes would get the blame, of course.

She was spiralling, she knew that. She couldn't help it. As they had arrived in the palace, the others fell away to their various tasks, Juárez leaving to follow up with the royal physicians and the remaining guards to their stations, or perhaps to a well-deserved break in a mess hall somewhere. She could do with a break, she thought. Just once. It would be nice. Perhaps even some sleep.

Finally, she was alone with Sylvian, silent as the grave, their footsteps echoing on the ornate tiles of the corridors. They had been left in an antechamber of the reception hall deep inside the Rose Palace. Lyta stopped pacing and took a deep shuddering breath which made Sylvian jerk as if she had kicked him in the gut.

'What's wrong?' he asked warily.

Lyta graced him with her darkest glare. 'Everything?'

Was it only last night they had fallen into each other's arms again like lovesick adolescents? It felt like a lifetime ago.

'Lyta,' he murmured and his voice was so gentle and so bloody *understanding* it felt like a blade in her heart. 'It will be all right. We'll talk to Annika and—'

'Would you ever stop calling her by her given name?' she hissed. 'She's the queen. The actual queen, Sylvian. Not some girl you sometimes have the good fortune to—'

She didn't see him move. That was the frightening thing. One minute he was standing there, relaxed, loose-limbed, radiating concern and affection and the next thing he had her pinioned, his body hard against her, his hand over her mouth. He was steel pressed against her, a living threat.

His breath whispered against her ear as she felt his chest heave and she shivered. She couldn't help it.

He could snap her neck in a second. It didn't do to forget that Sylvian Chant, noble royal bodyguard and all round fucking hero, was also a killer. She'd seen him fight too many times now, fluid and deadly as a blade, a weapon. He didn't hesitate, he didn't pause, he didn't stop. They had made him into a killing machine when they took him from Amberes all those years ago. They had bound him in service to the Crown, and unleashed him to slaughter their enemies at their whim.

He had even killed for her. And she had thanked him for it.

She'd just done something that was not only stupid but could be construed as a threat to the queen. The woman who owned him. How could she forget that?

'Don't,' he growled, soft and dangerous. His voice rippled through her body. 'Not another word. Especially not here.'

He was right. She was stupid and he was right and she hated it. She'd almost said the unthinkable, right here in the heart of the palace where anyone could hear them. Words that could see them both dead, and the queen too. Words that could also bring war on Amberes and destruction on the kingdom. She cursed against his hand, contemplated biting him anyway, but decided he'd just enjoy it and she wasn't going to be able to shake him off. He'd have to decide to let her go.

'Lyta,' he murmured. 'You have to be more careful.'

'When you two are quite finished,' General Vasquez's voice was cool and calm and made every hair on the back of Lyta's imperilled neck stand up. Had she heard too? No, she couldn't have.

Lyta would already be dead if that was the case. Not even Sylvian would be able to stop it.

The general knew the score as well as any of them. The woman was the power behind the throne, a master strategist. No wonder Francisco had left her here to guard the queen.

And yes, Lyta might be jealous of Annika and her hold over Sylvian, but when you got down to it, she was an Aspect of a goddess, and he was her champion. A paladin. Those kinds of bonds went far deeper than anything Lyta could forge with him. Ever.

She might steal him for a night, but he was never going to be hers. Never again. Why did her treacherous body make her forget that? She was smarter than this. And she was bound to a god too, a trickster and a thief. That had to count for something.

Slowly, she nodded and felt Sylvian's muscles loosen enough that she wasn't actually in fear of her life anymore.

'Be careful, Lyta,' he murmured, soft now. 'Please.'

Oh good, she thought, *manners, now he has manners*, and tore herself free of him as fast as she could.

'Her majesty will see you now,' said Vasquez, as if nothing untoward was happening at all.

She'd tell the queen what she knew and get the hell out of the Rose Palace and as far away from Sylvian Chant as she could. This had been a mistake. That was clear. She didn't need so brutal a reminder but there you had it.

The general was studying her. 'You may want to change first.'

Lyta glanced down at her worn jerkin and breeches, the boots that could do with polishing. Her own clothes. What she always wore. 'I don't think so.'

'The whole court is gathered.'

Lyta stared at the woman, who regarded her with an expression like stone. What was she thinking? They weren't going to blurt out details about the Imperial Church, dead children and gods and Viola Alderton in front of the whole court. No one wanted that.

'I can't make this report in front of a whole load of people, general.'

'You aren't going to be making the report yet, Cornellis. That will come later. This is a presentation. We have a problem and you'll help us fix it.'

Another one?

'What kind of problem?'

'A political one. Someone has been . . . indiscreet. I'll find out who eventually, but in the meantime we need to do something. And fast. Ystara has decreed it, apparently and Annika is determined. Your protection is paramount to her now, and she has need of your service in return. Sylvian, bring her with you and present your petition. Now. Before this whole thing gets out of hand.'

Something felt off about this. If Sylvian noticed, he said nothing, the mantle of the perfect soldier back in place once more.

Lyta, Eninn murmured to her. *Something's wrong.*

Oh shut up, Lyta thought at him as hard as she could and her own frustration and fear making her sharp. *That's all you ever say.* She was sick of this. Sick of palaces and queens and everything else. She didn't belong here and neither did Syl. Captain Chant, on the other hand, Captain Sylvian Chant . . . he did. Eninn was right again. Something was wrong. Not just the larger situation. Everything was wrong but this was a new development in the general wrongness.

What had Ystara decreed? She was here to give a report. Nothing more. There was no mention of political problems or being expedient, or petitioning for anything.

So why was the general eyeing her up like she was fresh meat?

'I think . . .' She stepped back towards the door. 'I think I'll just head home. I'll be safe enough there with Kit. Besides, he needs me. You never know what kind of trouble he'll get himself into when I'm not around. You really seem to have everything in hand and you don't need me to—'

'Nonsense, you're a royal employee, remember?' the general said in a voice that would not accept any argument. 'I'll be right behind you. Don't worry.'

Right behind her meant that Lyta couldn't instantly bolt in the other direction, even if she could have made it out of the antechamber. Even if Sylvian didn't have a death grip on her.

'What is going on?' she whispered to him.

He had a long-suffering expression on his face as he glanced at the general who nodded encouragingly and shooed them forward. 'I find it easiest not to ask too many questions and play along,' he replied.

'And that's worked out well for you so far, has it?'

A brief smile flickered over his mouth. And gods, the things she wanted to do with that mouth. A wave of need swept over her, pure lust which shook its way through her, followed by a very different sensation, a cold wash of dread.

Ystara, stop it! That was Eninn, a cry of outrage.

No. Lyta's mind flinched back from all of this, whatever it was. Too many gods, too many plans within plans, too much going on and she had no idea about half of it. They were trying to manipulate her and she didn't like it. Not just the queen, and the general. The gods as well.

'Syl,' Lyta whispered urgently. 'Your *friend* is interfering again and my *friend* doesn't like it.'

'I know. But I don't have the direct contact that you do.' His jaw was a hard line. A muscle twitched in it. 'General? What *is* going on?'

'I shouldn't have to give an order twice,' General Vasquez said curtly. 'Your queen is waiting, Chant. Move, and take your beloved with you.'

His *what?*

Sylvian paused, narrowed his eyes momentarily. Then he twined Lyta's arm around his and all but dragged her through the door.

Eninn? Lyta hissed. *What is going on? What is Ystara doing?*

She's . . . she's . . . Oh . . . That wasn't a good 'oh'. It was full of sudden understanding and agreement and things she didn't want to think about. It was a sound that made the bottom drop out of her stomach—the sound of two gods conspiring.

In the royal reception room beyond the antechamber it felt like half the nobility of Amberes were gathered. People packed together on either side, drinking sparkling wine from long glasses and eating tiny little fancies from large silver trays carried around by slightly harried servants. It was some kind of party, or reception, or . . . the gods alone knew what. Musicians were poised in the balconies, not playing anything at the moment but ready to do so. They seemed to have been interrupted and were shifting about awkwardly, trying to get a better view of whatever was going on beneath them. Everyone was, in fact. All the court, all the servants.

The stained-glass windows gave the room the appearance of a shrine, the light ethereal as it splashed across the walls and floor. The sense of Ystara was very strong now. When had she become so powerful? Annika sat perched on a dais, very pale all in jet-black, her stomach round and her feet propped up on a tiny stool, talking to a nobleman with a face on him like a smug peacock. She didn't look like an Aspect of a goddess. Just a very small, tired and irritable woman.

I know him, Lyta thought looking at the man. *How do I know him?* His eyes fixed on her as she and Sylvian were ushered through the gap in the throng, all eyes upon them. No, she'd never seen him before, but there was something so familiar about him.

Beatriz stood on the other side of the queen, dressed in a dark blue velvet trimmed with silver, a gown as fine as any other there, but her features were tight with stress. That couldn't be good either. The man on the other side of the queen glared at her. And Lyta recognised him now, who he had to be. She could see the resemblance. Older, harder, the man Sylvian had spoken of in such glowing terms. From the resemblance to Beatriz he was obviously an Alvarez.

'This really is a pressing matter, majesty.' His Andalusian accent was far more pronounced than Beatriz and Ben's. 'My cousin must see sense or I will be forced to—'

'Forced to do what, Baron de Marasso?' Annika's voice had that familiar cold edge that Lyta knew spelled trouble.

This was not good.

The veneer of politeness dropped from the nobleman's features. exposing a schoolmaster facing down an impudent child. 'You know very well what will happen if others learn what I know,' he hissed, loud enough for every ear in the place to crane towards him, longing for whatever scandal he had to share. Then he drew himself back and almost preened as if he'd already got what he wanted with that threat alone. 'All I ask is that you impress on my cousin that she must marry as I instruct her.'

'I do not agree to this,' Beatriz responded. 'I am the head of our House, cousin. Not you. I will pick my own husband, in my own good time, as is our way.'

Oh gods, poor Beatriz, Lyta thought. Was this what it was all about? Of course Ystara would take offence at this. Her cousin was trying to force her to marry and take control of House Alvarez through whatever stooge he foisted on her. And he'd chosen here, of all places, in front of the whole court to do it? No wonder Beatriz looked both mortified and outraged. She hid it well, but she wasn't fooling Lyta.

'Nonsense,' Annika trilled as if it was all a tremendous joke. Beatriz looked surprised but Lyta saw it for what it was—a calculated ploy, because nothing the queen did was without reason. This was designed deliberately to annoy him. And it worked. The queen was an Aspect too, of Ystara, the Goddess of Love.

Marasso's voice was almost a snarl, a man used to giving orders and not being dismissed. 'I warn you, my lady—'

Warn her? That was a poor choice of words. Unerringly his glare went to the other end of the room, onto Sylvian. His eyes were cold, and oh so knowing.

Shit, Lyta thought. *That. He knows about that.*

But *how*? And was he trying to blackmail the queen? Right out in the open like a fucking amateur? Someone had been indiscreet, the general had said. Did they think it was her? Did they think she'd blabbed about Sylvian and the queen and . . . oh gods defend her!

She'd almost blurted it out in the antechamber. Was that why she'd been hauled in here like this?

No. This was more. Eninn was roiling around in her head, up to something. He was always up to something. She knew that better than anyone. The gods played games of their own with human lives and Eninn and Ystara were no different. They had done it before and would again. She knew that.

But it felt like more, so much more.

'Warn me?' Annika replied, her voice a dagger of ice wrapped in that blanket of apparently light mirth. 'Oh *good*. I'm *so* glad. Warnings are *so* important, don't you think? Otherwise terrible things can happen. Very suddenly.' The tone on those last two words was not pleased, not in the slightest and if you could see past the beauty of her smile, her eyes were as hard as granite now.

'Let me tell you what I believe, what I have always believed. No one should be forced to marry, my dear baron. Not by family, not by necessity, and certainly not by me.' She pitched her voice so it filled the room. Everyone was already watching. Now they were transfixed and Lyta felt the power of the goddess fill the room. 'As you all know, Ystara guides me. Love is the only reason I will accept for any match. I was fortunate in my choice of marriage and wish all the same joy.' As a princess there hadn't actually been much choice for her, Lyta thought. She might love Francisco now, or have persuaded herself that she did. But choice? Lyta doubted it.

Her husband wasn't here, Lyta's racing mind supplied. Her husband wasn't her champion and had definitely not put that baby inside her. The queen hadn't married for love. She'd married for politics and she knew it. Her body wasn't even her own anymore. If it came down to a choice in the birthing bed of saving the baby or saving the queen . . . well, Francisco was young. He could marry again. The eligible princesses of the world would be lining up.

Annika waved one delicate hand at Lyta and Sylvian. 'Here is my most faithful bodyguard, who you tell me you value as a son, who has put aside his own ambitions in that area to serve us both for many years. Regard his lady and tell me do they not deserve the same felicity I enjoy with my most royal husband?'

Marasso fixed his glare on Lyta now, along with everyone else in the court, and panic welled up in her chest. Because the little she knew of Queen Annika was that the woman was a political animal who was never to be underestimated. And definitely not ambushed like this. Creatures like her were at their most dangerous when backed into a corner.

Did no one else understand that? Certainly not this arsehole.

But why was Annika doing this? What on earth was she talking about? What fairy tale was the queen spinning about her and Sylvian? And to what ends?

Lyta tried to stop. Sylvian pulled her forward, right up to the foot of the throne.

'You are going to pay for this,' she told him in as low a voice as she could muster.

'I know. But that'll have to be later.' He was just as quiet in return. His face was fixed on the queen, a picture of duty and stoicism.

'I will kill you in your sleep.'

'Promises, promises.'

'Shut up.'

'Gladly. I suggest you do the same if we want to get through this in one piece.' The problem was, he was right. And she hated that.

He went down on one knee and bowed his head and Lyta had no choice but to sink down beside him because he still had a death grip on her arm. She didn't curtsey. She was in breeches and a doublet. She'd look ridiculous.

More ridiculous than she already did. Maybe she should have taken the general up on that offer to change. It might have bought some time. But then she'd look just as ridiculous while also wearing a stupid gown. She didn't know any of this was going to happen. She wouldn't have had time to get away.

Eninn, what's happening? Oh she had an idea. She'd gone from one use to another. She was being used no matter what and she hated it. And her little god was not answering.

Worse, Sylvian was letting it happen. He was aiding and abetting in this travesty. They both were.

'Gentlefolk of Amberes,' said the queen in a voice like music that carried over the crowd and snared every single scrap of attention. 'You join us on a happy day. And at this time of year, it is fitting that we grant the dearest wishes of those faithful to us. It is our tradition, is it not? His grace, the Baron de Marasso, has reminded us of the joy of our marriage and we wish to share that joy. His niece has not yet made her own match, despite his determined efforts, but one day she no doubt will, and I would never force someone to wed without their consent.'

Like hell you wouldn't, Lyta thought as something the size and shape of a brick wedged itself in her throat. *If it suited you, you'd force a thousand weddings on someone. Anyone. You and your goddess both.*

'But I am of a mind to grant a petition today. Our faithful guard, Captain Sylvian Chant, hero of Montalbeau and Gravenenga, a true son of Amberes, sworn blood brother of our noble husband, and your king, beloved servant of us both—' She smiled at Sylvian with something like genuine affection. You couldn't mistake that, or fake it. Not this close. And the language she used, that could be misconstrued in so many ways, but she was doing it deliberately because . . . because . . .

Because if anyone said, 'She called him beloved', she could point to blood brother, faithful and hero . . . Because this was all an act and it was designed for her benefit, wasn't it? A performance. A show. Because words were Annika's weapons.

Eninn, help me. You have to get me out of this. Lyta could feel the trap closing. Eninn didn't answer.

'Some months ago our beloved Captain Sylvian Chant petitioned us to wed. As all here know his loyalty is unwavering and his heart is true. But it is a heart which is being pulled in more than one direction. His childhood sweetheart, Lyta Cornellis of your own Amberes, with whom he only reunited recently, and with whom he faced great peril in Montalbeau as they unveiled the treachery of Duchess Iseult against your king, is here with him today.

And Sylvian, I will hear your plea. I know what both of you have sacrificed in our service. Speak.'

A murmur ran around the court. Some of them knew this, more did not. It didn't matter. It was a show to them now, a performance and the queen was the Master of Ceremonies. Ystara was pulling the strings and probably drawing power from it. Love was her weapon, wasn't it? No wonder she was suddenly so bloody strong. They each had roles to play, even if Lyta barely recognised who the queen was describing apart from her own name. Montalbeau and the events there had been secret, but after the attack on the southern end of the city, which had led to the death of the duchess and the king's retribution on the Scholars' Tower, rumours had spread like wildfire. Francisco had naturally denied it all, which only made things worse. This was Amberes, after all.

Sylvian, Lyta thought desperately. *Don't you dare. Do not absolutely in any way, shape, or form dare. Please!*

'Majesty,' he said, ignoring the way Lyta's fingers dug like iron into his arm. Not that it made a difference. His muscles were so tense it was like she was trying to hammer those nails into even more iron. 'I am your willing servant, sworn to my king with my life's blood, now and always. I ask nothing more than to do my duty at your will and his.'

He didn't say anymore. And Lyta almost allowed herself to breathe again.

'And yet you have a request—one long-unspoken,' Annika said in that musical voice that wound itself around them. Ystara's power rippled through her words, shone through her skin. Did no one else see that? Or were they dazzled? She had every member of her court in the palm of her hand, didn't she? Enchanted with her. 'Don't be shy Sylvian. I will grant it and gladly.'

No one could have doubted the confusion on his face. It might look like bewildered hope, but Lyta knew him better than that. He had no idea what the queen was doing.

But Lyta did.

'Then I will speak it for you if you cannot heave your heart into your mouth,' said Annika, her voice changing subtly then to carry all the formality of a priestess, all the power of the goddess she could channel at will. Ystara seemed to shimmer through her eyes now, pale as ice and snow in her far-off home. Light streamed through the windows high above her and fell about her as if it was divine light. All around the audience chamber, people stared, struck by the wonder of the moment and Lyta knew that news of it would spread far and wide in no time at all. It was like a fairy tale, and the gods knew, the people of Amberes loved a fairy tale.

The city would know, the country and all the rest of the world, that Annika, Queen of Aragón, León, Castile and the Brabantine, Princess of Geatland, and whatever other titles they could add to her name like a series of invocations, spoke with the voice of a goddess of love and that word was law. That no one could undo this. No one would seek to try. No one but Lyta.

'And grant it too,' the queen continued. 'You are given leave to marry, and we will gift you a wedding fit for champions of this city. We will grant you lands and titles and you will be happy together. Has anyone a just reason why they may not be wed? Speak it now. This is my will, the will of my lord and husband, Francisco, your king, and the will of our divine lady, Ystara.'

Had everyone lost their damned minds? If Sylvian wasn't going to put a stop to his, she would. She had to.

You'll be safe here, Eninn told her, his voice no more than a murmur but as clear as if he stood right beside her. *This is for the best. You'll see. We've discussed it, Ystara and I. You can stay here, in the palace, and the Inquisitor won't be able to touch you. Rhiannon won't be able to embroil you in her mess. You'll be safe. He can keep you safe, in here. We can protect you. I'm sorry Lyta. I can't risk the Imperator taking us, either of us.*

What was he doing? What did he think he was doing?

Lyta opened her mouth to speak. To argue. To fight tooth and claw against being used in this manner by anyone, not by a queen, not by the man who supposedly loved her, not by her god, especially not at a time like this when they had so many other things to be dealing with.

But in that moment Eninn stole her voice away.

CHAPTER TWENTY

Kit

Kit sat in the middle of the printshop with the same pitiful bottle of brandy, having pushed aside one of the huge presses, and pried up the floorboards underneath. He didn't mean to. That's what he kept telling himself. But he'd drunk most of what was left in the bottle already and his head was spinning so it was better to sit down. And once he sat down he was close enough to the floor that it seemed like a good idea to dig up the bloody book anyway. He wasn't sure why. Perhaps it was calling him. It did that sometimes, in his nightmares, and in his daydreams, or when he was distracted, in those moments when he was alone. His imagination, he had always told himself, but now he wasn't so sure. What did that matter? Maybe the book could magically solve all his problems, had he considered that? And perhaps he wanted to look at it because right now it felt like the closest that he was ever going to get to Ben again.

Perhaps he was an idiot. That seemed like the most likely thing.

He'd hidden it for a reason. Right now he couldn't remember what that was.

He'd wrapped it in tissue paper and then in a soft cloth. As he peeled back the various layers, he saw the blue and gold binding, some of Jem's finest work. His blunt fingers brushed against the cover, as if it was his lover's skin.

It wasn't. And he would never touch Ben's skin again.

His stomach twisted. He was an idiot. A drunken idiot. A drunken unlovable idiot.

He had been a fool to think otherwise. He'd been so worried about hurting Ben, about not being good enough for him, and it turned out Ben thought he was a danger to Kit. It was laughable.

And he *wasn't* good enough for Ben, was he? Because he couldn't reassure the Seigneur of House Alvarez that he wasn't going to be in danger again, or that Ben couldn't hurt him.

Because Ben could hurt him. So easily. He just . . . he just had.

Kit knew he wasn't thinking right either, that the brandy which burned its way down his throat was making everything worse. Right now he didn't care.

His world was upside down and back to front, like the letters he'd loaded up in the compositor's stick to place so carefully in the galley when he printed this godforsaken thing. He had laid it all out in the chase, adding the spacing and framing pieces before tightening the quoins to hold everything securely together. Oh yes, he could do that. If only he could manage to hold his life together as easily. Those phrases were fixed forever now and he was falling apart. And yet he had printed them, those magical words that glowed and danced before his eyes and swept his mind away. He and Ben together, they had created this. And now Ben was gone and this was all he had left. Gods, he wanted something now that would sweep his mind away, and with it his pain.

So he opened the book and tried to read it again. Or rather, tried to focus his vision on the swirling letters and images it displayed to him.

He hadn't tried to read *The Book of Gold* since Ben first transcribed it. That had ended up with him senseless and on his knees. The typesetting job hadn't been as bad because he could focus on individual letters and words rather than sentences. He could use the frisket to block out half of it if he needed to and there hadn't been a lot of time for proofreading.

No one else seemed to have had a problem with it though. Jem had given him the funniest look when he asked if anything had happened. The bookbinder dealt with the exterior of a book, with the physical structure. He didn't much care about the content, not like Kit. When he asked Molly she had told him he should leave well enough alone and changed the subject, so perhaps she understood best of all.

Ben had understood. Ben had taken the manuscript from his trembling hands and told him it was going to be all right. That he would be all right.

But he wasn't. They weren't. They were over.

Kit knocked back more of the brandy and felt it punch the air from his lungs before burning a path down to his churning stomach.

'My word,' said Stirling. 'You are in a state.'

For a moment Kit thought he was imagining things. Kit hadn't bothered to light any lamps inside. All he had to see by was a flickering candle on the windowsill that had almost burned down. And the glow of *The Book of Gold*. Any other light came from the lanterns across the street. Stirling was a black hole in the doorway.

But Kit still recognised him. Couldn't fail to. He had come back.

'I locked that door,' he said, forcing his voice to be crisp and precise. He couldn't bear to let Stirling see him like this. Not when he was always so bloody perfect.

'I'm sure you did, Kit. I have a way with locks.'

'Nothing special about that,' Kit replied. Lyta had never met a lock she couldn't open. Even Kit had picked one or two in his time, not that he used that particular shady skill now.

His thoughts tangled on one another. Stirling shut the door behind him too firmly and something in the back of Kit's mind squirmed, something that knew danger when it approached.

Stirling had used him to wake the hand, had overpowered him, cut him . . .

And until he showed up Ben had been his. It might not have been perfect, but at least it had been . . . *something.*

Lord Stirling picked up the stub of the candle on the windowsill and used it to light one of the lamps, bringing it over to Kit.

'May I see?' Stirling asked.

Kit snapped the book shut and folded his arms around it, pressing it into his chest. 'What do you want, Piers?'

Stirling spread his arms wide. 'Just to apologise. I feel I caused a problem between you and Benedictus. That was never my intention. I got carried away with the need to find . . .'

His voice trailed off. The glare Kit sent his way should have made him burst into flames if there was any justice in the world. It didn't though and Kit thought miserably that this summed up his whole day.

'I don't want your apology. Go away.'

Stirling didn't. He sat down beside Kit on the floor, ignoring the hole in the floorboards and peered at the book in Kit's hands. 'Beautiful work. The binding I mean. Really, a work of art.'

Kit let his gaze drop to the azure Moroccan leather and the gilt decorations which traced their path over the cover, delicate gold-tooled dentelles of flowers and vines, and a rather elegant clasp. He didn't know where Jem had got that but he'd said it felt right. Perhaps the book had been speaking to him too, in its own way. He'd even gilded the edges of the pages. They gleamed in the lamplight.

'Jem's an artist,' Kit told him. 'I'm lucky he puts up with me.'

'Your work is famous, Kit. He's lucky to have you too. Without Typis Cornellis, he'd just be a bookbinder. A talented one, no doubt, but let's be honest, there are a lot of binders out there. Not as many printers. Few with your skill and certainly no others here with the king's warrant.'

Kit wrinkled his nose, suspicious. But nothing Stirling was saying was wrong exactly. It just struck him as a weird way of looking at it all.

'That was more accident than anything else. Besides, Ben was the one who—'

Who had talked Francisco into it, who'd spoken almost as quickly and convincingly as Lyta in that tower room where Kit would have said something stupid and ruined everything. Ben had brought him this far. And now he was gone.

'And how goes that great work?' Stirling asked.

What great work? The book? Well, not alchemy anyway. Kit didn't want to ever hear anything about alchemy again.

And the book wasn't going. It wasn't going at all. And without Ben it wouldn't. 'I'm still waiting on Ben's latest revised manuscript,' he mumbled, not wanting to say any more on the subject. Neither of the book or his former lover.

Former. That word stabbed at him even as he thought of it. His eyes stung and he looked away.

'Ah, yes,' Stirling had a laugh buried in his voice. It was gentle and kindly, but it was still a laugh. 'We scholars are known for that kind of thing.'

'What kind of thing?'

'Procrastination. I heard tell of a printer so desperate for the text that he ended up locking the author up in a room above his print-shop until it was done. Can I buy you another one of those?' He nodded at the empty bottle of brandy. Kit wasn't aware he'd finished it but he didn't care. Not anymore.

'No, it was awful. Lyta picked it up somewhere.' He didn't add that she had probably literally picked it up without any coin changing hands at all. He sighed, relenting. 'You can buy us a good bottle instead.'

He bent to replace the book in its hollow, realised that Stirling knew where that was now and froze. Why was Stirling here? Not out of concern for him. Or to buy him a drink. *The Book of Gold* was a thing of power, however. It might hold the answers he needed. And Kit knew Stirling would do anything to find Viola Alderton. Was that why he was really here? Of course it was.

But before either of them could say anything there was a knock at the door.

'Are you expecting anyone?' Stirling asked. That cool confidence seemed to have fled all of a sudden.

Kit shook his head. 'I wasn't even expecting you.' He hauled himself up, pausing only to make sure he was steady on his feet, and crossed to the shop floor.

He opened the door and peered into the dimly lit street outside.

A child stood there, lightly clad despite the snow which drifted down around him. It settled on his mousey brown hair and melted, dampening it, darkening it. He stood unnaturally still, without even shivering. He had to be freezing, but it didn't show.

'Are you all right?' Kit asked gently. He didn't *look* right and he was going to catch his death of cold standing out there like that. 'Are you lost?'

He wore the uniform of a Blacksmiths' Guild apprentice, the crest on his chest picked out in careful embroidery. Around his neck there was a chain of dark metal from which dangled a pendant. No, an amulet, marked with symbols Kit had seen earlier this evening in *The Book of Gold*. Something glimmered through the metal, gold and silver which seemed to move of its own volition, like threads or gossamer.

Kit blinked. It was a boy, although it was almost hard to tell. His face seemed to shift as Kit watched him, neither male nor female, young and shining with innocence. With otherness.

No, Kit thought, taking half a step backwards as his brain caught up with what he was actually seeing.

Just shining.

The light wasn't coming from the lanterns on the other side of the road. They were cold and dark now. It came from the child. The way Ben sometimes shone when the gods inside him became restless. When they took over and Ben was gone.

An amulet hung around the boy's neck like one of the ones Ben made.

But this child wasn't Ben.

Kit swallowed hard and hugged *The Book of Gold* closer, his fingernails digging into the leather so hard that a vague and distant part of his mind knew he'd leave marks, damage it, and then Jem would be so disappointed. But his body didn't seem to care.

The glowing child in the street held out his hand and waited.

'Piers,' Kit said, as the effect of the alcohol drained away and he dearly wished he had more. Fear made him sober, his stomach sick, and he did not like it one bit. His voice was as calm as he could manage right now, and that was not very calm. 'You need to go and get help. Get Ben.' No, not Ben. This was far too dangerous for Ben. Besides, Ben didn't want anything to do with him anymore. And Ben had made that amulet, his mind tried to tell him. Ben had made the thing hanging around the boy's neck—a thing designed to contain a god. 'Lyta. Get Lyta.'

Lyta would know what to do, wouldn't she? She was far more cunning than someone like Ben could ever hope to be. And if she didn't know, Eninn would.

He had to.

Please, Eninn, please, if you ever cared about either of us . . .

It wasn't quite a prayer. Kit wasn't sure a prayer would help right now.

But Stirling stepped past Kit and through the door, lifting his hands like a priest.

'Hail to you, Lord of the Crossings. Blessings shine on this night and—'

'The book,' said the child, ignoring Stirling entirely. The ground beneath them trembled. The snow spun around in whorls and spirals, no longer falling but buffeted in unnatural directions by another force. It hit Kit in the face and he found himself outside now. He wasn't even aware he'd left the shop, but he was standing in the street, out in the snow with only Stirling shielding him.

'I would have your name first,' Stirling replied, his voice darker, prickling with the kind of power Kit remembered from the Magister. He reached into his jerkin and pulled out a small vial of silver. Kit recognised the twisting coil of liquid metal inside. It was reacting to the child in the same way it had to the hand. 'It would be a shame if this escaped. It might call to that around your neck and disrupt it. It might open the veil and toss you back through.'

The child hesitated, its gaze now locked warily on the vial. Had Stirling just threatened a god?

No, this wasn't possible. This was a nightmare, or Kit was seeing things because he'd drunk far too much cheap brandy.

'Names are for mortals.' The scathing tone in so young a voice was unnerving.

'So are bodies like that one.' Stirling took another step forward into the slush of Twelfth Moon Street and Kit wanted to warn him, to tell him this was a terrible idea.

The child lifted his chin, defiant.

'I am Tamfana and this form is mine now. Freely given.'

'But that child is no Aspect or Nexus.'

'No. And yet it is mine. Your people work wonders, alchemist.'

'Only for a short time and the price is great.'

'Speak not of prices, mortal. My people died in their thousands for me. I am surely due one life. Besides I am not here to treat with you. I will treat only with him, the get of a lost god.'

He pointed at Kit with an unwavering finger and smiled again, so ancient and knowing a smile mismatched with so young a face.

Kit fought to retreat back inside, to get back into his shop and slam the door, but he couldn't move, fixed as he was in the glare of those bright and shining eyes.

The get of a lost god.

'I don't—' he started, swallowed hard and had to try again. 'I don't know what you mean.'

The smile spread, staining the innocence with something old and awful.

What had they said of the older gods? He'd always dismissed the tales of their bloodthirsty ways as propaganda. The Church Imperial had fought them and slaughtered them and then vilified anyone connected with them.

But now, seeing that expression, he wasn't so sure.

There was a vicious and sadistic pleasure in the eyes of that shining child.

'He is not for you either.' Stirling put out an arm and Kit found himself bumping into it. He hadn't even been aware he was moving again. He stopped, planting his feet firmly in the snow and fought to breathe. Was Tamfana doing this? Controlling him?

'When I give the word, can you run?' Stirling asked in a murmur, a calm enough question despite the words.

Not likely. If this child deity told him to crawl on his knees right now he suspected he'd drop and thank him for the privilege. It was more unnerving than he would have thought. Kit had never been religious but the raw power radiating off the small form rattled him to the core.

He swallowed hard, shook his head and ground his fingers into the surface of the book. He wasn't one to run away from a problem but right now running wasn't even possible. 'I can't.'

'Right then,' Stirling said, as if it was no more than a casual hitch in whatever grand plan he was weaving. He might not sound pleased about it but he wasn't going to let that stop him. It was a scant comfort. Kit managed to glance his way and saw his expression fixed and stony. 'Then you need to talk to it because it isn't going to listen to me. You, on the other hand . . . I don't know what it means but the hand responded to you as well. Something came through, something old and powerful, and it wanted you. And now this . . . We are going to have a very long conversation about you, Kit Cornellis, understand? As soon as it's convenient, anyway. But right now I'm going to tell you what to say. Repeat the words after me. Banishments are never fun and I fear this thing will not go quietly.'

This couldn't be happening. Kit wasn't going to be told what to do and what to say. Not by this child-god and not by Piers bloody Stirling. Lords and gods had no say over his life. The stab of rage made him stiffen, so alien to his nature and beneath his hands *The Book of Gold* warmed, the leather melding against his fingers. It was almost comforting. A part of him.

Whatever Stirling was going to say, another ripple ran through the air and the earth, like distant thunder, shaking the firmament. The child suddenly stepped back and froze, his face contorting first with shock and then rage. His bright eyes fixed on Kit and he snarled.

'No!'

The thunder in the air grew louder and the ground shook beneath them. Kit staggered back. 'What is it? What's happening?'

'This body is too weak,' the child growled. The amulet around his neck glowed, grew brighter, as if heating up. And suddenly the arrogance fled. The god in the human body looked scared. 'It cannot contain . . . I can't . . . I can't . . . Help me, Cornellis. I demand it. It is my right, my—'

The boy clawed at his chest, trying to get to the burning amulet to tear it off, and then, with a sickening crunch he arched backwards as if an unseen force grabbed his head and pulled. His chest wrenched itself open with a crunch of breaking bone and a splattering of blood, as something burst through from inside. Light coalesced in a will-o'-the-wisp that shot skywards. High above the roofs of Amberes it burst apart, the fragments falling like embers among the snowflakes.

The amulet shattered and the child fell back, lifeless and godless.

The street was suddenly completely silent. Snow continued to fall.

'Shit!' said Stirling abruptly. He dropped to his knees, grabbing the chain with the broken amulet. The silver in between the cracks, or whatever it was, had slithered away, gone with whatever quintessence of a dead god had inhabited the child. 'Shit, Kit. We have to get out of here. They'll be coming. Now!'

But Kit still couldn't move. 'Is he dead?'

Of course he was dead. What a stupid question. No one alive had a gaping hole like that in the middle of their chest.

He stared at the body and felt his knees begin to give. He wanted to close the kid's eyes. They were fixed sightlessly on the falling snow and the clouds and the darkness of the night. It wasn't right. Kit reached out.

'Don't touch him.' Stirling grabbed Kit's arm and pulled him away, through the snow and the slush which even now was turning scarlet. This time, Kit didn't even think of resisting. 'Hide that.' He shoved Kit's old red scarf into his hands. He must have grabbed it from inside while Kit stared numbly at the corpse. Kit hastily wrapped it around *The Book of Gold* with shaking hands. Stirling all but shoved him into a coat.

In seconds they were sprinting down Twelfth Moon Street and down towards Brewer's Lane. He hadn't a clue where their destination lay. And to be honest, he didn't care.

'It wanted the book,' Kit yelled, breathless. He was still clinging to it with one arm, crushing it against his chest as he ran. It felt like his own heartbeat, slamming against his body. The scarf didn't contain it.

'Probably sensed it the moment you opened it and came. It's powerful, more so than any relic I've ever seen. I had no idea how powerful. But he wanted you as well. Didn't you see that? You and the book. Down here. Quick.'

'He called me the *get of a lost god*.'

'I know. Try not to think about that.'

'*How can I not think about that?*' It came out as a snarl.

A *get* meant a bastard. At least in the street slang of Amberes it did. Did gods use slang?

'It's a bloodline thing,' Stirling said, pulling him down a laneway which he thought led towards the houses at the back of Swift Street, but he wasn't even sure which way they were running now. Or what they were running from. Something. Something terrible. 'I suspected it but . . . It's just— Look, I'll explain later.'

'You know what he was talking about?'

'I know. I promise. I know all sorts of things. Ben should have told you. He was probably afraid of how you'd react and I don't blame him, but he should have told you everything. He must have guessed, especially after the reaction of the hand in the cellar. He's a Divine Nexus. He draws gods to him.'

This time his voice came out as little more than a whimper. '*Ben knew?*'

How much had Ben kept from him? And why? Was this why he'd broken with him? To push him away? To protect him? Or get rid of him?

'Not now, Kit,' Stirling told him, all pretence at charm driven away by desperation. 'Just move. It isn't safe. Hold on to that book and stay with me, all right? We have to move. Whoever sent that thing won't be far away.'

'What was it?'

'A goddess. Tamfana. The August One destroyed her about 1,500 years ago. Wiped her followers from the face of the earth for good measure. And whoever brought her back is coming for us. They're getting closer.'

'Who are *they*?'

'The alchemists. Your city's alchemists, working with Charnock, in the Blacksmiths' Guild. Maybe others. He has a way of roping people into his schemes. Of finding out what they want and using that. This was his plan. This was always his plan, to reach out to the oldest ones, the really powerful ones. To bring them back and to trap them, to bend them to his will. To use the gods.'

He turned a corner into the narrow alley which was little more than a gap between buildings and led deeper into the heart of the Rookery. All Kit could do was follow.

CHAPTER TWENTY-ONE

Sylvian

'Did you know?'

The words were a cry of rage and betrayal such as he had never heard from Lyta before.

The sitting room in the eastern wing of the palace was beautiful, refined and far too small right at this moment.

Lyta turned on him the moment they were alone, the weird spell of silence which had come over her as they knelt before the queen well and truly broken.

'Lyta, please . . .' he tried to begin, but didn't get any further. She lunged forward, poking his chest with her finger. It didn't actually hurt, or have enough force to push him back. He stood there, trying to be patient with her, trying to wait, trying to see it from her side.

Because he did. Honestly he did.

This was not how any of this was supposed to go.

'Don't you *Lyta, please* me,' she snapped. 'What the fuck, Sylvian? What the actual fuck?'

Not exactly the way a man would hope the love of his life would respond to news of their impending marriage. But it wasn't the first time either. He heaved in a breath and fought not to grab her wrist and pull that poking finger away from him. Because if he touched her right now he wasn't sure what he'd do.

'She's the queen,' he said, as patiently as he could. His voice shook with the effort. 'I have to obey her.'

'You'll always pick her, won't you? Every time.'

The irony of that was not lost on him. 'Just like you will always choose Kit.'

'I have to. He's my brother!'

And this time he did yell. He couldn't help it. '*And she's my queen!*'

It shocked Lyta into silence for a moment and Sylvian tried to ignore the panic in her eyes, the way they darted around as she located the exits while at the same time making sure she knew exactly where he was too. He knew what she was doing—preparing for him to attack. Dear gods alive, did she think so little of him still? Did he blame her? He raked his hand through his hair and tried to pull himself together. He would never hurt her. Not willingly. But Lyta had seen too many men enraged in her life and instincts like that died hard.

Sylvian drew in a breath and then exhaled slowly, counting in his mind to calm himself. 'Lyta, Francisco is my *king* and she is his *wife*. I'm sworn to them by blood oaths. He carved those commands into my skin. Marasso showed him how, years ago.'

He shoved his arms out towards her, wrists upturned to show the old silvery scars from long ago. They were crossed by others, a lifetime of the sword and battle taking its toll on his skin. But they were still there.

Lyta stared, horrified and then drew back, repulsed, as understanding dawned. They were not dissimilar to Kit's, he supposed. Close enough to realise. But she said nothing.

'They mark me as the king's,' he whispered and he'd never felt it weigh so heavily on him.

Her touch was feather-light, a tentative caress. 'You had no choice. Not in any of it.'

He tried to smile. It was almost a relief to finally say it out loud to someone who didn't think it was to be expected, his duty, just and meet, or worse, an honour. 'Marasso did it first. Said that it was necessary if I didn't want to stay a conscript. I didn't understand what it was. Eventually he passed me on to Francisco and they did it again. But it binds me even now.'

'To Marasso?'

He shrugged and was about to drop his arms when she caught the right one and lifted his wrist to her lips. Her kiss on his skin was warm and gentle. It sent shivers of desire through him. And something else. A profound relief.

'To all of them in a way. But mostly to her, because of Ystara.' He pressed his hand to his chest, the ring cold around his finger. 'This. The two things combined . . . I don't know,' he managed at last. 'I didn't know and I still don't. Ystara is trying to protect you and this . . . This is the only way she knows how.'

'She has no right. I told you I couldn't marry you. I have responsibilities too, Sylvian. Kit needs me. I have to protect him. And not just Kit. I need . . . I need . . .' The words became gasps and she pulled his hand against her face, her tears warm and wet.

'What do you need?' he whispered, desperate for an answer. Because he wanted her and he knew she wanted him and it made no sense. 'Lyta, please, tell me.'

The words came out in a torrent. 'I need to keep *you* safe. I could never do that. I caused all our problems, I know that. And then I married Ranulf and got him killed, Sylvian. And I nearly lost you again. And again. And . . . and . . . I'll get you killed. I lost you before. I can't do it again.'

He stared at her in shock, unable to find his voice to reply. She thought she was protecting *him*? No, this was not how any of this was supposed to work. Lyta stared up at him, as if aware she had said far more than she had intended. Waiting for a reply. Dreading it.

His voice, when he could heave it into his mouth again, was carefully measured and gentle. Surprising even to himself. 'I swear to you on my life it won't come to that. On the queen's life. Lyta, you don't have to . . . I'm sorry. I will always be there for you. From this day on. I will always come for you.'

Lyta seemed to wilt a little at that, her eyes glistening, so blue, so bright, like forget-me-nots. He'd noticed those flowers when they camped on the road or before a battle, speckling in the long grass in the countryside, and had thought of her eyes for so many years. And hated every minute of the torment.

He had lost her once. And like Lyta, it had broken him. He couldn't lose her again. The same fear infected both of them, though they were trying to handle it in different ways. He only wanted to spend what was left of his life with her, looking after her, loving her, and yes, protecting her, as he always should have done. And Lyta, bless her, was trying to push him away in the belief it would keep him safe. She had always met a challenge by taking charge, by deciding what she thought was best and throwing herself into it regardless of what anyone else thought or wanted. And when it came to the people she cared about, there was nothing she wouldn't sacrifice. People like Kit. And him.

Even if the sacrifice was their happiness.

They had been forced into this. Annika and Ystara grasping at a solution and Eninn colluding, in order to protect Lyta from the Inquisitor, and perhaps Rhiannon as well. The gods always did what they willed, regardless of anyone else's wishes. And Ystara saw him as hers, her champion, and Lyta as . . . what? His reward?

The Baron of Marasso should never have forced Annika, and thereby Ystara, into a corner.

Marasso had been a good leader, Sylvian had always thought. What was he thinking now? Trying to bully the queen was never going to work. He had to have a reason, had to be doing it for her own good. Sylvian wanted to believe that. Surely the old man only wanted to protect Beatriz too by finding her a husband to protect her in this world. She was vulnerable in ways a man wouldn't be. Especially since the events with the duchess had weakened her. Beatriz didn't have the link to Eninn she once had and when she drew on the divine now, there was a greater cost. He knew that. Who wouldn't want to protect her?

'I hope you don't make a regular habit of swearing on my life,' said Annika from the doorway, her voice cool with disdain. He spun around, pulling free of Lyta, every ingrained instinct screaming at him as his bonds forced him to obey. Turning his back on Lyta, in favour of the queen, yet again, he cursed himself inwardly and knew there was no help for it. And it was another thing Lyta would blame him for. Rightly.

'Your majesty—'

The queen lifted one of her tiny, elegant hands and to his surprise waved his abortive apology away. 'Enough. I should be the one saying sorry. There was no choice. I had to shut that arrogant fool down and fast before he named you and me, and scandalised the whole court. We could never recover from that and Francisco would have no choice . . . It was the only thing I could think of and Ystara approved. Even Eninn agreed, I believe. Your own god, Lyta, wants nothing more than to protect you. And politically, you were . . . you were expedient, both of you, arriving when you did.'

Behind her, Vasquez and Juárez took up position on either side of the door. Beatriz followed them, making her way straight across the room to Lyta. She embraced the thief and somehow came away with all limbs intact. Lyta folded against her, her shoulders trembling and held on tight.

'It's my fault,' Beatriz said. 'I had no idea he'd found out anything, if indeed he really has, or was trying to bluff based on rumours, your majesty. My petition was never meant to cause this sort of trouble. He must believe he has support from my whole family to do such a thing. And others, far greater.'

She didn't say the king, but they were all thinking it.

Annika scowled. 'He's posturing for more than control of your House, Beatriz. When Francisco finds out what happened today there will be questions indeed. That was close. Far too close. The sooner the two of you are wed the better, to allay any rumours and suspicions he may stir up. It will not, alas, take care of everything, but it is a start and it saves face, which is the first—'

Lyta jerked back again, rounding on the queen. 'You don't get to decide that!'

There was a stunned and awkward silence. But Lyta wasn't repentant. More like enraged and Sylvian knew that in this mood she made the worst decisions. She always had.

'Lyta—' He tried one last desperate attempt to salvage what he could.

'No!' she shouted. 'The answer is no. You cannot tell me who to marry. I was married and I didn't get a choice in that either, and I am never going through that again. Do you hear me?'

Vasquez took a step towards her, but the queen shook her head and the general stopped, glowering at the thief.

Sylvian felt every word, every single one, like a knife in the guts. He couldn't show it. He couldn't move. He stared fixedly at Annika. Because if he looked at Lyta . . . if he made eye contact with her . . .

He hadn't felt so close to falling apart in thirteen years. And the last time, it had been her too. She'd left him behind and married Ranulf, but he'd found her again and he'd thought . . .

Gods, he was an idiot. Of course she didn't want him. He had ruined her life. Twice. He'd made her leave Ranulf to die as soon as she got him back. He was a monster made only to kill, entangled in blood magic and unbreakable oaths. He was bound to another woman, and dedicated to a goddess who wanted to run Lyta's life as well. He was more damaged than anyone else he knew. They both were.

Damaged goods, trapped in the machinations of gods and kings and who knew what else.

Annika cleared her throat and caught his attention immediately. Was she all right? In pain? Uncomfortable?

He winced. That was the other problem. He needed to protect her. Not just wanted to or was duty bound to do so. It was his first thought. Which meant Lyta would have to come second and she knew that. Exactly as she had said. They both knew it. Because Ystara willed it so.

'We can't do it,' he said, in a low, quiet voice that barely sounded like his own given his whirling thoughts. 'Majesty, it's not fair.'

Lyta glanced at him, surprise parting her lips.

'Life isn't fair, Sylvian,' Annika replied curtly. 'I thought perhaps you might have noticed. We all do what we must. And that includes you, Lyta Cornellis and Sylvian Chant. Enough.' She winced again. The next words came out almost breathless with pain. 'It is done. I have spoken. Ystara has spoken. The arrangements will be made.

You will be safe here inside the palace walls, Lyta, protected from those who seek to harm you. And here you will stay until . . . I—' Her words failed her, cut off by a sharp gasp.

Juárez caught her as she fell, yelling something Sylvian couldn't even process as he too surged forwards, swooping in with the need to protect her. Too late.

All was chaos as Vasquez barked out orders and they lifted her to a chaise. She was too pale and ungainly with pregnancy. There was something on the floor, not water, not blood either. He didn't know what it was and he didn't know what to do. She cried out, a desperate cry, her head thrown back.

'Beatriz,' he yelled. 'Beatriz, quickly!'

'The royal physicians—' Vasquez began.

'No time for it. Beatriz is right here. Now.' He had never countermanded a superior officer in his life but right now he didn't care. He'd deal with those repercussions later.

Beatriz didn't hesitate. Though she no longer had the power she had once wielded, she knew far more about healing than anyone else, magic or not. She was kneeling by Annika moments later, speaking to her in a rapid but calm voice, a song of reassurance and comfort as she pressed her hand to the queen's stomach, her face fixed in concentration.

'Send for boiling water and clean cloths,' she said. 'Now.'

'Lady Alvarez—' the general began uncertainly. This wasn't a battle to be won or a plot to be uncovered. She had no more experience of childbirth than Sylvian did. She was scared.

Beatriz rounded on her.

'I swear on the goddess Ystara, I'll do all I can. On all the gods of Amberes, if you wish it. They are with me, and Ystara guides me now. You have given all you can to her in service of this moment. Your physicians are little more than butchers. They'll cut our queen apart to get this child and you know it. Let me try to save both. Take my head if I fail.'

She shouldn't say such things. Francisco would do it. But of course, Sylvian realised, Beatriz knew that.

This was all happening too early. Not wildly early, but the queen should not be in labour yet. Her time was still weeks away. Sylvian had no real idea. Time seemed to have turned to jelly in his mind. He couldn't breathe. His chest locked and his heart thundered inside him. The ring on his finger burned like ice.

'Do it,' Annika snarled suddenly. She grabbed Beatriz's hands, knotting their fingers together, pulling the woman closer. 'Help me. Please. By my lady goddess and all her light. Help . . . But—but you have to save the child. You have to. Nothing else matters, Beatriz. Save the baby.'

'If I can, Annika.' She closed her eyes and that warm golden glow Sylvian knew too well seemed to seep in through the floor and ceiling, sliding through the air.

The door opened and closed as Juárez went for help and a pair of arms slipped around Sylvian's waist. Lyta pressed her face to his back, though she said nothing. Just held him.

'What do I do?' he asked.

'You keep out of the way,' Lyta said. 'And if they ask for anything, you do it. Okay? She's going to be all right, Sylvian. Beatriz will make sure of it. You know that. Women do this every day.'

Did he? He didn't know anything right now. How could he? He could feel the goddess panicking. Ystara had planned this for her own ends. Annika was her Aspect and Sylvian her champion, her Chosen. And this child was special. Boy or girl, it would inherit everything Francisco had to offer. They would be adored and loved and given anything they wished for. But more than that. This child was Ystara's and always would be. Sylvian was just the means to an end. Maybe they all were. King, queen and bodyguard. A goddess worked her own will.

And now he was useless. There was no one to fight, nothing to kill. He was a brute with a sword and skills which had no place here.

If they lost the child or the queen, or both, Francisco would kill every last one of them. And that was nothing to what their goddess would do.

'Breathe,' Lyta told him. 'You have to breathe.' How was she so calm?

Annika cried out again, the sound strangled and awful, like someone with a mortal wound on a battlefield, one of those lost souls that haunted his nightmares. His whole body stiffened.

'Look at me.' Lyta pulled him around to face her, pressed her hand to his face and made him do just that. To really look at her.

Her skin was pale, freckles standing out across her nose and her eyes, red-rimmed and still feverishly bright with tears, were calm now. 'Lyta?' he gasped, horrified at the weakness of his voice.

'I know, love. I know. Just . . . just come here.' She pulled him to the other side of the room and they sank down to sit against the wall, staring at the flurry of activity swirling around the chaise as screens were set up and hot water and towels brought in by white-faced servants. Beatriz was a bright glow, her eyes closed, her head bent over the queen. It was too much for her, Sylvian wanted to say. Too much of a strain. She didn't have the easy link to power she had once had. But no one, not even Beatriz, was going to listen to that now.

'Breathe,' she said, in a firm, clear voice, echoing what Lyta had said earlier, though her attention was all on Annika. It was a voice you wanted to believe in. A battlefield commander's voice. 'That's it. Breathe. Steady now, steady.'

Everything blurred around him. Everything except Lyta, and her voice telling him it would be all right, and her hands in his. She was his anchor in this storm and he clung to her.

Annika screamed again, a raw guttural noise of an animal in pain. He'd heard people talk about the wonders of childbirth, about the beauty and the simplicity but this . . . this was none of those things. Perhaps it was all a lie so women didn't refuse entirely to get pregnant ever again.

Too many died, he thought grimly. As many as soldiers. More, if you counted them all up. In peace, in war, in their droves.

If she died—his heart almost wrenched out from inside him—if she died . . .

'Push,' Beatriz commanded. 'Push Annika. Now!'

Another snarled cry, raw and terrible and then . . . the honeyed light was so bright, filling the room and everyone in it, drawing on something in each of them. Sylvian could smell lavender and gardenias, he was sure of it. Not scented oil in water, or a fragrance wafted through the room, but the actual scent of living flowers in full bloom. At the same time he knew that it wasn't natural, wasn't real, that it came from somewhere other and divine.

'Ystara, save them,' he whispered. 'My lady, please save them. I'll do anything. You know I will. Anything you want.' The ring seemed to tighten on his finger and he knew he'd regret that somehow, that she'd exact a price. She always did. But right now he couldn't bring himself to care.

And then there was another cry, sharp and outraged, like a cat or a bird, a sound so alien to his world that it brought him back up to his feet as if he was hooked on a line.

He heard Annika sob, and Beatriz murmured something to her and his vision almost went, blurred at the edges. It felt like something finally tore inside him, something so deep that he didn't even know what it was. Part of him. Definitely part of him.

But it wasn't part of him anymore.

His child was crying, a high, plaintive wail.

'Lyta?' His voice grated inside his throat.

Her hand still held tightly to his, the only thing keeping him where he was. 'What is it? What's wrong?'

'A new king,' he whispered. He didn't know how he knew that. His son. He had a son. And he would do anything to protect him.

He felt her press her forehead against his back and squeeze his hand. But she didn't say anything.

There was more activity behind the screens. Servants bustled out, grinning from ear to ear, smiles which faded when they saw Vasquez by the door, standing there like a living warning.

Beatriz emerged, wan and exhausted but satisfied, drying her freshly washed hands. 'Mother and son are well,' she said and her legs almost went from under her. Juárez steadied her. Sylvian hadn't even seen him move. He guided her to a seat and knelt beside her, speaking intently to her. 'I'll be fine,' Beatriz replied. 'If someone would please send for my brother . . .'

'Your cousin is close by, my lady,' said one of the attendants.

Her hand tightening on Juárez's in genuine horror. 'Oh, no . . . don't trouble him. I just need a moment.'

She needed far more than that. Sylvian knew what magic of that kind did to her and he suspected she'd had far more to do with the outcome than she would ever admit. She'd saved him from the brink of death. She'd healed Lyta too.

And as for events surrounding the death of the Duchess of Montalbeau . . . well, he didn't want to think about that now.

Beatriz was a powerful Aspect, channelling divine power from any god who would lend it. Perhaps right now they all owed Beatriz far more than would ever be acknowledged. Echoes of Ystara's power shimmered beneath her skin, draining away now. And with the goddess went the remains of Beatriz's strength.

'Fetch my lady's brother,' Sylvian told the attendant, but he didn't get any further.

'Sylvian,' said Vasquez. He snapped to attention. 'She wants to see you.'

Why? Why would that even be a thing? The queen had what she had always wanted.

But he walked forward without hesitation, Beatriz and Lyta left behind, and passed through the barrier created by those elaborately decorated screens.

Annika lay on the chaise still. Her gown was a pool of ruined silk on the floor but she was swathed in blankets and carefully cushioned. And at her perfect breast, a small, even more perfect being suckled contentedly. The queen smiled up at him.

And it was the old smile, the one he remembered when she had first arrived, the one that had stolen the hearts of all who saw it, from commoners to kings, before stress and fear drove it away, when Francisco had first sent him to her with his wild plan which had led them here.

'Annika?' he whispered. He had to whisper. His voice was too loud, his whole being too large and clumsy to be so close to such a tiny, precious life.

'I thought you'd like to see him,' she said, and she sounded like a girl instead of a queen. No, not a girl. A woman, a mother. Her hands trembled slightly as they tightened around her child. 'Perhaps hold him? This is Alejandro.'

He couldn't. He shouldn't. It was a terrible idea.

This boy was not his child. Would never be his child.

But the dusting of black silky hair on the tiny head, and the eyes so dark a brown they were almost as black said something different. He had heard they all had blue eyes when born. Not this one.

Sylvian knelt beside her and reached out one hand, touching the child as if he was made of glass.

There was still something of heartbreak in Annika's eyes. 'Thank you,' she whispered. 'We owe you everything. And he'll have everything, Sylvian. Forever. I swear it on my life.'

He tried to smile. 'I should go,' he said. 'I still have to talk to Lyta.'

'I'm sorry about that too. Truly. If the baron had not forced my hand, I would never . . .' Except she would have. She had. And if the need arose, she would use him and Lyta and any of them again. She was ruthless. Perhaps she didn't want to be, but she was in the end exactly who she was always going to be. A queen. 'Can you talk her around? I could try.'

He shuddered, not even sure if an answer existed for that.

But when he left Annika, as her various maids and the royal physicians swooped in around him like a horde of revellers to wait on the queen and the future king, to see to their every possible need, he found that Lyta was gone.

Of course she was.

What else had he expected?

CHAPTER TWENTY-TWO

Kit

Their luck—if you could call it luck—didn't last. Stirling didn't know the Rookery and Kit tried to warn him he was doubling back but he didn't listen. Why would he listen? He was a lord and Kit was drunk. Except he wasn't anymore. He was exhausted and afraid and so confused he didn't know which way was up anymore.

They were cornered behind the Temple of Lost Gods. The moment the two of them stepped out into the square, a dozen men swept around them, cutting off all escape.

Winded and broken, Kit doubled over, trying to catch his breath.

'Well gentlemen,' said De Werve. He was leaning back against the wall of the temple gardens, as if he was waiting for someone. Them, it turned out. 'Quite the chase. Are you going to come along quietly now? Don't make us do more damage than we need to. Some of these lads don't know their own strength.'

Apparently the laws about carrying arms within the city walls didn't count anymore if you were a member of the Glorious Company of Blacksmiths. Crossbow bolts were trained on Kit and Stirling from all corners of the square.

'*Self-defence*,' they would say and spread their hands wide, helpless. '*You know how dangerous this place can be*.'

'You don't want us dead, De Werve,' Stirling replied. He still sounded full of bravado, as if this was no more than a casual conversation outside a bar. But his hands were clenched into fists at his side.

'You don't need to be dead, Lord Stirling. Writhing in agony isn't dead, is it? And we thought you were one of us. Letters from old Master Dee himself. Even he's dancing to a royal tune now. Thomas did warn me you'd try something, you and the girl. Your hands have never seen an honest day's work, have they?' He turned his glower on Kit. 'You however, Master Cornellis, I'm heartily sorry you're involved in this. I admired what you tried to do earlier this year, standing before the king like that. We free men of Amberes should stand together.'

Free men of Amberes? No one had stood beside him when he'd been accused of sedition over a pamphlet, Kit thought bitterly. De Werve had been noticeably absent at his trial. He didn't say anything though. There was clearly no point.

'We don't want trouble, gentlemen,' De Werve said when the silence dragged on. 'Come along with us now. We can discuss matters in the guild where it's safe.'

'Was it safe for Viola Alderton?' Stirling asked. 'What did you do with her?'

De Werve snorted out a laugh. 'Is *that* who she was? Well, she's most likely dead by now. Raving mad, at least. She tried to stop us at the Imperial Temple, the fool. They'll take care of her now and no one will miss her.'

'Her brother will,' Kit cut in. 'And he commands quite the following in this city. He'll want words about it.'

De Werve scowled, fixing him with the most unpleasant glare. 'I'm not afraid of Lord Charles Alderton and his thugs, Cornellis. I'm an alderman of this city, first among the free men of Amberes. I'm going to be the next mayor as soon as Marasso takes command.'

So that was it. That was how it hung together. Marasso would become Governor in place of the queen, Ursel would be ousted, and De Werve would step into the gap. It sounded so simple. No wonder he wasn't afraid of Alderton if he planned to rule this city in all but name.

He ought to be afraid though. Once Alderton found out they'd done something to his sister, every knife in the dark Amberes had to offer was going to be out for De Werve. The mayoral chain of office wouldn't protect him. Didn't he realise that?

The guildmaster waved a dismissive hand at them. 'Enough. No one is telling tales. Especially not the two of you. No need to cause more trouble.'

'Trouble?' Stirling said with a grin Kit was beginning to recognise as dangerous. 'I quite enjoy a bit of trouble myself. What about you Kit?'

'Not a lot,' he muttered, as if that was going to help now.

'Where's the fun in that?' his companion replied and hurled something at the blacksmiths, whatever he'd been holding in his clenched left hand. At the same time, he turned, pulling Kit down underneath him as a deafening explosion tore through the square.

Dazed, his ear still ringing, Kit pushed himself up, just in time to have Stirling grab his arm and scramble forwards, down the next alleyway. Up ahead it split either way but as Stirling headed right, Kit grabbed him, pulling him left.

'Dead end!' he yelled, but his voice still sounded far away. He knew this place better than anyone. They were around the back of the Temple of Lost Gods, near Tavern Lane. It was a warren of alleys and places to hide. 'What did you do? What was that? Gunpowder?'

'Something like it. My own devising.' He sounded positively gleeful. It was a nightmare. 'I wasn't lying about studying alchemy. Good, isn't it?'

Good was a relative term and Kit was fairly certain it didn't apply to anything connected with them right now. 'We need to get to safety. Find somewhere to hide and get word to Lyta and Syl. Or Ben. Ben could help, couldn't he?'

There was a door left ajar ahead. Whoever hadn't locked it would probably be regretting that when a horde of angry men poured through it, but Kit couldn't think about that right now. He shouldered it open the rest of the way, pulled Stirling inside, and slammed his full body weight on it. There had to be something in the darkened room to block it with. It was a store for wood and old junk by the look of it.

'Here,' Stirling had found a wooden bar. He shoved it into place and for a moment they both stood there, breathing hard. Kit's hearing was slowly clearing and the near silence seemed doubly loud. 'Ben can't help us. He's too deeply involved. We can't trust him. He's an Alvarez and they're . . . they're after power too. Always have been. Juan Alvarez de Marasso is going to move against the queen somehow, a coup in all but name. Your sister and that guard maybe though . . . Can she get us through to the queen? If only I had more evidence, but I think it's too late now. We'll have to go with what we have and hope we can still reach Viola in time.'

Kit rounded on him, pushing him back with his free hand. 'What? What is going on? What do you mean?'

'It's a plot. Against your queen, I think. Or the king. Take Amberes back maybe, use Marasso to do it. Free men of Amberes, didn't you hear him? I don't know the details. They want to call back a lost god, a powerful one. That's what Charnock does. Look, it's far too much to explain. He's using the relics of the oldest, most powerful gods to connect with them, to use them and their bloodlines. And De Werve wants this city for himself, as Mayor or as something more. There're probably a few of them involved, pulling strings, jockeying for position—courtiers, aldermen, priests . . . I don't know. Normally I'd leave local politics alone but with Viola missing and Ben Alvarez involved, and Marasso right next to the queen and now you . . .'

'But Ben would never—'

Before Stirling could answer though a voice called out. 'Who's down there? What's going on?'

The glow of a lantern appeared in the corridor beyond the storeroom in which they found themselves.

Kit cursed softly to himself and then tried to make his voice as gentle and inoffensive as possible.

'We don't mean any harm,' he called up. 'We needed shelter. Just give us a few minutes and we'll be on our way. I swear it.'

An elderly woman appeared with her lantern, peering at the two of them. 'Sanctuary, is it? Well, a temple is the place for that, of course it is. But people usually use the main doors.'

Kit stared at her, understanding finally catching up with him. 'Auntie Florrie?'

'Kit, my lovely, what trouble have you got yourself into? That's not like you. Come on, both of you. Skulking in my storeroom, I don't know. Come inside.'

*

Florrie prepared a herbal infusion in her narrow little kitchen, making sure they both sat down at the table. She cut them thick slices of a lemon and poppy seed cake and fussed over them like they were guests there on a feast day afternoon.

'We can't stay,' Kit tried to tell her again. 'There were people after us and—'

'Well then, you don't want to be outside in the dark, do you? I remember the trouble you children used to get up to, you and Lyta and those awful boys, don't think I don't. You aren't the first to hide out in here from another gang. So sit still and eat up.'

She poured the steaming tea into mugs and pushed them into their hands.

'We're most grateful,' said Stirling, all charm. 'You really have saved us, ma'am.'

'I'm sure I have,' she chuckled to herself and sipped her own drink. Kit ate the cake, mainly to keep her happy and Stirling did the same, though rather more delicately than Kit did. He had manners, Lord Stirling. They were another weapon, Kit thought, another tool he used on a daily basis to carry out his missions for his queen. 'And who was after you in such a hurry?'

'The Blacksmiths' Guild,' Kit told her. 'I think they're involved in this business with the robberies and the children. But I don't know why.'

'You mean they broke into my temple, knocked out our Alaric and murdered that poor little lad?' Florrie gasped. Her look of horror made him wince. Perhaps he shouldn't have blurted it out like that.

How did he explain what he'd seen tonight? He didn't want to. She wouldn't believe him anyway. And then he'd have to get into Stirling's wild theories . . .

'I—I—Sort of? I don't know.'

If it was the same as the boy possessed by Tamfana, who had come for the book, Kit didn't quite know what to call it. The children were dead, that was for sure. But who had done it and why was another matter. Murder? Maybe. Certainly something more than misadventure.

'We really need to make our way to the palace,' said Stirling.

'Best wait until sunrise. Won't be long.' She pushed more cake at him. 'It's a long way at this time of night and there's bad people about.'

'Perhaps we could summon the watch?'

Florrie didn't quite laugh in his face, but the smile was unmistakable. 'You aren't from around here, are you? Summon the watch? Ha.'

'They aren't going to come into the Rookery after dark,' Kit told him with rather less humour. 'She's right. We should wait for sunrise, go then.'

'Kit, I'm not sure—' His own argument was lost in a yawn.

Exhaustion was catching up with both of them fast, now they were sitting in a quiet safe place. Or as safe as it could get. Kit wasn't sure even the head of a guild was going to have his men breaking into Florrie Stone's house in the heart of the Rookery in the dead of night. Not unless they wanted a riot on their hands.

A wave of tiredness swept over him, his eyesight blurring until the table was swimming before him and the cake crumbs had got far too large.

'You don't remember your da, do you pet?' Florrie asked. Kit turned his attention back to her, frowning. His father? What was she saying about his father? Bemused, he shook his head.

'You resemble him more and more, you know.' She was smiling at him fondly now, watching him intently with eyes sharp as an eagle's.

'He was gone before I was born.' Kit yawned, trying to cover his mouth.

'Well, now,' she murmured, pouring him some more tea. 'He didn't have a great deal of choice in that, did he? He never could stay long. That's the way it is with the likes of him.'

'Did you know him?' he asked, stifling another yawn. Now the adrenaline was wearing off, he was exhausted. His head ached and his sight was growing darker at the edges. 'I thought he was a sailor or . . . or a traveller.'

'A traveller, yes. That's a word for it. And yes, I knew him. He adored your mam, he did. Moved mountains for her, or he would have done if he could. And for you and Lyta too. He only was able to come back for a time because he loved her so much. Just a few days at this time of year. But he did, for her. Until she passed anyway, the gods rest her. I suppose that broke the last tie. For a while, anyway.'

Kit had never heard any of this before. Lyta didn't remember him either and Kit barely remembered their mother beyond a gentle caress, a soft laugh and somewhere warm and safe to hide.

'What was he like? Who was he?'

'Soni? Well, he was like you, Kit my love. Very like you. In looks, and in heart too. Loved this city, he did. It's like his very nature, Amberes. And this was his time of year. Always was. That was when he'd come to visit her, on the longest night of the dark days.'

Both he and Lyta had been born in early autumn so Kit guessed that made sense.

Tiredness swept over him again, but he needed to find out more.

'*Soni*,' he asked. 'What kind of name is that? Where was he from?'

'Oh that weren't his real name, pet,' she murmured. Her voice was a lullaby now and he was drowning in it. He struggled to keep his eyes open and something felt off. He clung to her words, trying to focus. 'Just a nickname she called him. His real name was far too complicated for a lover's murmurs.'

'What was it?' He had to know.

'Cissonius.' She smiled at him, her eyes keen. 'Druon Cissonius Antigonus.'

Kit frowned, trying to untangle what he was hearing. Three names, like in Caput Mundi. Was he an Imperial then? A soldier? And the middle one . . . 'Cissonius? Like the goddess?'

She gave a soft laugh. 'Somewhat like her, yes. But not a goddess. Not him. Druon was a giant, they said and he guarded us, right up until the Church Imperial came. When they started killing gods.' That couldn't be right, Kit thought. That was hundreds of years ago. But he didn't interrupt her. He didn't seem able to find his voice. 'He was betrayed, my love, by those he trusted most. They cast him out, but he could still reach us, those who loved him most—once a year, when the veil was thin. That's when he came to her and she welcomed him with joy. Like in the old stories. Now look at you. You're exhausted, you boys. You need to sleep. We'll talk more another day. I'll tell you all the stories you want. Into the parlour, both of you. You can sleep on the floor in front of the fire.'

There didn't seem to be any point in arguing. If he put his head down on the table now, he'd pass out and Florrie wasn't someone with whom to argue. Her stories weren't even making sense to him anymore—one minute talking about his parents, and then about gods and things that happened when Amberes was little more than a tolled river crossing rather than a thriving city, hundreds, if not a thousand years or more ago. As if he was missing parts of the conversation. Florrie bustled them both out of the kitchen. Kit stumbled after her, aware of Stirling following a little more reluctantly.

The house was so familiar. He'd grown up in a house like this. Until it burned down, Lyta's house had been like this. There was a kitchen for living, and a parlour for good, and upstairs no more than three rooms. She had a sheepskin rug in front of her banked fire, and pulled a mass of knitted blankets from a cupboard.

He had a name for his father. Something to do with the goddess of the bell, the patron of Amberes. Had he come from the Latinate States or Caput Mundi itself? A traveller maybe, or a trader, maybe even a representative of the Imperial Church or one of their guards? Was he a Patrician who had taken a local lover? But Druon was a local name. It had to be. It was so familiar. He remembered it from old songs and stories, didn't he? The old god of the river. Who named their sons after dead gods?

As he slumped down in front of the hearth like a tired old dog, the book still wrapped in his faded red scarf acting as a pillow, he was already falling asleep. Stirling let out a low, soft groan and flung one arm over Kit's chest, already unconscious.

For a moment, he started. Stirling wasn't Ben and it was strange to feel another's touch. But the night was pressing in on the edges of his mind and he couldn't keep his eyes open any longer. He drifted in and out of the edge of sleep, some part of his brain still trying to figure out why what Florrie had said about his father was disturbing him so much. It didn't make sense. He didn't like things that didn't make sense.

But his body was like lead and the edges of his consciousness drifted away.

Somewhere beyond the parlour, Florrie opened a door. 'Inside,' she said in hushed tones. 'They won't give you any trouble now.'

And by then, it was far too late.

*

Kit awoke with a thundering headache and the feeling that something had crawled into his mouth and died. It was so much worse than a hangover. It was only when he tried to move his aching body that he realised that there were iron manacles on his wrists, and wherever he was, it was not Florrie Stone's neat, warm little parlour in the Rookery.

This was a cell, the type of place that made his heart give a lurch of remembered despair.

His body moved in spite of himself, and instantly crashed back down as the chains holding him snapped taut. The floor hit him hard, driving the air from his lungs.

'Yes, I wouldn't bother with all of that. Even if we weren't shackled, there are iron bars and some rather intricate locks between us and a way out. We aren't going anywhere for now.' Stirling sounded defeated. It was not encouraging since up to now he'd been irrepressible. Kit squinted through the dark. He could make out the other man on the other side of the cell. Bars had been fitted floor to ceiling between the stout wooden door into the room and the place where they sprawled. There was a door to their cage, securely locked, straw on the stone floor and an unnerving quiet.

They weren't in Old Steen. The smell was wrong for one thing. He couldn't hear the river or the groans of misery and anguish. It lacked the all-pervading sense of hopelessness, not to mention the stench of so many prisoners huddled together waiting for the end.

Kit shuddered, trying to push those memories away again. That wouldn't help.

'Where are we?'

'Damned if I know. I presume they took the book.'

Kit cursed softly. It was gone. And it would hardly have been difficult to find. 'She drugged us. Florrie drugged us. But—but she drank the tea as well.'

'I suspect the cake,' Stirling muttered. 'Never did like poppy seeds. I'm sorry, Kit. I was stupid. Very stupid.'

'So was I. I trusted her. I've known her all my life. She let them in to take us, De Werve and his gang.'

'She must have. I don't suppose you can get out of those shackles?'

Kit hadn't even thought of trying. They were snug around his wrists, and chains ran to rings fixed in the walls. He tried to undo them but his fingers were numb and useless. He wasn't sure how they were sealed.

'No, you?'

'I've been trying for an hour. I assure you if I could I would have.' And he said he had a way with locks. Lyta would laugh in his face.

'What do we do?'

'For now? We wait. I don't think there's much more we can do. I'm sorry, Kit. This is all my fault.'

They didn't have to wait long. The sound of voices filtered through the stone halls of wherever they were being kept as someone approached deep in conversation.

'—most useful, I'm sure, for experimentation, if nothing else. An enormous source of power. Truly, this is a wonder. Excellent work, De Werve.'

'Charnock,' Stirling said, the single word seething with hatred.

'But I don't understand,' said another voice and Kit's head shot up. Far too familiar a voice. 'He just handed it over? Willingly?'

'Well, I wouldn't say *willingly*,' said De Werve with a nasty chuckle. Lantern light spilled across the floor of the cell as the door jerked open and Kit blinked furiously, trying to see even though his eyes burned in the glare. He had to see, he had to know.

Ben stood there, holding the lantern for De Werve and Charnock, his eyes wide and luminous, his mouth forming an O of surprise as he stared at them.

'Sacrifices have to be made, Alvarez,' said the guildmaster. 'Your cousin understands that. I thought you did as well.'

Charnock's hand fell on Ben's shoulder, rubbing it affectionately. 'Don't worry about my prize student, De Werve. Benedictus understands the nature of the great work. It's to his benefit. And that of the gods inside him. They are all in agreement. It's all about bloodlines and his is one of the most special ones, royal and divine . . . ancient. Of course the Alvarez line is too precious for experimentation, but there are others, as you see here, and they are much more closely related to our ultimate goal. You can trace only a few people back to the gods themselves. But a single generation? That is rare indeed. For some reason Amberes is a focal point. It gathers them here, calls them back—a future area for study perhaps? We should make a note of that, Ben.'

His voice was a droning noise, smothering the screaming that had started up in Kit's mind. He sounded like he was lecturing even now. Nasal and self-absorbed and not even really talking about real people but animals or minerals or . . . or *things*. 'Perhaps the city itself forms a Divine Nexus. Like you, Ben my boy, drawing gods to yourself. We're going to pull those gods out of you in no time, just as you wanted. You'll see. A normal life awaits. You can take your place in your family, study as you will, have your own mind back. The baron will see you well placed with the new king and all will be well. He is your family, after all, and we know the gods will smile on you. How could they do otherwise? That's worth any price, isn't it?'

Kit locked his gaze on Ben's trying to communicate something, *anything*—an inarticulate cry, a desperate plea for help. But Ben stood there, his features frozen in that mask Kit knew too well, before he turned away, all his attention on Charnock and De Werve. Then he smiled.

'Absolutely, Master Charnock. Any price. We all have our parts to play in the great work.'

CHAPTER TWENTY-THREE

Lyta

Lyta hadn't expected to feel such heartbreak. She was all ready to flee the palace, and maybe the city too. Panic had settled in the pit of her stomach, sending acid up into her throat until she thought for sure she'd throw up right there on top of the formal furnishings and finery. And then the queen went into labour.

Annika always had to have the last bloody word, didn't she?

Sylvian had looked so lost, so helpless and so patently terrified. She'd never seen that before. Not Sylvian. Stoic endurance or furious rage, that was what she knew, not the sheer blind terror she'd seen on his face. So she'd held him, and sat with him and tried to be there for him as long as it took. Because . . . because she had to.

Eninn tried to comfort her too, but she wasn't listening to him right now. She might never talk to him again. He'd conspired with Ystara to put her in this impossible position. And if anyone used the words 'fate' and 'destined' and 'meant to be' she would happily knee them in the balls, even if it meant finding a body to stuff Eninn into in order to do it.

But the baby had been born and the queen was saved, Beatriz had done whatever Beatriz did and once more Sylvian was Annika's faithful servant. He had walked away from Lyta without a backwards glance the moment she called.

If Lyta had ever doubted of how little importance she actually was to him, that showed her.

So she took the opportunity that presented itself and slipped out of the door before anyone noticed.

'Is there news, Mistress Cornellis?' asked a voice she remembered too well. Turning, she found the Baron de Marasso waiting for her at the turn of the corridor. He had armed men with him, and not the usual guards Lyta expected in the palace. They had that air of a soldier, as Sylvian did. They all looked to Marasso. His own troops then.

'News,' she said carefully. 'Yes. She's fine. They're both fine.'

He stared at her intently. 'A boy or a girl?'

Lyta hesitated. 'I'm sure there will be an announcement very soon.'

Marasso seized her arm, pulling her closer, all pretence of civility gone. He shook her. 'A boy or a girl? Tell me, woman.'

Lyta tried to tear herself free and failed. His grip was like iron. 'A boy, all right? She had a boy.'

Marasso beamed, and released her. 'The best news we could have hoped for. Our god will be pleased. And where is Chant? I need words with him.'

'Still with her, I think,' Lyta replied, more unsure now. What god was he talking about? 'He and Beatriz and . . . What are you doing?'

'Hmm?' He was staring at her, as if he was examining her. 'They tell me there isn't a lock you can't open, Mistress Cornellis, not a thing you cannot steal.'

'Oh, really?' And who might *they* be, she wondered.

'Indeed, and that there's nothing you wouldn't do for your brother. A fine man. I met him briefly. I thought for a moment Beatriz had set her cap at him to annoy me.'

Oh, you have no idea, Lyta thought vindictively. *And I can't wait until you find out the truth.*

She kept her voice cool and calm, 'Can we get to the point, my lord baron? It's been a long day.'

He smiled, a nasty smile which hooked something in her chest. 'I'm sure it has, and it's not over yet. I have a job for you. Things will move very fast now. Very fast indeed. I need you to fetch something and bring it to the Blacksmiths' Guild.'

'I'm not your servant.'

He reached out as if to grab her again and Lyta darted back, evading him effortlessly.

Then he dropped something in front of her. It was a scarf, badly knitted and old, but she would have known it anywhere. Her mother had made that sad, faded thing for Kit, years ago, and Kit had darned it so often it was as if he'd made half of it himself. So had she, when he was too busy. He treasured it and he'd been wearing it in the cold of late. In the snow. It still had a darker patch of his blood from when they had been attacked because there hadn't been any time for laundry.

Lyta couldn't move. She stared at it for a long moment as understanding clawed its way up her spine, and then she slowly lifted her gaze to meet Marasso's. That smug smile was back.

'What have you done to him?'

'Nothing. Nothing at all. He's perfectly safe. I'm told he's a pillar of the community, your brother. He's probably charming the alchemist as we speak. Master Charnock was incredibly eager to make his acquaintance following his encounter with you.'

Lyta sucked in a breath, ready to tell him that Kit had no interest in alchemy or blacksmiths or . . . and then her brain caught up.

Charnock had Kit. Charnock who wanted to work out how Eninn had got into her mind, who was obsessed with bloodlines and gods and was not above sacrificing children in his quest for his so-called *enlightenment*. No, not that, not really. Power and control, more like.

That bastard had Kit.

'If they hurt him '

Marasso held up a gloved hand, the fine leather creaking in a soft threat. 'Why would they do that? All you have to do, my lady, is to fetch a relic and bring it to them, and then Kit is free to go.'

'What *relic*?'

'Brabo's sword. They had one of those . . .'—he curled his lip in distaste—'*children* in place to take it, but the Alderton girl interfered and that plan failed.'

Clémence, Lyta thought. *She had a name, you bastard, and it was Clémence.*

'So we made a new plan,' he went on. 'Your Sylvian told me all about you. Back then, when he was just a boy with a broken heart.' He smiled his thin smile. She hated it. 'And more recently too. You only have to see him look at you, or mention you, to know that he really does think very highly of you. Others tell me you're a master thief, and you've already been in there to work out the lie of the land. Shouldn't be a problem for you at all.'

They wanted the sword Inquisitor Tiberius had bragged about in the Imperial Temple, one of the greatest treasures of the Church Imperial. Was that all? She started to shake her head. It was suicide. Madness.

The power of a god had burned inside those children, like the kid in the printshop, in Clémence, now dead on a slab somewhere with the royal physicians. Had De Werve sent her to steal the sword? Viola had tried to stop her and had been trapped by the Church Imperial, doomed to die. What would happen to Lyta if she stepped into this maelstrom now?

But what else could she do? They had Kit. And Sylvian was right about one thing. Her little brother always came first.

'Should you have any further doubts,' Marasso went on, 'there's the matter of Captain Chant. Your lover—the queen's lover—he's been very busy, hasn't he? The king knows, of course—he gave the command—but everyone else . . . well . . . how long would he survive do you think if that was made public? Francisco would have to act.' That was what Annika had said as well. That if Marasso made that public, Francisco would have no choice. 'In fact, a loyal servant could do that for him and no one would question a thing. It's treason, did you know that? To lay hands on the queen.'

He'd been hinting at that to try to force Annika's hand on the matter of Beatriz's marriage. Now he was saying it outright. Something had changed. Some kind of endgame reached. He was making his move. Problem was, Lyta didn't know what it was.

'You leave him out of it. He's sworn to her and Francisco has made sure those bonds are unbreakable. He's loyal to death.'

'That's what I'm counting on, my dear. Who do you think originally formed those bonds, prepared the ground as it were? He was loyal to me first. Maybe that can save him, but you never know with Francisco. He's fickle, as I'm sure you've noticed. There's always the danger that Sylvian's usefulness has now passed, isn't there? That is, if Francisco makes it back here at all.' He cocked his head to one side, waiting for her to say something.

The baby. They had the baby now. That was all they wanted. The king, the queen, the whole court . . . An heir had been born, and she wouldn't put it past Francisco to have sat back and waited for Sylvian's usefulness to Annika to pass. To send Marasso to do his dirty work.

She might despise the king for it, but he was nothing if not pragmatic. She didn't have an answer.

She'd heard the tone in Sylvian's voice, that knowledge he couldn't possibly have had, the devotion. And she knew that while she might steal him away from Annika from time to time, she could never tear him away from the prince. His child—a chain in human form.

Marasso was far too keen on a newborn prince in a different way. If Francisco didn't come back from whatever expedition had taken him away, that left a weakened queen, and Marasso as his appointed governor, someone strong to take control, to act as regent for a helpless babe. He thought he could control Sylvian, and perhaps he could, between blood and magic. Who had made those bonds? Sylvian's first commander, that was who. His god would be pleased, he had said. The god of a soldier, of warriors . . .

Kyron.

Bile rose in the back of the throat.

A lot could happen on the roads back to Amberes. Even to a king.

'Fuck you!'

Marasso reached out and grabbed her pendant, ripping it from her neck. The chain broke as if it was a thread and, as this was no rival god, there was nothing Eninn could do to stop him. Even if the pendant heated up, the gloves probably protected him. 'I can always find a use for a man like Sylvian Chant again. He's a warrior, descended of warriors. I saw that from the first moment I laid eyes on him, even when he was a lowly conscript devoid of hope. You broke him, Lyta Cornellis, but I rebuilt him. He loved me once as well, like a father. And deep down, you know he loves with all his heart. That kind of love doesn't fail. Do you think he won't cooperate with me if only for your sake, Lyta? Do you doubt him so?'

Lyta hissed, baring her teeth, and Eninn growled deep inside her, but there was nothing they could do. The Baron de Marasso smiled that vicious, knowing smile and flicked his fingers at her in a curt gesture of dismissal. 'Better get going, Mistress Cornellis. Time is short. You have work to do.'

*

It wasn't hard to get out of the palace. Everyone was completely distracted by the queen and the baby, and by wild rumours and speculation about what had happened. If anyone recognised Lyta as the woman in the audience chamber, where Annika had spun that twisted tale of childhood sweethearts reunited and used them both for her own ends, they didn't stop her. Those in charge of security were always far more concerned with who was going in rather than who was going out.

The night-time world of Amberes folded itself around her like a blanket of darkness. There was a fight breaking out down one alley, a gaggle of prostitutes plying their trade on the edges of the Great Market and a drunken sing-a-long in the nearest tavern on Exchange Street. Snow was falling heavily now, blanketing the world in white, smothering sound, dulling the stench of the city and freezing the canals. Only the Scaldis flowed on.

The great bell started to ring from the top of the tower above Cissonia's temple, ringing for joy, in celebration of the birth. Riders would be dispatched, and would thunder their way across the continent with the news. Heralds would be making haste to all the points in the city to proclaim it: *A boy has been born to the king, a son and heir.*

In the darkest days of the year, a future king had been born. She'd heard stories like that, had grown up on them like every other child in Amberes. They usually ended badly. Not for the king, naturally, but for everyone around him. Especially the commoners.

Like her. Like Sylvian.

Men like the Baron de Marasso always had their way. They knew that.

The last place she wanted to go was Cutlers Lane and Janlow's bar, but she needed to get to the heart of the matter fast. She needed help and Sylvian and the Alvarez siblings were out of the question. Alderton was not going to invite her into his fine house in Falconbrook. Even if he did she was not going to go. The last time had been a time too many.

The bar reminded her too keenly of the way her life could have gone. It would have been dark, bitter and terribly short.

That was what Janlow had planned for her and Kit once upon a time. The least of what he had planned. She had no doubt they would have been long dead by now. Ranulf had saved them both.

And now dark, bitter and terribly short might be their future fate again.

Marasso and De Werve couldn't hurt Kit yet. They had to give her time. They wanted the sword, that was all. A powerful relic of the enemy of Amberes. Yes, getting into the Imperial Temple was not going to be easy, but it could be done. She had to do it.

But not alone.

*

Some attempt had been made to clean up Janlow's bar on Cutlers Lane. The dull-eyed girls and boys lounging in the corners were dressed a bit better, and there was a flood of light from a dozen new lamps. The bar itself was still the same, running right across the back, but had been topped with a slab of pale marble which put her in mind of a morgue. And there were actual tables and chairs rather than the things that had been cannibalised from old barrels she remembered. Well, it had been years.

As she entered she caught movement from the corner of her eye, large figures turning towards her, watching her, and the sound of conversation drained away. They knew who she was. How could they not?

Janlow rose from the table where he'd been sitting, his lizard eyes making her feel the urge to wash every inch of her skin. Still handsome, although his nose had been broken one or two times too many now, mostly by Sylvian. He wore more expensive clothes and now sported a glittering earring in his left ear. A diamond maybe? Had he turned over the diamond traders outside the South Gate? She couldn't imagine him buying it fairly.

'Lyta? What a pleasant surprise,' he drawled.

The urge to wash was replaced by the desire to peel off her own skin as a more definitive solution.

'Janlow, I need to see your boss.'

He tilted his head to one side like a great cat and blinked meaningfully. 'I'm my own boss, love.'

Lyta smiled her nastiest smile. It was all front but she didn't have time for his bullshit now. 'Well we both know that's not the case. Maybe I should find Frida and let her pass on the good news. I've found his sister.'

There was another flurry of movement behind her. Someone left, no doubt to carry the word of what she said to Alderton. She didn't much care. She wanted this over and the fastest way was to make him come to her. Forcing his high-and-mighty lordship to soil himself with this dive was the icing on the cake.

'Have a seat, Mistress Cornellis,' said Janlow. 'I'll fetch you a drink, will I?' He pulled out a chair at the same table where he'd been sitting, dusting it off sarcastically.

Drink something here? Not a chance. It wasn't snobbishness. She didn't want to mysteriously pass out from whatever he'd no doubt slip her. She pulled out an entirely different chair, fixed her back to a bare bit of wall and sat down with her legs coiled under her, ready to make a break for it if needs be.

This was not safe. Nor was it a good idea. But she was all out of good ideas.

He slammed his tankard down with a bang that would have made anyone else jump out of their skin, and sat down at the other side of the table. On purpose. The room was far too quiet.

Everyone was watching the two of them. Their history was well known here.

'Are you celebrating?' she asked.

'There's a new prince. Course we're celebrating.'

She nodded slowly and said nothing. She wasn't celebrating, that was for sure. And no one else here was in a party mood either.

'No Sylvian?' asked Janlow. 'Thought he was your dog these days.'

'He's the king's dog and you know it,' she replied and hated herself a bit for saying it. Sylvian's loyalty to Francisco was absolute and the king had already passed him on. He belonged to the queen, and if Marasso had his way, he was going to belong to the baron again, with no choice in the matter. But she wasn't going to say that to Janlow. At least now she knew he didn't really have a choice, but she wasn't sure if that made it better or worse.

'Yeah, I heard something like that.' He narrowed his eyes. 'What are you really doing here, Lyta?'

'I told you. I found her. She's in deep shit. The kind that doesn't sit right with me. Call it a peace offering. He asked for my help, remember?'

'Yeah but . . . Well, no one expected you to actually do anything about it. Not after . . .'

'After you kidnapped me and stabbed me in the back?'

He gave a brief, gruff laugh. 'That wasn't me, my love.'

'I'm not your *love*.' She said it more out of an instinctive reflex reaction than anything else. This was a terrible idea. Viola Alderton was in a cage in the Imperial Temple, being tortured, and would very soon be burned alive. And Lyta needed to use them to get in there for an entirely different reason. The possibility of rescuing Viola was slim, and she was using it as an excuse to get help. She was probably going to get them all killed.

Well, better them than anyone she actually cared about.

Janlow smiled that brilliant smile of his and didn't reply. He didn't need to. She didn't have Ranulf's protection and she wasn't even sure she really had Sylvian's anymore, not now he had a son, albeit one he could never acknowledge. He would still be devoted to the child, would do anything to protect him, even if she was the price. *A new king*, he had said, rather than his *son*. Long before anyone had announced whether Annika had delivered a boy or a girl, Sylvian had known.

She tried not to think of the baby, or the queen, or Sylvian's face when he'd heard the newborn wail. Annika had him forever, if she wanted him. And why wouldn't she want him?

And now Marasso was going to use Kit to get to Lyta, Lyta to get to Sylvian, and Sylvian to get to the prince and the queen. With enough leverage, he could seize power here in no time at all. Tonight. She didn't know where that would leave them.

So much for her letting Kit have his respectable life. She had fucked that up as well, just by being *her*. If she didn't pull this off, she dreaded what Charnock would do to him.

The door opened again and this time there was no mistaking the man who entered. Lord Alderton's eyes were ringed with dark circles and hungry for information. They fixed on her like she was a rock in a torrent. Behind him, Frida slipped inside, wearing the livery that Janlow didn't seem to feel the need for.

'Where is she, Cornellis?' Alderton asked, the bark of command highlighting his hoarse voice.

Lyta rose wearily. She was going to have to work with these people. Her stomach was full of lead and her head full of panic. But there were rights and wrongs, and sometimes there wasn't any choice anyway.

'You're not going to like this,' she told him. 'She's alive, but not for long. Not if we don't move fast.'

*

It was not a plan. They were not her crew. Lyta didn't trust any of them as far as she could throw them. Frida and Janlow had both betrayed her to varyingly dangerous degrees and Alderton regarded her as little more than a guttersnipe who had a skill he needed and could be discarded as soon as she ceased to be useful.

Eninn was chattering away now but not actually helping. He was instead listing how bad an idea this was over and over again, and all the ways it could go wrong. And it would go wrong. It always did.

If that was you in there, she asked him eventually, *would you want someone to come? Anyone?*

It's not the same thing, said the god in her head. But it was. She knew that. *Go back to the palace. It's safer there.*

No it isn't. And I'm not leaving Kit to die.

At least with that he stopped arguing against her plan. Not against the details though. That would be far too much to ask for.

Frida wasn't much better. She never took her eyes off Lyta, hand straying to her knives far too frequently for comfort, watching her like she'd lost her mind. Lyta didn't mind the knives so much, although they were a bitter reminder of how Frida had betrayed her. She kept her hand on the belt knife which had once been Sylvian's as well. She wasn't much good in a knife fight, not like Frida. But that didn't mean she was an idiot either.

Besides, Frida had a wheellock too. Lyta would probably never get the knife out of her bloody belt.

'Tell me again how this is a plan?' Frida asked.

'Have you got a better one?'

The answer was no. The answer was always no. There was no way other than this to get into the Imperial Temple, not for them, and Lyta hoped that the Inquisitor was still interested in tormenting her and Eninn for reasons of his own. Because if he wasn't they were stuck.

So she stood at the gates with Alderton, Janlow and Frida, any of whom could literally stab her in the back at a moment's notice, and asked to see him.

The guards manning the gate, who were trying very hard to look like nothing more than simple acolytes, stared at her like she was mad.

Perhaps she was.

'Ready for this?' she murmured to Eninn.

'Of course I'm ready,' Alderton growled and Lyta flinched. She'd thought she'd been too quiet for him to hear.

You have to be more careful, Eninn told her. *And no, I'm not ready. I'll never be ready. But I know what to expect now.*

She only hoped he really did. The divine presence of the August Imperator in here had shaken them both. She didn't want to lose it in front of Alderton because Eninn was having another panic attack.

Just walk in the front gate and ask to speak to the man in charge. She felt like having a panic attack herself.

They knew about Eninn. They knew about *The Book of Gold*. They probably knew all about Ben Alvarez as well. And here she was, marching into the monster's den for a woman she didn't even know, with only enemies around her.

Not your brightest moment, Cornellis. Not by a long shot.

She should have at least told Sylvian what she was up to. Because if she vanished in here, he'd never have a clue what happened, would he?

Or perhaps they'd tell him. Simply to goad him into doing something equally stupid. He would too. Marasso was the kind of sick bastard who would enjoy that.

I'll always come for you, he'd said.

Not this time, Syl.

Inquisitor Tiberius appeared with a flock of dark-robed acolytes around him, not so much attendants as guards. She was instantly reminded of Sylvian, Juárez and the others. Praetorians were not allowed in the city, but if no one admitted what they were, who would know? But she saw it now. They must have been at prayers or some kind of ceremony. The Inquisitor was wearing official robes this time, a long draped toga and a cloak of dark reddish purple, the colour of wine, or blood. It might not be Imperial purple but you didn't get that colour cheap, and Lyta felt a chill of premonition as he came towards them across the first courtyard. Were they too late already? There hadn't been any smoke, or any sign that there was anything untoward going on inside the temple. She'd paid several of the local kids to keep a very close eye on things. And they were good at what they did.

And you surely couldn't burn a goddess without any signs, could you? There would be smoke at least, and screaming . . .

Get me to her, said Eninn. *I'll do what I can to help. I'm ready this time.*

Lyta pursed her lips and nodded, praying he was right. Although who she was actually praying to was a question she no longer wanted to probe too deeply. Because she had always prayed to him, much good it had done either of them.

'Lord Alderton,' said Tiberius, expansively, holding out his hands in greeting. A ruby sparkled on his finger. Lyta's gaze locked on it and that familiar magpie bit of her brain sparked with awareness. She knew that thing. Or something very much like it. She'd last seen it on the headless corpse of the Magister. Honestly, she'd thought it had been buried under the rubble of the Scholars' Tower. Shit. This was not good. She couldn't believe it was going sidewise quite so quickly. 'An honour to meet you.'

'Don't kiss that ring,' she hissed beneath her breath to Alderton, who cast a bemused glance at her, a haughty dismissal. The lord from Albion had no intentions of kissing an Imperial ring. He didn't show deference to anyone except his queen. And even that was questionable given the queen in question had kicked him out of the country.

'Hardly,' he murmured. Then he turned his attention back to the Inquisitor and gave a curt bow. Respectable enough. He was here as a supplicant after all, not a superior. He wanted something. Desperately. 'Lord Inquisitor, you do us a great honour at this late hour.'

It was almost midnight, Lyta thought. Only late by some standards.

'It is not yet the hour of Vigil but we were already in preparation. Come inside and be welcome. Mistress Cornellis, I had not thought to see you quite so soon.' He even smiled at her and she felt something inside her—something that suddenly felt distinctly like prey—shrivel up as small as it could in an effort to hide.

Don't lose it Eninn. I need you now.

'It's a matter of some urgency,' she said as calmly as she could. 'We need to discuss your prisoner.'

'My sister,' said Alderton firmly. 'And a loyal and beloved subject of her royal majesty of Albion.'

'I see.' Tiberius didn't seem surprised. Not even slightly. So he'd known who she was, had he? Lyta's mind flicked through a number of options. Something was wrong here. She could feel it. Something had changed. 'Do subjects of her majesty commonly claim sanctuary in the temples of the one true god?'

'Sanctuary?' Lyta spoke before Alderton could reply. She wasn't sure what he'd say. 'She didn't look like someone seeking sanctuary earlier.'

'Miracles can happen at the strangest times, can't they?' He smiled at her. That winning, handsome smile which made her want to retreat as fast as possible.

'May we see her?' Alderton asked, surprisingly calm. 'I would like to assure myself of her safety. You would be merely indulging a fond brother. I'm sure you understand.'

Lyta decided she had underestimated him. There was no bluster, no threat. He almost managed to sound meek.

'Of course, Lord Alderton. Please, follow me.'

Lyta, Eninn whispered. *This feels like a trap.*

Lyta gritted her teeth so she wouldn't tell him to shut up and either inadvertently insult someone she shouldn't insult or give them away entirely. He owed her this. And he knew it.

But he was right. It did feel like a trap.

Because she was pretty sure that's what it was. But the only way out of it was to go right through it.

CHAPTER TWENTY-FOUR

Sylvian

Searching the palace for Lyta was a fool's errand but what was he, Sylvian reasoned, but the greatest fool who had ever lived? The problem was, he couldn't leave Annika, not at a time like this. He had his duty.

And Lyta had the whole city of Amberes in which to get into trouble of her own. An entire city, which she knew like the back of her hand, in which to hide from him.

At least she'd stayed a little while, when he had needed her most. That was a small grace.

He circled round, back to the royal apartments and saw Vasquez standing outside the queen's bedchamber.

'Royal physicians are in with her now,' she told him.

Sylvian felt that awful pang of concern again which he knew was amplified by his connection to her. On his finger the ring hummed against his skin.

'Is the queen all right?'

'Yes. Don't worry. They're checking her over. Perfectly standard, or so I'm informed. She's exhausted and she lost blood but she's strong. So is the young prince. Like a lion, that one, with a roar in him too. They've whisked him off to the nursery already to give her some peace and quiet. There's a veritable army of nursemaids. Lady Beatriz went with them to be sure, on the queen's command. It seems she has changed her mind about the Lady of House Alvarez at least. Word has been sent to the king.'

Sylvian nodded. There was absolutely nothing he could safely say about any of it anyway. Vasquez knew everything.

'Did you find Lyta?' she asked, after an awkward silence. Was that a kindness? He wasn't used to that from Vasquez, though it was not impossible.

'She's left the palace. I'll have to search the city and hope she wants to be found.'

'We'll find her, Sylvian. I can set Juárez on it, if you want.'

That was another twist of the knife, Sylvian thought. Then again, Juárez may have a better chance of getting her to listen to reason than he ever had. And he was a better tracker than Sylvian.

'Where is he?'

She almost smiled. It was hard to tell in a face like granite but he was sure there was a crack. 'Ostensibly guarding the prince. Lady Beatriz asked him to accompany her. He's smitten.'

'With the baby?' Juárez had never struck him as particularly paternal but you could never tell. Devotion came in many forms and the boy would be their king one day. Each of them was bound by an unbreakable bond to serve and protect the king and his family.

Vasquez actually laughed this time, so alien a sound that Sylvian almost went for a weapon in case this was some kind of impersonator in her place. 'With Lady Beatriz, you idiot. She's in there too, bossing all those nurses around. That woman could teach drill sergeants a thing or two, and you bodyguards as well. Hasn't left the child's side.'

That couldn't be good. Why would Beatriz be refusing to leave the baby? Was he ill? Weak? What was she protecting him from? Was she keeping him alive?

'Maybe I should check on them.'

'Maybe you should. Juárez will not thank you though. I, however, will be most grateful. I don't need all the guards distracted. One of you is bad enough. Off you go.'

The nursery was not far. Up a flight of stairs and along a corridor. He was almost there when Beatriz's cry broke the calm and he pitched himself forward, sprinting for the open door, weapons already drawn. A flood of nursemaids filled the corridor, scattering around him with screams of alarm. There wasn't time to stop and question one. He plunged on.

Juárez lay face-down on the floor, blood spreading out in a widening pool around his still form. Beatriz was clutching Alejandro in her arms, a tiny swaddled bundle with that familiar dark hair. Baron de Marasso and his men surrounded her.

What had happened here?

'Luca?' he said but his friend didn't move.

'Sylvian, help!' Beatriz called out.

'Captain Chant, stand down,' Marasso snarled at him, the tone of command so familiar. And the urge to obey him, as he had always obeyed him before serving the king and Vasquez directly, shuddered through him. 'You don't understand what's at stake here.'

At stake? They had the prince, that was what was at stake. His friend was down and Beatriz was in danger.

But Beatriz was Marasso's family, his blood. Why would he harm her? What was going on?

'Sylvian please,' she tried to say, her eyes huge. But at the same time he felt something surge through him, renewed strength, and he had no doubt as to where it came from. Beatriz was anything but helpless. If she was involved with Marasso, she'd be trying to slow him down, not strengthen him. 'He's going to take the baby. He's going to kill him.'

Marasso grabbed her arm, a knife digging into her side and he saw her go white, stiffening.

'I'm serving my kingdom and my god, you stupid bitch.'

'Your god?' Sylvian murmured. '*Kyron*? What does Kyron want with a baby?'

And when it came down to it, that didn't matter either. Marasso was trying to take the baby, to betray the queen, whatever he had planned after that. The old man, the man he'd looked up to, served and followed, who he'd allowed to bind him in oaths of blood and loyalty, to mark his body . . .

The scars on Sylvian's arms burned but he gritted his teeth and pushed the pain down. This couldn't be happening. What was Marasso doing?

But he knew.

Marasso, a traitor . . . The thought shuddered through him, stealing his breath, like claws in his heart. The old man, the commander in whom he had put all his faith in years ago, who had saved him, had the prince and intended to sacrifice the child? It wasn't possible. The deathly calm of battle settled over Sylvian's mind like a blanket of snow even as his body went on the attack. They were good, Marasso's men, but only good enough to fight as a pack. They must have surprised Juárez because he should have been able to take them in a fair fight. Not that any of this was fair.

Sylvian snarled as his sword tore through the nearest man's stomach and he kicked another aside, sending him to his knees. Beatriz was trying to both shield the baby, and protect herself from her cousin's blade.

One of the men got in a lucky blow and Sylvian went stumbling backwards. Juárez surged up, grabbing one of Sylvian's attackers by the knee and slammed a dagger into the leg, right at the femoral artery. Blood washed the other bodyguard's face scarlet and his teeth stood out white as bone. A kick to the face sent him sprawling back and as another man went to stamp down hard on his stomach, Sylvian threw a knife, embedding it up to the hilt in the bastard's chest.

'Juan, stop this. You have to stop this.' Was Beatriz trying to reason with him or command him? It wouldn't work. Not now. Sylvian had seen that gleam in the old man's eyes before. The commander would not be swayed. 'Ben will never agree to this.'

Marasso's voice was a bark. 'Like he has a choice? That stupid boy has no idea. He's a sleepwalker, your brother, blinded by his thirst for knowledge and completely under the sway of the gods he has imprisoned. He doesn't even realise it. When we release them they will make him crawl.'

Two more of Marasso's men came at Sylvian in a wild flurry of movement and savagery, scars on their arms old and as deeply embedded as his. They were dedicated to the baron, he'd give them that, but they were just soldiers. They didn't lose themselves in battle like he did. He twisted, taking them both at once and snarled as his sword bit through leather and flesh.

And then everything went still. Horribly still.

He could hear other royal guards coming up the corridor outside, roused by the nursemaids, could see the bodies sprawled around him, the empty cradle and Juárez, lying face up now, struggling to breathe, his eyes going glassy.

'Stay back,' Sylvian yelled. 'Do not endanger the prince.' Any more swords in here and there would be no protecting anyone. No one would walk away.

'Let us go,' said Marasso. He was holding something out to Sylvian, a dangling silver necklace with a small misshaped pendant hanging from it. The chain was tangled in his fingers where they held the sword. He dug the knife even closer to Beatriz as his other arm encircled her. 'Let us go now or you'll never see her again.'

No. Not this. He couldn't make this choice.

'What have you done to Lyta?' he growled. The ring on his finger burned with his anger. And fear. A cold terror washed over him at the thought of something happening to her. There was no other way Marasso could have got the pendant from her.

'You will never know if you don't get us out of the palace right now. You'll never see her again. Understand? Do as you are told, you Amberes dog. I give the commands and you obey them or there will be consequences.'

Consequences. There were always consequences. He couldn't risk Lyta. But he couldn't risk Beatriz, or Alejandro either.

Marasso's power wound around him. He was an Alvarez too, not as potent as the siblings perhaps but the same blood flowed in his veins. And he knew ways to use it that Beatriz would never consider. Sylvian remembered the knife digging into his skin, old wounds burning beneath all that came later.

His breath seemed to clog in his throat, choking him. The bastard had lied to him, then and now, but he couldn't seem to move.

'That's better,' Marasso's voice almost purred, and he seemed to relax a little. 'You always were the best of them, Sylvian. I should have kept you close, but at the time I thought placating the selfish fool would serve me better. But you have a new prince to protect now. Obey me and no one gets hurt.' He tugged Beatriz back against him, which made Alejandro wail and Sylvian's heart jerked up like a fish on a hook. He couldn't let him hurt the baby. And Marasso knew it. Sylvian almost lowered the sword in defeat.

Beatriz shook her head. It was the smallest gesture, but Sylvian understood. She pulled the baby closer, her arms trying to shelter him from this. Alejandro let out a long continuous wail. Marasso snarled in frustration, turned to her as if to strike her, or the child.

And that was all Sylvian needed.

He had a new prince to protect. And he would.

He surged forwards, even as Beatriz threw herself and the child aside, going down in a flurry of silk skirts, rolling aside still cradling Alejandro. Losing no time, the baron dropped the knife and brought both hands to the hilt of his sword, parrying Sylvian's blow.

The clash of steel on steel was deafening, but Sylvian knew it like a song. Not in his heart. In his blood, in his guts.

'They're going to kill your lover, Sylvian,' Marasso said, with a rush of spite Sylvian would never have thought possible from him. Stern but kind, fair, that was what he had always thought. Not anymore. The mask was gone. 'They'll use whatever wretched gods they can and tear your red-haired thief apart from the inside.' His swordsmanship was still the finest Sylvian had ever encountered. This was the man who had taught him the blade, to love it, to dance with it, to live to the full by being willing to die. 'You were my man first and can be again.' He pressed forward, throwing Sylvian back a step or two and they broke apart, circling each other. 'Come with us. We'll make the prince a god and all will be as it should be.'

'A god?'

'Yes, a god-king we'll be proud to obey. Our warrior god, the one we were born to serve. Not an arrogant fool like Francisco. He thinks himself another Imperator, but we can make the child so much more. Kyron has chosen him. They can do it, the alchemists. Charnock can do it. Imagine. We will conquer the world, and you and I will be his instruments, his weapons. The Church Imperial will not compare to the things we'll do.' Spittle flecked the corners of his mouth. 'Serve me again, boy. I'll raise you higher than you could imagine.'

'A god-king?' The breath caught in Sylvian's throat. That was what they were planning? He thought of the children who had died, of Lyta, of Kit . . . and he hesitated.

His son. Marasso was talking about making his son a god.

'Sylvian, no,' Beatriz whispered. She had backed into a corner, no escape available to her because the two of them blocked her only way out. In the corridor outside, only a sea of weapons awaited.

'Shut up Beatriz and know your place!' Marasso roared. 'Your brother understands what is at stake here. So does Sylvian. So should you. Our family line, our future, everything! Kyron will bless us all. We will sit at the right hand of the throne. We'll guide him as he grows and mould him into a true king. The king we need. I'll be as a father to him.'

'Francisco is his father,' Sylvian said, the edge of steel in his voice making no difference to Marasso.

'Is that the line you're still going with?' Marasso shook his head. 'Francisco is dead in a ditch by now. We laid an ambush for him that even he won't see coming. The queen is just a woman, still laid up in her birthing bed and she can be dealt with easily. You will obey me, Chant. Isn't it better for you, and for your Lyta, to have a strong hand guiding your lives? Better for everyone?' The power he wielded, his voice and his will, scorched through the marks in Sylvian's skin. 'Do as you're told, boy, and stand down.'

Enough, Sylvian thought. That was enough. Marasso didn't care what happened to Lyta, or to Sylvian. He didn't even care what happened to the baby. They were all just a means to an end. He knew that. He had always known that. Marasso didn't give a damn about anyone but Marasso.

He'd heard enough. They were all betrayed, all used. Who needed more details? He caught Beatriz's eye and her anger blazed there. She was not part of this. That much he could cling to.

'Ben would never agree to this,' Beatriz said. '*Never*. I don't know what you and those wretched alchemists have done to him but—'

'Ben has his own ambitions, ridiculous though they are. All he wants is peace and we can grant him that. The gods inside him want out and they will agree to anything. Even to deceiving him. Ben doesn't even realise how much he has aided us all in this. No, Ben will do as he's told and if he does, he'll get to keep on playing with his metals and his charms, free of the gods inside him. It might save his sanity. He can spend the rest of his life buried in his books. That's all he's interested in. Now for the last time—'

Sylvian took his opening. Marasso moved too late, distracted by Beatriz. The baron may have taught Sylvian swordsmanship, but Amberes had taught him to fight. He went low, dropping to his knee and coming up under Marasso's reach, his own blade skewering the baron before his old commander could react. The sword went up through the baron's body, under his ribs and tore him open when Sylvian twisted it savagely.

Marasso fell with a dull thud in the sudden silence, a sound echoed around the room, Lyta's necklace still gripped in his fist. Sylvian bent down to grab it, pulling the chain free of the twitching fingers, and lifted the pendant to his lips. It felt like a shard of ice.

A warning. She was in danger. She was in terrible danger.

You'll never see her again, Marasso had told him.

But he had promised. He had sworn that he would come for her when she needed him. Always.

And now . . . now . . . she needed him.

'Sylvian,' Beatriz gasped and held out the wailing baby to him. He dropped his sword and seized the child, cradling him against his body, terrified that he might do more harm than good, while Beatriz threw herself at Juárez's still form. 'Luca? Luca, please, wake up!' She pushed her hands against his wound and let that golden light flood her, enveloping him. And though she had said she had far less power than before, she threw everything she had into Luca Juárez's failing body. 'Don't leave me. Don't you dare leave me.'

All around him the palace was in uproar but all Sylvian could do was hold a screaming baby and watch Beatriz trying to save the life of his brother-in-arms. Finally, Juárez seemed to breathe again, without that terrible juddering rattle, and his blood flow subsided. Relief painted itself across Beatriz's face.

'I think he'll be all right. I think . . .' She slumped down beside the other royal bodyguard, holding him close, already weak from saving the queen and the baby, now as exhausted as Sylvian had ever seen her. Her breath was no more than a whisper, her skin like old ashes.

When the general arrived with all the guards she could muster, Sylvian tried to give a report but his voice failed him. Alejandro wailed. He had a pair of lungs, that was for sure, and part of Sylvian wanted to join in.

Lyta, they had Lyta. He wasn't even sure who. The Blacksmiths' Guild? The alchemist? Beatriz had insisted Ben wasn't involved but he was an Alvarez and the baron hadn't been shy about implicating him. Lyta had been so angry with him about whatever she had seen at the guild, and about his association with this Charnock character.

And now, dear gods . . .

The next thing he knew the queen was there. She gathered her baby son in her arms and finally . . . *finally* . . . the child calmed, hiccoughing against her shoulder. Annika made soothing noises, whispered endearments and Sylvian faced her, aware of the wildness surging inside him, needing a command, needing her to tell him what to do.

It was like a wolf tearing at his heart and his guts, desperate to be out, to hunt, to kill. He met Annika's gaze and saw it reflected there. Perhaps it came from Ystara herself. Perhaps it was the rage he could no longer control. He didn't know and he didn't care. It was a force he could use. But he needed the command. He couldn't leave her without it.

They had been betrayed. All of them.

'Take Lady Alvarez into custody,' said Annika. 'Get Juárez to the physicians. Go quietly, Beatriz. We will speak later.'

Beatriz didn't argue. Perhaps she couldn't. She didn't have any strength left in her and Sylvian feared she was too broken to defend herself now. She had nothing to do with her cousin's plot, he knew that, but would anyone else believe her? And what of Ben? She might believe her brother innocent, but like Lyta with Kit, Beatriz was blind where Ben was concerned.

'Sylvian?' Annika prompted, and he found his voice.

'Majesty, they have Lyta.'

It was all he could say. The words were too great, too dangerous, too terrible. If he said more he feared he would lose his mind and run wild.

'Then you had better go and get her back,' Annika said. 'Do whatever you have to do, Sylvian. I release you from your duty and your vows to protect me. The Crown and the city need you now. If a single guild can stand against us, do what they will with our citizenry, then we have already lost Amberes. The others will see and they will know, so we must be swift and decisive in our response.' She spoke as a queen and he knew orders when he heard them. He knew what she meant as well. This was a revolt and it had to be crushed immediately, because otherwise it would spread. And Francisco's retaliation to something like that would be horrific.

But then her voice softened, dropping to something low and infinitely more dangerous.

'And if they have hurt her, in any way . . .' She fixed him with that silvery glare, held out her hand and he saw Ystara in her eyes. There was no doubt of it. Sylvian slid the ring from his finger and offered it to her. When she took it, the rage inside him rose in a wave in response, the rage of a goddess thwarted, divine fury. Betrayed by her own brothers and sisters. 'Kill them all.'

CHAPTER TWENTY-FIVE

Lyta

Viola Alderton knelt in the temple. She was dressed in the white robes of a new acolyte, her head bowed before the statue of the Imperator and she didn't move. She might have been a statue herself. Bandages were wound around her palms but otherwise there were no signs she was ever injured. Lyta remembered the lash cutting into her back, the blood and the ragged flesh, but there was no trace now. Had they healed her, somehow?

'Lady Viola?' Tiberius said in that gentle, charming voice that set every one of Lyta's nerves on edge. 'Your brother is here.'

The girl turned towards them and Lyta frowned. She barely looked like the same woman. These placid features carried no signs of torture or misery now, her hair a fall of silken gold, and Eninn gave a murmur of unease as they saw her. She had been allowed to wash and dress befitting her station, but she seemed . . . diminished. Empty.

The goddess is gone, he said.

Lyta covered her mouth as if coughing. 'What do you mean?'

Gone. Like she was never there. What have they done to her?

But she had been there. Lyta knew that. She could still hear her voice, still remember the divine madness in the girl's eyes. She probably still had bruises where the caged woman had grabbed her.

Alderton ran towards his sister and swept her up in his arms, talking to her in hushed tones, his concern evident.

'Not a prisoner then,' said Janlow. 'Not really anything like you said, Lyta.'

'No,' Lyta agreed warily. 'Something's going on. Something weird.'

'I don't like weird,' he muttered, shifting uncomfortably. 'It never ends well.'

On that she had to agree. But not out loud. Not with him.

Tiberius was standing close by and she didn't like the smile he wore either. 'A miracle,' he said again with deeply formal tones. 'Our August One delivered her, healed her and made her whole. Mighty is his name.'

'How?' Lyta asked before she thought better of it. She heard Frida hiss softly in warning but it was far too late. Tiberius was already smiling at her. Why was he always bloody smiling?

'We can work wonders here, Mistress Cornellis. I told you as much. A god is only a parasite in this world. We can remove that. It has always been our mission, you see?'

A parasite. She felt Eninn bristle but tried to hold still. She couldn't afford to give anything away right now.

But it wasn't an answer, was it? She asked again, a bit more petulantly. '*How*?'

He shrugged and strode forwards, beckoning her to follow. On the altar, at the foot of the statue of the Imperator, there was a short sword, not much longer than Sylvian's belt knife. It was flat, no wider than her hand at its broadest, and had a tapered point. Not elegant, or decorative, but each edge had been sharpened until the steel gleamed. The hilt had ridges for grip and a round knob at the end. There was a single word engraved on it—*Brabo*. It was old—no, ancient—but beautifully cared for. It was surrounded by row upon row of candles and their light flickered in its sheen.

That was what she was here for. For Kit.

Tiberius wrapped his fingers around the hilt and lifted the sword, the edge scraping against the stone so loudly that Lyta flinched. A chill surrounded the blade, a sense of something primordial and dreadful. Something she didn't want to stand anywhere near. The candle flames flickered wildly as it passed by.

'Behold the gladius of Silvius Brabo, Prince of the Church Imperial, blessed of the August One, he who freed Amberes from its dark god Druon and brought enlightenment to your people. He cut off Druon's right hand and threw him in the Scaldis rather than pay another coin in tribute. Is this not a tale of your own people?'

Lyta frowned. Yes, there was some old story about a giant and a hero, and cutting off a hand. But a Prince of the Church Imperial? That wasn't part of it.

'The Church never ruled here,' she said carefully. Because *fuck off with your imperialist bullshit* might offend. 'And I've never heard of any Brabo except from you.'

I have, Eninn whispered in the back of her head. *He was their general, the one who hunted us, the one who almost killed us all. It's still called the* Brabantine, *Lyta, for the blood he spilt here.*

Good to know, she thought. Not something she was about to share.

'We've lived in Amberes all our lives,' Janlow cut in. 'Don't know any Silvius Brabo. Sounds like a knob.'

Thank you Janlow, she thought. Very helpful. Insulting their god-slaying hero while the man in front of you is holding a sacred and very sharp weapon. Maybe they'd be lucky and Tiberius wouldn't deign to sully the gladius's point with their mortal blood. Didn't mean he wouldn't use something else though.

If Tiberius was tempted, he didn't show it.

'It kills gods,' he said softly.

'You killed the goddess in her?' Lyta asked. She didn't know anything about Rhiannon but she doubted that she'd deserved it. She wasn't exactly relishing the thought of telling Lord Stirling about that. Albion would lose their collective minds if their royal goddess was actually dead.

'Banished perhaps. Exiled. She is gone, is that not enough?'

Oh, Lyta thought and had to fight an insane urge to giggle. *He doesn't know. He hasn't got a clue how it works. He has a magic sword and he doesn't know what to do with it.*

'Gone?'

'It amounts to the same thing,' Tiberius told her curtly. 'They call it the Nether. I believe you have heard of that at least.'

Ah, that was more familiar ground. How did he know about that?

'You said you were going to burn her,' Lyta said, almost absently, desperate not to give anything else away. 'What changed your mind?'

'We aren't animals, Lyta. There was always a choice. Viola chose the blade and thus saved herself. Did you think we meant to cut her head off? It was always her choice—give up Rhiannon to the blade, or burn with her horse goddess. She chose wisely. After you left she seemed to finally come to her senses. I was most relieved.'

A shiver of warning ran a cold finger down Lyta's back. She forced herself not to show it and fixed her full attention on the gladius instead.

'Is that what the child who broke into your temple was after?' she asked blithely. 'That knife?'

He executed a couple of moves with it, cutting the air, twisting it this way and that, turning it in a circle. A swordsman at practice, expert and casual with familiarity. Oh he'd handled weapons like that many times. And he was probably showing off a little. She wasn't impressed. He had nothing on Sylvian.

'I assume so. But they were possessed by a god, weren't they? That's what you believe. Had they touched it, it would have killed them. Perhaps it did.'

Let him believe that, Lyta thought. It was probably safer. Charnock's crappy alchemy had killed Clémence and all the others. No magic sword necessary.

Alderton rejoined them, his sister at his side, her head bowed to avoid eye contact. 'With respect, Inquisitor Tiberius, as the head of our family and custodian of my sister, I will be taking her back home. Imperial law means that my will overrules her whims, as I'm sure you will agree.'

Ah yes, Lyta thought, that charming attitude of the Church Imperial to women. It pervaded the Latinate States. Try to argue your way out of that. She'd told Alderton it was their best card to play.

'Even when she expresses such newfound devotion?' Tiberius turned, pointing the gladius directly at Alderton now, staring down its length. He was playing with them, Lyta thought. Arrogant arsehole.

Alderton didn't flinch. His smile turned thin and humourless. 'She's just a girl. What does she know of devotion or anything else? A child beguiled first by an errant goddess and then enchanted with those who rescued her from that. Women have no place in your Church. She needs to come back to her family now. So we can reform her ways.'

If Kit had said that about Lyta she would have kneed him in the balls so hard he'd have spat them out six yards away.

But then Viola spoke, her voice soft and musical, her tone all innocence, and Lyta was suddenly certain, all an act. 'My lord Inquisitor, I am so grateful for all you have done in liberating me. But my brother speaks true. It is my duty to return to my family. I have so much for which to atone.'

The girl's hands clasped a little too tightly in front of her, her fingers knotting together. Lyta stared at the bandages on them. Was that where she'd held the blade? Had she let them cut her? They weren't the only ones desperate to get out of here. Viola Alderton was no fool and Lyta had had enough of these games.

'Frida, now,' Lyta said.

Frida slung the pack from under her cloak and pulled out the hand of glory. It was somewhat worse for wear after whatever Ben had done to it in his cellar but there was no one there when Lyta had dropped by to pick it up earlier so she couldn't exactly ask. She'd persuaded the servants she was meant to be there and grabbed it. Apologies could be made later on.

Frida tossed it to Lyta who thrust the wick into the candles flaming in the votive rail while Janlow and Alderton drew their own weapons to engage the militia closing on them.

'Quickly,' Janlow snarled. She ignored him, cupping the flame to protect it while it took.

'Don't do this Mistress Cornellis,' Tiberius began, and he sounded almost resigned. Like he'd expected something. Not the hand, maybe, but something. 'I can help you as well—'

Help her? Not a chance in a million hells.

The silvery flame finally caught the wick, guttered wildly for a moment, and then the magic of the hand spread out like a concussive wave. It hit the guards, still masquerading as acolytes and they went down like sacks of wheat. Alderton swayed on his feet but Lyta grabbed his arm, willing him to stay with them. Whoever lit the candle controlled its power, or so Eninn told her, and she needed them still. Janlow stepped in beside Frida, and made some sort of protective sign on his chest. Lyta wasn't sure who he was praying to and she didn't want to ask.

Tiberius and his men sank down too, captured effortlessly by sleep.

'I don't want your help,' Lyta said to the Inquisitor. 'And I never will. Right, Alderton, get your sister. Time we were getting out of here.'

'Will the spell hold?' Alderton asked.

'It had better.'

Step two, Lyta thought. 'Frida?'

Frida was already rummaging in the back. She withdrew a huge crossbow fitted with sights and trailing a length of rope. The thing had a kick like a mule and when she fired it up into the dome, she had to take a couple of steps back to steady herself.

But Frida never missed a shot. The bolt sank into the roof right beside the oculus opening. Both Frida and Lyta seized the other end of the rope and pulled. It held fast.

'Go,' Lyta told her and Frida began to climb, shimmying up the rope with practised ease while Lyta held the end fast. As soon as she was at the top, she secured a rope ladder and let it snake down.

'Alderton, Viola, go.'

She didn't want to be last out, but there wasn't any choice. She sent Janlow up next and grabbed the sword from where it lay beside the unconscious Inquisitor. They might have let Viola leave with her brother. She hoped Alderton hadn't figured that out yet but didn't have time to worry about it. What was done was done now. The sword though? They would never have let her take the sword. Oh Tiberius was going to lose his mind when he woke up. Which would be soon, because she couldn't carry the lit hand and climb at the same time. But she couldn't leave it in their grasp either. It was too powerful a thing, a relic of the god this sword had slain.

This, Lyta decided, was the tricky bit.

Be quick, Eninn told her, which was not actually as helpful as he thought.

Lyta hooked the sword onto her belt, smothered the flame, dropped the hand back into the sack and climbed for her life.

She was only halfway up when she heard people stirring below, but she forced herself on, hand over hand, as quick as she could. Once someone had the bright idea of a crossbow of their own, she was in real trouble.

She felt the first pursuer start to climb the ladder behind her, felt it shaking and begin to strain.

Above her she heard their voices rise in argument and then Janlow leaned into the oculus, knife in hand, blade against the left-hand rope of Frida's ladder. He locked eyes with her and grinned.

Her throat closed tight and she made her body keep going, faster and faster. Danger behind her and danger above. If he cut the ropes she'd be done for. If she was lucky the fall would kill her. If not . . . Tiberius could do with her whatever he wanted. And she knew how they felt about thieves. And about Eninn.

Her life right now, was in the hands of Frida, Alderton and Petrus Janlow.

Fuck! She should never have trusted them, none of them. Why hadn't she gone first? Idiot.

'Don't you dare!' Viola Alderton gasped, her voice ringing out through the night. 'Charles, by all that's divine! Stop this. She saved me. We still need her.'

Lyta could have kissed her. It might not do any good but what did that matter right now?

'Petrus, wait,' Alderton commanded and Lyta caught the flash of annoyance and disappointment on Janlow's face. But he obeyed all the same and Lyta managed to breathe again.

As Lyta reached the top, it was Frida who grabbed her hands and hauled her to safety. She rolled onto the rooftop and then onto her belly, gazing back down into the heart of the Imperial Temple as Janlow sliced through the ropes and the ladder, and her pursuer fell. He landed lightly, she saw and let out a string of what she presumed were apologies, on his knees before the Inquisitor.

Tiberius Octavius Aurelianus was awake again and stood, gazing up at her.

But instead of anger and outrage, he had a strangely knowing half-smile on his handsome face and Lyta decided it was time to get the hell off the roof no matter who she was with.

CHAPTER TWENTY-SIX

Kit

There was a strange half-light in the dungeon and Kit could almost see now his eyes had become accustomed to it.

What kind of guild headquarters had a dungeon anyway? It was probably originally a cellar. But guilds tended to enact their own justice if they could. So he guessed it made sense. This way dirty laundry didn't get flaunted in front of the rest of the city, or worst of all, the other guilds. The Worshipful Company of Art and Word had been known to destroy printing presses and melt down type of those who transgressed their rules. But that was a far cry from chaining people up underground.

'Kit? You still with me?'

Stirling kept trying to make him talk. It really wasn't helping. Kit didn't want to talk. In fact his brain wanted to shut itself down entirely and let his body follow it to the darkness. Perhaps he'd find his own Nether, and lose himself in that.

He ought to be angry, he knew that. He ought to be enraged. Ben had betrayed them, Ben who he loved with all his heart, Ben who had looked him dead in the face and said they were finished, supposedly to protect him. But it had been a lie. All of it. Perhaps all along.

Because one thing Ben was right about. Kit didn't know him, not really. He'd fallen in love with a man caught in an enchantment, been further beguiled by a man with a host of gods living in his head, who barely knew himself sometimes. Kit had no idea who Ben Alvarez really was. Common sense had tried to warn him, every instinct that had always served him had warned him about getting involved with a noble, but he hadn't listened. Ben's mind, his heart, his wit, his body . . . it had all been far too tempting. Kit had fallen in love and fallen hard.

But in the end . . . well, old loyalties always won out, didn't they?

What was Kit to him but a printer who was desperate for a fuck?

'Kit?'

'Yes, still here. Not going anywhere. You?' He jerked on the chains again for good measure and felt the bands crushing his wrists dig in to the raw flesh there again in a stab of grounding pain. That was real. Nothing else might be. But this was.

He was going to die in here. They both were. And that was only if they were lucky and the alchemists didn't have anything worse planned for them.

Lyta would come for him, wouldn't she? She wouldn't give up until she found him. But Lyta had other things on her mind and she didn't even know he was missing. Probably. Who was going to tell her?

Maybe Jem, eventually. Tomorrow or the next day. Or at least she would find out he was missing, but she wouldn't know where he was, would she? Maybe she'd guess. He had to hope she'd guess. But by then it would probably be far too late. They weren't going to let him go. They weren't going to let him live. Not when he could identify people. They weren't exactly hiding their identities to begin with.

No, they didn't intend to let him out of here alive.

He thought of that kid, the way his eyes had rolled up in his head, his voice choking, right before his chest exploded. These people did stuff like that to kids. They wouldn't hesitate to get rid of a printer from Amberes.

'We are never getting out of here,' he muttered.

There was another rustle of movement and the sound of Stirling's own chains clanking. 'Never say never,' he mumbled. He had something in his mouth, mangling his words. 'It doesn't pay to be defeatist.'

Was he trying to pick the lock?

Kit let out a long rush of breath. It was what Lyta would have tried to do. Stirling sounded like Lyta. Like Lyta when she was listening to Eninn and setting out to cause the most chaos she could possibly cause.

All he'd wanted was a quiet life. His work, his business and some peace and quiet. He'd been an idiot to dream about love as well, but he'd thought he had a chance. For a little while. And now . . .

'Kit?' That voice brought his head around so fast he felt his neck crack. That wasn't Stirling. 'Kit? Are you there?'

On the other side of the cell, Stirling went as quiet as a corpse, whatever he was trying to do instantly halted.

Kit swallowed hard on his suddenly tight throat. It was like trying to force down a jagged lump of coal. 'Where else would I be?'

Ben unshuttered a lantern and Kit shied away, blinking as the light blinded him. Ben crouched on the other side of the bars, his face lined with concern and grief. The door was open behind him and beyond it an empty hallway vanished into darkness.

'Hold on, I'm going to get you out of here.'

'Won't your mentor be upset with you about that?' Kit jerked his arms again so the chains rattled. The pain was worth it for the wince Ben made. He hardened his beautiful face a moment later. He pulled out a huge metal key and fitted it into the lock of the cell itself. It turned smoothly, well-oiled and cared for, and the gap in the bars swung open silently. Ben stepped inside.

'This isn't what I intended. None of this is—'

'What did you intend?' Stirling asked coldly. 'Or did you simply not think that far?'

'You know how important this work is, Piers. The possibilities, the wonders . . . If I can't focus anymore because of the things in my head—'

Stirling's voice turned scathing. 'Well, as it's all about *you*, Ben—not dead children, or Viola and whatever they did to her—that's *fine*.'

Ben stared at him, his eyes wide, the lantern light making the colours of autumn in them glow. 'Piers, you don't understand—'

Stirling let his head fall back against the wall and hit it several times.

'*Dead children*,' Kit reminded Ben, his voice glacial.

Ben wilted. He hunkered down in front of Kit like some kind of penitent.

'I swear, I didn't know about that. There are pieces of my memory missing, Kit. The gods maybe, the amulet . . . I don't know. On my honour.'

'Not a lot of that left right now, is there?' Stirling said.

Ben glared at him over Kit's shoulder, which reminded Kit once more that he didn't really know this man. Every inch of his body, perhaps, but not what lurked inside. Gods, he was a fool. So was Ben.

Ben let out a long sigh and turned back to Kit. 'Beatriz is going to kill me.'

Kit decided he'd had enough of this. Ben didn't get to indulge in self-pity. Not now. 'Not if the rest of us get there first. You sold us out.'

'Oh, for the sake of the many gods,' Ben muttered. 'I did nothing of the sort. Hold still. Whatever you do don't move.' He laid his soft fingertips on Kit's arm, and the contact sent a shudder through him he didn't want to examine. Kit still wanted him, he realised. Ached for him. How could he not? But he couldn't trust him, not anymore. He winced and bit into his lower lip, holding still as instructed. Ben unstopped a small vial he'd taken from his pocket and poured it on the join of the shackles. 'It'll take a few moments.'

'Is that acid?' Kit exclaimed, jerking back, far too late now. The metal was hissing and a sharp smell rose in the air.

'*Aqua regia*,' Ben corrected him. 'Don't worry, the shackles should come off before it touches your skin.'

'So the answer is yes, Kit,' Stirling interrupted and thrust his own wrists out as if to receive a blessing. 'It's acid. A combination of acids, one of the strongest mixes at an alchemist's disposal. They use it for the transformation of base metals into gold, and to make living silver. It's a vital part of the great work, isn't that right Ben? *One* of the great works anyway.'

Ben poured some of the solution on Stirling's shackles as well. It hissed and frothed. 'Maybe stop talking so you don't breathe in the fumes,' he replied coldly. Seigneur Alvarez indeed.

Kit felt the metal give and tore his hands free before the acid could go any further. The chains thudded back against the wall and before he knew what he was doing he seized Ben and flung him back beside them, holding him there, his forearm across his lover's throat.

'What are they doing? What's your involvement in this?'

To his horror, Ben's eyes filled with sudden tears as they fixed on his. He saw terror there and regret, along with endless shame. The fear directed at him would have made Kit baulk had the shame not been there as well, which told him Ben knew how bad all of this was. He knew what he'd done and had helped others to do.

'I'm an idiot.' He said the words so quietly and in tones of such defeat that it punctured the rage in Kit more completely than any other argument could have. 'I didn't think. I'm meant to think, Kit. It's the one thing I'm supposed to be good at.'

He lifted the amulet he wore in a shaking hand to show it more clearly to Kit. 'I made it to keep the gods at bay. And I thought, if I could block them from my mind, it might be as good as getting them out of it, like rewriting the book was meant to, then it would be easy to go back to a normal life. There's so much I want to—to do, to be. And I can't, not with them there. But the amulets didn't work the way I thought and the gods and I . . . we sort of bleed together.

'Charnock can help though. He can take gods out of relics and put them into people. And he says he can do it the other way around. He did it before he says, learned it from a magus in the Latinate States, or maybe Doctor Dee, I don't know. He refined it, perfected it. He wrote to me. He'd heard of my research and then . . . It's an unstable process, so we were working together since he came here to fix that, to make it safe. For all of us. But I think he . . . I think . . . I think Kyron, and maybe Gloir and Nimyeh . . . They saw Eninn run free and Ystara use her ring as a relic and tie herself to Sylvian and Annika, and they want to be free so much. I think, those moments I don't remember, that they worked with Charnock.' Tears spilled out of his eyes, matting the lower lashes and his lower lip trembled. His excuses ran out. 'I'm sorry,' he said.

Kit didn't know what to do with that. He was still furious. 'You should be.'

'I swear I didn't know about the children. Or the rest.'

'What rest?'

'The baby prince, and Lyta and . . . Gods, you don't know, do you?'

'They know nothing, Benedictus,' said another voice behind them, on the other side of the bars. With a deafening clang the cell door slammed closed. 'They aren't on your level. They'll never understand the complexity, let alone the necessity.' The accent, rough with the tones of Albion, never as refined or cultured as Stirling's, made Ben flinch in Kit's grasp. Kit jerked him closer, though whether to protect him or to use him as a shield, he was no longer sure. 'Don't hurt him, Master Cornellis. Things will go very badly for you if you do.'

'Charnock,' Stirling growled, shaking off the iron shackles as if they were nothing but paper now. Not that it mattered. Charnock was not alone. There were five guards with him, filling the narrow space, and more outside in the hallway.

The lean, ferret-faced man grinned unpleasantly at his countryman. 'You came all this way for nothing, Stirling.'

'I came for Rhiannon. And Viola.'

'And now you've lost both. The Church got the goddess, and Viola . . . A goddess in your brain does tend to do a huge amount of damage physically and mentally, doesn't it Benedictus? Especially if you're mortal. And that's all you want to be. Isn't it? For him? What a waste that would be, but if it's what you want . . .'

'Kit,' Ben breathed, soft as a lover's plea. 'Let me go. Please.'

Kit couldn't help it. He loosened his grip and Ben pulled away. Charnock nodded to the guards who opened the cell door for him, leaving Kit in the cell. He'd been in on it. Maybe not all the way. Maybe they'd used him and his brilliant mind, but he'd definitely been involved. Whatever his reasons, whatever he believed . . . He must have guessed. He *should* have guessed.

But Ben had always been one to lose himself in his work. That had seen him trapped in the Scholars' Tower to begin with, heedless of the path down which his research was leading him. And the gods had used him as surely as Charnock had.

He'd got lost, he used to say. But never so lost as now. But the one thing Kit knew about the Alvarezes, they didn't give up.

Ben advanced slowly and carefully on Charnock.

'I won't let you hurt him,' he said. He pulled off the amulet, discarding it on the cell floor and his body began to glow. He was brighter than the lanterns, drowning them out until they were more like shadows. Words and symbols skirted over his skin as the gods locked within him took hold of him again. So long denied, they came on with a vengeance and Kit heard the echoes of their voices in Ben's words. The guards murmured uneasily, stepped back, raising weapons, but Ben ignored them, all his attention fixed on the alchemist. 'You cannot make Kit agree to help you, and without his agreement, your plan falls apart. I will never let you hurt anyone again. *We* will not allow this to continue.'

Charnock smiled, a sight which made Kit's heart lurch up in alarm. He was halfway up to his feet as Charnock spoke, his voice so smug and calm. 'You think too much of yourself Seigneur Alvarez. Divinities, control your vessel.'

Ben choked, froze and then dropped to his knees, clawing at his throat. The light in him died.

'What are —? Kyron? Gloir? Nimych, please . . .'

The words and symbols still slid across his skin, but there was no light now. No power. Nothing.

He sprawled on the floor, and the alchemist kicked him hard, sending him rolling to one side. With a strangled sob, Ben curled in on himself.

'I think not,' said Charnock. 'Your work, Benedictus, is extraordinary. Combining metals and their properties with the symbols, in such artistry . . . Honestly, I would never have thought of it. But we have an agreement, your gods and I.' His eyes flashed with a strange kind of obsessive jealousy. 'That's my skill, you see? I find brilliant people and I make deals.' He'd used Ben to get to the gods inside him. And he was still using him. He clearly intended to keep on doing it. He raised his voice abruptly, a certain formality infecting it. 'Divinities, take him and make him yours at last. Wipe the slate clean. We don't have time for his reluctance now.'

A shudder ran through Ben's body and his body convulsed, as if twisted from inside. He begged, a strangled inarticulate string of words. And then, slowly, he dragged himself to his feet, his eyes aglow, not a trace of Ben Alvarez remaining in them. Kit threw himself at the bars, as if he could tear them open, trying to reach Ben. Or what might be left of him, if anything.

Charnock turned on him. 'Don't think I've forgotten you, Cornellis. I didn't really believe it until I met your sister, that old tale of Amberes, of a brother and sister of a bloodline unsurpassed, wild children of the oldest of gods, here. For a while I thought it was him.' He cast a dismissive glance at Ben but then reached through the bars quick as an adder, grabbed Kit's jaw and held him like a specimen to be examined. 'But then I saw her and I knew the truth. You and your sister. Just left here in Amberes. Waiting. It's probably why you were so drawn to him. Ben is, after all, a Divine Nexus, created to attract all that is divine to him. I expect you weren't able to resist.'

He tilted Kit's face one way and then the other and there was nothing Kit could do to stop him. Not now.

'Perfect,' he said. 'And there's no minor deity to rid you of first.'

When he released him, Kit's legs almost went beneath him. He caught himself on the bars.

'Bring him with us,' Charnock told the guards who had accompanied him. 'It's time this was over and done with. The veil is only thin enough for a little longer. We must act now. I'd invite you to watch, Lord Stirling,' Charnock sneered, 'but I think it's better that you rot in here. I'll find a use for you eventually. Maybe Gloir might take a fancy to you after all. As you said, you're still an alchemist.'

Ben followed Charnock from the prison without a backwards glance.

Two guards seized Kit and dragged him from the cell, leaving Stirling behind.

CHAPTER TWENTY-SEVEN

Lyta

Lyta hadn't reckoned on ice and snow on the rooftops of Amberes. It took longer to get back down to the ground than she would have liked, and dark as it was, the way proved treacherous more than once. No one spoke, no more than to give a bark of warning, or in Alderton's case, to check on his sister.

Viola had grown quiet again and by the time they were clear and back on solid ground, she was cold and shivering. Alderton took off his cloak and wrapped it around her.

'What were you thinking?' he asked softly, more human than Lyta had ever heard him.

'There's too much to explain,' she whispered. 'I'm tired, Charles, so tired, but I finally feel more myself now I am free of that dreadful place. We have to stop Charnock. He believes he must act tonight. If he succeeds all will be lost, Amberes will fall, and Albion will be blamed.'

'Enough of this nonsense,' Alderton's voice turned gruff . 'We're going back to the house and I am locking you in your room until I can secure passage home. We have indulged you far too much.'

But Viola ignored him. She stood, staring up at the full moon overhead. 'Where's Piers?' she asked and for a moment Lyta didn't think she was talking to them at all. 'Where is he? Did they kill him? Thomas said he'd kill him. They'll want to silence him. He shouldn't have come after me.'

'He was well enough last time I saw him,' Lyta tried to assure her.

'*Piers*?' Alderton had taken on that cold, thin tone which probably meant that if Charnock hadn't killed Stirling, Alderton was more than happy to see it done himself. 'What were you doing with Lord Stirling?'

They had almost reached the Rose Palace. Sylvian was in there somewhere and Lyta needed him, wanted him, but there wasn't time. Besides if she set foot in there Marasso would know. Alderton and the others would be safe in there, could claim sanctuary from the Imperials if they dared to give chase outside of the temple. Alderton could explain and they would have to listen to him. Now he had his sister back, they could tell all without embarrassing their queen.

This was her cue to leave. She needed to get to the guild with the sword before anything happened to Kit. She backed up and promptly bumped into Frida.

'Where are you off to?'

Lyta cursed softly to herself, but she wasn't going to be able to slip away quietly now. 'They have Kit, Frida.'

But Frida kept her voice low and careful. 'I can't let you hand her over to the alchemist instead.'

'And I have no intention of doing that. They want the sword. No idea why.'

'It kills gods,' Viola whispered, and the weight of sorrow in her voice made them all stop and stare. Lyta hadn't been aware she was listening, or even how she could have heard the two of them. But her attention was on them now, unwavering. 'It is a powerful relic, the most powerful in Amberes I think. He will use it in combination with the others linked to that old god. Be careful Lyta. Please. It's dangerous. I'm too weak to be of any help yet. Without Rhiannon . . .'

The horse, the relic . . . 'I don't have your relic. I gave it to Sylvian.'

A smile flickered over her lips. 'You were right not to bring it with you. Who knows what the Inquisitor would do with it. Besides, I don't know if I would be strong enough to use it and if I'm not, I'll lose her forever. Or lose myself. Piers will know. He always knows. He's her servant first.'

There was a sadness in those words which Lyta found far too familiar.

'I have to go,' was all Lyta could say in reply to that.

'I'll come with you,' Frida said suddenly.

'Why?' It came out louder than she'd thought, louder than was safe.

Frida sighed her long-suffering sigh. 'It's Kit, isn't it?'

Lyta swallowed, emotions clawing around in her chest that she couldn't quite examine right now. Before she could say anything, Frida turned her attention on Lord Alderton and took charge of the situation.

'Forgive us, my lord, but we have to stop these alchemists before it's too late.'

Alderton eyed her shrewdly. 'I owe you, Mistress Cornellis and I pay my debts. I will raise the alarm at the palace. Try not to get killed. Mistress Elwyn, I value your service and my offer still stands to you, Mistress Cornellis. Perhaps even on more favourable terms.' The sneer that twisted his mouth undermined that thought, even if Lyta would have considered it to begin with. 'Maybe. We'll have to see how this falls out.'

Not on your life, Lyta thought. But she had to take the offer at face value for now.

'Please get word to General Vasquez and Captain Chant,' she said. She didn't add *and anyone else who might listen.* 'Tell Sylvian . . . tell him I'm all right and whatever the Baron de Marasso says is a lie.'

'Marasso?' Alderton leaned in closer, clearly intrigued. 'What does the baron have to do with this?'

'He's the one behind this, who told me they had Kit. He's in this up to his neck, so warn the queen. I think he has designs on the throne himself. She'll probably be delighted for an excuse to be rid of him.'

More scheming and trickery to delight him, Lyta thought bitterly, and not even the good kind. The likes of Lord Alderton lived for that. He'd use this to scale some kind of hierarchy Lyta couldn't even visualise.

She turned her attention to Frida instead. 'You heard Viola. Charnock and De Werve have Kit and whatever they're doing, it happens tonight. I don't want him hurt in all this. We need to get to him as quickly as possible.'

'On that we agree. My lord?' Frida seeking permission, that was new. Whatever he had on her still held firm. Haldevar's death maybe, and with it her reputation and continued survival in this town? Maybe she liked working for him.

Alderton nodded. 'Go.'

*

They made their way up Meir and across Cornmarket Street, hugging the edge of the frozen canal almost as far as Johannesport.

The Blacksmiths' Guild loomed over them. There were furnaces at work even now. Smoke poured from the chimneys and the gates were firmly closed against the city and the night. Here in the heart of Amberes, thinking itself greater than the rest of the city, it was a viper curled up, waiting, Lyta thought and an unexpected rage rippled through her. How dare they? How dare they do this in her city? In her home? How dare they threaten her brother?

If the guild succeeded in this treason, what would the king do to her city in return? Because she knew Francisco wouldn't let this stand.

She and Frida stopped on the corner before the bridge. She glanced at Frida who was gazing over the canal there, towards the area where Haldevar's shop had once been.

'You ready?' she asked, drawing Frida's attention back to the here and now. She needed her fully here, not focused on regrets and loss, on her own terrible mistakes and betrayals.

Frida shuddered, so small a movement you'd barely notice it if you didn't know her as well as Lyta did.

'How do you want to play this?' Her expression was fixed with determination.

Lyta let out a long breath. Once again, a plan might have been nice. But there were some plays that were as old as time and they both knew them inside out.

'I'll give them what they want. You stab them in the back.'

'Playing to our strengths then,' Frida replied taciturnly, and stepped back, vanishing into the darkness.

For a moment Lyta hoped her smart mouth hadn't pushed too far and Frida's described role in this wasn't too on the nose. But the time to worry had passed. She heaved in a deep breath and walked up to the gates.

The smith on guard was not impressed at being hauled out of his cosy little gatehouse. He probably hadn't been dozing, she decided—he was too clear-eyed for that—but she was willing to bet that he had a stove or something in there and had been nice and warm.

'I need to see De Werve,' she said. 'Tell him Lyta Cornellis is here. I have the sword and know where the girl is if that's still of interest to him.'

Neither of those things were a lie. She stood firm, confident enough that the message would bring the guildmaster out fast enough. Or maybe Charnock. Who knew?

They made her wait, the bastards, out there in the cold. When they finally opened the gates, there was no sign of De Werve or Charnock. No one senior at all, just a collection of guards who glared at her and ushered her inside.

If there was one more guard once among their number when they closed the gates, they didn't seem to notice. At least, Lyta hoped she was counting right.

This was the plan, she told herself. Stick to the plan. And pray that Frida didn't decide to double-cross her again. It was a risk. A huge risk.

But it was for Kit and she had no choice.

They brought her in to a long corridor and spread out. 'Weapons,' said the leader. Lyta casually removed her knife and handed it to him. It was pathetically small in his big hand. He discarded it with a disdain that was actually insulting. That knife had saved her life. Sylvian had given it to her.

Carefully she removed the sword next, holding it like the relic it was. She actually saw the light flare up in his eyes. He was a smith first and foremost, after all, perhaps even a bladesmith by trade. She could tell he couldn't wait to get his hands on it, whether to examine it or test it out.

'Stand down, journeyman,' barked De Werve as he stepped through the door at the far end, his face lighting up as he saw Brabo's sword. 'That weapon is a relic. It belongs to our lord, Gloir.'

Like fuck it does, Lyta thought, though whether that thought was her own or Eninn's was anyone's guess. Gloir would probably wet himself if faced with it.

Luckily she managed to keep her mouth shut. She didn't like the guildmaster but now was not the time to call him out.

'I've done what you wanted. Where's my brother?'

De Werve snatched the sword from her, his face as avaricious as the guard's had been, but there was no one here to tell him no. He tested the weight, twisting it this way and that so the edge caught the light of the candles and lanterns, wickedly sharp. Lyta imagined it slicing through the skin of Viola's palms as she clutched the blade and it tore away her goddess. Eninn gave a hiss of concern but she had to ignore him. This was not the time.

'It truly is Silvius Brabo's blade then,' De Werve murmured. 'Honestly, I thought they might have made it up. But this is magnificent. I've never seen a relic like it. You can feel the power in it.'

Not so much power, Lyta thought, *as malevolence*, but again, she kept that to herself.

Survival instincts, Eninn told her. *You're growing.*

It wasn't the moment to laugh either and there was nothing to laugh about.

'My brother,' she said again. 'Marasso promised—'

De Werve was still fascinated with the sword. 'I doubt that. The man doesn't make promises. Just threats. You brother is here waiting, Mistress Cornellis. And Master Charnock will be delighted to know you're here as well. He's most eager to work with you both. But where's the Alderton girl?'

'Safe,' Lyta said. 'Once I have Kit, I'll tell you where.'

'Oh I don't think there's any need for that,' said another, familiar voice. A far-too-familiar voice. Lyta turned as Petrus Janlow entered the hall behind her, Viola Alderton's arm firmly in his grip as he dragged her behind him. 'The gang's all here, Lyta, my love. And some of us actually deliver on our promises.'

CHAPTER TWENTY-EIGHT

Lyta

It was surprisingly warm in the cells beneath the guild, at least compared to being out on the streets or up on the roof of a temple in the freezing wind. Lyta wondered if there was a furnace somewhere nearby. Handy for getting rid of corpses, she supposed. It was too quiet as well. No movement outside, no one casually passing by.

'I was hoping for a rescue,' Stirling said. 'Not company.'

'Well, you shouldn't have got yourself into this in the first place,' she told him. 'Nor my brother either.'

'His boyfriend got him into this and you know it. If we're generous, it was the gods in his head. Maybe.'

Lyta snorted out a bitter laugh. It wasn't even vaguely amusing. 'Oh believe me, I'm going to have a lot of words with Ben very shortly. He's not going to enjoy a single one. I warned him. And I am *not* feeling generous.'

I've got a god too, she had told him once and had meant it as a threat. Eninn might not have a scrap of power left to him, but he was still there. Together they would come up with something. Maybe De Werve and Charnock didn't think Eninn would be able to help her.

More fool them. Trickster gods are the ones to watch out for. He sounded more confident than she felt though. *My siblings will pay for this.*

How he'd make them pay, with no power of his own, she didn't know, but she needed to trust him now. A god without power, a god trapped inside her head.

And even if all his luck was on her side, they were facing Ben's gods and Brabo's blade before even reaching Charnock, and whatever he was planning to do to Kit.

'Can you get us out of here?' Stirling asked.

'After all the effort I went to get in? There's gratitude.'

'As I heard it you were double-crossed.'

She shrugged. 'Wouldn't be the first time.' Janlow. She should never have underestimated the bastard. She thought Alderton had pulled his fangs. She didn't know what had happened to Alderton either. Hopefully he was still in the palace trying to rally help and not bleeding out in an alley somewhere. How Janlow had got Viola away from him and here so quickly was another mystery Lyta was going to have to untangle later. Preferably while holding his head underwater or something equally effective. But that could wait. It would have to wait.

They hadn't bothered shackling her but they had locked her in the cell with Stirling. His wrists were chained together but not secured to the walls. A pair of mangled cuffs hung behind him but she didn't have time to get the details. She supposed that showed her where they thought the real threat came from. More fool them was right. He'd explained how he and Kit got here, including the betrayal of Florrie bloody Stone. Once the Rookery found out what she'd done, and the fate of all those children, that would be the end of her saintly grandmother act. They'd run her out of the city, and just that if she was lucky. All those children, sold on the promise of a better life and offered up to gods who killed them. By people who should have cared for them. And Florrie had known. She must have known. And then she had handed over Kit as well.

Lyta wasn't sure which she wanted more, to kill the woman herself or to let the mob have her.

But that all depended on there being a future for any of them.

'Time we got out of here,' she told Stirling. 'They have Kit and they have Viola. I need to know where and what they're doing. Then we need to stop them.'

'The locks might be a hindrance to that,' he muttered darkly. He'd been in here too long now, she thought and clearly that had wounded his pride. Couldn't get himself out, and he hated it.

Lyta was already at the lock to the cell, pulling out her picks. 'These locks? A kid in Amberes could open these. Did they give you trouble, my Lord Stirling?'

'Lyta, this is serious,' he replied. 'We have to stop them. They'll kill Kit.'

'Oh this is my reaction to serious,' she told him. 'You should hear me when it's life or death.' The giddy elation of riding on the back of a wild stallion composed entirely of raw terror was getting worse. Eninn never helped with that, she knew it. 'I need some muscle. Lift this,' she tapped the barred door. 'Right there.'

Stirling grabbed the metal and lifted it, exactly as instructed. She and Sylvian had done this what seemed like a million years ago, when they'd been kids breaking into whatever took their fancy. Long before Ranulf had taught her the fine arts of burglary. It was easy.

'I'm almost insulted,' she told him as the lock gave and the cell door opened. 'Right, where did they take Kit?'

'Charnock's laboratory would be my guess. It's not far from here. That's where he conducted his experiment with the girl when we were last here.'

The girl, Lyta thought with a pang of anger. Clémence. Dead in the Imperial Temple because Charnock had sent her after the very sword Lyta had delivered. That was how he'd done it, wasn't it? Get an impressionable child supplied by Florrie, stuff them full of a god, and send them off to do his bidding, stealing the relics he needed. The coin, whatever he'd wanted from the Temple of Lost Gods, and the sword. They had even come to the printshop for *The Book of Gold*. And if Charnock had that, with all its secrets, they might be in more trouble than she already feared. He had Kit. Why not the book as well?

She bent her skills to the cuffs instead, forcing their lock to open and letting them clatter to the floor of the cell. Stirling rubbed his wrists gratefully.

But Lyta needed to know the rest, anything he might have overheard while in here.

'What does he want with the sword?' she asked. 'And with Viola? And Kit for that matter? The truth now.'

Something flickered in his gaze and then he relented. He wasn't defeated, not Piers, Lord Stirling, but he knew he had no choice but to tell her everything he knew. He rolled his aching shoulders and rubbed the chafed wrists again as he spoke.

'Charnock is obsessed with the old gods, with their power. Rhiannon is one of the oldest to walk this earth still. He stole her relic, which contains much of her power and fled here. Viola followed, determined to retrieve it for Rhiannon. Well, you know better than I how that ended.'

'She's alive. She said . . .' Lyta hesitated.

'She's alive for now. He'll get to her next, I'm sure of it. It's only the temptation of what he might be able to do with Kit.' He frowned. 'Druon is an ancient god, older even than Rhiannon and she remembers when the rocks themselves were formed. Lyta and if you and your brother truly are of his bloodline, he can bring him back. He might even be able to control him. *Blood and silver*. But he's made other promises too. To ensure Ben's cooperation, he bartered with Kyron, Nimyeh and Gloir. New bodies for them, new lives. Freedom.'

Lyta growled under her breath. 'They always were treacherous bastards.' Was that her or Eninn? Again, there was no way of knowing right now. 'And Marasso?'

'Kyron will be king,' he said, his voice bleak. 'Marasso will steal the prince and . . . I don't know all of it. But from what I can glean . . .' He shuddered. 'Can you imagine, a god in the body of the heir to the throne?'

It was horrific. 'Given how quickly the process killed the other children, no.'

'But they were just human. Not . . . well, whatever the prince is. Royal blood is meant to be special, isn't it? He's the child of an Aspect and—'

Lyta gave him a dark look and he swallowed back the next words, realising he'd better not pursue that. Or even mention what he suspected. She had other concerns. She could only pray they couldn't get to the prince, that Sylvian would protect him. 'Yeah I get it. But why do they want the sword?'

'Charnock's ritual needs enormous divine power. That sword is a direct link to Druon—the weapon that killed him. It kills gods, countless gods. How much divine power do you think it contains?'

How many gods had the Imperial forces killed with it? Lyta didn't want to think about that.

'But Charnock isn't interested in a child. Certainly not a baby. A god like that, in so helpless a form? No, that's Marasso and De Werve's plan. He wants one of us, me and Kit. Why?'

'Your bloodline. Charnock saw it in you. And that awful woman, Florrie, said as much. You're the line of Druon, his blood in your veins.'

'That's impossible. He died centuries ago.'

'He's a god, Lyta. It works differently. Don't you see that?'

Did it? She tried to question Eninn but he had gone suspiciously quiet all of a sudden.

Stirling went on, adamantly. 'I have a theory about your father and—'

Her father. Who the hell knew who he was? This was a waste of time. Time Kit probably didn't have. If Charnock tried to put a god in her brother in all likelihood he'd end up like little Clémence with his chest torn open. She was under no illusion that Charnock had somehow perfected his ritual in the short time since she'd seen it last.

'I don't care about the theory. Are you going to help us, or will I lock the door again and leave you down here to rot?'

'You might leave me here anyway.'

'Always a possibility. I don't like you much.'

He gazed stubbornly into her face with something akin to hope. 'Is it true about Viola? She's here?'

Lyta nodded slowly. 'Last chance. Time's running out.'

'I can take you there, if you help me find her. I'll help you.'

She only hoped that was true.

*

The guild was still mostly asleep which was one saving grace. Anyone out and about at this hour they could consider part of the conspiracy, or blindly following orders, and therefore a threat. They skirted along the edges of silent corridors, keeping to the shadows.

By the time they reached the level where Charnock had his workshop, Lyta was really starting to worry. Where was everyone? They hadn't seen a soul since they climbed the stairs.

Voices drifted down to them and she signalled Stirling to stop.

'The guards say the army is moving in, clearing the Guild Quarter. They're coming.'

'Let them come,' said De Werve. 'It's not going to matter when we unleash our god on them. I'm heading to the gates to assess the situation. Hold every approach to the shrine, every doorway, understand?'

'Guildmaster, the army is going to fall on us like wolves. We are not soldiers.'

'You are now,' he dismissed them. 'Holy soldiers in the service of Druon. And the city will not let us down. Others will come. Go. He will reward us all.'

And then he was gone.

The muttering among the remaining smiths told Lyta that not everyone shared his conviction. There might be some grounds for hope after all. But they were still armed guards with orders and she and Stirling had no weapons but their hands. She had hoped sneaking would be enough, but now it was going to come to a confrontation. Maybe if she could distract them long enough, pretend she was lost or drunk or simply stupid, then Stirling could—

The sound of a brief and brutal struggle put that out of her head. No one cried out. There wasn't time. When it all went still, Lyta held up her hand to stop Stirling moving and peered around the corner.

Frida stepped over the two bodies slumped on either side of the door, dressed head to toe as a Blacksmiths' Guild guard. Lyta wondered who she'd left lying in a corner to get the outfit and hoped she'd hidden the body well enough.

Stirling moved faster than Lyta would have expected and before anyone knew what was happening he had Frida in a headlock, the inside of his arm tight against her throat.

'A friend of yours?' he asked.

'For a certain value of friend,' she muttered. 'Took you long enough.'

Frida smiled that cold and calculating smile, and you'd never have thought Stirling could break her neck or choke her out at any second. She still had her knives and Lyta knew you could never discount Frida.

'You didn't stay put,' she replied. 'I had to double-back to find you. Sneaky. So, Janlow double-crossed us.'

'And you're surprised? Maybe you really are slipping in your dotage.'

Frida bared her teeth, muscles tensing, and Stirling tightened his grip. 'Call off the new attack dog, Lyta. We've common ground here. Alderton's going to be furious and when he's furious, he gets even. He's alerted the palace and they're on the way. The smiths are in an absolute panic, but they're manning the walls ready to make a stand. They say their god is coming. Or *a* god anyway. They might need one. I guess your Syl has raised every armed force in the city and is bringing them here. We have to get our people to safety before he rains fire on this whole place. If you think Francisco would raze it to the ground, have a think on what Syl and his sweet little golden-haired lover will do.'

'She's not his—' Lyta blurted out before common sense could catch up and swallowed down the rest of it. Frida was goading her. She lived for shit like that.

Time for winding each other up was over. Lyta lifted two of Frida's knives and nonchalantly handed them to Stirling, who finally released the other woman.

Frida glanced at him, all cool disdain. 'I'll want those back when we're done.'

'They're good knives,' he said by way of agreement. 'You picked well.'

'Lucky I have more.' Of course she did. She'd probably take half an hour to divest herself of weapons. 'Ready Lyta? Not that I'm asking you to trust me.'

'Well, I know better than that, don't I?'

Stirling cleared his throat. 'There's history here, clearly, but again, we don't have time. If they manage to perform this ritual and call Druon through . . .'

'Disaster,' Frida agreed. 'Destruction. Probably of the whole city.'

'What else is new?' Lyta asked. They didn't have time to worry about that. In fact, they didn't have time at all. 'We're going to have to split up.'

Frida rolled her eyes. 'Oh yes, because that *always* ends well.'

CHAPTER TWENTY-NINE

Kit

The guards were not gentle as they hurried Kit up several flights of stairs and into a chamber much like the heart of any temple Kit had ever been in.

A sacred space. He could feel that the moment he stepped inside and a shiver ran over his skin. He'd always avoided temples. It had been easy growing up. Lyta never visited them. No one they knew did if they could avoid it.

The presence of this place washed over him like a wave of cold water. It wasn't the Shrine to Gloir. Not anymore, if that was what it once had been. This was cold and dark and empty. Waiting.

Waiting on a lost god to return.

Candles had been lit in the various corners, but they did little to warm the place, only cast their flickering light on the circle in the centre of the room, the hollowed-out dip in the floor surrounded by eldritch symbols drawn in chalk. He recognised them from *The Book of Gold*, and from Ben's skin.

Ben's work then. Or something they had garnered from Ben's work.

'What have you done?' Ben took it all in, clearly sickened. That couldn't be good. If he was horrified by what he saw here . . . Or rather the gods inside him were . . .

This had been Gloir's place. But no more.

Charnock pushed him aside, fearless now. 'I improved on your shrine. Transformed the place. And it works. Wait until you see how it works. It's all about the great work, is it not? We can reuse this place, time and again. And with your amulets, we'll have an army of gods if we want it, all bound to obey, all faithful to us. Man ruling gods. Can you imagine it?'

'You can't do this. Man cannot rule gods.'

A faint glow was trying to force its way through Ben's skin. Were his gods finally catching up? Did they realise what a terrible mistake they had made trusting Charnock?

'What trickery is this?' Kyron asked. 'We had an arrangement, alchemist.'

'One he never intended to keep,' Kit said and Kyron glared at him. 'Don't you see that? This was never about you. It was all to get to Ben, and all that he knows, all he can discover and figure out. *His* mind. Not yours.'

Ben pushed his way to Kit's side, reaching out for him. His fingers brushed against Kit's neck for a moment and the touch sent a shiver of need through him. Regret too. They weren't getting out of here, Kit thought. Not both of them. Probably not either of them.

Ben tried to say something. His eyes flickered through all the whirl of colours Kit associated with his lover, and then flared gold.

Kyron's hand clamped on Kit's throat like iron, pushing him back against the wall by the door, far more powerful than Ben would ever be. Kit couldn't fight him. He was staring into Ben's eyes, his beautiful multifaceted eyes, but he couldn't see him. Not anymore. The things that looked out hated him. 'Silence, Cornellis. You cannot reach him now. He is gone. We are all that remains. We will be set free and I will rule this sorry collection of kingdoms. I will create a new empire and tear down the throne of the Imperator. You think I won't deal easily with the likes of you?'

'We have a king,' Kit gasped out. Perhaps imminent death made him reckless. 'Don't like him much but the position is occupied.'

Kyron, the God of Warriors sneered. 'Not Francisco. His son. Charnock has promised me his son. And then I will be king and god both.'

'You're going to possess a baby?' His eyes flickered to Charnock, appalled.

Charnock shrugged, watching all of this with interest. 'Who wouldn't want a god-king? Powerful, strong, a divine warrior to wear the crown and vanquish all your enemies.'

No one would want that, Kit thought frantically. No one sane. 'He isn't even a day old!'

'What is time for a god?' Kyron snarled. 'I grow tired of this and tired of your constant interference. We don't need you, Cornellis. Ben will obey now. He has no choice in the matter.' His grip tightened again, cutting off Kit's breath.

The cool tip of a sword slid between the two of them, pressed hard against Ben's throat. The god in him froze.

'Don't harm him, divine one. We can't be having that. Our Kit is special,' said Florrie Stone. 'Back up, that's a good lad. He's still needed or none of this is going to work. I've spent my life watching over him and his sister, just to bring us here and now. He carries Druon's blood and that is our part of the deal, is it not?'

Kyron drew back Ben's lips in something halfway between thwarted rage and disgust, baring all his teeth. But he stepped back, releasing Kit who gasped for much-needed air. He didn't quite slide to the ground but he had to hold himself up against the wall. He could sense their fear now, all of the gods.

That was what Charnock had been waiting for. Which meant . . .

'Your Lyta came through,' Florrie told him. 'Walked right in with this treasure, and the hand of glory too.' She tossed a sack to Charnock who seized it gleefully and hurried to the centre of the shrine with it. He was laying out the various relics around the sunken hollow in the centre, all surrounded by those swirling designs Kit knew from *The Book of Gold*. Charnock had been studying it.

Florrie patted Kit's face fondly and he couldn't move. 'There's some that say she's not half the thief she claims but, I don't know, Kit my love. Can't think of anyone else who could have done it. Her and Eninn were made for each other.'

He had to stop this. He needed to reason with her. She was from Amberes, from the Rookery. She had to listen to him.

'Eninn's a god of Amberes too, Florrie. He won't be happy.'

'When we have this?' She showed him the sword she carried in far-too-confident a hand. 'Who cares? This sword kills gods, Kit. It's the sword of Silvius Brabo, the one that slew my lord Druon. And now it is ours at last and we can use it to bring him back for once and for all. Through blood and sacrifice. Through the lore of silver. No one is going to care what a little god of nothing thinks when our true god is back from the Nether. Oh he'll want to run and hide then. She showed us the way though, your Lyta. Made that tear dragging the Trickster back through with her. And suddenly the veil was like spiderwebs, the Nether right there in reach, especially as the year went on and the liminal days came closer. Alaric felt it, in the Temple of Lost Gods, the poor stupid boy. He told me.'

She reached out to stroke Kit's hair back from his face, almost as if she was petting him. Kit flinched, but there was nowhere to go now. He might be able to overpower her, even if she didn't have a weapon, but the guards were still watching. And he'd have to abandon Ben for good. 'Lyta would have been a fitting way of reaching back in for Druon. But I think it was always meant to be you in the end. You always had the good of this city in your heart, my boy, always stood up against injustice and our invaders. That's all we're doing, pet. Taking back Amberes from the invader, on behalf of its true god. Thomas, it's time. We can't wait any longer. Enemy's at the gates. Time's wasting. Time to bring him home before that foreign bitch's army breaks through. Then we'll teach them all to fear us. Men and gods. He will bring you all into line.'

'You cannot do this,' Nimyeh interrupted, her voice so calm and reasonable she might have been somewhere else entirely. Or perhaps it was something of Ben still. Gods, Kit hoped there was still something of Ben in there. 'It will not work. You need a willing vessel for a god with the power of Druon, his bloodline, untainted.'

'And we have one,' Charnock told her with a maniacal grin. 'We have Kit here.'

'He would never be such a fool as to agree to that,' the Goddess of Wisdom scoffed. And in that she was right. It was the only hope he still had. If he didn't agree, they couldn't do it. Was that what Ben had been trying to tell him back in the cell? Not to agree? If he didn't agree, their plan fell apart?

'Wouldn't he?' asked Charnock, grinning at Kit. There was madness in his eyes. If Kit had thought Ben overzealous in the pursuit of his mysteries, Charnock put that suspicion to shame. This was obsession.

Kit was trapped, his back to the wall, with Charnock bearing down on him. He glanced at Florrie, still holding the old sword, plain and unadorned except for the words carved on the blade. Lyta had brought it. What had they done to her?

Too many questions. No one to answer them even if he had time to ask them. He was all out of time.

'Give me the sword,' said Charnock, approaching like some kind of stalking cat. Kit didn't like that, not one bit.

'No,' said Ben, and it wasn't Kyron this time. 'We do not agree. We never agreed to this sacrilege. You cannot bring him back and Cornellis is not yours to sacrifice.' Gloir. It had to be Gloir. Tears spilled from Ben's eyes, tears of betrayal and genuine grief. 'This was my shrine, the heart of my people. And you've corrupted it. You've—'

They never got to hear what else the God of the Forge and the Hearth thought that had been done.

Charnock seized the weapon from Florrie, grabbed Ben by the scruff of the neck and slammed the blade into his stomach.

Behind him, Kit saw Ben fold over, like Charnock had landed a fist to his gut. But the awful noise Ben made told him it was much worse than that. Charnock pulled back and stabbed again, twice, three times, before releasing Ben's body as if he was no more than a sack of meat.

Ben dropped to his knees, clutching his stomach.

'There,' Charnock said. 'An incentive, Cornellis. If we're quick, you may have time to save him. Gods can heal even wounds like that. But only if you're quick enough. And you'll need a god first. Ben's all out.'

Kit scrambled to Ben's side while Thomas Charnock and Florrie Stone set to work preparing the shrine for whatever ritual they were going to begin. The watching guards clustered by the door, eager to be out, unwilling to flee in case there were repercussions. As if he didn't matter anymore, as if neither of them mattered.

Ben was bleeding from a savage stomach wound, the whole front of his clothes black and slick with blood. Kit knew the type. It wouldn't kill him yet. It would be slow and awful. Agony. He'd seen too many in street brawls and tavern fights. Clearly Charnock had as well. He knew exactly what he was doing. Ben's face was chalk-white.

'How did this happen?' Kit whispered at last. He wasn't even sure how he forced the words out. He gathered Ben's shivering form in his arms, trying to staunch the blood. Pointless. It painted his hands red. But that didn't stop him. 'Ben? What were you thinking?'

'They . . . they're gone Kit. I can't feel them. They're . . .'

The sword killed gods, wasn't that what Florrie had said? Ben's hands slipped against Kit's, trying to hold him, their strength gone, those long, delicate fingers scarlet. No gods now, just Ben, pale and terrified. 'I swear to you, I didn't know. I wouldn't have.' Dying, Kit thought. He was dying. In agony. Trying to confess. 'You know I wouldn't have. It was . . . theoretical, something to figure out and Thomas was so . . . so helpful, Kit. I was running out of time. Oh gods, this is all my fault. I just wanted to stop them, to get them under control, to find a way to help them. . . so we could . . . so you and I could have a normal life. Without . . . Without . . .'

His voice seemed to fail in his throat and he looked away, devastated now he fully understood what he had done.

'But the gods had their own plans,' Kit murmured. He hated them. He had never hated them quite so much as now—Kyron, Gloir and Nimyeh.

'They were so angry when Ystara escaped but they didn't. Angry with us, not finishing the book. With you. With me. And they chipped away at my mind, my memories, my—my soul . . .'

And now they were gone. Somewhere. Betrayed, as they had been betrayed so many times because they never bloody learned.

It hurt, the thought that he had lost Ben so easily, that Ben had inadvertently let him get himself tangled up in this and that Kit hadn't even noticed. What kind of lover was he? It hurt more than he would have thought possible. That pain that made him human, he thought, the pain that told him he was still himself. And any moment now, he was going to lose even that pain. He was going to lose everything.

Kit reached out and pulled Ben against his chest, cradling him. He didn't know what to say. He wanted to comfort Ben, but he couldn't. To tell him it would be all right would be a lie.

If Lyta was really imprisoned here, they wouldn't hold her for long. And if anyone was attacking the guild headquarters, it would be Sylvian, trying to reach her. And once Sylvian had found Lyta, they would come for him. And even so . . . .they would still never get here in time.

And what would Charnock do with Lyta if he caught her?

These zealots believed they were the children of a god. That was what Tamfana had called him—*the get of a lost god*. Maybe he could hold things up. Maybe he could delay them long enough for help to come. And maybe . . .

If he shared blood with a god, maybe he could reason with him? Lyta and Eninn managed.

He had to try something. Anything.

'What will happen, Ben?' he whispered, his own voice scraping inside his throat. 'If I let him in?'

Ben face paled and his eyes went wide. 'Don't even—' His words cut off, strangled by pain as he tried to move, to twist around towards Kit.

The guards shifted uncomfortably but didn't actually do anything to tear them apart. Perhaps they were as worried about this as Kit was.

Well, no, given what he faced right now, no.

Ben bit back whatever he had been about to say but it didn't matter. Kit had his answer. He smoothed his hand down the side of Ben's face. Kit loathed the thought of that bastard alchemist from Albion doing this to his . . . *his* Ben. Gently, he pressed his lips to Ben's hair and held him. Ben trembled in his arms, spasms of pain running through him as he bled out. There was nothing Kit could do to stop it. Maybe Ben had caused this. Part of it anyway. And maybe he had been naive. And maybe the gods from *The Book of Gold* had deceived him. That didn't actually change anything. Not here, at the end.

'It's going to be all right,' he whispered, deciding maybe it wouldn't hurt to lie a little. Just this once. 'I'll make it better.' Because there was one thing he could do. There had always been one thing he could do.

He might be a no one. He wasn't noble born or rich. He didn't have the divine in his mind like Ben and Lyta or access to their power like Beatriz. He couldn't fight like Sylvian. He was just a man, no matter what Florrie thought. He had no idea if her wild tales about his father were true, but he'd never seen any evidence of it.

Rose gold and alabaster, the Magister had said of him, like he was a statue of an old god. But he'd dug into Kit's brain and tried to remake him and he hadn't found anything divine. Except maybe those words.

They were going to kill him with this stupid ritual, he knew that. They were going to force a god into him and it would eventually rip its way out of his chest like the others had, but maybe he could hold out long enough to heal Ben, or at least for Lyta to get here. He knew she would come for him. She always did. And maybe she could save Ben if he couldn't.

Maybe.

'Kit?' Ben murmured. His tear-filled eyes were unfocused and distant, and Kit was struck again by the colours, like all the shades of autumn swirled up in a breeze and captured in glass. It was one of the first things he'd noticed about Benedictus Alvarez, before he knew him, before he loved him. The first time he'd seen him.

No, he'd loved him then. He just didn't know it. He loved him still. He always would. It didn't even matter if Ben didn't love him back. They owed each other nothing.

But still, he loved.

Ben found his voice again, no more than a whisper, stretched and thin. 'You can't, Kit. This god, he's one of the old ones, one of the oldest. Kyron and the others remember. And they fear him. He has no pity. Not for the likes of us. He demanded tribute from the city when it was nothing more than a river crossing and some wattle and daub shacks. Always a tribute, a sacrifice, in gold and in blood. There was a statue once, made of alabaster, decorated with gold. They used to kill people for him there. His sister is the patron of Amberes now but he—'

'The Church Imperial killed him and sent him to the Nether, didn't they?' Kit interrupted. 'They wrote that history. They used that sword.'

'Yes, but . . . Kit . . .'

'And he's still strong enough to find a way back from time to time?'

'That's what the stories say but, Kit, *please* you have to listen . . .'

He bent his head and kissed Ben with all the determination and willpower he could muster, silencing him and driving all arguments from his mind. The bloody fingers of Ben's hands dug into the fabric of his shirt as Kit tried to sear this into his memory. Because it would have to do.

He should never have let Ben drift away, let him lose himself in his work like he did. This was as much his fault. He should have been more aware of what was going on and less concerned with his own problems. None of that mattered now. He was going to lose Ben. At least he could try to protect him one last time.

The caress of his hand along Ben's jaw, his fingertips tracing the stubble there and the smooth skin beneath, that was all he had left now. Just these few moments.

'Promise me one thing,' he murmured against Ben's throat as he pressed another kiss there. Ben's pulse fluttered in a wild staccato and he made a helpless sound. 'If this works, if I'm gone . . . get that sword and use it on me. Or tell Sylvian to. He'll do it if you . . . if you can't.' He choked, and had to swallow hard to force himself onwards.

Ben's grip tightened and he jerked back, letting Kit see those kaleidoscope eyes again. One last time. The shock in them, the horror.

He knew what Kit was asking.

'It'll be all right, heart,' Kit whispered, as he gently lay Ben down on the cold stone of the shrine floor, ignoring the way Ben tried to hold on to him. But the dying Seigneur of House Alvarez didn't have the strength to stop him. No one did.

Charnock smiled. Kit hated his smile more than he could ever have imagined hating anything. Even Florrie paused, watching him intently. No smile from her. That matronly old woman was gone.

'You need a willing vessel if this is to work,' he said, amazed at the way his voice rang out around the room, how strong and certain it sounded. 'If you let the others go, Ben, my sister and Piers . . . if you let them all go, I'll do it.'

CHAPTER THIRTY

Sylvian

The last person Sylvian expected to arrive as he gathered every guard the palace could spare and sent runners with orders to the barracks, as he summoned up as much of an army as he could currently muster from wherever they were stationed around the city, was Lord Alderton, looking haggard and angry, never a good combination.

'Chant? Lyta Cornellis sent me.'

The words sounded like nonsense, or possibly a sick joke. Sylvian carefully did not react.

'Where is she?'

'She went to the Blacksmiths' Guild. They have her brother.'

That made everything slot into place. Marasso had thought he had Lyta in his power, and through Lyta, Sylvian as well.

That had not worked out so well for him.

And still, Lyta had walked into the jaws of danger for Kit. He should expect no less at this stage.

Alderton swiftly filled him in on their mission to rescue Viola, and Lyta's theft of Brabo's sword. It was a military report, precise yet detailed in all the right ways. He appreciated that, even if the news didn't fill him with joy.

'Your sister is safe?' Sylvian asked.

'Yes, she's—' Then he seemed to pause, searching the courtyard where Sylvian's force was marshalling. 'They were to find you here while I talked to the queen and the general. I left her with Janlow.'

It was like watching Alderton's stomach fall out right in front of him. Sylvian had seen that happen in battle more than once. Alderton's face was suddenly a mask of horror. Sylvian didn't blame him. The thought of any young woman at the mercy of Petrus Janlow . . .

Alderton composed himself with impressive control. 'It—it seems . . .' Something caught in his throat.

'Janlow has double-crossed you. He probably sensed a payout. He may even have been part of it all along. I'm sorry, Lord Alderton. I know him of old. I suspect he's already taken Viola to the alchemists.'

It took a moment, but to his credit that was all. Sylvian may not like Charles Alderton, but he had to admit he respected him.

'I'll have his guts,' Alderton snarled and Sylvian pondered offering to help him, when this was all over. Why not? He'd enjoy it. But Alderton got there first. 'May I offer my sword, Captain Chant? My countryman Charnock has a lot to answer for, as does my supposed associate. It's the least I can do.'

He had a point, and having him there as a witness for his queen when one of them tore Charnock's head off would only help. If Alderton or Stirling did the deed it might even ward off any unpleasant political repercussions.

But the wolf in Sylvian's chest, the clawing rage that still filled him, wanted De Werve, wanted Charnock, wanted to deal with them as he had deal with Marasso, and if any of them had hurt Lyta—

*

It was near dawn as they reached the guild, the watch and the royal troops from the barracks already surrounding its walls. Behind the gates, the guards shifted uneasily and when Sylvian approached the gates, De Werve was waiting on the other side.

'This is guild ground, Captain Chant,' he said by way of warning more than greeting. 'We have agreements with the Crown.'

'Those agreements don't involve kidnapping citizens of Amberes and representatives of other royal courts, guildmaster.'

'We have done no such thing,' he blustered. 'And you will not attack. The people of our city will not stand for it. You of all people know this.'

The arrogance of the man. Did he believe that he commanded Amberes now? The aldermen were not exactly beloved by the rest of the city. They might be watching intently, and if the Crown showed weakness now they would never govern this city again. And if Francisco thought an uprising needed to be put down, he would do it. Brutally.

His bodyguard could do no less. And he had the power of the queen behind him.

'The people aren't here, De Werve,' he said. 'And I come from this city. Who's to say they won't stand with me? And I stand with my king.'

'Your king? Your king is dead. The Baron de Marasso will—'

'Juan Alvarez is dead, not Francisco.' He only prayed that was true, but he couldn't imagine any ambush, not even one engineered by Marasso himself, actually succeeding against his king. No, Francisco was very much alive. He would know otherwise. He'd feel it. Of that he was sure. 'I executed Marasso myself for high treason and treachery. It was quicker than he deserved. You stand alone, and when the king returns he will not be pleased.'

A shocked silence rippled along the walls of the guild compound. Sylvian let it travel, waiting for it to sink in. 'Are you going to surrender now?'

'Never!' De Werve snarled at him. 'This is my city, Chant, not yours and not that upstart from Castile's. It will never listen to you. What are you but a gutter rat who clawed his way out through blood and shit? I'm an alderman, like my father and grandfather. My family ruled Amberes for generations before your bastard king's father took it by force. It will be mine again.'

Amberes was watching, the city poised, transfixed by this spectacle. Very well, thought Sylvian. He could give them a spectacle.

'What is Charnock planning, De Werve? This is your last chance.'

'They're going to call the old god, our god, the first god of Amberes, and he'll remake this city into the glory it was always meant to be. We'll be free of your bastard king and his ilk. To Amberes, City of Lost Gods, all things return. Druon will reward me. He'll reward all of us! You'll see.'

Condemned by his own mouth as a traitor.

Sylvian didn't have patience at the best of time. He was a man of action, unleashed at his king's command. He had never really had need of patience.

Now, he didn't have to wait any longer. He'd given De Werve a chance. He'd let his people know their position was hopeless. Maybe they'd turn and run. That was their decision. His queen had told him to do what he had to do.

Without another word, he walked back to his men, leaving De Werve standing there, staring at him. Once there he faced the gates again and saw De Werve backing slowly up, confused. Let him worry. It wouldn't be for long. Sylvian raised his hand and let it fall, knowing that behind him the message was relayed back with ruthless efficiency, one thing you could rely on among Francisco's troops. He drew his sword and waited. His men followed suit, the sound of blades being drawn hissing in the silence.

For a moment all was still and quiet. Amberes watched and waited with him. A night bird called out and his men shifted into readiness.

Cissonia's bell began to ring, steady, solemn, again and again.

Projectiles soared through the air with a soft *whoosh*, released by trebuchets at the barracks, so close to the Guild Quarter that they didn't even have to move them beyond the mustering ground. Someone cried out as they realised what was happening but by then it was far too late. Inside men and women ran, scattering across the courtyard and from the walls of the compound.

A stone the size of a carthorse slammed through the gates, while pottery jars rained down on the building surrounding them, on to the manned walkways. The sound of them breaking was obscured with screams moments later as they burst into flame and lit up the night.

The army had alchemists too, and they excelled at what they did. A second wave hit the walls and the towers.

It was fast and brutal. No argument and no defence.

Time to show them battle-hardened soldiers, Sylvian thought and roared the command to attack.

The guild men were not warriors. Not really. Even if De Werve had convinced them otherwise.

Keep command, a soft voice whispered in his ear. It almost sounded like Vasquez and for that he was grateful. He didn't want to think what Marasso would say to him now. *Keep control and keep your troops in check. If you lose them now they will riot and the city will suffer. If that happens you will never win Amberes back again.* The soldiers stationed here were bored and hungry for war. They had never feared violence. He remembered Gravenenga and all that had transpired there, all the horrors of Vermand. Not here. He could not let it happen here.

Just the smiths. Those were his order. Just this one guild. Take as many captive as possible. But there were already dead and dying bodies scattered around his troops as they flooded into the broken headquarters. The gardens were ablaze.

It wasn't even an attack, not really. It was a rout.

De Werve hadn't expected this. He was an alderman, a councillor, an idiot, too puffed up with his own importance. He thought he had Marasso's protection.

He'd thought wrong.

It was over far too quickly for the wolf. Sylvian growled, seeking something, anything else to attack. He stalked across the shattered gates, the metal twisted and broken. De Werve lay underneath it, a beautifully worked floral-wrapped bar embedded like a spike in his chest. His eyes stared glassily upwards, fixed in surprise, and his mouth hung slack.

Sylvian gave him a kick, to make sure.

Francisco would have his head mounted on a pike. Or send it back to Annika. Maybe he should do that.

'Captain,' one of his lieutenant jogged up to him to report almost nonchalantly. A veteran, that one, unshockable. 'We've secured the compound and rounded up their troops. Most of them surrendered. A few took off.'

'Any injuries?'

'Scratches and bruises, sir. But we still have to get through to the sublevels. They've fallen back there.'

Naturally they had. It was common sense. Which meant close combat, hand to hand, in confined quarters, a brutal and bloody pitched battle.

'So be it. Give them one chance to surrender. And get the apprentices clear first. I'm going after the others.'

Alderton fell in beside him, sword in hand as Sylvian headed for the main building with its shattered doors.

'Effective,' he said.

'I aim to please.'

'After that display,' he said sardonically, 'I don't think anyone doubts your aim, Captain Chant. Where are they keeping their captives?'

'The true believers have fallen back to the deepest part of the compound. That's what our intelligence says. They're protecting Charnock and the hostages. Ready to fight our way through?'

Alderton grinned and the wolf inside Sylvian recognised like. No wonder the Virgin Queen didn't want him in her glittering court. He was dangerous.

After a brief flurry of fighting, on the first turn of the stair down, the smiths had formed a blockade. It might even have been effective if Frida Elwynn hadn't been coming from behind them. The battle there was just as brief and brutal. Sylvian directed his troops on past her and she bowed her head to Alderton.

His servant, Sylvian remembered. He might not trust her but Alderton did. Frida was about as trustworthy as a lawyer with a big payout coming in, but she knew the way around here somehow and Sylvian wasn't going to argue with that. She had a twisted loyalty to Alderton and that meant she'd get the girl out at all costs. Especially if it meant landing Janlow in it—a goal with which he heartily agreed.

'My sister?' Alderton barked. It was both a question and a command.

'Lord Stirling is on it, my lord,' she replied, wiping blood from her face. Not her blood, Sylvian noticed.

'Lord Stirling?' Alderton sounded like he didn't quite believe that. 'What's he doing here?'

'He has been most . . . helpful. Works for your queen, I believe. He thinks Charnock is planning to use Viola as a hostage.' Alderton's scowl darkened. Frida didn't elaborate further.

'Where is Janlow?'

'Gone, I reckon. If he knows what's good for him. I came to clear the way down here when we heard the noise you were making outside. Took you long enough,' she told Sylvian as she pushed her way towards him. 'Lyta's gone after Kit.'

Of course she had. On her own. 'Where?'

'There's some sort of temple and they're digging in around it. Some nasty surprises planned. Or at least there were.'

The power Ystara had instilled in him snarled and an image swam through his mind. It had been the Shrine to Gloir, he realised. And then wondered how she knew that. Maybe Gloir had told her. Maybe she just knew. How she was communicating with him was another question he didn't want to dwell on now. He was her Chosen, he knew that, but Annika had released him. Not Ystara, it seemed. She was as angry as he was. She and Eninn had a deal and that meant protecting Lyta.

The need to tear someone limb from limb was growing beyond his ability to control and he was starting to fear he'd lose it and turn on those with him instead of the enemy.

The hunter thrummed in his blood, made his teeth ache. He had to keep things together. He didn't like to admit it, but if this kept up he'd be relying on Frida to do the thinking.

Other urges were taking over from rationality. Not just the need to destroy his enemies and protect Lyta. The wolf in him wanted her so much it was almost unbearable. This was neither the time or the place but part of him would have happily dragged her into a room and—

What had Ystara done to him? He was barely in control anymore. The need to fight or to fuck something royally up was overwhelming. At this moment, either would do.

'This way,' said Frida, and they followed her.

Sylvian didn't believe in leading from behind, never had done. It wasn't Francisco's style and so he'd learned from the best. Or the most reckless. It was easier, he thought, when he wasn't trying to keep his king alive at the same time. Hand to hand meant short blades, knives and fists. Fighting dirty. He dodged a hammer, and grabbed the weapon from the man wielding it, dropping low and using it to shatter the bastard's knees before he could react.

They found Stirling engaged hand to hand with a knot of smiths who took one look at the troops approaching and either fled or surrendered.

'Where's Viola?' Alderton roared, ignoring everyone else as he bore down on his fellow countryman. 'You were meant to protect her, you fucking zealot.'

Stirling backed up, his hands raised in defence.

'I'm trying to find her. De Werve has her locked up somewhere. If we could find him . . .'

'Dead,' said Sylvian. 'Try something else.'

And then he remembered the horse, that little bone relic Lyta had given him for safekeeping. Viola had told her to give it to Stirling.

'Here,' he said, digging it out of his pocket and thrusting it towards the other man. 'Does this help? She said you'd know—'

'Captain Chant!' Stirling exclaimed, pouncing on it, his eyes wide. 'Yes. Yes it very much does. Where did you—? No, no matter. Lyta, I suppose. She is a wonder.' He cupped it in his hands and pressed them to his forehead, closing his eyes. The air seemed to shimmer around him. Magic or the divine. Sylvian couldn't tell and didn't care. 'Yes, this way. Follow me.'

He took off like a hare along the corridor and all they could do was race after him, almost losing him around a corner, where they found him on his knees, picking a lock. He wasn't as good as Lyta—Sylvian could see that right away—but he was determined.

'Is she in there?' Alderton asked again, this time in his own language.

'Yes.' He said something else, too quick for Sylvian to catch.

'Open the door,' Alderton told him. 'We'll do the rest.'

'For once, my lord, your wish is my command.' Sarcasm dripped from his words, but at the same time, the lock opened and Stirling pushed the door open, staying on his knees.

Just as well because the crossbow bolts went right over his head. He rolled aside before they could fire again.

Sylvian attacked. He didn't think, he didn't plan, he moved on instinct alone, a wild and free thing, made to kill and alive with the fulfilment of that need. Every nerve in his body fired. It was like breathing, like the beating of his heart. The knives were an extension of his hands, sweeping lines of death which sliced through the throats of two of the guards inside the door as they tried to escape.

Someone shouted but Sylvian didn't even process the words. They didn't matter. Sylvian grabbed the guard who came at him by the arm, slamming his sword into the wall and twisted his elbow, planted a knee in his guts. There wasn't room for swords in this narrow corridor and only a fool would try.

The blast of a wheellock exploded past Sylvian's ear and he dodged aside as another body fell. Frida was busy then. She'd got far too comfortable with that particular weapon.

'Syl, focus!' she roared at him. He ducked as a figure came at him with another huge hammer. It crashed into the wall beside his head and stuck there, while the man tugged at it pointlessly.

It was all the opening Sylvian needed.

He used his bare hands, locking them around the smith's throat and slamming him back across the desk in the corner, pinning him there.

'Where are they?'

'You're too late,' he croaked, his face turning purple beneath Sylvian's grip. 'They're already in the shrine. Already calling him forth.'

The man convulsed, coughing up bloody foam, his eyes rolling up in his head. The pain written on his features was terrible. With a rattling breath, he twisted violently beneath Sylvian and then fell still. Sylvian let out a careful breath and released his corpse. 'What the fuck was that?'

'Poison,' said Alderton, all too calmly. 'Cantarella, if I'm any judge. Must have had a vial of it in his mouth. Zealots love poison, don't they Stirling? A shame. I would have liked a word or two.'

There was a girl in his arms, honey-haired and beautiful, her face buried in his chest. Viola Alderton. Her brother held her close, his eyes filled with justified rage, his bloody hands trembling against her, smearing the white material of her gown.

Five dead bodies lay on the floor. There was no one else in the room.

Sylvian didn't have time for this. 'Where's Lyta? Where is the shrine?'

'They've corrupted the shrine,' Viola Alderton murmured, her voice soft as falling rain on the old windows of Amberes. 'Turned it into something ancient and cold. Gloir's Guild is no more. He lost them. He is lost. I feel his pain echoing through every stone of this place. Oh, Piers,' her voice hitched in horror and she pulled away from her brother, reaching for Stirling. 'He's dying. They're all dying . . . They are betrayed.'

'Come,' said Alderton. 'No more talk like this. We must get you to safety. Frida, help me. Captain Chant, my thanks, but we must leave now.'

Good, Sylvian thought. Better they were out of here and out of danger. Even if the creature clawing inside him, desperate to find Lyta, seethed beneath his failing control. Ystara save him, he couldn't see them to safety. He had to find her.

'We can't leave.' Viola held out her hand, so small and slender a hand. 'You have the horse, don't you, Piers? This is the time. There's no other option.'

'Viola, he's right. We have to go,' Stirling argued, even as he dug into a pocket. 'Surely this can wait. It's too much for you. Too powerful. She will destroy you. Everything you are.'

'I have to do this. It is my duty. Rhiannon is our mistress. We must trust in her now.'

'Viola, please . . .' he whispered, as if still clinging to a vain hope he knew was lost already. 'There has to be another way.'

'No,' she said implacably, her fingers twitching with impatience. 'I have to, Piers. You know that. Charnock must be stopped. I can't do that alone. Not as Viola Alderton.' She smiled and touched his frowning face briefly. 'I'm sorry, Charles. For everything. We're both sorry. But it has to be this way. You know that. Duty to her, first and foremost.'

Viola stepped away from him.

When Stirling pulled out the little horse figure, she snatched it from him and pulled it tight against her chest, clutching it close as she closed her eyes. It was an expression of prayer, of devotion, of ecstasy. Alderton might call Stirling a zealot, but his own sister was clearly much worse.

From all around them came the noise of galloping horses, from the walls, from the ground beneath and the ceiling above, echoing through them. Sylvian felt it shaking its way through in his chest.

Alderton gasped and staggered back but Stirling dropped to his knees, his face lifted to her in adoration.

'Rhiannon,' he whispered. 'Goddess mine. Bless and protect us, Queen of All.'

Viola Alderton smiled, but the woman standing before them wasn't Viola Alderton anymore.

CHAPTER THIRTY-ONE

Kit

Rose gold and alabaster.

Those words had rung through his life. Maybe not voiced out loud, not before the Magister, but always there. There had once been a god in Amberes who fed on blood and death, who revelled in suffering, who exacted toll after toll on its people.

Florrie used to tell them the story when Kit was little.

They said he'd been made of rose gold and alabaster.

To Amberes, the city of lost gods, all things return. That was the motto of the city. It was carved on the Temple of Cissonia, and over the Anchor Gate, the oldest one in the city walls. It was written at the core of every man and woman born here. They were all waiting.

All things returned. Even their lost gods. The ones who had bled the people dry, who had worked them to death, who had demanded adoration and sacrifice in equal measure.

Now he saw Florrie Stone, the hunger and the madness in her eyes, part of him wondered if they had deserved it. She was a monster but she prided herself as the heart of this city, the Saint of the Rookery, caring for its lost and abandoned children, keeping the memory of the lost gods.

Those same lost gods—or one of them in particular.

A city, he had once written, when he was sketching out ideas for pamphlets which should never have been printed, could be a caring parent or a ravenous beast. It needed its people. They were its lifeblood. But it could turn on them quickly. At the worst, a city used them, enslaved them, saw them as little more than livestock.

It wasn't a particularly subtle metaphor, but that hadn't mattered at the time.

Not until it actually got printed anyway. The great and good of Amberes had not liked that analogy at all, as it turned out. The duchess had been especially enraged and her revenge had been terrible. Would any of this have happened if it had never made its way to the press, or if he had never put pen to paper? He would never have met Ben. And right now, that might not have been a bad thing.

Ben was dying.

He didn't know any details about the story of Druon the Giant and Silvius Brabo. He didn't know the tales of Cissonia, the goddess in the bell. It was all faded into forgotten history as the world lurched onwards and new gods rose and fell.

But Florrie thought that was his father. That somehow a dead god had made his way back from the Nether to get his mother pregnant and bring him into the world. Him and Lyta. No one could deny that they were siblings. There were two of them, brother and sister, in the story too—Cissonius and Cissonia. But she was the only one who survived.

Fitting, he thought.

Where was Lyta? Safe? She had to be safe. But knowing her, she'd be hurling herself into danger at this very moment. She'd be trying to reach him. She fought the whole world, Lyta did, and always had done. She was like Amberes itself. No one controlled her. Not a man like Charnock, not a god, no one.

Keep her safe, he prayed, to no one in particular. Any of the gods lingering near this place were not likely to grant him any indulgences now. Not Nimyeh, not Gloir. Definitely not Kyron. Were they already dead? Ben had thought so. Had the sword consigned them to the Nether, or done something worse? But Kit prayed nonetheless. *Please, keep her safe.*

Charnock approached him warily, as if he expected some kind of trick, for Kit to attack him or to try to flee. The manacles he brought with him this time were different, etched with gold and other metals, more like bracers linked by a thick chain than what they'd put on him as a mere mortal. They had markings like the amulet Ben had worn, though these were cruder, as if daubed by a less artistic hand. They glowed with a dull silver light as Charnock slid them onto his arms and secured them.

'There, just a safety precaution. They'll keep him in check until we've worked out terms.'

The metal sank icy needles into his skin and Kit felt all the bravery drain away. They were actually going to let the old god go free?

No. One look at Charnock's face told Kit that was never going to happen. This was how Charnock intended to keep Druon under his mortal thumb. Ben's work again, but twisted.

The alchemist grabbed the chain connecting them. Kit stumbled as Charnock jerked him forward, and he heard Ben whimper something, a plea or a prayer, perhaps just pain forcing its way out again, his voice echoing around the chamber. Kit couldn't tell. It felt like something else was whispering in his ears now, loud and urgent, words he couldn't quite make out, or maybe a language he couldn't hope to understand.

Something from far away, reaching out to him already in this benighted hole.

Kit flinched, couldn't help himself, and jerked back, the need to protect Ben too strong for him to stay still.

'You want to make it worse for him?' Charnock asked. 'By all means. I can I can inflict such tortures on him before he dies, and gladly.'

He dragged Kit into the pit and secured the chain to the ring sunken in the middle. Standing over him, Charnock crossed his arms.

'He's a whining little aristocrat, Cornellis. He may have brought us the final mile, but it's my work that got here. Gods, I followed word of him here in hopes that . . . But look at him. Pathetic. Well, he's free of his gods, like he wanted. And you'll thank me soon. You'll finally be free of him.'

'You used him,' Kit said, amazed at how calm his voice sounded.

Charnock bowed sarcastically. 'It's what I do.'

'Viola as well?'

He barked out a laugh. 'I'll deal with her soon enough. And your sister. You know she's coming for you, don't you? I'm counting on that.'

A flare of something like rage burned up inside Kit's chest. It didn't even feel like him. And yet, it did. It was both part of him and part of something ancient buried in his blood. 'Leave Lyta out of this.'

'You really are not in a position to make demands, Master Cornellis. What goddess will I make her? An amenable one, I think. I've made more of these beauties.' He indicated the manacles. 'I'll have Viola and your sister both, chained and obedient at last. I shall raise an army of gods at my command, with you at their head. Shall we begin? Florrie, if you will.'

The old woman murmured a prayer, again words at once familiar and strange to him, words that should have had a place in the Temple of Lost Gods except they felt distinctly profane as they reached his ears.

'Hail to you, Lord of the Crossings. Blessings shine on this day. We give you tokens and offerings, trophies of your enemies, the marks of their passing . . .'

Kit's heart pounded inside him and he struggled to catch his breath. Charnock was pouring living silver onto the ground around the hollow and it crept sluggishly towards the slope, finding little groves and channels carved there, an intricate pattern spreading out around him, which turned bright and shone like moonlight. He consulted *The Book of Gold* carefully, and added more, drawing something strange at the edge in blood. Ben's blood? Where else would he have got so much of the stuff?

Blood binds, silver wakes.

'What is that?' Kit asked, trying to turn around and see what was happening, but the chains still held him in place. He couldn't get away now. Something told him that even if he wasn't chained he wouldn't be able to get out. Not anymore.

Florrie shouted out something now, a summons, an entreaty. She plucked the hand of glory from the table, and held it up. The light flickered as it caught fire but Florrie didn't hesitate or stop to wonder at it. She flung it into the hollow which held Kit. It burst against the silver, shattering into motes of light all around him.

The ground shook and dust fell from the ceiling. He could feel a great presence surging in the air, invisible and terrible, ancient and so hungry. It gnawed at the edges of him, ready to force its way through him.

Was this what those children felt when they died? Had they been pulled apart from within to let a monstrous god of long ago through into this world again? Suddenly volunteering in order to save the others seemed like a terrible idea.

A mist rose, and from that mist came something else, something which grew like a plant, all vines and thorns, twisting through the air around him. It tangled in on itself, a crystalline form of rose gold, liquid but not liquid, gaseous but not gaseous. It changed as he watched it, hypnotic, enthralling as it built itself up, layer upon layer, all around him. As Florrie stepped forwards, priestess in this corruption of a ritual, the crystalline structure closed around them, sealing them away and Kit realised it did matter. It mattered very much. She was going to kill him. This might be Charnock's great work, but it was Florrie Stone who would be the midwife to a lost god.

Behind them the door burst open but it was too late. It was all far too late. He knew that now as rose gold light from somewhere else swirled around him and turned to glass.

He twisted, trying to see what was happening as Lyta skidded into the room.

She couldn't be here. Not Lyta. Not for this.

'Lyta, get out!' He yelled as loudly as he could. 'Take Ben and get out!'

'Stay where you are, Lyta my love,' said Florrie with that smile he'd once found so trustworthy, so comforting. 'Bear witness. You can't help him now. No one can. He belongs to all of us, to Amberes. A sacrifice to bring back our god, our true god.'

She drew the sword with its razor-sharp edge and the name of a long-dead hero engraved on it, and sliced through the skin of his chest in a deft and practised movement. Kit screamed as the line of ice became burning pain. His blood splattered on the ground, on the markings and the living silver and all of those intricate, terrible symbols. The cut wasn't deep but that didn't matter. It wasn't the blade of Silvius Brabo that would kill him. He was no god. Not yet.

It was his blood they wanted, spilled into the living silver—binding and waking.

Light and sound exploded, a volcano erupting through him, incinerating all that he was, all that he had ever hoped to be. He heard Lyta scream his name but it was far too late. Everything was far too late. He had agreed to this, that was his mistake. He had agreed and let them bind him, and let them bring him here and now he was lost.

Everything was pain, a pain of molten gold and of cold stone sliding through his veins and in his mind, coiling through his guts and making his heart burst inside him.

Kit knew no more.

CHAPTER THIRTY-TWO

Lyta

Lyta kicked the door open and the guards scattered. They hadn't even bothered to lock it, the arrogant bastards, as though no one could hurt them here and no one was coming to help Kit. As if she wouldn't always come after Kit. It was her purpose, her only reason for being. It had been all her life. 'Look after Kit,' her mother had said that time and again, even as she lay dying, and to be honest Lyta had done a piss-poor job most of the time.

It had taken her too long to get here. That was all she knew. Far too long. She took in Ben sprawled on the ground in a pool of his own blood, Charnock reading aloud from *The Book of Gold*, some kind of spell of summoning and Florrie Stone . . . What the hell was Auntie Florrie even doing here?

Sorcery, from the looks of it. A ritual. Something made of blood and silver. And nightmares.

The stab of betrayal in Lyta's guts almost took her breath away. She had trusted the woman. So had Kit. All their lives. In everything. She was meant to be the Saint of the Rookery. She was meant to care for all the lost children.

Not hand them over to die. No saint her. There were no longer words enough for what she was.

Florrie grinned like a skull and spoke of Amberes, and sacrifices and raised the sword.

And Kit . . . her Kit . . . lost in a maelstrom of light and metallic sparks, of gold and silver, of a mist so thick it had to be impossible to breathe, she saw her little brother on his knees, throw back his head and let out a silent scream of agony. Blood poured down his chest. He was bleeding. Kit was bleeding.

'No!' she roared and threw herself forward, but someone caught her arm in an iron grip and pulled her aside.

'*Enough*,' said a voice that was not Viola Alderton's voice. It could never belong to a mere mortal.

Inside Lyta's head, Eninn gave a shout of his own, some kind of recognition or jubilation. '*Rhiannon?*'

She nodded to Lyta, a brief incline of her head, and then raised her hands. '*Stop this abomination!*'

The swirling mass around Kit froze, hung there for a moment and then crashed to the ground, shattering to flakes of snow.

'No!' Charnock howled. 'You can't stop this, not now. This is my life's work. I will bring you all to heel, divine monsters, you thieves of freedom.'

He threw something at the goddess, a fine net of silver and she staggered back, clawing at it. Crashing into Lyta, they both went down, Rhiannon struggling vainly to free herself and Lyta half-pinned under her.

Stirling stepped between them and the alchemist. 'Always a knave's trick, Thomas.'

Charnock grabbed the sledge hammer which leaned against the wall unused. 'You have no power without her. Everything you are is tied to her. You're just a half-rate alchemist, aren't you? You never had the courage of your convictions. I'll teach you a lesson now, boy. You didn't even bring a weapon.'

But Stirling grinned, spreading his hands wide, beckoning the other man forward. He didn't have a sword, not that Lyta could see. But he slipped to one side effortlessly as the hammer crashed down where he had been only moments before. He danced, and Charnock heaved up the hammer again, swinging it wide.

Stirling was playing with him, exhausting him. But there wasn't time for that. Kit didn't have time. Lyta heard rather than saw

Sylvian arrive, heard the guards fighting and dying and heard him shout her name.

Snarling, Lyta finally struggled free and ripped the net from Viola, flinging it aside. 'Enough farting around,' she hissed at Rhiannon. Maybe you weren't meant to talk to a goddess like that. Lyta didn't care. Not anymore.

'Agreed,' the goddess growled and something flashed in Stirling's face, his eyes narrowing. And if Lyta had ever doubted what he was, she didn't now. He was as Chosen as Sylvian was. And his goddess was one of impossible power. Perhaps neither of them had a choice in that service. But Stirling didn't care. He revelled in it.

Stirling moved so fast he was a blur, twisting to the side and bringing his foot down hard on the back of Charnock's knee. The alchemist collapsed with an aborted cry, as Stirling pivoted, and brought both fists crashing into the back of his neck.

Stirling grabbed Charnock by his hair, slamming his face down into the stone of the floor.

'I don't need a weapon when my lady is with me,' he said. 'You betrayed her. And you'll have many long hours in the Tower to contemplate what that means.'

Sylvian had reached Lyta's side, that same wildness in his eyes, desperation and rage. But she launched herself forwards before he could stop her, sprinting for the centre of the shrine.

Kit wasn't moving. He lay there, face-down, enchanted metal cutting into his arms and he wasn't moving. His blood was mixing with the living silver and acid and gods alone knew what else pooling around him. All their potions and vials and concoctions. She didn't know and didn't care. She had to get to him.

There was a rip in the world above her brother. She could see it, feel it, that terrible cold sucking sensation which had engulfed her when she'd dived into the Nether after Eninn. And it was growing. Something was clawing at it from the other side, opening it further. If she got too close it could pull the two of them through again and this time she wasn't certain she'd find another way out.

There was something waiting on the other side.

'What is it?' she hissed.

Eninn's voice trembled. '*It's him. The oldest of us, the strongest of us. All the gods of Amberes are nothing to him, Lyta. He's coming.*'

But she fixed her eyes on her brother's still form and hurled her body forward. She crashed into the circle, just in time for a knee to drive itself into her solar plexus and knock all the fight from her.

Someone grabbed her by the hair and hauled her to her knees. Lyta gasped for air but it was pointless. Brabo's gladius jabbed at her side, not deep enough to cut, but a clear warning, and Florrie—Auntie Florrie who had never had an unkind word, was always there in times of need, the one person in the Rookery anyone could turn to when everything went wrong—held her in an implacable grip, like an animal ready for slaughter.

'I might have known you wouldn't give him up. Two peas in a pod, you are. Both of you special in more ways than you'll ever know. I've watched over you, tried to keep you safe, even tried to prepare you for a great destiny and all you've done, time and again, Lyta Cornellis is land yourself in trouble.'

No old woman should be this strong. It was unnatural. They stood in the circle of summoning, over Kit's still body and the tear in reality was growing.

'Can you close it?' Stirling yelled from somewhere on the other side of the chamber. 'Rhiannon? Can you close it?' At least they were trying, but it didn't seem to be working from where she was.

Through it, Lyta could see the endless dark of the Nether and the wandering ways, the stone doorway and the desert that had led her back here with Eninn.

'Let her go,' Sylvian growled. He circled the hollowed-out heart of the shrine like a caged animal seeking an opening. But there was none, not while Florrie had Lyta at her mercy.

'Come and get her, Ystara's dog,' the old woman snarled. 'But you'll never be quick enough. He's coming. And he will destroy you for standing against him. Cissonius will return and reign over all. He'll fill his children with gold and glory, and Amberes will be free.'

'No it won't,' Lyta rasped. 'It'll just be enslaved to someone else.'

'Perhaps,' Florrie smiled, a savage and vindictive expression born of rage and disdain. 'But it will be *my* god in charge at last. Cissonius will take Amberes as his own once more and he will make it great. The Imperator will fear us. So will every king and queen.'

'*You don't even know what he is*,' said the goddess Rhiannon. '*None of you do. He's the oldest of us. He isn't content with service or devotion. He won't reward you. He doesn't understand. Listen to me, woman—*'

'The goddess of another land? I think not. You have no place here, grey mare. And when he comes he will destroy you too. He'll suck the divinity from your veins. Aye, and rip the Trickster from your mind too, Lyta. He's learned from the Imperator. He won't make the same mistakes again. They wanted their own god-king, these free men of Amberes, and that ambitious fool Marasso. And Charnock thought to control him. As if that was possible. Now they will finally see what he truly is.'

Eninn was squirming, trying to find some way to wriggle free but Lyta couldn't move. The Nether was too close, sucking away at all things divine.

Rhiannon stayed out of reach. She was angry, but not a fool.

And Lyta was trapped here with Eninn, right on the edge.

'Kit,' she hissed. 'Kit, wake up.'

He stirred at the sound of her voice, groaning Lyta's name as he rolled on to his back, his eyes glazed with pain. Florrie glanced down, that horrid smile turning fond as she beheld Kit. She released Lyta and raised the gladius again. 'Hold still, pet. I'll make it quick.'

'Eninn,' Lyta called out. 'Eninn, listen to me. I have a plan.'

No you don't. You never do. What are you—? Lyta, no!

'You can run, you can hide. You can escape with your heart and your wit. I know you can. That's what you do. So run.'

In her mind she saw his golden curls and mismatched eyes, saw the fear in them, the pleas, the denial. *Lyta, don't do this. You need me. You have always needed me. You're a terrible thief. All you are is lucky and that's just because of me. Lyta, please,* please *listen to me.*

'I'll find you,' she told him. 'Trust me. I will. I promise. Just run.'

Lyta threw herself between Florrie and Kit. The blade slid into her body, moving like acid inside her, through her. She couldn't scream, couldn't draw breath. It was cold, the cold of the Nether, the cold of death. The wandering ways slid along her veins. All she could manage was a strangled gasp of surprise.

Florrie jerked back from Lyta in something like appalled shock and Lyta fell. The blade tore free, leaving that shard of harrowing ice spearing her, as she collapsed across Kit. Maybe she could still protect him, shelter him. He squirmed beneath her, trying to rise, trying to do something. But she was a dead weight, bleeding out, trapping him on the ground.

Beyond the tear, light flared, bright and terrible. It illuminated the desert like sunrise, but there was no sun there. There should be nothing at all but lost hopes.

Lyta, what have you done? Eninn wailed and it felt like a hurricane stuck inside her mind, ripping him away, like finger nails clawing at the edges of her brain. *Lyta!*

She couldn't hold on to him. What *had* she done? The blade was dangerous, an enchanted object. She knew that.

A god-killer, not an idle title, a weapon of the Church Imperial. Her thoughts were becoming harder to follow now, draining away like her blood. Her breath came in gasps and little more. What had Tiberius said about it?

The desert beyond the tear grew sharper, as if coming into focus through a spyglass. Lyta could smell the air there, hot and dry. And across the space between, step by step, a figure was approaching. A figure made of fire and nightmares. That was where the light was coming from, she realised, that ruddy light, like bronze or gold dipped in blood, the parched air, the smell of nothingness. There was no sun there. But there were gods and the most terrible of them all slouched towards her across the Nether.

'Lyta? Lyta, hold on.' That sounded like Sylvian's voice. It had to be. But it sounded so far away, wavering and strange. And the screaming in her head was drowning it all out anyway.

'Close enough, dog.' Florrie grabbed Lyta by the hair again, hauling her up. Through the haze of agony and blood loss, she could see him now, a shadow bearing down on them, deadly in his grace. He was sketched in darkness but full of the fire of Ystara. And he was beautiful.

But Florrie had her as a human shield and he couldn't, or wouldn't come closer. 'I tried to warn you, Lyta Cornellis. I could have made you great, you or your brother. You were born for it. But if you'll willingly give an old god your blood—' She brought the blade to Lyta's exposed throat like a butcher at a slaughterhouse, ready to slash her open and bleed her out for once and for all. 'You can be his first sacrifice. It's fitting, don't you think? You've always been willing to die for your brother, even if he never appreciated it. But he will now. Your brother and your father both.'

'Frida, now!' Sylvian snarled.

Something small and bright as silver flew from the left and slammed itself into Florrie's neck, sending her staggering back. A throwing knife, Lyta thought with a strange and absent sense of recognition. One of Frida's throwing knives.

Florrie opened her mouth to speak, but couldn't form words, couldn't draw breath. She dropped to her knees, bringing Lyta down with her, and the gladius clattered from her limp hand.

Viola stepped up to the edge of the tear into the Nether, her arms held out wide. Light blazed from her body and she poured every last ounce of strength into the tear which lead to the Nether. Wind pulled at her, whipping her hair around her, as if it would drag her through, but she didn't stop. Behind her, Stirling held her fast, his arms wrapped around her, rooting her in this world.

There was a sound like a clap of thunder and the tear above them snapped shut. Viola fell to her knees and still Stirling held her close, muttering prayer after prayer as he held her limp form. Slowly, the light faded and the smell of candle smoke and blood washed over Lyta in a wave, replacing the hot dry air and the emptiness. The sudden silence felt like an assault on her senses, as if something equally vital and terrifying had been cut off. She tried to breathe, and she couldn't. So she held on to Kit instead. He heaved in a breath and shuddered. Kit was still alive. At least she had that.

'Never liked that two-faced old bitch,' Frida spat. She wiped a bloody hand across her face and exhaled. She had circled around while Sylvian distracted the old woman. Now she took one last look at her handiwork and nodded, turning to the young woman from Albion who still glowed faintly like the dawn. 'Lady Viola? Your brother will be here momentarily. Please don't run off again like that. It vexes him.'

Viola was leaning heavily on Stirling now, the two of them pale and exhausted, drained. Whatever she had done to close the way to the Nether had taken its toll on her, goddess or not. Like Beatriz, Lyta thought.

And now she was Frida's problem. Frida Elwynn, wrangling a goddess . . .

Lyta laughed and it hurt like nothing had ever hurt before. The mirth turned into a gasp of agony and light danced in front of her eyes while shadows ate away at the edges of her vision. Not good. Not good at all.

'Lyta?' Sylvian scooped her up. Normally she'd tell him to put her the hell down and to stop doing that because she had two perfectly good legs. But no, Sylvian kept doing this, as if she was helpless. And she wasn't. She just needed a moment. She wasn't sure what had happened to those legs, but they weren't working anymore. And she kind of liked it when he held her like this.

What had she seen through that tear? What was that being that had been moving towards her, blazing and terrible? And hungry. So hungry.

'Kit, is he—?'

Sylvian turned her around. 'He's fine. He's all right.'

A shape that looked much like Kit was struggling up from the ground. He barely glanced at them but staggered over to the sprawled body bleeding on the ground in the corner. 'Help, someone, please, help.' His voice was so faint, desperate. He was down on his hands and knees, holding Ben Alvarez.

Viola sighed. 'Take me to him, Piers.'

'You haven't the strength.'

'I have to. Now.' And Stirling didn't seem to have any capacity to argue with her.

'Poor Ben,' Lyta murmured. She was feeling dizzy now. It was so strange.

'Poor Ben nothing,' Sylvian replied curtly. 'It's his fault we're—'

'No. That's not . . . he didn't—' Her voice came out as little more than a whisper. She couldn't catch her breath, not really and the world was melting away. It was so dark and cold. Everything was so cold.

She heard, rather than saw, Alderton and the host of soldiers arrive, and the unmistakable sound of Sylvian hurling orders around to anyone who got within earshot would have made her smile if she could have figured out how the muscles of her face worked. He sounded frantic.

But it didn't matter. Nothing mattered. There was a soft mist closing in on her, red-gold and pale as bone. It ate away at her vision and turned her skin numb. She thought she could smell lavender. Far away she heard the rumble of those bronze battle horns again, like wild animals calling out, echoing over an empty plain.

'Lyta,' Sylvian's voice rumbled where her face pressed to his chest. 'Please, hold on, my love. Hold on.'

She dug her fingers into Sylvian's uniform and tried. She really tried.

CHAPTER THIRTY-THREE

Sylvian

It was not the first time Sylvian had paced outside a room waiting to find out if Lyta was still alive. It would probably not be the last, he reflected bitterly. But that didn't make it any easier. He had carried her back here, shaking off any suggestions of handing her over to someone else, or of reporting in first. He was fairly sure he had snarled like an animal at one of the lieutenants who ran off crying to Vasquez. They could report what they wanted. He didn't care. Not anymore. Only Lyta mattered.

When Beatriz finally opened the door and let him into the tiny room in the palace garrison, he stared at her for a long moment, trying to read her grey, bleak face. She was wrung-out, and between the queen, Juárez and now this, he wasn't surprised.

'Is she—?' He couldn't say it.

'Go in and talk to her,' Beatriz told him wearily. 'She'll be fine. But one of these days the two of you are going to push things too far even for me.'

He seized her in his fierce embrace, squeezing her tight until Beatriz gave a cry of alarm which brought Juárez up to his feet from the bench opposite them. Which he really shouldn't have done either, because he wasn't entirely healed yet and Beatriz would have very stern words with him in a moment.

Sylvian's fellow bodyguard seemed to have appointed himself as her guardian now. If the king wasn't lucky, he was going to run out of men soon.

But right now, Sylvian didn't care about anyone else.

Lyta was trying to sit up on a sea of pillows. Someone had bathed her and changed her clothes for a linen nightgown. They had even brushed her hair until it shone. Not that it helped. Lyta was profoundly irritated and he loved her for it. The scowl belonged there on her face.

'I don't know what you're grinning at.' Oh good, petulance.

'I love you too. When are you going to stop going off on your own?'

'Well, you were busy and there was a tight deadline.'

He sat on the edge of the bed and held out his hands, waiting. It didn't take too long. Her fingers brushed against his and then they intertwined. Lyta leaned forwards resting her head on his chest. She felt so right there, tucked in against him.

'That was too close,' he murmured at her.

'Maybe you could have been faster. When you come to the rescue with a whole army, you shouldn't be late, Syl. Come on your own instead. Other people slow us down, you know?'

The corners of his mouth twitched. 'I know.'

There was a long moment of silence, of acknowledgement while she struggled to find words.

'You came for me,' Lyta murmured.

'I always will. I promised, remember?' He stroked her hair with a hand which trembled more than he would have liked to admit.

'Everyone else is okay?' she asked after another long pause when she just breathed and he resisted the urge to pull her even closer. He was still terrified of hurting her more.

'Yes. Viola was able to save Ben's life. Kit's fine too. He went home.'

She shoved at him, annoyed that he saw through her so clearly. But he did. He knew her. Kit had gone home, to the printshop. He hadn't stayed with Ben. Sylvian didn't want to break that to her yet, or ponder on what it could mean. Nothing good. 'And the baron?'

'Marasso's dead, love. His supposedly brilliant ambush cheered Francisco up no end as it turned out he was bored stupid in Westphalia. He's fine too, on the way back here as we speak, to see his son. Everyone else is safe now. Oh, that reminds me.'

He fished her necklace out and handed it to her. Lyta snatched it from him. She cupped it in her hands like a treasure, staring and took a moment too long to reply. She sucked in a breath, and then let it out, long and uneven, shuddering. 'Not . . . not everyone.'

Sylvian opened his eyes. She was gazing into the distance, her blue eyes like a piece of the sky through broken glass. 'What is it?'

'He's gone, Sylvian.'

'Who?'

Tears filled her eyes, matted her lashes together and spilled down her face. For a moment he didn't know what to do, what to say. 'Lyta, what happened?'

'Eninn. I think . . . I think I killed him. There's an empty place in my head where he used to be. Or . . . or he got pulled back into the Nether. Or the blade took him. I don't know. But it's my fault.'

Arguably it was Eninn's fault as well, because it was always Eninn's fault, as far as Sylvian was concerned. He made Lyta the wild card she was. Sylvian knew better than to say something like that right now.

He carried on stroking her hair, unable to think of anything he could usefully tell her.

'I had to save Kit,' she whispered at last.

'And you did, heart. He's fine. He's back at the printshop already bossing everyone around. He . . . he took the book and what was left of the hand. Said he'll hide it again. Better this time.'

He didn't mention the haunted look in her brother's eyes. Or that he and Ben had not exchanged a single word right up to the moment Ben had been escorted off to be interrogated by General Vasquez. Time enough for all of that.

'What now?' she asked.

'Whatever you want, Lyta.'

Her lower lip wobbled. He wouldn't have believed it if he didn't see it himself. 'But you . . . the queen . . . and . . .'

Words failed her.

Sylvian smiled. At least he could promise her this. 'Whatever you want, my love. I'm at your service now.'

'Does she still want us to get married?'

Ever since the queen had released him, he felt as if he was a kite untethered. Lyta was all he had to ground him.

If Annika had noticed that the bond between the bodyguard and herself was gone, he didn't know. She had released him to go after Lyta, so he assumed she must. She was only concerned with Alejandro and the imminent return of her husband, who having heard reports of his new son and the attempted kidnapping, was racing across the continent to be with her again, with only a brief skirmish to slow him down. Sylvian had largely been left to his own devices. Which meant he had spent most of his time sitting in or outside this very room. He had tried to pray, but it hadn't helped.

He wasn't sure who he was praying to. Ystara maybe? But she wasn't answering. He wasn't sure where she was either. Since the wild rage had passed, he couldn't sense her quite the way he had. He didn't know what to do about it either. Something told him she may have released him for now, but she wouldn't give up her Chosen quite so easily.

After they got out of the Guild Quarter, and returned to the palace, Vasquez had to persuade him to release Lyta to the healers and to be honest it was only because Beatriz had appeared that he had agreed. Alderton, Voila and Stirling had fled back to Alderton's house in Falconbrook at the first opportunity and the young woman embodying the Goddess of Albion was staying very quiet indeed. Sylvian felt keeping it that way was probably the best bet.

He didn't want to explain to Annika that the Sovereign Goddess of Albion was walking the streets of Amberes. Not even now.

As for Kit and Ben . . .

Benedictus Alvarez's blind stupidity had almost cost them everything. You could blame his childlike wonder in all things related to the gods, or the insidious nature of Charnock's manipulation, or the betrayal of the gods who lived like parasites in his mind, but the upshot was the same really. Ben was under investigation and when Francisco came home it might get bad indeed. He'd been released from custody, Juárez had told Sylvian, but was confined to his sister's house pending further questioning. The plans their cousin had laid implicated both of them, rightly or not, and House Alvarez was going to suffer for it. Beatriz saving the queen and thwarting Marasso's kidnap attempt might be the only hope they had.

Kit was both heartbroken and betrayed. Sylvian didn't blame him.

'Frida saved my life,' Lyta said after a while. She had been so quiet he'd almost imagined she was asleep. But clearly she had been mulling over events. Dwelling on them. Each and every thing. He didn't like that.

'That she did.'

'A few times, actually. Do you think she meant to?' When he shrugged, unable to think of an answer, she scrunched up her face. 'You heard what Florrie said, about Kit and me?'

'Florrie Stone was a mad old woman obsessed with an ancient death cult. I wouldn't set too much store by her words. The Rookery is sharing some stories now and it isn't pretty. We're still rounding up any associates, but we won't stop until we have them all. The cult is finished.'

'And her god, her Cissonius or Druon, or whatever he was? Did you see him?'

Sylvian swallowed hard as his throat tightened. He had seen something beyond the veil. He'd seen it fix its sights on Lyta and seen it draw back its lips from sharp teeth. He'd felt it hunger for her blood. And if that was her father . . .

'Whatever it was, it's gone. The tear closed. Viola made sure of that. Annika's going to have half a dozen of her natural philosophers pouring over it. She's handing them the whole Blacksmiths' Guild, to take over the work of the alchemists and to make sure that nothing like that ever happens again. She's probably going to blame Albion.'

She had made that perfectly clear. Apparently Francisco was delighted with that prospect. He was always hungry for another war.

'Poor Viola,' Lyta murmured. She sounded tired now. 'It wasn't her fault. She was trying to stop Charnock. Do you think they'll blame her over there as well?'

'Depends on how much their queen likes her. And how they really feel about Rhiannon walking among them. I'm not even sure there is a Viola Alderton anymore. You didn't see her back there, all she did.' He shuddered and pushed the thought away. 'I should let you sleep.'

But her hands in his tightened to iron. 'Don't you dare leave me.'

Sylvian settled back on the bed with her curled in against him and held her until her breathing deepened and she fell still. If he had it his way, he would never let her go again.

*

Annika summoned them long before Sylvian was ready. Lyta looked positively rebellious. Thankfully it was Juárez who came to find them and, despite everything, she seemed somewhat inclined to listen to him. If Sylvian hadn't seen the way his fellow bodyguard followed Beatriz around like a puppy he might have been jealous.

However, the dress was a step too far.

'What is *that*?' she asked, as if someone had suggested she wear freshly butchered animal skins. Knowing his Lyta, she'd probably be happier in freshly butchered animal skins. But this gown was green as the richest leaves of holly, trimmed with pearls and embroidered with golden threads in intricate patterns around the bust, the cuffs and the hem. It would suit her. Annika must have chosen it herself. She had an eye for things like that.

'You have a royal audience,' Juárez told her calmly enough.

'I don't *want* a royal audience.'

'Well, nonetheless, you have one. Aren't you lucky?'

'Lucky,' she told him with scorn. 'That's a word for it. Not one I'm overly fond of anymore. I have another.'

Juárez kept his face completely solemn, but didn't give her the chance to voice that word. It would only be obscene. 'The queen is most insistent, Mistress Cornellis. And her majesty cannot be kept waiting.'

And somehow that was that. If he'd tried it, Sylvian thought, she'd have laughed in his face.

Lyta cast the other royal bodyguard a sly look as she vanished behind the screen to change. 'Is Beatriz going to be there? Is that why you're in such a hurry?'

It didn't help Juárez's professional image that he went scarlet as a berry. He didn't answer.

'Sylvian, help me do up the back,' she commanded triumphantly, and he had to smile. As he did so, tightening laces, he planted a series of lingering kisses on her bare skin, mapping a trail up the back of her neck. She was wearing the necklace once more, a line of silver against her pale skin. He had found a silversmith to repair the chain, unsure that it helped, but it was the least he could do if it offered her any comfort at all.

She pressed back against him and that was a whole other distraction, her body against his. 'Trying to make us late?' he asked. 'You know, if we wait until later we can take our time.'

'Is that a promise?' she murmured, the depth in her voice indicating the effect he was having. He knew the feeling.

'If you want it to be.'

As they reached the audience chamber, she slipped her hand into his. 'Stay with me,' she whispered.

She had got very good, all of a sudden, at handing out orders, he thought. Not that he objected. Not anymore. He was just relieved she was still here.

Annika was dressed in silver, the colour of her goddess, bringing light after the darkest days, with a delicate crown of white gold, jewelled chains dangling from it framing her delicate face. Holly heavy with red berries, long loops of ivy and garlands of mistletoe decked the audience chamber, and fires blazed in every hearth. It was almost homely, if such a room could ever be said to be homely. Outside, beyond the walls of the palace, festivities would be in full swing by now. The great bonfire would be blazing, lighting up the darkness. Music and dancing, people skating on the canals regardless of city ordinances, the Midwinter Fair filling the entire Great Market with spiced wine and honey cakes, but in here, Sylvian held Lyta's hand and stayed by her side, and it was all he wanted.

The court had gathered for the last night of the darkest days, ready to celebrate the Solstice and the return of the sun, although a significant number of the aldermen were absent. Still being questioned by Vasquez, he supposed. Ursel was exultant, courting the queen as he shepherded his newest allies to meet her. The make-up of the new city council was liable to transform utterly. Sylvian hoped Ursel wasn't the only one putting forward names and made a mental note to mention that worry to Vasquez. So far it seemed that the cult of Cissonius didn't extend as far as they had feared, but no one wanted to take any chances. It had drawn in a guildmaster, a pillar of the community in the Rookery and a baron of the royal court, all for their own reasons and none of them altruistic. It had corrupted the alchemists and many other members of the Guild of Blacksmiths.

Sylvian bowed as they reached the foot of the dais and Lyta sank into an unexpectedly graceful curtsey. He hadn't thought she would bother.

It would take a lot to make Lyta forget the last time they'd knelt here. And he still didn't know how that tangle of emotions was going to play out.

He would give her time, he had decided. But he would not give up.

'Captain Chant, Mistress Cornellis,' said Annika and smiled. Her smile was like the sun coming out between clouds, and yet the hold she had wielded over him in the past was a faint whisper now. She wore Ystara's silver ring on her own finger now. Her own champion, perhaps, or a champion for her son. He didn't know. He was just grateful for his own release from the role. 'You have done us a great service once more, and we owe you more than we can ever articulate.'

More than she could ever admit either. Not publicly.

'I hope this will go a small way to reward you.' She handed him a scroll which he took with murmured thanks. It bore the royal seal, ribbons and a wax disc dangling from the heavy vellum. There was something faintly ridiculous about it. 'Let the world know how my husband values your service. Let this also be our wedding gift to you both.'

Lyta tensed like a coiled spring and Sylvian wilted internally. So Annika wasn't giving up on that then. Neither was Ystara. The Goddess of Love was still fixated on the two of them. She gained power from love and the demonstration of that love. From people like them. And Lyta was bound to dig her heels in.

Joy of joys.

With that they were dismissed. It took all of a few minutes and they were ushered to an antechamber. They might be favoured but that didn't mean they had much of a place among the great and good of Amberes. Or that Annika wanted her court to have a front row to any potential meltdown Lyta might have over this wedding gift business. His queen was no fool.

'What is it?' Lyta asked, her voice still worryingly small. That told him she didn't want to fight about this marriage thing either. Not yet anyway. And that she was worried about what Annika had in store for them next.

Because Annika was always planning something, and it was too easy to get swept up in those plans.

Sylvian unrolled the scroll and studied it carefully. Then he read it again unable to believe it the first time. Had the queen lost her mind?

'She's . . . she's giving us *Montalbeau*.'

Lyta snatched it out of his hands. 'She's *what*?'

'This has to be a mistake.' And there it was, coming right out of his mouth: the understatement of the century. He had known Annika had let him go far too easily. It had been Ystara's decision, not hers. A queen did not give up anything that was of use to her.

'*In recognition of acts of loyalty, on the occasion of their marriage*,' Lyta read out loud. 'So how do we tell her that there's not going to be a marriage? And what's a *margrave* anyway?'

'A lord charged with defence of a region. Comes from a military term from long ago. It doesn't matter.'

His throat tightened and he turned away from her, walking to the small mullioned window which overlooked Cissonia's Tower and beyond it the market. Amberes spread out beneath them, and now with the midwinter festivities, it was alive, thriving, a whirlwind of activity, noisy and barely governable again.

Like her. Like the woman he loved more than reason. More than life itself.

'Why would we want to go back to Montalbeau anyway?' she asked, the words still pouring out of her. 'The place is full of nightmares and regret.'

That was true as well.

'Lyta,' he began carefully and turned to face her. His voice failed.

She had that flustered, exasperated look on her face. She was still holding the scroll but her hand was shaking. Her hair caught the light like a fire, and she was beautiful, even if she was angry. Perhaps she always would be. Angry. Beautiful. Both. 'I won't *marry* someone because the queen tells me I have to.'

It was his turn to be reckless, it seemed. Instead of arguing, Sylvian went down on one knee.

'Lyta,' he said again. 'What if *I* ask you? What if we could make up for lost time? What if we could be together, because we *want* to be together? Like we always should have been?'

Lyta stared at him as if he had spouted gibberish instead of what he had imagined was a perfectly good proposal that most people would be pleased to hear. '*What?*'

'What if we *want* to?' Was he making a fool of himself? Would she say no yet again and he'd be left kneeling there like an idiot, rejected and abandoned? *Again.* And with that thought came a new kind of anger. It wasn't fair. None of it was fair. 'What if I want to marry you, for *you*? What if it was all I *ever* wanted? I can't conceive of the years left to me without you, Lyta.'

'You think you have years?' The sharp words always came out first. Then she faltered. 'But I . . . Sylvian . . . you're . . .'

He'd never thought he'd actually see her lost for words. It was a novelty. Strangely it gave him a new kind of courage. 'I want you. I always did. Surely that's all that matters in the end. I'm still yours. I always was.'

'I'm a thief.'

'You're *my* thief. That was always the case. You know that. Nothing has changed that, heart.'

'And Montalbeau is a fortress of nightmares.'

He swallowed a laugh. 'I don't want Montalbeau. Just you. We don't have to live there. We can burn it to the ground if we want.'

An unexpected smile flickered over her face and she reached out for him, letting the scroll clatter to the polished floor. 'That would make a fitting pyre for Ranulf, wouldn't it? Nothing like a spot of light arson as part of a celebration.' Her voice came out in a sigh now and Sylvian rose slowly, carefully to his feet, still holding her. She let him pull her closer, her body moulding against his.

'Well?' he asked, brushing his lips against hers, his hands finding the curve of her waist and holding her close.

'I want you,' she breathed. 'Just you. I always did.'

And those words were all he needed to hear.

CHAPTER THIRTY-FOUR

Lyta

It was probably madness. She'd lost all her wits in the darkness of that corrupted shrine in the guild, but what was done was done. She had Sylvian, even if it meant marriage and a cursed castle in the mountains to the south that she had vowed never to set foot in again. Annika needed someone to hold it, she supposed. It made Sylvian nobility, probably, and there had been mentions of a string of titles attached to it. Margrave, whatever that was. She didn't know or care.

If the queen thought that would keep Lyta in check, she had another think coming. But Annika was not that stupid. She probably had something else up her sleeve. She had her precious son now, and Francisco would come back to her and pretend like he had never been away.

Perhaps getting Sylvian out of Amberes for the time being was a very good idea indeed. It had to be better than being locked up in the palace. Lyta had stolen a relic from the Imperial Temple. And they knew it was her. No way she could deny it. The Inquisitor would come after her. She had no doubts about that.

The thought of Montalbeau, though . . .

She shuddered and pulled the cloak a bit tighter around her. Sylvian walked beside her as if he didn't feel the cold. The snow was still falling thick and fast. It felt like this winter would never end. The city hummed, a suppressed energy which signalled its slow reawakening. The year had turned, the days were getting longer again, if only by a little so far. But soon the winter would pass and trade would roar back into Amberes from every corner of the world.

They didn't make it as far as the printshop when a group of men surrounded them. For a moment she thought of running, but to be honest, she was so sick of running, she didn't want to. They were too well-groomed for Janlow's men, too quiet and well-disciplined for the usual street thugs. They were Imperial troops.

Sylvian's sword slid from the scabbard with a threatening hiss.

'Praetorian Guards are forbidden to enter Amberes on pain of death,' he said in a voice that almost sounded reasonable. If you ignored the gleam in his eyes.

So that was what they were. She'd thought as much. Elite troops assigned to guard Patricians of the highest rank. Usually the Imperator and his family or closest supporters.

'Mistress Cornellis,' said Tiberius, pulling down his hood to reveal his unnaturally handsome features. He stood in the heart of them, completely unafraid and unrepentant. 'Captain Chant.' He didn't sound in any way worried, not even with Sylvian looming over him, ready to attack at the slightest provocation.

'Inquisitor,' Lyta replied carefully. It didn't do to forget what he was. Not that his title would protect him if she gave the word. She hoped he knew that too.

'Are you quite well? You had something of an ordeal, I believe. I'm glad to see you recovered.'

Lyta narrowed her eyes, glanced at Sylvian but didn't flinch. 'What's it to you?'

'There is still the matter of the sword you borrowed. Without leave.'

Ah, she thought, casually taking in the stock of the men who surrounded them. 'Sorry about that. I needed it.'

'So I heard. And that did not work out so well.'

Who had been blabbing to him, she wondered, really not enjoying this. She kept waiting for the violence and the shouting, perhaps even the blood but it didn't come. And she could still feel the cold of that ancient sword sliding under her skin. She was lucky to be alive.

Eninn was lost somewhere out there. She didn't know where but she could feel that he wasn't entirely gone. Just gone from her. Separated. Instead, deep inside her was a cold and hollow place, like she had been scooped out and filled with ice. She had hoped that somehow Eninn would do what Rhiannon had done. But she had not been wearing her pendant. Sylvian had taken it from Marasso's corpse, and he hadn't been close enough. Whatever little power Eninn had still possessed, it hadn't been enough to work one last miracle. Not even to save himself. If he had managed to hide somewhere, it wasn't in her pendant. And she couldn't find him.

Even though she had promised him.

'I think that's probably enough conversation for one night,' Sylvian interrupted. 'It's too cold to linger and we have places to be.'

Tiberius smiled, that thin, hard, shining smile, like a knife's edge, Lyta thought. Dangerous. He was so dangerous.

'Very true, Captain Chant. Or is it Lord Chant now? Sylvian, an interesting name is it not? It comes from our language, did I tell you that? From Caput Mundi itself. Although we would say Silvius, like the hero in the legend, the man called Brabo, who became lord of these lands—the Brabantine. Perhaps you should keep the sword, my lord, my lady.' And he bowed, deeply, gracefully. A bow of respect, one soldier to another. Lyta didn't miss that it was directed not only at Sylvian, but at both of them.

The Praetorian Guards followed suit and Lyta felt a chill run through her that wasn't entirely to do with winter.

Tiberius stepped back, clearing her path and his men did likewise so they could pass by. Part of Lyta wanted throw a well-crafted insult in his face, but right now she couldn't think of one. Why was he trying to claim Sylvian all of a sudden? What was this business with the sword? And what was the unexpected respect about? Instead of arguing she got the hell out of there as quickly as she could.

Even the Imperial Church wasn't afraid in Amberes anymore: going around claiming its soldiery as their own, parading about with their elite militia, and gifting Sylvian a sword with a huge weight of baggage behind it. It had to mean something and nothing good.

They had come at them armed, without fear. Even if all they had done was make veiled threats and promises.

'What did happen to the sword?' she asked as quietly as she could.

'Kit took it. Along with the book and anything else involved. He was very thorough.'

'Are you going to ask him for it?'

Sylvian didn't answer.

Lyta wasn't sure how she felt about that.

But she noticed that he didn't resheath his own blade until they reached Twelfth Moon Street.

*

Kit was back at the printshop, hiding in plain sight. He was busily surrounding himself with the familiar, keeping himself as occupied as he possibly could. He always did this when he was in real pain. Lyta knew his ways far too well. When she entered, half a dozen apprentices looked up, stared open-mouthed and went horribly silent.

Great, she thought, word had spread about what had happened, or Annika's offer, or half a dozen other problems she found herself tangled up with now. You could always rely on the Amberes gossip to spread at the speed of a whisper. Usually elaborating beyond all reason as it went.

Or perhaps, she realised, they were staring at Sylvian in that familiar mixture of horror and awe, which was probably fair. He certainly looked fearsome, this newest lord of Amberes.

'Kit?' she called. He was stooped over the block where he set the type for whatever piece he was working on now. He was tired, she thought. Worn-out. He shouldn't even be here. He should still be resting. She shouldn't have agreed to stay at the palace with Syl, even if she had been assured it was for her own safety. And perhaps it was, because Inquisitor Tiberius had found her the moment they left.

But she should not have let Kit leave either. He shouldn't be here on his own.

Although what he should be doing, she had no idea. Where else was there?

Ben's house, maybe.

Kit tried hard to hide the wince when he noticed her studying him. He failed miserably.

'Lyta, Syl,' he said by way of greeting and turned his attention back to his work.

At the far side of the room Jem caught her eye and nodded upstairs. He didn't look much happier. Clearly they had all noticed the state of Kit.

'I need to talk to you,' she told her brother. 'We both do. In private.'

To her surprise he didn't argue, which was probably a bad sign too. Just rolled his eyes and then headed for the stairs.

In the little sitting room, she shut the door. Kit stood by the window, winter light streaming around him. It illuminated his red-gold hair, gilded his pale skin.

'You all right?' she asked. 'We barely got a chance to talk.'

'I've been worse,' he replied, although he didn't sound it.

'Did you talk to Ben?'

Kit shook his head. No emotion in his eyes, no obvious hurt or regret. He was just numb. Empty. Oh, this was not good. Not good at all.

'Don't you think you should?' Sylvian asked him. There was a degree of care in the words, balanced and empathetic in a way she wasn't sure she'd be able to manage. He was good at it, the sympathy, kindness. That thing that no one ever expected of him.

'I don't know what there is to say.' She heard the break in his voice and rushed to wrap her arms around him. He might be almost twice her size but he was still her little brother. Kit tensed as she did it, but he didn't pull away. Finally he relaxed enough to let her hug him properly. 'Are you all right?'

Lyta laughed. 'Me? Fine. The queen is still interfering but no, fine.' She'd wanted to ask his advice but couldn't find the words now. It seemed like a small and petty problem. Or not—*the queen wants us to become nobles and is intent of handing over a castle complete with nightmare underground labyrinth where we all almost died. I still have nightmares about it. It's probably cursed. Oh and my husband died there so we could escape.*

Had Annika really thought that through? Or had she grabbed at the first thing of value with which she could try to bribe Lyta in order to get her, and therefore Sylvian, out of the way. Or to keep them indebted to her.

'She is trying to reward us,' said Sylvian. 'But I'm not sure she truly understands what she's doing.'

A knock at the door made them all turn. Lord Stirling stood there, carrying a pile of books. Lyta scowled at him and he took half a step back.

'I can come back,' he said warily.

'No, come in Piers,' Kit replied before Lyta got a chance to tell him where to go. 'I'm glad you came back. I thought you were leaving.' So he was Kit's friend now. She wasn't sure how she felt about that either. Far more trouble than he was worth that one. Still, he had done his part in a jam. Perhaps if he was actually leaving she could be magnanimous.

'Our ship sails this evening,' Stirling said. 'I've taken Charnock into custody and will bring him to Elizabeth's justice. It will not . . . be kind, I think. Well, he wanted to get inside the Tower, I suppose.' He sighed and offered Kit the pile of books. 'I came to give you these. You may find them of interest? They are rare manuscripts, in a number of languages, and no one else has put them into print. I've added my own notes and the necessary translations. And I wanted to say a proper farewell.' Again he paused and gave a wary smile. 'And apologise.'

Kit frowned as he took the books, his hands very gentle on their older well-worn bindings. 'Apologise for what this time?'

Stirling shrugged and gave a soft self-deprecating laugh. 'Whatever needs apologising for, I suppose.'

An awkward silence filled the room.

'How is Viola?' Lyta asked. Because there was no easy way to ask '*Is your girlfriend still a goddess?*' and someone had to say something.

'Safe,' Stirling said. 'She's coming back with me to report to the queen and Lord Burghley. So is Charles, for the time being. I think he believes it's his path to redemption, but I wouldn't count on it. Some grudges are bigger than that. And we may well still have a war on our hands. But Rhiannon has hope.'

'She's still a goddess then?' Lyta asked, surprised to find a way after all. 'Not sure your queen will like that. It kind of messes with the royal authority, doesn't it?'

Stirling smiled. It was a troubled smile. 'Well, quite. But we will do what we can. And if my goddess has hope, so do I. We're going to visit the seers at Aquae Sulis in the hope they have some insight. They're half-divine already.'

Albion would be an interesting place for the time being. She didn't envy him. She didn't envy any of them.

Alderton leaving Amberes though. Wonders would never cease. How many times had she prayed for that? She wondered if Frida would go with him. She couldn't picture it, but then Frida had surprised her more times than not.

Frida had saved her life back in that chamber. Once she would not have thought twice about that, would have expected it. When Frida was her friend and partner in crime. But now . . . now she didn't know where they stood. Perhaps she never would.

'Any word on Janlow?' Kit asked.

'In hiding,' Sylvian told him. 'Alderton's put a price on his head for betraying them and the general wants him for questioning. It's going to make life very uncomfortable for him for a while. He might even have to up sticks too. Can't imagine him outside the walls of Amberes, but I can't imagine he'll live long if he stays here.'

That was delightful. Lyta even found herself smiling. Who said vindictiveness was a bad thing?

'And you, Lyta?' Stirling asked. 'I hear you're a baroness or something?'

She made a face which only went halfway to showing her distaste for it all. 'Or something.'

'You're a *what*?' Kit exclaimed. It was the most emotion she'd seen out of him since she got here.

'It's not—' Uh, this was awkward. She pointed at Sylvian. 'It's his fault anyway. Look, never mind, I'll explain later. Annika's been meddling, that's all. We'll figure something out.'

Stirling laughed. 'Only you, Lyta Cornellis,' he said with genuine affection which surprised her. And maybe she thought she didn't loathe him as much as she wanted to. But that might just be because he was leaving her city. Then his tone changed, became more solemn. 'I'm not only here to say goodbye,' he told Kit. 'Ben wants to see you.'

Kit said nothing, but Lyta got the impression he'd been waiting for this. He swallowed hard, his throat working as he failed to find words, and then slowly nodded again.

Acceptance, resignation, dread . . . she wasn't sure which.

*

In the end, Lyta managed to persuade Kit to get it over with as quickly as possible. Otherwise he was going to carry on torturing himself and that wasn't going to help anyone. So the three of them, Lyta, Kit and Sylvian, made their way to Beatriz's house on Crescent Street.

To no one's surprise, Juárez was there, sipping tea from an incongruously small porcelain cup, in Beatriz's parlour. He almost dropped it as they entered, so flustered that Lyta thought he wanted the floor to open up and swallow him whole.

'You're feeling better then,' she said as she sat down opposite him while Sylvian stood behind her. Looming. It had always been his greatest skill. Well . . . she thought of the things they had done last night, and what she planned to do with him later. Maybe not the greatest.

Juárez cleared his throat nervously. 'Lady Beatriz has been most diligent and—'

That just made Sylvian growl. Juárez might be his friend but this was Beatriz and Lyta knew Sylvian had complicated feelings about the protection of women in this city. Even from his friends.

'Oh, I'm sure she has,' Lyta replied with a sly smile. His face turned even more scarlet. She hadn't thought that was possible. 'You weren't the only person stabbed, you know?'

Beatriz stifled a laugh which was full of affection.

'Where is Ben?' Kit asked in muted tones, and the amusement threading through the room faltered. Lyta was reminded of how uncomfortable he had been when they first came here, so many months ago. He was much worse now.

'He isn't allowed to leave the house,' Beatriz told him, more soberly. 'He's barely left his rooms. Losing the gods, his injuries . . .' But then she shook her head. 'I think he's been waiting for you.'

Kit hesitated, his jaw tightening.

'I should go and see him then.'

Kit took himself off and Lyta sat there, feeling more and more unsure. Heartbreak was never easy to deal with, even if it was someone else's. Not if you cared about them. Both of them, as it turned out.

It was only when they heard the crash that all four of them rose as one. The house shook, suddenly, and something like thunder rolled overhead. No, not thunder . . . the sound of great bronze horns, like the warriors of old carried into battle, their long plaintive roar vibrating deep in the chest. Lyta knew that sound. Far too well now.

Sylvian moved first, shaking off the shock, with Juárez behind him. They sprinted up the grand staircase. At the end of the corridor, the door to Ben's room swung open, half off its hinges as if someone had taken a battering ram to it. The air hung heavy with the smell of rain on earth and fresh vegetation—petrichor, once called the blood of the gods.

Kit stood unmoving in the middle of the room while Ben sprawled back on his bed, staring, wild-eyed at the threat.

And he was clearly under threat.

'Don't,' he yelled when he saw them, flinging out his hand as if to ward them away. 'Stay back. It isn't safe.'

Slowly, Kit turned his head, looked over his shoulder at Lyta. They made eye contact, but Lyta knew the being she was staring at in horror wasn't her brother. Not really. Kit might have been in there somewhere—she hoped, dear gods, she hoped he was still in there somewhere—but he wasn't in control. Something else wore his face, something ancient. His eyes spilled golden light down his cheeks and the smile, the slow cynical smile, that was not and never had been Kit.

'What . . . what are you?' she gasped.

But Kit, or whatever lurked inside him, didn't answer. He frowned at her and then, finally, pure confusion flickered over his face. For a moment she thought it was Kit. It *had* to be Kit.

He gave something like a sob of despair, her name tangled up in a net of pain and confusion. Then he folded up, dropping to the floor, unconscious, golden light still spilling from his eyes.

Author's Note

The Lore of Silver grew out of three things—the wacky world of alchemists in the 16th century, the wild adventures of relic thieves down through all the centuries, and of course Lyta, and the big question of what would she do next after *The Book of Gold*?

Once again I have been playing with history, both real and imaginary. I am not actually portraying real figures from our history, but an alternate world where history and reality are significantly different from our own, although it perhaps sometimes carried echoes. Any mistakes are either deliberate or accidental, but they are entirely my own.

I've been fascinated by alchemists for years. The history of alchemy is long and complex, full of secrets and esoteric lore. A lot of this was mainly because they wrote in code to keep their discoveries secret, code that was often misinterpreted which added to the mystery and the accusations of occult practices. We've all heard of the quest to turn lead into gold, or to create the Philosopher's Stone, but alchemy was about far more than that. It was both a spiritual journey and a scientific adventure. At this turning point of history, alchemy began to transform itself into chemistry and the philosophical and esoteric side began to fade away. But before that happened, before the enlightenment and the advent of the scientific age, all these elements still operated in tandem, a complex thing of many moving parts—science and magic hand in hand.

Of course, in Amberes, that means gods as well. And their relics. More about them in a bit.

Dr John Dee is probably one of the most famous figures of the period when it comes to alchemy, and has made many appearances in fiction, but he was by no means alone. There was a real Thomas Charnock, though not a lot is known about him. Born in England in the early 1520s, he described himself as 'an unlettered scholar' and probably learned alchemy from his uncle (also Thomas Charnock). He was conscripted in 1557 and before leaving for Calais, he destroyed all his equipment in a rage so no one could steal his work. Four written works are attributed to Charnock, including *The Breviary of Naturall Philosophy*, better known as *The Breviary of Alchemy* (1557). They were collected in Elias Ashmole's *Theatrum Chemicum Britannicum*, in 1652.

By 1562 he was back in England where he married one Agnes Norton. He sought patronage from Queen Elizabeth and promised her the philosopher's stone 'uppon payne off losing my hedd' if she would let him work in the Tower of London, but she refused. He died in 1581 but for at least a hundred years, the story goes, no one would live in his house for fear of demons. The threat of the alchemist lingered on long after he was gone.

Between the defeat of the English at Calais and his return to England and marriage, there appears to be no record of what he got up to, which is where the alternative history of Amberes steps in. I shamelessly stole his name, in true Cornellis style, but I'm sure he wasn't as terrible as my version. Apologies to all friends of the real Thomas Charnock.

Lancel Ursel is another real figure I purloined for the world of Amberes, based on Lancelot II of Ursel. He came from one of Antwerp's many political dynasties and was Mayor of Antwerp thirteen times. His brother-in-law was Jan de Werve, Lord of Hovorst, another alderman of Antwerp and member of the intricately linked noble houses of the time. Both were prominent aldermen and served the city, Ursel being key to saving the cathedral from fire in 1533 during which he was gravely injured, and de Werve losing his life trying to protect the City Hall during the sack of Antwerp by mutinous Spanish soldiers in 1576. The Van de Werve and Ursel families are among of the oldest noble houses in Belgium and are still extant today. I shamelessly stole the names again. Apologies to all friends of the real Ursels and de Werves.

For as long as there have been relics, there have been relic thieves. Generally, they stole to order. And often *furta sacra,* or holy theft—the theft of a saint's relics and moving them to a new shrine—was seen as entirely legitimate, directed by God, the saint themselves, or the Church (or at least by those who were in charge of the new shrine). Relic thefts were often highly organised operations, and the thieves themselves could be treated as local heroes. Or the worst kind of villains, depending on where you stood. Any bit of bone or scrap of wood could be passed off as a relic with the right story attached to it. The most famous relic thief is, to this day, Deusdona, the ninth century deacon who pillaged the Roman catacombs and sold relics across the Carolingian empire. With the sack of Constantinople in 1204 thieves fell on the city in search of relics.

By the sixteenth century the demand for relics was so great that theft and fraud were rife. Every altar was required to house a relic and the veneration of relics had been reaffirmed by the Council of Trent. The sixteenth century reformer John Calvin noted that if all the relics were gathered together in one place 'it would be made manifest that every Apostle has more than four bodies, and every Saint two or three'.

Such thefts are not a thing of the past either and this in part inspired the relic thefts in *The Lore of Silver*. In March 2012, the heart of St Laurence O'Toole, the patron saint of Dublin, was stolen from Christ Church Cathedral. The thieves hid overnight in the cathedral and lit candles before they left. Despite the many things of value there, they took nothing but the heart. However, in 2018 the heart was found in a public park following a tip off and the story goes that the thieves believed that they had been cursed by the theft and wanted rid of it.

The heart was not alone. A 14th-century crucifix containing fragments of the 'true cross' was stolen from Holy Cross Abbey in Co Tipperary in 2011, and St Manchan's Shrine dating from the 12th century was stolen in June 2012.

At the time we joked that someone was trying to build a Franken-saint. Which, when you think about it, is a rather terrifying concept. But it planted the seed of an idea.

The power of a relic—a body part of a saint, something which belonged to them, or which has simply touched or been touched by them—is still potent to believers today. As I wrote *The Lore of Silver* the idea of relics transformed into evidence of the enduring power of the gods of Amberes, and the promise that *To Amberes, All Things Return*.

Or is that a threat?

Lyta could never back down in the face of a threat.

As to what Lyta will do next?

I still don't really know. I got a bit of an answer but there is more to come in book three of the Feral Gods.

Whatever she wants, I guess. Hopefully I'll find out soon. Writing these books does very much feel like being along for the ride and writing up the incident report.

Acknowledgements

Second books are always a little tricky. You've pulled it off once. It can be done again, surely. And then the fear sets in.

Many thanks to everyone who loved and supported *The Book of Gold*. It is so good to know I am not the only one with the strange early printing obsession. It helped so much in keeping me going when writing *The Lore of Silver*.

For handholding and off-ledge persuading, and listening to me howl and complain, eternal thanks to the fabulous Lady Writers Social Club—Sarah Rees Brennan, Catie Murphy and Susan Connolly; and to the irrepressible Naughty Kitchen—Alison May, Jeevani Charika (Rhoda Baxter), Janet Gover, Imogen Howson (grammarian extraordinaire), Kate Johnson and Sheila McClure. I couldn't manage without any of you.

Many thanks as well to my wonderful first readers and friends, Kate Pearse, Kari Sperring, and Jeev again. I can't tell you the comfort I feel when I hear back from you. You are so wise, witty and kind. And as always I look forward to reading your wonderful words in return.

Huge thanks are also due to Dr Liz Bourke for helping me with the translation of Marcus Aurelius and putting up with so many rounds of 'couldn't the word also mean this, like if you squinted at in a bad light? Please? Pretty please?' You've been such a stalwart supporter for so long and you are the best. I definitely owe you.

More thanks to everyone at Hodderscape, especially Molly Powell, Sophie Judge and Priya Das. Once again I am so grateful for the marvellous cover by Micaela Alcaino. Look at those details! Really, look at them. There are key elements of the story woven seamlessly into that beautiful image. She is such an incredibly talented artist and I count myself lucky to have her work grace my books.

My agent Sallyanne Sweeney has been with me through thick and thin for more than ten years now and it is absolutely not a word of a lie to say none of this would have happened without her support.

And finally, to my long-suffering (*ha-ha*) kids—Diarmuid and Emily—and of course Pat, my husband, always my hero and partner in crime.

About the Author

Ruth Frances Long writes romance and fantasy from the heart which often strays into weird and wonderful liminal places. In 2015 she won a European Science Fiction Society award for *A Crack in Everything*. She also writes as Jessica Thorne, was longlisted for the RNA Romance Fantasy award in 2020, and wrote a tie-in novel for the music festival Tomorrowland. She lives in Ireland and works in a specialised library of rare and occasionally crazy books. But they are mostly under control.